Love, Life ‹

Jane Hugen-Tobler

For Jason

Thank you for all the dog walks and talks

Love recognizes no barriers. It jumps hurdles, leaps fences, penetrates walls to arrive at its destination full of hope.

Maya Angelou

PROLOGUE

LONDON 1927

When she thought about her old life, Margaret felt that she had been reasonably happy as an English teacher at Camden School for Girls. The girls had loved her and another young teacher, Daphne, had been her closest friend. Sharing a love of literature, they used to meet fortnightly for book club, taking it in turns to select a book. The one who chose would make notes, picking out their favourite parts and hosting an evening in their study with philosophical discussions, tea and toast. Margaret could almost smell the toast cooking as she pictured them sitting in her tiny study gingerly holding the bread in front of the fire on a long brass fork, trying not to get burnt as the heat travelled up the handle. This was one of the things she missed most in her new life; yet before, she had always felt an absence, as if she was waiting for something important to happen to make her feel complete.

Rummaging through the trunk she had brought with her from home took her back. It was brown leather with metal clasps and her old initials, DMF, embossed on the top. Her real name was Dorothy, but she hated it, and from a young age had decided to change it, preferring her middle name. She felt so strongly about this that she began refusing to answer anyone who didn't call her Margaret. She kept the trunk's key well hidden under a pile of clothes, at the bottom of a drawer. This was because the trunk held not only her personal possessions and treasures, but her private thoughts in the form of the diaries she had kept since she was a teenager. Secretly, she wrote poetry in a beautiful black leather journal given to her by her cousin Alice. Her dream was to one day write a book.

Breathing in the scent of the leather she turned the key and snapped open the clasps. Inside, her previous life beckoned her back. Opening the journal, she turned to the page where she had composed her latest poem. Her act of rebellion and only outlet.

Twin Beds

The empty bottle squats
Accusingly between us.
As you grip it, your hand
Turns green, deformed,
Like a dragon's talon.

We share breath,
Yet the chasm is
Tangible.
Inside I am awash
With uncertainty.

It is impossible,
Although I have tried
To pinpoint
Exactly when
Indefatigably,

Seeping like a slow leak,
From a broken sand timer,
Our bed
Developed
No man's land.

I long to taste you,
To acquaint myself
With your moles
And return to when
Everything was possible.

Instead we
Make a
Pathway
And sleep in
Twin beds.

Sighing, she returned the journal and began trawling through birthday cards, letters and photographs before choosing one that caught her attention. The photograph showed her and her two sisters smiling for the camera when they had spent the day at the beach. It had been a lovely day and one of the last they had spent together as a family before… She shivered and returned to that day, turning her back on the present, remembering the scent of the seaweed spread across the sand and the thrill of catching crabs with a net. It had been blustery; the wind had stolen her words and flown them like a kite as she had called to her sisters to explore the murky pools filled with emerald fronds concealing the treasure within. Her reddish shoulder-length hair had been hidden beneath a green felt hat that kept threatening to blow away. Looking critically at the photograph she decided that her large amber eyes were her best asset, but she frowned at her mouth. She hated the way that when she smiled widely her teeth looked crowded. Scrutinising the image of herself she wondered if that was what Leslie disliked about her.

PART ONE

ITALY 1927

The small Italian piazza in Civita was sleeping. It was overlooked by the peach coloured church that had guarded it like a faithful sentinel for hundreds of years. The statues on its walls stared blindly, their faces changing from dove grey to rubicund as the sunlight swept across them and rose above the steeple. Seven chimes announced the new day. Doors and shutters began to open, bright awnings fluttered in the wind, and the silence became peppered with morning sounds. Birds trilled, there were calls of *'Buongiorno'*, and the sound of neighbours passing the time of day, while the scents of coffee and baking bread mingled in the air.

Ricardo, a tall bearded man with raven curls and dark eyes, strode along the road. Whistling, he ducked under the archway leading from a narrow side street into the square, passing plant pots that gleamed as the sunlight played over their vibrant colours. Lilac and magenta lobelia peeped out from beneath salmon and scarlet geraniums as he trod the worn flagstones - which bore witness to more than two hundred years of visitors - each one polishing and shaping the stone. He pushed open the wooden door to his brother's *osteria*. Inside stood a long wooden counter, and, behind, the wall was decorated with wooden shelves housing bottles and glasses, as well as jars filled with coffee, sweets, candied lemons, biscuits and pickles. Along one side of the square room stood a tall oak dresser covered with blue china plates, bowls and cups. On the worn wooden floor were ten small tables, often pushed together for large parties. Corrado's cooking was famous in the area; he was especially celebrated for his lemon creations. He kept his recipes a secret, but his cooking validated the belief fiercely held by Tuscan men that both their food and women were superior to those in any other Italian province.

'Corrado,' called Ricardo, 'I've a message from Giverny. She wants you to come home to dinner tonight. She's worried you're not eating properly now Mama's gone, bless her soul.' He crossed himself and muttered a prayer.

'I don't think your lovely wife should be worrying about me wasting away!' Corrado said as he walked in. 'I've just been so busy here every night I stayed late.' He opened the red shutters, allowing the sun to enter and bathe the floor, turning it the colour of honey.

'Give me a hand, we can sit out.'

Between them they moved some trestle tables and chairs outside into the square, which was coming to life.

'I've just got to check on my bread. Coffee?'

Nodding, Ricardo settled himself contentedly, enjoying the early sun and looking forward to catching up with his brother. Across the road the butcher's wife was sweeping up; children walked to school; and a donkey and cart driven by an old man smoking a pipe bowled past.

'*Buongiorno,*' Ricardo called.

The old man waved back. A podgy white bull terrier, sunbathing on the worn mushroom- coloured cobbles, momentarily lifted his head as Ricardo gave him a stroke on his soft pink belly. Then he resumed his sleeping position. The greengrocer, Christiano Barbieri, whistled as he arranged his boxes bursting with vegetables and called over.

'Tell Corrado I've got some asparagus. He was asking for some.' He pointed to a fan of spears like a green and purple peacock's tail standing in a wicker basket.

'He'll be over in a minute.'

The brothers had a good relationship now, but it hadn't always been that way. Ricardo, the eldest by fifteen years, used to be jealous of his younger brother. Their father, Amedeo, had died when Corrado was young, which had devastated the whole family, particularly Ricardo. He had adored his papa and spent every spare minute with him, learning how to farm and listening to his stories about his youth travelling around Europe. An intelligent man with a penchant for languages, Amedeo's hopes for a long career as Professor of Languages were dashed when his father became ill. This meant Amedeo had to take over the family farm and settle down with Mara.

Both boys had happy memories of their childhood. Despite their mother being thirteen years younger than her husband, she ruled the roost. After Ricardo, the two of them had tried for many years to have another child, each pregnancy ending in early disappointment. Agreeing to one more attempt, had Mara prayed constantly to Our Lady, promising that if her wish was granted she would never complain again and would do anything to make her family happy. She would never admit it, but when Corrado was born he became her favourite. She delighted in teaching him to cook on sunny afternoons, when she would stand him on a chair and watch him gently prod at the dough with podgy hands. Then they would eat hot bread straight from the oven, laughing as golden butter dribbled down their chins. Corrado also had a special bond with his grandmother, Nonna, who was always telling him stories. Consequently, Ricardo felt he was out on a limb, as if Corrado was the chosen one. When their father died, most of the responsibility fell on Ricardo's shoulders, but both boys had had to grow up fast and help their mama run the farm.

Fortunately, Ricardo's life changed had when he met Giverny. She was staying in Bolsena at her uncle and aunt's hotel by the lake. He happened to be helping out with some gardening there. Initially, it was her wide smile that captivated him. They secretly swam in the lake together, and when she returned to her home in the north they wrote love letters to each other for a year, planning how to be together, as her family were against her moving so far away. Eventually Giverny managed to persuade her parents to let her return the following summer. Ricardo proposed, and they had a wonderful wedding. Giverny was a godsend in several ways. She was a hard worker who pitched in with everything on the farm, working tirelessly during the harvest and never stopping even when she became pregnant with their first child. She was also a peace-maker and through her the brothers learned to love each other again.

The family recovered from Nonno's death and were blessed when Giverny gave birth to a baby girl, Gabriella. She grew, nourished by the goat's milk and cheese they made at the farm, and the family was completed by dark-haired noisy twin brothers. Corrado was seven when his niece was born, and she became like the sister he had never had. He was fiercely protective of her and he became the one she ran to when she grazed her knees. They sat and read stories together; he taught her to climb trees and gave her piggy backs. The farm flourished for several years until a tragic accident occurred. Mara adored her granddaughter and had passed her love of horses on to her. She taught Gabriella to ride when she was tiny, and gave her Belleza, her much-loved pony. Together, they loved to explore the hills and valleys around the farm, and on particularly hot days would ride to Lake Bolsena nearby for a refreshing swim. Gabriella was proud to be seen with Nonna, as she knew everyone, which meant they could barely ride past another villager without having to stop and chat.

Mara went riding to Bolsena alone one day and didn't return, so Ricardo went to look for her. He found her lifeless with a broken neck, her Thoroughbred horse trembling beside her. Corrado took the horse up to the lemon grove. Blinded by tears, he pulled the trigger. The horse fell. As the bang ricocheted around the hillside he felt as if his heart was being ripped from his body. Overcome, he lay beneath the lemon tree and wept. Ricardo found him digging an enormous grave for the horse. Gently taking the shovel out of his brother's blistered and bleeding hands, he finished it while Corrado stood by, his tears falling into the hole as he remembered standing with his Mama cutting tomatoes, laughing as she taught him how to turn them sideways to always get circles. Picturing her face, he clung to the memory of the way her eyes used to narrow as she concentrated and tasted her dishes for seasoning, and how she would throw her head back and laugh with her mouth wide open when he said something funny. Their shared grief brought the brothers closer together and made them appreciate family even more than they had before.

Corrado brought out two steaming cups of coffee as a short man with a grey suit, tie and hat walked past them. They couldn't see his eyes because he wore dark glasses, but he stared at them without speaking and continued through the square before turning left past the church. Ricardo looked at Corrado and frowned.

'Why's he got his eye on us?'

Corrado shrugged in reply. Ricardo picked up his coffee, his large brown hand dwarfing the cup. He sniffed it deeply before taking a sip, wiping his moustache and letting out a satisfied sigh.

'That's better. Now I'm awake. So, dinner later?'

'Yeah.'

'I think Giverny has an ulterior motive.' Ricardo chuckled, and his brown eyes shone with mischief.

'What d'you mean?'

'Well, she might have invited someone else.'

'Like who?'

Ricardo smirked.

'Oh! I get it. It's another set-up. No way. It was a disaster last time, with Isabella.' Corrado stood up, gesticulating. 'No. Tell Giverny I'm not ready to settle down. I want to see the world first, or at least some of it. If she has her way, I'll be married with loads of little ones running around, just like you.' He slumped back into his chair and scowled into his coffee cup.

Ricardo laughed and clapped his brother on the shoulder. 'But you're such a good-looking boy! All the girls want to marry you.'

'*Va al diavol!* Get lost!'

'Ha ha. Got you. No-one else is invited. She just wants you to bring a lemon tart. You know it's her favourite, and as you've been here all week we've missed you being at home. You know, you could be a bit friendlier to women. Whenever they talk to you, you look bored. You never smile.'

'That's because I am bored!'

Punching his brother on the arm, Corrado laughed too, before taking out a packet of cigarettes and offering it. Both men looked almost identical as they faced one another, except that Ricardo had a beard and Corrado's dark hair was shorter and wavier. Patting his pocket for matches Corrado lit both their cigarettes. The smoke swirled lazily over their heads, past the white awning and the *osteria* sign. They sat in companionable silence.

'Papa, Uncle Corrado.' A tall, dark curly haired girl ran to join them.

'You've finished chatting, then,' said Ricardo to his daughter.

'Morning, Gabriella, and how are you today?' Corrado smiled. 'Come with me and I'll see if I can find you something to take to school.'

She followed him inside as he bent down and pulled out a large glass jar from under the counter.

'Want one of these?' He handed her a lemon biscuit dusted with sugar. Her lips were quickly dusted too.

'Right. Come on, madam. Time for school.'

Gabriella's lip curled and she shook her curls and frowned at her father.

'I hate school. Why can't I stay here and help Corrado? You know I want to be a cook like him.'

'But what will the sisters say if you don't go? And Uncle Corrado's got work to do, and so have I.'

'I tell you what, I'll come and collect you later from school and we'll go and pick some lemons,' said Corrado.

'All right, but don't forget.'

'Promise. I'll be up this afternoon. Tell Giverny yes to dinner and I'll bring Gabriella home.'

'*Ciao*.' Ricardo walked with Gabriella along the road, stopping every few yards to chat to the locals, who he had known all his life.

'Come on.' Gabriella pulled at her father's arm.

Two ladies dressed in black with identical faces, their skins so covered in branching lines that they resembled rivers drawn on a map, sat on the church steps taking in the beautiful morning and watching the tall man and his daughter head towards them. They knew everything about everybody, having lived in Civita their whole lives, more than seventy years. The steps of the church and their windows were their seats in the theatre of the square. Nothing escaped their attention. The smile of a girl falling in love, a frown from a husband whose dinner was not ready on time, the despair of an unrequited lover as he recited poetry to his bored girlfriend. They heard frustrated mothers berating their husbands and children for making a mess. They even heard the wheedling tone of a wife asking her husband to get in the washing that hung along the balconies adorning the piazza like royal boxes at the opera.

'*Buongiorno,*' they said in unison.

'Morning, ladies. How are you both?' said Ricardo.

'Not so bad, young man, but we're getting older...' began Adriana, the younger of the two.

'... And we can feel it in our bones,' finished Rosetta. They both laughed, showing their pink gums.

'How are those little rascals of yours?'
Gabriella pulled at her father's arm again.

'Cheeky as ever! See you ladies later, *ciao.*'

Leaving the square to walk up the slope to the school, Camillo, the butcher, stepped out of his shop into their path. A portly man - bald with a bulbous nose and black moustache stiff as a yard brush - he was wiping his bloody hands on the white apron that covered his ample stomach. He had been busy arranging the day's meat in the window of his small, dark, cool shop.

Shuddering, Gabriella stared through the window at the pig's head that gazed back at her with blind eyes and a gaping mouth. It seemed to be laughing. The fat chorizo garlands festooned across the window, interspersed with pigeons and rabbits with lolling heads, looked like a grotesque celebration for the dead. Turning away, she stood back in the sun and enjoyed the feeling of it warming her face.

'Hello my friend. How's things?' said Camillo.

'Yes, we are all very well, and you?'

Camillo's deep brown eyes darkened and turned black, as he frowned and leaned in to half whisper to his friend.

'Have you heard about Ciro? He's left because of that *bastardo*, Nicolai.' He sneered.'Sorry for my language in front of the child.' He nodded at Gabriella. 'But…' He spat on the ground. 'He's trying to take over, and who knows who'll be next, eh?' Camillo flung his hands upwards before turning back to his shop doorway. As he went he muttered about what he'd like to do to Nicolai.

'What's he talking about, Papa?' Gabriella stared up into her father's eyes, which mirrored her own.

'Nothing for you to worry about. Now, race you up the hill!'

Corrado waved to his old friend, Christiano, the greengrocer, who was polishing his oranges before standing back to admire them.

'I'll be over shortly,' he called.

Christiano waved back and straightened the white fedora he always wore pulled down over his ears. Having once sported a long glossy mane, he had never quite got over the cruel loss of his pride and joy. Despite this, he was a jovial man who always shared the time of day with anyone who came to his shop. His wife, Carlotta, was the opposite.

Christiano had a set daily routine: he opened his shop from seven every morning until eleven, and then sat outside in the piazza to wait for his friend, Davide, the baker from Bagnoregio. Davide would cycle up the huge hill to Civita. He'd arrive breathless and boiling, wiping his brow with the scarlet handkerchief he always carried. Together, they'd share several glasses of grappa and lunch at the *osteria* before playing dominoes and cards until two o'clock. Then Christiano would stagger across to his shop and go upstairs to bed and Davide would wobble back down the hill to take his own siesta. Christiano rarely surfaced again until evening, and Carlotta - secretly renamed Crudela by the local children - took charge of the shop once her husband was in bed. They didn't just sell fruit and vegetables but sweets as well. Everyone knew the time to buy from their shop was in the morning, but sometimes unfortunate children were sent on errands by their mamas to pick up things forgotten earlier in the day. The mothers knew that the only way they could persuade their children to run the Carlotta gauntlet was to bribe them by giving them a little extra money for sweets.

Taller than her husband, Carlotta towered over the unfortunate children that entered the shop and glared at them.

Thin and angular with long greasy hair, she had a mouth that was constantly pursed disapprovingly. When she spoke, it was as if she had been eating the sour grapes that are cast aside during harvest because they have never been kissed by the sun. Rumour had it that she had once been happy and laughed and joked like her husband. This seemed inconceivable as they were so ill-suited now. Her greatest wish in life had been to have children, but unfortunately every one of her eleven pregnancies had ended prematurely. Sorrow had turned her into a gorgon. As a result, everyone tried to be kind to her, but generally kept out of her way.

Taking his basket Corrado crossed the piazza, enjoying the early sun chasing away the shadows.

'*Ciao.*'

'*Ciao*, Corrado. Look I've got what you wanted.' Christiano pointed to the basket of asparagus.

'Perfect for what I want to make today. I'll take half of those, please.'

'So, what's on the menu for lunch?'

'Well, I'll lightly grill these spears with salt, pepper and a drizzle of olive oil, and finish them with a grating of Parmigiano and a squeeze of lemon. No other accompaniment is needed - this dish will speak for itself. And, I'd like some of those.' Corrado's eyes lit up as he pointed to a basket crammed with zucchini crowned with delicate orange flowers. 'I'll make *fiori fritti*. Can you get me more of these for Friday? I need as many as possible for the party, I'm going to stuff them with ricotta.'

Christiano filled Corrado's basket. 'I can get you as many as you need. You're making my mouth water. I can't wait for lunch.'

'*Ciao*.'

MARGARET

Returning the photograph to the mound inside the trunk, Margaret scooped out her diary and opened it before sitting on the bed to flick through her entries. Turning the pages, she longed to turn back the clock, longed to return to the time when she had been innocent - before she had allowed herself to be swept away on a tsunami.

5th March 1927

Tonight I went to a big company dinner with Father. He introduced me to his new business partner, Leslie Mallows. He's very tall and blonde with piercing arctic blue eyes. I sat next to him while we ate and he talked to me all evening. He asked me about my job and told me he likes reading too, although he's crazy about cars and has two of his own. He seems a very interesting character, although he's quite a lot older than me. I think he must be in his mid-thirties. As we stood up to leave I noticed he had a slight limp. It doesn't detract from his attractiveness. It makes him seem more interesting. I didn't dare ask him about it, but Father told me on the way home that he was injured during the war. They are opening a new steel factory together, specialising in making sheet metal car parts. Father also told me that he intends to hand the company over to Leslie when he retires and suggested that he might be a good man to marry. I laughed, but he didn't. I realised then that maybe he was serious.

10th March 1927
Leslie has written and invited me out to dinner with him tomorrow and I have agreed.

11th March 1927

We had a lovely time at a little restaurant tucked away in Mayfair that I haven't been to before. He really is frightfully charming, and we drank champagne all evening. He is so attentive and different from boys my age, who seem so childish by comparison. He knows so much. I found out tonight that he read History and English at Oxford University, so we talked about books all evening. He knows so much about everything.

31st March 1927

Leslie asked me to marry him! I'm so excited, and we're having a party next week. My ring is beautiful. It looks perfect on my finger. I can't wait. We can spend evenings discussing books and go out to dinner and have parties.

Sighing, Margaret sucked the pen, remembering her excitement, before turning the page to her wedding day.

1ˢᵗ May 1927

Today was the big day. Mother couldn't stop crying every time she looked at me in my wedding dress. The wedding was capital, all the guests agreed it was a frightfully good do, and Father made a lovely speech about giving me to a worthy man. I think deep down he was worried I'd never marry, as I had turned Tom down last year. Leslie is different. He's seen the world and is the most handsome man I've ever met. I can't wait for him to make me a woman.

Why, why, why? What was I thinking? Slamming the book shut Margaret threw it on the floor.

LEMON PICKING
ITALY

Whistling to himself as he kneaded his pizza dough in his kitchen at the back of the *osteria*, Corrado looked out of the window at the sun shining on his pots of basil and oregano and thought about the dishes he was planning to cook that day. First, he carefully washed the zucchini flowers and began to make the batter, before checking on his famous onion soup. People came from miles around for a bowl at lunchtime. The air was filled with the aroma of the sizzling, sweet onions as they gently caramelised. Removing the lid, he took a long sniff, before giving them a stir. The door opening made him turn.

'*Buongiorno.* We're not open yet,' he called, and walked behind the counter still whistling. The man from earlier, wearing a trilby, appeared in the doorway. Taking off his dark glasses he smiled cruelly. It made him look like a dog snarling. Corrado's whistle died abruptly.

'*Buongiorno*,' said the man, undoing his coat to reveal a grey suit with matching silk tie. Selecting a cup, he poured himself a coffee from the steaming jug on the long bar in front of him. Taking a sip, he studied the room.

'You have a nice place here, my friend. They say your cooking is the best in town.' He took another sip before striding to the end of the counter and taking the transparent cover off a cake. Picking up a knife he pointed it at Corrado.

'I'll have to try it for myself.' Cutting a slice of cake, he took a large bite. Corrado watched the crumbs fall on to the wooden floor that he had already swept ready for the day.

'Mmmm,' the man took another bite. 'Lemon, *delizioso*.' Brushing the crumbs from his tie he sat down, still holding the knife.

'What do you want, Nicolai? I'm busy,' said Corrado.

'That's no way to greet an old friend, now is it? It seems to me you're doing very well for yourself here.' Nicolai began to use the knife to clean under his fingernails. 'My friends and I will be back later to try some more of your famous food.' He stood up, put on his hat and glasses, and carefully put the knife back on the counter. '*Arrivederche.*'

'*Merda*!' Corrado went back into the kitchen and realized his onions had started burning. He tipped them into the bin and began peeling some more. All his food would be late now, as the onions needed to cook for at least two hours to make them sweet enough. Working his pizza dough, he imagined it was Nicolai's head he was pummelling.

*

Later, as Corrado drove his niece up the steep stony hill to their family farm, a black Labrador followed by two mop haired boys came hurtling down before stopping breathless in front of the car. Corrado leaned out of the window and stroked the dog's ears.

'Hello, Nero,' he said, before turning to his nephews.

'Whoa, you trying to get run over? Now who's who? Tomaso?' He pointed at the nearest nephew, who shook his head with a big grin.

'You're rubbish! You never get it right. I'm Alfredo, and he's Tomaso.' Alfredo pointed to his twin, who was getting in the car. As they drove up the hill the dog raced behind them, black ears flapping. The boys loved it when Uncle Corrado came and played with them. He gave them piggy backs and stood in goal while they tried to beat him at football. They drove up and got out, avoiding the chickens and ducks clamouring around their feet.

'*Ciao.*' Corrado kissed Giverny on both cheeks. She put her bundle of washing on a table so she could kiss her daughter.

'Quick, get changed if you're going lemon picking. Don't

forget your hat,' Giverny called to her daughter, who had already run inside.

The twins began to chase the chickens until their mother stopped them.

'You two do something useful, find the basket and collect the eggs.' As they ran off towards the field to the left of the house she added, 'And no breakages this time, or there'll be trouble. Do you hear?'

Gabriella ran out of the house.

'Ready.'

'Mama's rose garden is looking wonderful.' Corrado strode over to admire the lines of passionate red, sweet pink and creamy ivory roses tinged with the palest blush, before inhaling deeply.

'Mmmmm. She would have been proud of it. This was her favourite time of year.'

'Oh, I nearly forgot. Here's the lemon tart I promised you.' Corrado produced it from the back of the car with a flourish and a smile before placing it on the table next to the washing.

Giverny began pegging out the linens. 'Mmmm. *Grazie.* Don't be late,' she said, mumbling because there was a peg in her mouth.

'Come on, Nero. Good boy.' Walking back up the hill with the dog, Corrado and Gabriella reached a low stone wall, covered in deep green velvety moss. Corrado helped Gabriella climb it before jumping over himself. They continued walking for a long time as the spring sun cast long shadows on the path ahead.

Eventually Gabriella looked up at Corrado pleadingly.

'I'm tired, we've been walking for ages,' she said.

'Let's have a quick stop, then.' Out of his large canvas knapsack Corrado took a package. Opening it, he produced two fat slices of lemon sponge cake covered in white icing. The zest in the cake contrasted deliciously with the sugary topping and made Gabriella's lips tingle. Nero made short work of the dropped crumbs and in return for the treat allowed himself to become a pillow for Gabriella. Lying in the sunshine she and Corrado listened to the sound of the crickets, and watched bees commandeer the delicate field poppies that danced and swayed, sprinkled across the otherwise barren scrubland like scarlet butterflies. The rough parched grass tickled Gabriella's legs, and made her wriggle. She sat up and turned her head to one side.

'Who's that singing?'

'That's the sisters in the Abbey, it's not too far from here, over that hill and down in the valley. Our lemon grove is on the edge of our land and theirs begins right behind it.'

'What do they do, apart from sing and teach at school?'

'They pray and garden and look after people.'

'They sound like angels.'

Corrado smiled and nodded as they both listened to the distant sweet strains.

'I'm not sure which smells better, the sunshine or the cake,' said Gabriella.

Corrado lit a cigarette and inhaled deeply, letting smoke trickle from his lips. He laughed.

'It's not the sun you can smell. It's the lemons. We're getting close now, come on.' He pulled her to her feet, and they walked on towards a lemon grove. Its waxy deep green leaves stood out against the delphinium sky.

'Now, have a sniff.' Corrado inhaled deeply. 'That's my favourite smell.' He smiled at his niece as she wrinkled her nose. 'You look like a rabbit when you do that.'

Before them stood a magnificent lemon tree. The sound of crickets became deafening as they breathed in its citron aroma. Ivy tendrils dripped from its branches like bracelets. Clusters of fungi protruding from its forks covered the lacy ochre lichen on its bark. Its crowning glory was the fruit glistening in the shadowy sunlight, shining leaves forming a protective canopy over the ripe yellow lemons, like little parasols. Gnarled, the Italian sunset reflecting off it, the tree creaked and seemed to sigh, as if trying to tell them about the many tableaux played out beneath it. Corrado put down his knapsack.

'I remember the first time I came here with Nonno, my papa, and he said to me: "This tree is special; it's seen many things. It's very old. Hundreds of baby birds have been born and nurtured to maturity within its branches. They have taken their first timid flights, while their parents anxiously watched over them, willing them to fly safely. Families of rabbits have made their burrows within the sturdy roots beneath, sharing them with earthworms and bustling beetles. And the biggest secret of all is that this tree grows the best lemons that I have ever tasted."'

Gabriella smiled up at him. 'I like thinking of it being a home to lots of birds and animals. It's a very useful tree then, isn't it, to them - and to us, as we get to eat the lemons?'

'Yes and not many people know that this is here you know, and that's the way we want it to stay, so make sure you keep it a secret, *si*? When Nonno planted some of these trees, I was with him. I was a few years younger than you, about eight or nine. The lemon grove around the special tree needs replanting every fifty years, but the big tree is more than a thousand years old. One day you might help your papa plant some new trees.'

They picked the lemons until Corrado's bag was brimming,

before turning down the hill in the gathering gloom as the last rays of the sun filtered through the trees, turning the lemon grove into a golden crown.

'Can you teach me to cook some of your recipes?' Gabriella asked.

'Ah, you want me to give away my sugary secrets do you?' Laughing, he brushed back his fringe from his eyes as they trudged back in the dying light. 'Yes of course I will. You can help me cook at the weekend.'

CORRADO AND GABRIELLA

Returning to the farmhouse, the family home that the brothers had lived in all their lives, a delicate smell greeted Gabriella and Corrado as they pushed open the large oak panelled door and entered.

'Mmmmmm.' Gabriella drank in the aroma of garlic, onion and tomatoes frying gently in olive oil. It was the signature smell of her childhood. At a later date, whenever she cooked the same dish herself, she would feel comforted by memories of her mother and home.

The white walls blushed in the dying sunlight and shadows played over the large dresser higgledy piggledy with crockery, children's drawings and photographs of family. Oak beams were adorned with herbs and spices interspersed with garlic plaits and onion rings hanging on hooks. Above the busy, black range, great copper pans were hung. Steam rising from the bubbling sauce clouded the reflection of Giverny, stirring. A petite woman with long black hair that fell in a thick plait like a rope down her back, her face could never be described as classically beautiful; but she had a generous mouth, and when she smiled her eyes lit up and she became very attractive.

Grabbing both of her arms Corrado gave her a resounding kiss on each cheek. 'Mwah, mwah, smells fantastic.'

Giverny smiled, a tired smile that didn't really reach her eyes.

'What's wrong?' He put an arm around her shoulder and frowned as he peered into her face.

'Nothing. I just have a bit of a headache.' She brushed an errant strand of hair behind her ear. 'And those little boys are wearing me out, but they're in bed now.'

'Right. Sit down. I'm taking over, no arguing,' he guided his sister-in-law to the long, scrubbed table that had been in the family for years. He had watched his mother and grandmother at this table, pounding pasta into silky dough before stretching it into long swathes ready to hang to dry like washing from the long slats fixed to the ceiling. Sturdy and strong, the table had groaned under the weight of all the feasts necessary for christenings, weddings, birthdays and funerals.

'Where's Ricardo?'

'Feeding the buffalo and checking the goats and sheep. Gabriella, go and shut in the ducks and hens, quickly before it's too dark.'

'So, what can I do?'

'It's pretty much done, really. I've finished the stew. It just needs some parsley. *Grazie*, Corrado.'

'Where's the wine? You could do with a drink. No, I'll get it.' He stopped her from getting up and fetched two glasses, filling them generously with Chianti. Returning to the stove he dipped a spoon into the sauce. After tasting it, he took a pinch of sea salt from the large terracotta bowl beside the range and ground some between his fingers, enjoying the roughness before sprinkling it in, giving it the stew last stir and adding some fresh green parsley.

The kitchen was silent as the four of them savoured each mouthful of perfectly seasoned veal cooked in wine with chilli and tomatoes.

'Delicious.' Corrado pushed his plate away and wiped his mouth with his hand.
Across the table his niece was trying unsuccessfully to stifle a large yawn, which didn't go unnoticed by her mother.

'Right. Bedtime, Gabriella.'

Gabriella wrapped her arms around her mother, who buried her face in her daughter's hair, inhaling her sweet smell and hugging her tightly.

'Good night.' Gabriella blew her papa and Corrado a kiss.

Gabriella sat in her wooden bed covered with a brightly

coloured patchwork quilt, writing her diary. The walls were covered in drawings of horses and ponies, and under the window was a wooden bookshelf containing fairytales about knights and princesses. On the windowsill sat her pride and joy - a gift from her Nonna – a set of Russian dolls with pink painted pinafores and green headscarves. When she was little, she had spent many fascinated hours taking them apart and arranging them in perfect lines before putting them back together. Her mouth began to wobble, before a plump tear fell on to a yellow square of patchwork. Stifling a sob, she put her diary back under her pillow.

Walking past her room Corrado heard a muffled noise and poked his head round the door.

'Ah, what's up?' Corrado wiped her tear away and took her hand.

'I miss Nonna,' she sobbed.

Stroking her hair, Corrado held her until she quietened. 'I know, I miss her too, every day, *innamorato*. Your bedcover reminds me of her.'

'She made it, didn't she?'

'Yes, and every square has a meaning you know, a memory. This one,' he pointed to a green and white checked square, 'is part of an apron she used to wear when I was young like you. She was very happy. She sang all the time while she was cooking.' Corrado sighed.

'What did she look like when she was young?'

'Well, you know, her eyes were chestnut, the same as yours, and she'd put her hair up with pins, but curls would escape and snake down her back. She had one that would always fall over her eyes, and she would push it back behind her ear. What I remember most is the way she was always cuddling your papa and me. She worked so hard, helping run the farm and cooking, always cooking. I can picture her now pounding a great mound of pasta, a smattering of flour on her cheek and her black curl hanging down, totally engrossed, caressing the dough before dominating it into the shape she wanted. I always wanted to be close to her, she was my world. I wanted to please her and spend every minute with her, and I realised that if I shared her passion, I could.'

Gabriella pointed to a white square covered in tiny yellow roses. 'What about this one?'

'That was her favourite dress. She used to wear it for best, but one day it got ruined.'

'Why what happened?' Gabriella sat up and wiped her nose with the back of her hand.

'Well, she and Papa were going out after dinner, I was quite little so I can't remember where, but she had an apron on and we were about to eat. She asked Papa to shake up the dressing, but the cork was loose, and it poured all over him and some went on Mama's dress.' Corrado laughed at the memory. 'He looked so funny with oil dripping everywhere, like he was melting. We all laughed, and they didn't go out in the end. So, Mama kept a bit of the ruined dress for the quilt because she had loved it so much.'

'That's a funny story. Did Nonna teach you to make everything you cook now? She started to teach me before she got ill, and then she was too tired all the time.' Gabriella sniffed and her eyes began to fill up again. Corrado hugged her tightly.

'Listen now. If you promise not to be sad, you can help me make some of the dishes for the big *festa* next weekend. Do you remember last year's?'

'I was allowed to stay up until midnight! Tell me the story about why we have it again,' she pleaded.

'What, again!' He laughed. 'Not tonight, it's too late. You'll hear it on the night of the party when I make my speech. On Saturday we have to get up extra early to prepare the food before we go into the village for the procession of the Madonna. And this year is special for me and Giuseppe as we are the icon bearers. I'm going to need your help, so get some sleep now.'

Gabriella nodded, her eyelids drooping as Corrado kissed

her goodnight and pulled the quilt around her.

Back in the kitchen Giverny and Ricardo were deep in
discussion.

'It's Roberta I feel sorry for,' said Giverny. 'He's making
everyone turn against her.'

'We saw him this morning, didn't we?' said Ricardo.

'Nicolai? Yeah he struts around like he owns the place.'
Corrado picked up the plates and stacked them.

'I saw Camillo earlier, he was fuming. He told me that Ciro
took his family and left because Nicolai was extorting money
from him. Who the hell does he think he is?'

'He came into the *osteria* after you left and started throwing
his weight around, threatening to come back with his new
fascist friends.' Corrado frowned in disgust. 'Now he thinks
he's a big man with them behind him. I've got the feeling he's
going to try to get money from us next.'

'Luigi always looks unhappy, too. That family have been
through so much with Barbara leaving. And now this,' said
Giverny.

'Giuseppe hates him. The other day, I heard from Antonio,
you know, Beppe's brother from Bagnoregio, that Nicolai's
playing around with Pamela that lives at the top of the hill.'

'That whore! But Roberta's pregnant. What a total *stronzo*.'

Giverny finished clearing the table. 'Poor girl, she's so young, stuck with him and still reeling from her mother leaving.'

'Who knows what Giuseppe will do if he finds out. You know what he's like.'

'Yeah, I wouldn't like to be in Nicolai's shoes then.'

'I've promised Gabby she can help me cook on Saturday, is that all right?'

'Of course. She's growing up fast. She's determined to carry on the family tradition. Keeps asking if she can leave school and work with you in the *osteria*.' Giverny laughed. 'I think she thinks if she goes on enough she'll wear me down.'

'She's always been like that when she decides she wants something, hasn't she? Like when she learned to ride a bicycle. Even though she kept falling off and hurting her knees she wouldn't give up.' Ricardo smiled proudly at the memory of his daughter waving at him as she wobbled down the drive, laughing because she had finally mastered the trick of it.

'The same with riding, Mama said she was a natural straight away. Once she decides she's going to do something, woe betide anyone who gets in her way,' said Giverny. 'But I'm not giving in to her about school.'

CORRADO

Taking himself off to the library, his favourite room in the house, Corrado closed the door behind him, waiting for calmness to descend on him as the scent of wood, dust and leather brought back floods of memories. Shutting his eyes, he pictured his father seated at the large wooden desk under the window, his glasses perched on his nose, reading. He had passed his love of books to Corrado, and from an early age had introduced him to Homer's *Odyssey*. As a professor of languages, he would read it in Greek and translate to his wide-eyed son Odysseus' arduous journey and his battles with the Cyclops and the Sirens. He would also tell him about his own travels abroad. This had ignited a desire in Corrado to see the world for himself, and he used to pore over atlases and attempt to roll his tongue around foreign words and place names. The scrapbook Corrado had filled with his father's tickets, stamps and grainy photographs of himself, dapper in a light suit and trilby, laughing in some far-flung place, had long ago been assigned to a trunk in the attic.

The room was wallpapered in books. Leather-bound large

tomes full of facts about science, history, politics and geography dominated one wall; however, Corrado preferred the others, novels that he loved to get lost in, reading about adventures and battles. Sitting in the worn leather chair that still bore his father's imprint he thought about his conversation with Gabriella. He desperately missed his mama, too. Opening one of the desk drawers he took out a box. Inside was a photograph of his mother under a lock of her dark hair. Tears filled his eyes as he looked at it.

'Mama, I miss you. I feel so guilty. I'm losing my faith. I can't believe in a God who takes away everyone I love. First Nonno and Nonna, then Papa and now you. Why?' He slammed the drawer shut. 'I don't want to be here anymore. I want to get away. But I can't because I have to put the family first and be responsible. I feel dead inside. On the surface I look like one of the ducks on the pond swimming calmly along but, underneath I feel like I'm slowly dying. I'm paddling like fury, trying not to lose my mind. When you died I couldn't bear it! I still can't. Then I wanted to end it all, throw myself down a ravine - and if it hadn't been for Giuseppe, I think I would have. Luckily he found me under the lemon tree.'

Corrado remembered that day so clearly because it was a turning point in his life. He had been pacing up and down beneath the tree when he had seen Giuseppe walking towards him. His fury had taken over. And he had screamed at his friend.

'What's the point of it all? Why do I have all this responsibility? I didn't ask for it. Nonna made me promise to stay and keep her secrets, but I don't want to be here any more. I hate it.' He had broken down then, and Giuseppe had held him in his arms until his tears subsided. They had been friends for 21 years, since birth, but had never really had a conversation before, a real one, that wasn't about football or girls.

'I know it's not the same because my mama isn't dead. Although she's dead to me, since leaving with that *stronzo*. Nothing's the same for me anymore, either.' Giuseppe had said. 'Papa's angry all the time, Roberta's married and having a baby. I want out. Let's both go.' He had turned to Corrado with eyes full of intent. 'Why not? What's stopping us? Neither of us is happy. Let's secretly start making plans and then we can tell everyone just before we go.'

'Where, though?'

'Haven't you always wanted to go to England? Lots of people do it, why not us, eh?'

'I know it's always been my dream to go to London and open an *osteria*, but what about you?'

'Sounds good to me. We could buy a farm. We've both got money, our inheritances from our grandparents, we can use those.'

Since that day they had been formulating a plan. However, after talking to Gabriella Corrado felt torn again. He looked at the photograph once more. 'I'm sorry, Mama, but for the first time in ages I feel something other than the sense of dread I get every morning when I wake up. I know it's a cowardly thing to do, but we're leaving. I've learnt to carry on, but I can't love. That's why I ended it with Isabella. I'm terrified of being hurt and losing love again. Now I feel like a fraud. On Saturday it's the *festa,* and I'm to be the icon bearer but I'm not sure I have any faith left. Now I'm 21, I have to take responsibility and be an adult, but I feel too young. When Ricardo was my age he was about to be married and wanted to be a father. I'm not ready! I'm going to have to pretend and smile, all the time loathing this life, this empty life. I think Papa would understand my wanting to leave, but I feel you would be disappointed in me and I can't even think about Nonna or Gabriella.' Replacing the box back in the drawer, he sighed before going to bed.

ITALY 303AD

'The day began like any other. Camilo Amerigo, affectionately called Milo by his mother as she kissed him goodnight, lived with his family on a farm near Bagnoregio. Each day he woke at dawn to graze goats across the neighbouring hillsides. Mist enveloped the garden, turning it into a silver spidery paradise. Cobwebs clung in cradles, tiny strands of pearls slung between the roses, and lavender bushes glistened in the light of the watery sun as Milo waved goodbye. After countless thistles and bits of scrub grass had snatched at his feet while he followed the goats, he sank down gratefully beneath a cypress tree, its shadow the shape of a long feather. As the sun was reaching its pinnacle, the shade became a cool cloak, comforting him while the heat of the day and the gentle sound of the goats' bells lulled him to sleep.

Groggily he pushed his curly hair from his dark, sleepy eyes, drank some water and ate a hunk of the bread his mother had packed him, before scanning the horizon to see the goats disappearing over a hill. Hastily he leapt to his feet, imagining his father's wrath. He was always getting into trouble for not watching the herd properly. Running towards them made them run away faster. Their bells clanking wildly like a deranged orchestra, they scattered in all directions. Once he caught up with them, they stopped and began to nibble at the grass by their feet. Panting, he bent over to catch his breath, and suddenly heard singing floating across the hillside. Milo cocked his head in surprise. The singer sounded so sad. His deep voice singing a prayer had a haunting quality. Milo felt drawn to follow it.

Resonating across the valley, the voice led him to a high stone wall which he skirted until he found a gate. He turned the wrought-iron latch, but it wouldn't move. Looking around, he discovered an old olive tree whose branches leaned over the wall like a shady canopy. Hoisting himself up, he climbed until he could stand on the wall and circle round an old building built of stone, the colour of the rich honeycomb he sometimes stole from the bees nesting high on the hills. The building glowered balefully in the sunshine, choked by thick branches of ivy that infiltrated the windows and rooms upstairs. There was no one in sight; he looked below and saw what once must have been a beautiful garden planted with bushes and flowers. The rosemary bushes had turned woody and the convolvulus had taken over, giving the space a melancholy feel, exacerbated by the singing coming from within. Milo's curiosity got the better of him, so he jumped down, and a myrtle tree broke his fall. Running towards the voice, he found it coming through a wall at the side. There was a high window there that he couldn't reach, so he called out.

"*Buongiornio.*"

The singing stopped. "Who's there?" A weak voice called.

"Camilo Amerigo. I heard you singing and…"

"Thank you, Madonna, Holy Mother, for answering my prayers. My name is Ansano and I've been imprisoned here by Roman soldiers."

"Why?"

"They found me walking in this valley three days ago. They beat me and left me here to die."

"Where are they now?"

"I don't know. They haven't been back since they threw me in here. I thought I would die. I haven't eaten or taken water since. Do you have any?"

"Yes, but how will I get it to you? The window's so high up."

"Is there anything you could climb on?"

Finding an old, marble bird bath, pockmarked with algae, near a fountain that had long dried up, Milo dragged it over the grass using all his strength and set it under the window. Clambering up, he stood on his tiptoes and could just reach the ivy-covered sill. He took his bag with the bread and water and swung it over the ledge.

"Stand back." Milo heard the bag hit the floor, and then the sound of the man greedily drinking and eating.

"Thank you. You have saved my life."

"There are olives on the trees outside, I can collect some for you."

Heading off to collect fruit from the garden, Milo tried to think what to do. After throwing in the olives he had an idea.

"Ansano, I will get my father to come back with me and try to help you. Eat these and wait for me to return."

"Thank you. God bless you."

Milo ran home like a whirlwind, driving the startled goats before him. They bleated indignantly, but were relieved when they finally found themselves back in their field. Milo shut the gate and raced to find his father, colliding with him coming around the corner from the barn.

"Whoa! Why are you in such a hurry?"

Breathless, Milo blurted out his story. His father, Lazzaro, a burly weather-beaten man, put his hand on the boy's back. He had huge hands like paddles, too big to help his flock of sheep when they were lambing. That was his wife and daughter's job, to coax the little lambs out when the sheep were in trouble. Nonetheless he was gentle and loving as he patted his son.

"Calm down and catch your breath."

As they walked to the house Milo explained about Ansano. His father's big brown eyes turned serious and he frowned. "If we took a rope could you fit through the window?"

Lucia, Milo's mother, smoothed back her glossy dark hair as Milo told her his story and narrowed her eyes. "But what if the soldiers come back?"

"There was no one there, Mama, except Ansano, and we can't leave him to die. He was starving."

"We'll go back with a rope and check before we go in. If we get him out, we'll bring him back here."

Lazzaro and Milo rode on donkeys, taking water and a rope.

"What is this building, Papa?"

"It's an old monastery. Monks lived there until they were murdered by the Romans for their beliefs some years ago."

"We'll have to climb over, the gate's locked."

They tied up the donkeys and Camilo shinned up the tree again while Lazzaro kept watch.

"Go and tell him we're here."

Throwing the rope over the wall, Lazzaro followed it down as it slid snakelike to the ground and walked towards the sound of his son's voice.

"This is my Papa, Ansano, we've brought a rope to try and rescue you."

Lazzaro fastened one end of the rope securely to a tree a short distance away, threw the rest over a broken piece of balcony that jutted out above the window, and pulled on it to check its strength. Then he tied the other end around Milo's waist, went back to the first tree and hauled until Milo reached the windowsill. Milo breathed in, ignoring the foliage and small branches digging into his legs and back, slithered through and landed with a crash at the feet of the man imprisoned inside. Looking up he saw a young man wearing a tattered green tunic. He couldn't help recoiling in horror and gasping as he saw Ansano's cuts and bruises. Ansano's face looked like a map. It was covered in congealed blood, with a broken nose at an odd angle, and black rings round his eyes so dark they resembled volcanic craters. Despite this, Ansano smiled through his cracked lips.

"I imagine I look gruesome, sorry."

"My mama will clean you up."

Untying the rope around his own waist and wrapping it securely around Ansano's, Milo pushed him up the wall and over the sill. He was very weak, but Lazzaro took the strain as he emerged blinking into the brightness. Then Lazzaro lowered him gently to the ground. The rope was untied and used to lower Milo.

Ansano rode back to the farm on the donkey. Once there, Lucia fussed over him, bathing his wounds and feeding him before putting him into a soft bed. As he drifted off to sleep, Ansano felt that he had gone to heaven. The following day he told them his story.

"I was born into a noble Roman family and lived a rich life. Our farm was full of glorious fruit groves where I played. I had a wonderful nurse, Maxima. She adored me and secretly baptised me as a child and brought me up as a Christian. I believed I was meant to fight the Romans and their barbaric practices, so I openly declared my beliefs. This was during the time when Emperor Diocletian was persecuting anyone who did not adhere to traditional Roman religious practices and sacrifice to the Roman gods." A lone tear slipped down his swollen cheek. "I don't regret this. However, it led to myself and Maxima being whipped. It killed her. I continued to preach until my father denounced me to the authorities - he was scared that punishment would be meted out to the rest of the family. This led to me being found and imprisoned. I cannot stay with you, it's too dangerous for you to have me here. Milo, to thank you, I give you all that I have." He took a tiny worn leather bag from his tunic and handed it to him. "Plant these seeds and be always blessed."

A few days later, Lazzaro was at the market when he heard that Ansano had been caught and immersed in a vat of boiling oil before being decapitated. His head had been placed on a stake as a warning to other Christians that their beliefs would not be tolerated.'

THE FAMILY REUNION
ITALY

The villa looked stunning against the cerulean sky, like a huge square present. Bottle green ivy clung to its crevices; the sandstone beneath was almost obscured, and the windows had to be constantly reclaimed as the leaves on the thick writhing branches twisted and curled, trying to shut out the light. Tiny silver lizards scuttled up and down the walls using a labyrinth of secret passages known only to them. The morning had been spent changing sheets and dragging mattresses from the attic to make beds up all over the house for the family. The other children enjoyed the chaos when everyone came to stay for the party, but Gabriella felt slightly apprehensive as the brown truck trundled up the track beeping, narrowly avoiding an angry goose with a death wish. She stood behind her mother, squinting into the sunlight as her siblings lined up, forming a welcoming committee, under the cloudless sky.

She loved her cousins coming, but Eduardo, the eldest,

was two years older than her and she always felt awkward whenever they met. She was really looking forward to seeing Emilia; they were the same age and got on so well when they got together. Their birthdays were only two days apart, both of them would be fourteen soon, and they used to pretend they were twins. They did look very alike with their long black ringlets and nut-brown eyes.

Giverny remembered watching the bonfire pile grow day by day as people from the village brought up planks of wood and all their rubbish and meticulously placed it in position. The lighting ceremony had been magical. It had taken a little while to catch as her uncle and his friends used flaming torches to light it underneath. Once it had got going, the fire had roared like a wild animal and seemed to be alive as its flames and sparks reached up to the sky. Smoke had swirled around the crowd. making them cough and surge back as one. It had felt dangerous, and Gabriella and Emilia had held hands so they didn't lose each other in the crowd.

In the back, everyone was waving as the car came to a halt and three dishevelled, curly haired children - two boys and one girl - tumbled out. Giverny grabbed them all in a big hug, giving them resounding kisses on both cheeks.   'Benvenuto! Goodness you've all grown so much.'
Laughing, they pulled away and their mother, Giverny's older

sister Giulia, took their place. The sisters cried as they hung on to one another.

'I've missed you so much, *sorellina.*'

'It's so wonderful to see you,' said Giverny.

Ricardo slapped his brother-in-law on the back before hugging him and helping him with the slightly battered suitcases.'Good journey?'

'Not too bad,' said Abramo as he hugged Corrado. 'This is for you.' He carefully lifted out a large wooden barrel full of olive oil. 'Last year's,' he said, handing it to Corrado, who shouldered it with a grin.

'*Fantastico. Grazie.* I was hoping you'd bring some.'

Extricating herself from her aunt, Gabriella took a deep breath before forcing herself to overcome her shyness.

'Would you like some lemonade?'

Her cousins trooped after her into the cool of the kitchen, blinking a little as their eyes adjusted to the slight gloom after the glare of the garden.

'When are the others coming?' asked Eduardo, a handsome boy of sixteen with his mother's dazzling smile.

Gabriella took a stone jug from the larder. It was filled with lemonade she had helped her mother make the day before.

'Alfonso, Ricco and Piero are coming later,' said Alfredo.

'And Santo and Sergio are coming soon, their mama is bringing lake fish for the antipasti.'

Tomaso held out a matchbox to show Marcello, the middle cousin aged eleven, a year older than the twins. 'Look at my spider. I caught him yesterday in the barn and-'

'Will you stop getting that thing out! And get some glasses.' Gabriella glared at her little brother. 'Mario and Christina aren't coming now as their mama isn't well.' Gabriella passed them all a glass.

'I needed that,' said Emilia draining her drink. 'That's a shame about Mario. He's so funny. He always makes everyone laugh.'

'I know,' said Gabriella 'but there'll be lots of other people here anyway. Alfredo and Tomaso, show Marcello and Eduardo where they're sleeping. Emilia, you're with me, come on.'

Gabriella's shyness vanished once she was alone with Emilia, helping her unpack. 'I can't wait for tomorrow. Do you remember last year when Papa's friend Giuseppe got so drunk he fell asleep in the chicken shed?' She giggled.

Emilia laughed. 'Didn't get much sleep though, did he, with the cockerel crowing in his ear?'

'Come on, I'm dying to show you our new buffalo.' Gabriella stood up.

Emilia put her nightdress on top of the soft pink and purple feather quilt on the camp bed ready for later, then followed her cousin downstairs.

Nero pattered after them as they left the villa and crossed the yard. Lined up along the low stone terracotta wall were pots of all sizes housing different herbs. The first one was filled with silvery sage, its leaves covered in soft down like a newborn baby's hair. The lilac flowers on the chives stood out like pom poms on a woollen hat, and a shock of crocodile-green parsley frothed out in all directions. Emilia laughed because the pots reminded her of heads with different unruly hairstyles. They passed the long wooden pergola dripping in vines, with small grapes like tiny emeralds that would soon become swollen and juicy.

'I hope we have breakfast out here like we did last year.'

Remembering eating at the long table under the swathes of fruit made Emilia's mouth water. Giverny had made buttery flaky pastries, and they'd had cold meats and cheeses, the perfect way to start the day.

Opening a gate, the girls walked into a wide field full of curling golden wheat, each ear reaching up to the sun, a congregation at prayer, interspersed with sprinkles of cornflowers glowing like a reflection of the sky. The next field they entered was a meadow of luscious grass.

'Luciana,' called Gabriella, and a shaggy great buffalo reared her head and ambled towards them.

Backing off, Emilia stood back by the gate.

'It's fine, don't worry,' Gabriella reassured her. 'She's really gentle. And look, here come her babies.' She pointed, and Emilia couldn't help but smile as the two calves followed their mother.

Luciana stopped in front of Gabriella and gave her a sniff, her horns standing out, dark against the sky, as Gabriella rubbed her under her bushy chin. 'See she loves it. We've had her since she was young and now these are her little ones. This is Liliana and the brown one is Valentina. Look, you can stroke them.'

They stood next to their mother. Liliana had a copper coat so fluffy she looked like a sheep that needed shearing, Emilia stroked her soft pink nose and ears. She did the same to Valentina, who was an exact replica of her mother but in miniature. 'They're lovely. You're so lucky to have these, we only have chickens.'

'I saw them being born. It was so exciting. We've got more but they're a bit older and two more are pregnant. Right, we'd better go and help now. We have to pick some tomatoes and herbs on the way back.' Gabriella gave the buffalo one last caress before shutting the gate.

'We need to go past the ducks and chickens to get some eggs.'

Chickens congregated around their feet clucking loudly as Gabriella threw them some corn before putting speckled brown eggs from the hen house in her basket.

'Hello girls. Here you go.'

Approaching the vegetable garden Gabriella broke into a run. A huge brown buffalo bottom protruded amidst the carefully tended rows of lettuces and the tall tomato plants that glowed in the late sunlight. The garden was immaculate, weed free and carefully planted.

'No, Carlos. Out.' She pushed the buffalo's muscly shoulder. Gazing at her with his liquid brown eyes he completely ignored her, chewing slowly. She pushed harder and shouted at him until he began ambling towards the gate. He still stopped every few seconds to pluck leaves that took his fancy, though. Following behind as Gabriella walked him back to the field admonishing him all the way, Emilia tried not to laugh at the sight of the great beast in disgrace walking meekly next to his tiny owner. Carlos kept turning to look at Gabriella as if he was listening. Once he was back in the right place, Gabriella ran back to the vegetable garden and helped Emilia fill the basket with tomatoes and basil.

'He's always escaping and coming here and helping himself. He's really funny though and very gentle. But I won't tell Mama. She gets so angry with him and she's got so much to do with everyone here.'

ITALY 333AD

'Brimming with anger and sorrow when he heard what had become of Ansano, Milo was beside himself, so he took the seeds he had been given and walked to a hill on the family farm and planted each one. It was hard work as the ground was parched and split in places, baked by the sun, looking like pieces of a giant jigsaw puzzle. Crying as he cut into the earth, he felt that saving Ansano had been so futile. "We should have left him in the old monastery. At least then he wouldn't have been boiled alive in oil." Trembling, he thought about the agony Ansano must have suffered, and fat tears plopped into the holes he placed the seeds in.

Meeting Ansano affected the rest of Milo's life. He became a serious boy who spent his days trying to be responsible, learning everything he could in anticipation of one day taking over the farm. He and the seeds grew together. He became a kind and gentle man, and they turned into seven saplings that stood strong on the hill, forming a lemon grove.

The farmland around the trees changed once they had grown. No one made the connection for a long time. It began imperceptibly. The goats, sheep and cows grazing on the land became plumper than they had ever been and produced more offspring. Their milk tasted different too, sweeter and creamier, making the cheeses they sold the most popular around and in constant demand.

It wasn't until Milo was in his forties and had children of his own that the biggest tree gave its first fruit. Great lemons appeared, the size of grapefruits, knobbly with thick skin. They were the juiciest and sweetest that he had ever tasted. After marrying Cara, his childhood sweetheart, the two of them had been blessed with five daughters, all healthy and happy except the youngest, Viola, born prematurely. She had survived - but was always sickly.

Returning home one day, Milo found his wife on her knees praying in a desperate, wheedling tone and wringing her hands next to Viola's bed. The curtains were drawn. The room had a musty smell, as if death were nearby waiting in the wings. His daughter's cheeks were flushed and rosy as the poppies that sprinkled the hillsides around their farm; she wasn't responding to the cool water being squeezed on her face gently by her eldest sister and could not be woken.

"Papa what shall we do?" Milo's other daughters looked to him with quivering lips and terrified eyes.

Holding back his tears, Milo ran to the lemon groves, where he prayed to Sant Ansano to help him. Picking the biggest lemon he could find, he ran down the hill into the kitchen before squeezing it into a cup with some honey. Returning to his daughter's side he gently lifted her little head and forced some of the liquid down her throat, all the time muttering prayers to Ansano and begging God to save his baby.

After what felt like an eternity, Viola opened her little brown eyes and coughed and spluttered. Holding her head, her father gave her more lemon juice to drink, until her cheeks lost their red tinge and natural pallor returned to her skin. The room erupted with noisy crying as Cara and the girls threw themselves on Viola's bed, hugging her and thanking every saint they could think of.

From that day onwards, Viola's sickliness disappeared, and Milo knew that the lemons grown on the biggest tree had to be sacred. Hadn't Ansano blessed the seeds when he had handed them to him all those years ago? Swearing his immediate family to secrecy, he never told another soul about the lemon tree except for one family member, his favourite granddaughter. Years later he told her the secret of the tree and made her swear that one day she too would choose one special person in her life to tell and keep the family story alive forever. Unfortunately, not everyone that knew about the power of the lemons used that knowledge for good.'

LONDON
1927

Leslie Mallows and Edward, Margaret's father, became
acquaintances when they both frequented the Raleigh Club in
Regents Street. The all-male clientele was comprised of high
ranking ex-military men like themselves. Edward was a
retired commodore, and Leslie, a retired army brigadier.
Leslie had decided to invest in a new business, and once they
started talking, they bonded over their passion for cars.
Edward decided that Leslie was exactly the type of man he
wanted to work with and wished his daughter to marry, so
wasted no time in both working out a deal and introducing
them. After their first encounter it all happened very fast.
Before the couple knew it, they were having an engagement
party and the wedding date was set. Arriving home alone
after the party, Leslie headed straight for his drinks cabinet.
Slamming down the lid he poured a full glass of whisky
before taking a large slug. The liquid washed over his tongue,
burning it. He drained his glass and refilled it, spilling some
on the highly polished wooden top of the cabinet before
gulping it back.

Arriving home alone after the party, Leslie headed straight for his drinks cabinet. Slamming down the lid he poured a full glass of whisky before taking a large slug. The liquid washed over his tongue, burning it. He drained his glass and refilled it, spilling some on the highly polished wooden top of the cabinet before gulping it back.

'Damn!' Wearily he wiped the alcohol away with his jacket sleeve. When he woke up in the early hours with his head resting next to his empty glass he groaned, holding his head. He went into the bedroom, where he looked into the mirror and barely recognised the reflection staring back at him. His suit and bow tie seemed to mock him; they didn't go at all with his bloodshot eyes and ashen face. 'You are a man of honour,' he said to himself as his thoughts raced. 'I can't back out now. How would I explain myself to Margaret's mother and father? Worse – how could I explain it to her? I'll just have to try and make her happy.' He glared at his reflection in the mirror. 'What the devil are you doing? How could you let yourself get carried away with this dream of an ideal life?' He smashed his fist into the mirror, sending silver shards of glass cascading down around his feet. They hit the floor like hailstones. Curling up on the cold floor he began rocking back and forth, his head in his hands, the blood on his knuckles trickling down and staining his shirt.

Eventually, he crawled into bed.

In the small hours he was woken as usual by his nightmare, which always started at the same point: back in the trenches.

Aware of the stench of sweat, filth and fear that lace the air, the order comes and he and his fellow men run towards the enemy. The deafening sound of the gunfire matches his heartbeat. He feels he is about to explode. In his peripheral vision Leslie sees his comrades mown down, as if a Greek god were playing an incongruous game of skittles. His leg buckles where he has been hit. Next to him Jonny, his best friend, calls for his mother. Dragging himself to reach Jonny, Leslie cradles him in his arms, the reek of blood assailing his nostrils.

'It's all right, Jon, I'll save...'

His words die in his mouth as he sees that where Jonny's eye once was is now a gaping, bloody cavernous hole. Vomit rises like a volcano inside Leslie and gushes over his jacket sleeve. Turning back to his friend he strokes his hair.

'I want my mother. I want to go home. Please take me home. I'm scared.' As Jonny begs, Leslie doesn't know how to respond.

'I'm going to get you back home. Your mother is waiting to see you. She'll look after you it's all right.'

Rubbing the place where the bullet had entered his leg, Leslie awoke in a cold sweat. He stared round the room, bewildered, before crumpling, curling up tightly in a ball and sobbing himself back to sleep

ITALY

The kitchen was alive with chatter while pots and pans bubbled on the range, promising a flavoursome dinner. Ricardo filled glasses with grappa and *liqueur al limone*, made from a secret family recipe, as they all caught up on each other's news.

'How's business your end, Abramo?'

'Not too bad. The olives are growing well. It all looks very promising this year, and we're still selling a fair amount of chickens, what about you?'

'We've bought some more buffalo, so the herd is expanding, and we're making lots of mozzarella now. I think we're having some tonight, aren't we, Corrado?'

'*Si*, it won't be long now and ...'

The arrival of three black haired brothers - Alfonso. Ricco and Piero, musicians and cousins of Giverny's - stopped him.

'*Ciao*, sorry we're late.'

'*Benvenuto*, welcome,' said Giverny kissing them all warmly, 'what a shame Mario and Christina can't make it. How is your mama?"

'I think she's on the mend, but the others didn't want to leave her, so they stayed. But they all send their love,' said Ricco.

'Good. So glad she's getting better. Come and sit down and have a drink. Where are your things?'

'We left our bags and instruments in the car. We'll get them after. Where's everyone else?' asked Piero.

Ricardo filled up his glass. 'The children are collecting eggs and picking basil and tomatoes for the *primo*. Paolo's hoping to come later and-', he was interrupted by the doorway filling up with a beaming family 'Ah, here are the Baronis.'

Vito and Maura were Giverny's uncle and aunt, and had two sons, Sergio and Santo, the same age as Ricardo and Corrado. They lived close by at Bolsena, where they owned a hotel overlooking the huge lake there. It was through them that Ricardo and Giverny had met. Maura, a big woman, bustled into the room, hugging everyone and squashing them into her ample bosom, as Vito, a thin man with a drooping moustache, brandished a large box at Corrado.

'There you go, should be more than enough.'

'*Grazie.*' Pumping Vito's hand, Corrado opened the box to see little parcels of seafood. Lake fish were a delicacy, and Corrado intended to use them to make antipasti for the party.

Giverny got everyone seated and smiled as she looked

around the long wooden table. It was lit by thick white candles and covered in plates of food. Long wicker baskets held golden loaves of ciabatta, and everyone was chatting easily as they ate the basil, mozzarella and tomato salad drizzled with olive oil and balsamic vinegar.

'This is fantastic.' Guilia used a chunk of bread to mop up the last bit of food on her plate. 'The richest mozzarella I've ever tasted.'

The murmurs of approval coming at her from all directions made Giverny beam.

'*Grazie mille*. We are blessed with very fertile land for grazing. I love making it. Tomorrow I'll show you our two new calves. Gabriella has named them Valentina and Liliana; they're such soft creatures. Baby buffalo are adorable. I enjoy milking them but now we've expanded, I can't manage the whole herd on my own, so Isabella, my friend from the village, has started working for us. She's really good.'

'So, what's on the menu for tomorrow?' Abramo arched an eyebrow at Corrado.

'Crostini, different antipasti, thanks to Vito and Maura.' He nodded across the table at them. 'Crab and lemon spaghetti. Camillo has given us a piglet to roast. And lots of lemon tart and ricotta and honey from our bees for afters if we can fit it in.' Corrado smiled. 'And of course, don't forget, we'll have

Giovanni's punch to get the evening going.'

Groaning filled the air because Giovanni's punch was lethal. It was secretly referred to among the family as Roulette Punch because Giovanni's father, who had invented the recipe and brewed his own grappa, had gone blind. Its strength was legendary. No one had the heart to tell Giovanni not to bring it. He was so proud to continue the family tradition.

'Don't worry about that!' Abramo rubbed his stomach and laughed, making them all join in.

'Papa, can we play a game after dinner?' Marcello looked at his father hopefully.

'Yes please, can we?' Emilia joined in.

'Of course.' Giverny smiled at the children. 'Do you want to play the grab-the-sweet game?'

They nodded, and Gabriella clapped her hands.

'I love it when you come. We never play games otherwise.'

Once their secondi, *spaghetti alle vongole*, was just a memory, the table was cleared, and Gabriella was sent to the larder to find the lemon sweets which were meant for the following day for the children.

'It's a good thing you helped me make extra this year.' Corrado relieved her of the large glass jar.

'Now how many do I need? Will you boys count for me?'

Tomaso was counting up one side of the table and Alfredo

the other when the door opened and Paolo, another cousin, appeared in the doorway with a slightly wild look in his eye. He was brandishing a half empty bottle of grappa.

'*Buonasera, come stai?*'

'Ah, Paolo, *bene grazie.*' Disappearing momentarily in a flurry of hugs, Paolo resurfaced, laughing, before running his fingers through his unruly mop of curls, and sitting down.

'We're playing the card game where you grab the sweets. Remember last year I kept winning?' Eduardo nudged Paolo. 'Are you going to play?'

'Go on then, but first I need a glass.'

Ricardo filled up the glasses as Eduardo dealt the cards.

'So, boys, how many sweets do we need? Did you count up?'

Tomaso nodded. 'Fifteen.'

'But," said Alfredo, 'you put one sweet less, or everyone will get one and no one will be out.'

'You're both right. Well done. Now do you want to put the sweets in a long line down the middle of the table? And I've got my eye on you, no eating them!'

The cards were passed around and the room rang with laughter and shouting as the first person to get four of the same cards grabbed a sweet, swiftly followed by the others. Guilia was out first, followed by Giverny, so they washed up as the game continued.

'It's so lovely to be all together again isn't it?' Guilia, up to her elbows in hot water, scrubbed the plates while Giverny dried and put them away. 'They all look so alike there's no doubt they're related.'

'I know. I wish we lived closer,' said Giverny, 'but it's wonderful to see everyone. Are you looking forward to tomorrow?'

'I am. Are you? I know it's a lot of work for you all with the party after.'

'It's worth it though-' A loud guffaw interrupted her. Paolo and Ricco were wrestling over a sweet. Ricco won as Paolo fell off his chair. Giverny raised her eyebrows at her sister.

'Oh dear, he looks like he might have had one too many.'

Guilia joined the others at the table, and Giverny sighed happily as she listened to snippets of conversation punctuated by laughter as everyone talked at once. Ricardo was telling a story about playing football at school, and he and Corrado having a fight, and how their mama had given him a hiding when he got home, because he had punched his little brother. The twins were going into great detail to anyone that would listen about how difficult their spider had been to catch and put in the box. Looking over her shoulder, Giverny saw Santo, her favourite cousin, sitting back from the table and not joining in. This was because, Maura had confided, he was broken-hearted. The girl he loved had jilted him. Santo was her favourite because when they had been young and the boys in the town used to tease her mercilessly, he had never joined in. Always kind, he'd also saved her life. Once, when she and Guilia had been staying at the hotel they had taken the boat out and swum in the deep grey waters. It had been full of tiny black fearless fish, the same delicious-tasting kind that would be cooked for the party the following day. Letting the boat drift near them, they had swum lazily around it. The sun had freckled their brown skin, turning the water as silver as the mullet swimming in shoals below them. Sergio had challenged them to a race. They were all to swim out to a buoy some distance away. The first one back at the boat would win and not have to row to shore. They had all started together, but Guilia had soon lagged behind as she wasn't a strong swimmer. Three of them were neck and neck when Giverny had got cramp. Sergio hadn't even noticed, as he surged ahead, determined to prove his strength. The pain in her legs had begun to pull her under. Her mouth had filled with water as she had tried to call out, and she had begun to panic. Suddenly Santo had been by her side, and he had held her up, kicking his legs and pulling her towards the boat. He had talked calmly to her all the time.

'It's all right. I've got you. We're nearly there.'

Clinging to him, tears and lake water had blurred Giverny's vision, but she had been so relieved to be safe. They'd always had a special bond since then. Family gatherings were something she loved. She thought of them as being like a jigsaw - when everyone met up they all locked into place. They all found their niche. She went over and put her arm around Santo.

'How are you?'

'A bit sad, but I'm trying not to spoil the party, sorry.'

'You're not.' She squeezed his arm. 'You know where I am if you want to talk.'

Marcello won the game. The cards were put away and they all sat around the table peacefully drinking coffee, except for Paolo, who was arguing with Sergio about four sisters who were coming to the party.

'No.' He waved his finger. 'Agnesa is the most beautiful. It's her eyes.'

'I know. But haven't you noticed Allegra's dimples when she smiles? What do you think, Corrado?' said Sergio.

Corrado shrugged disinterestedly.'I don't know.'

'Come on. You're a man, aren't you?' Paolo punched him on the arm.

'Well,' began Corrado, 'I'm not sure, because I think

personality wise that Allesandra is the best. She used to make me laugh at school.'

'She's pretty keen on you too. You should marry her. *Bella cosa tosto e rapita* – a pretty thing is soon taken.'

'Shut up, I'm not getting married.'

'Which one do you think Giuseppe will be after?' said Ricco.

'Did I hear my name?' A tall man with a curly black moustache wearing a grey fedora strutted into the room. Taking it off, he tossed it on to the hat stand before gazing into the mirror and smoothing his hair.

'*Ciao*. We were talking about you, not to you.'

Stroking his moustache between his forefingers and thumbs, Giuseppe curled it and laughed.

Corrado hugged him. 'We were discussing the merits of the Rosato sisters and wondering about your preference.'

'Well, I think from a beauty perspective Agnesa has the best eyes, like a beautiful gazelle. Although Alonza's freckles are very pretty, and Allegra has the best legs. It's a hard decision, but I've got my eye on someone else.'

'Who?'

'Viviana Vanore, from Bolsena.'

'Isn't she going out with one of the Panzica brothers?'

'So? Have you seen this face?' Giuseppe swept back his

fringe. 'She won't be able to resist me. I started chatting to her at the coffee shop the other day. Is she coming tomorrow?'

'I think so,' said Corrado. 'You'll have to ask Giverny, she sent out the guest list.'

Eduardo took some plates over to his mother, and as he returned sat down next to Corrado.

'I think you might be taller than me now.' Corrado gave his nephew a playful dig in the ribs. 'How's the studying going, do you still want to be a doctor?'

'Yes. I'm working hard. I'd like to go to university abroad, but I'm not sure yet.'

'Where are you thinking of going?'

'London or Paris.' Eduardo shrugged his shoulders.

'I've always wanted to go to London,' said Corrado, 'ever since Papa told me about his travels.'

'So,' joined in Abramo, 'what's stopping you?'

'I don't know.' Corrado frowned. 'Family, I guess, and that's another reason for not getting married and tied down. I'd love to open an *osteria* and cook proper Italian food for the English. Papa said their food wasn't much to write home about.'

'Yes, I've heard that too. Well, Eduardo, if Corrado moves and you go to London too you'll be well fed.'

They all laughed, except for Gabriella, who turned her big brown eyes on Corrado reproachfully. 'You're not going, are you? You promised me you'd teach me to cook.'

'I did. And I will keep my promise. You're going to help me cook tomorrow for the party, aren't you?' Corrado sighed and turned away to hide the guilt clouding his expression.

Gabriella nodded and smiled. 'Yes. Emilia and I are in charge of all the tables too, and-'

Paolo suddenly interrupted her, saying in a loud voice. 'I had a run in with that fascist Nicolai earlier. I don't know who he thinks he is, acting like he owns the place.'

Ricardo looked serious for a moment. 'I don't know why he's being like that. We've all known him for years, and he and Corrado were in the same class at school-'

Paolo snorted. 'None of that matters to him, he's got new friends now. Ones who protect him. Fascists just like him.'

Giverny shepherded the children up to bed. 'It's late and we've got a big day tomorrow, come on, now.'

'Don't forget, Gabriella, we've got a cooking date in the morning It's an early start.' Corrado winked at her.

'I'll be up. See you in the morning.'

LONDON

Leslie played his part at the wedding. He was a genial host and made sure that all Margaret's friends and family thought he was wonderful. Margaret had butterflies as they arrived back at the house which was to be her new home. It had been left to Leslie in his father's will. It was huge with eight bedrooms and a large garden. She was looking forward to becoming its mistress and getting to know the staff, although Leslie had given them all the night off. He wanted to be alone with her. Their wedding had been such a whirlwind that she had only been to his house once before. She felt slightly shy as they got out of the car. They barely knew each other. Excited, she couldn't wait to find out all about him - his habits - what he liked and what he didn't. She wanted to be the best wife ever and make him so happy.

'I've got something to show you. Shut your eyes and take my hand.' He turned her around. 'Now you can open them.'

Before her stood a beautiful black shiny car with silver headlights glinting in the moonlight.

'Oh! You've got another new car.'

'Isn't it beautiful? It's an Austin Seven, the latest model.'
His eyes shone and he reminded Margaret of a little boy.

Laughing, she said, 'It's lovely.'

'I know. I did a deal and got it for you as a wedding present. Do you like it?'

'For me? Really? Oh, Leslie, I don't know what to say. Thank you so much. It's frightfully generous of you.'

'Tomorrow you can look inside. I got it partly to make it up to you, because we're not going on a honeymoon. Setting up the business with your father means there's too much to do. Once it's up and running properly, you and I can go away together anywhere you like.'

Picking her up and crushing her cream silky dress, which rustled noisily, he carried her through the door and over the threshold.

'Welcome home, Mrs Mallows.'

'Oh Leslie, I can't believe I'm finally a married woman. I'm so happy. And I can't believe you've given me my own car! I love you.' Throwing her arms around his neck, she rained a little flurry of kisses on his neck. He put his mouth to hers and kissed her hard before setting her down in the large hallway. Margaret stopped, struck by the huge chandelier illuminating the dark wooden panelling covering the walls.

On the wall facing her was a long picture of a hunting

scene. The fox was on the far left, its brush trailing just in front of a pack of hounds cheek to slathering jowl, murder in their eyes. Riders followed, hunched over muscular horses as they galloped as one, baying for blood. The only flashes of colour were the fox and the huntsmen's scarlet jackets.

'Let's have a drink.' Leslie took her arm and led her past the grand staircase and into the drawing room. He opened an old carved cabinet.

'I'm not sure I want any more,' Margaret said. 'I've drunk so much champagne. Wasn't it a lovely party? We got so many presents-'

'I'm having one, anyway.' Leslie selected a crystal decanter full of whisky, tipping a generous measure into a matching glass. Banking up the fire he poked it to get the embers ignited. Sinking down opposite her new husband in one of the leather armchairs, Margaret looked around. The walls were papered in a bold green leafy pattern on a cream background, and there was a large oval mirror with a dark wooden frame above the fireplace. The fire filled the air with a soft sizzling sound as the logs got going and the flames took hold. An ornate silver candelabra, housing three dripping white candles which wavered gently in the slight draught, stood on the mantelpiece. On the opposite wall, a picture of her new husband in his full army regalia glared sternly down at her above large photographs of cars. She hoped Leslie would never look at her like that. Below the photographs was a large, full, wooden bookshelf that she looked forward to exploring. Leslie watched her as she removed her white satin shoes. She buried her stockinged toes in the soft pile of the large Wilton rug that covered most of the parquet floor. Smiling at him, she flung her shoes to one side. He looked away.

'I'm so glad to get them off. I'm sure my feet are covered in blisters after all that dancing, but it was so wonderful. Everything was just wonderful, don't you agree?' Bending forward, Margaret stretched her feet out in front of her and massaged her toes.

'Would you like me to do that?' Leslie asked in a thick voice, before kneeling in front of her and reverently taking one of her feet in his hands and rubbing each toe. Then he abruptly stopped and walking towards the door.

'I'll be back in a moment.'   Margaret wondered why his voice sounded strange, but he seemed back to his old self when he returned. Although she felt nervous as they went upstairs, she was excited to see their bedroom.

It was large with two windows and a high double bed covered in a white counterpane. All the furniture was old and dark like the wooden floor. Margaret felt a pang when she saw that her trunk had been placed in a corner.

'I thought you would like this room. It looks over the garden, and next door is a dressing room for all your clothes.'

'Thank you, but aren't we going to share a room?'

'Of course. I just thought that as we have so many rooms you could have one of your own. Also, since the war I find it difficult to sleep sometimes. So when that happens, I will go to my room down the hall and leave you in peace.'

When each seed pearl had sparkled in the candlelight at the party, she had felt like a princess. Now, after one more twirl, she carefully removed it. Trembling, she put on her new underwear, squirted her neck with the Chanel Number 5 Leslie had given her and wrapped herself in a silk dressing gown. Then she took a deep breath and opened the bedroom door. She was surprised to discover that it was now in darkness, the only sound Leslie snoring. Tiptoeing over to the unoccupied side of the bed she climbed in quietly and shut her eyes.

As tears escaped down her cheeks, she brushed them away and put his behaviour down to tiredness before falling asleep herself. When she woke in the morning, she wondered where she was before remembering and turning over murmuring, 'Good morning.' There was no reply. Leslie's side of the bed was empty.

2nd May 1927

I don't know what to do. Leslie has gone out without telling me and I don't know where he's gone. Last night was a disaster. I was so nervous about our wedding night, but by the time I'd got changed, he was asleep. Perhaps he was exhausted after all the excitement of the day. I feel so disappointed. I decided to unpack my things. Yesterday Leslie told me I could have my own room and use the adjacent one as my dressing room. It has a large walk in wardrobe, so I put my clothes away. I opened a door on the right which held a tower of boxes, I peeked inside the top one to find the most gorgeous pair of shoes. I took them out, they were black and white leather with a low heel, and tried them on, they fitted perfectly. I riffled through the other boxes and saw they all held shoes my size. Leslie is so generous! As well as giving me a car, he's bought me a shoe collection to die for. I can't wait until he gets home to thank him.

COOKERY LESSONS

ITALY

Twittering birds outside her window, and the sun peeping through the gap at the top of the curtains, woke Gabriella. A bubble of excitement began to build in her as she remembered that today was the day she was going to cook with Corrado. She felt she had to prove herself and was determined to do everything he asked perfectly. She slipped on her clothes quietly so as not to wake Emilia, and crept downstairs. Corrado was already in the kitchen.

'Morning. This is for you,' he said, giving her a red and white gingham apron.

'Thank you.' She put down the book she was carrying and put the apron on.

'What's this?' Corrado picked up the book. There were recipes written on each page in a careful hand.

'I started making that with Nonna.' Gabriella smiled proudly. 'And I'm going to add the recipes we make today.'

'You'll have to do that later. You're going to be too busy cooking First, we're going to make the pastry for the lemon tart. I'll get the butter, sugar and flour from the larder. You get the eggs from the basket.'

'How many eggs do we need?'

'I don't know yet, definitely four for now, maybe five. We'll see how we get on. Now, pour the sugar into a bowl, that brown one over there. Cut up the butter into little chunks. Your mama makes the best butter; look at it, all golden and creamy. Mmmm.'

'I helped her make this.'

'That makes you the best butter churner too. This bit's hard work to start with. That's it. Keep mixing.'

While Gabriella stirred, Corrado selected several large lemons with knobbly skin and began zesting them and then skillfully squeezing them, filling the air with a delicious sweet aroma.

'I think it's well mixed now.'

'Let me have a feel.' He took the spoon from her and gave the mixture a stir. 'Perfect! Now for the eggs. This is the best way.'

He took a brown speckled egg and cracked it one handed, letting it fall into a small blue bowl before putting the empty shell to the side. 'You have a go.' He poured his egg into the butter and sugar and threw an egg to Gabriella. 'Catch!'

Laughing, she caught it. 'Got any tips? You made that look very easy.'

'The trick is to make the egg believe you're in charge and do it fast.'

She cracked it and quickly and threw it into the bowl along with half the shell, making Corrado laugh.

'Maybe you need a bit more practice.' He watched her trying to get the pieces out with a spoon and picked up the other half of the shell, dipping it in so the pieces stuck to it. 'It's easier like this. Add the egg to the mixture you've made, gently at first, and then beat it hard so it makes a noise.'

'Why do you only do one at a time?'

'It curdles if you put in too many at once, like putting lemon juice in milk.'

Continuing to combine the eggs made Gabriella's arm tired but she didn't complain. 'I've used four, what do you think?'

'Looks good - now the flour. Gently fold it in a bit at a time.'

'How do you know how much to put in?'

'By the feel of it and the look of it. That's it.' He watched her hand. 'Now caress it; love it; turn it over gently and keep going.'

'How can I write the recipes in my book if I don't know the measurements?'

'Eventually you'll remember how to do it and you can just put in the ingredients. Now you need to bring it together.'

He showed Gabriella how to scrunch it together and make it into a firm ball. 'Feel how it's all together, no crumbly bits? Stroke it gently now, like when you rub Belleza's nose to say goodnight after a lovely ride. Carefully roll it out to the sizes of your tins, leaving an overlap.'

'I've done this before, making jam tarts with Nonna.'

'You have to make sure there are no cracks or holes, or it won't work.' He taught her how to use her thumb to smooth any small splits. 'Now we'll blind bake it in the oven for a short while for around ten minutes on a low heat so the bottom has a chance to crisp up. Then we'll leave it to cool. We need lots of eggs now, nine or ten. Also more sugar, cream and the lemon juice I squeezed. Can you boil the juice up with the sugar until it dissolves, and I'll whisk the eggs? They must be mixed gently until they are just broken up. Good cooking is all about textures and making sure it feels right. Then I'm going to pass them through a sieve into a jug.'

'What's the zest for?' asked Gabriella.

'We need to boil the cream with the zest and also leave that to cool slightly. Then we combine the juice and sugar, mix with the eggs and add the cream. The cream mixture has to be passed through a sieve first to get rid of the zest. Once it is all mixed together we have to let it rest.'

'It's quite complicated, isn't it?' Gabriella stretched her fingers.

'It's quite a tricky one to get right. Over the years some have gone wrong, and every time that happened I had to look back and work out why. Finally, pour the cooled mixture into your pastry case and bake quite low until it is just set with a slight wobble.'

Soon the table was creaking under the weight of the pies, alongside a mountain of lemon biscuits. They hung the silky pasta they had made above their heads like bunting before stopping for a rest.

'Our pies are looking just right. Well done. Shall we have a taste?'

The smell of lemon was so strong as Corrado cut them each a slice that Gabriella's mouth started watering. He passed her a piece of tart as yellow as egg yolk. The pastry had a slight crunch to it as she took a mouthful. There was an explosion of flavour in her mouth.

'That is so good,' she mumbled.

Corrado smiled. 'Yes. The contrast in flavour and texture are married perfectly together. You're a natural.'

'Are you feeling nervous about today?' said Gabriella. 'I mean carrying the statue?'

'A little. I had a dream last night that I dropped her. To tell you the truth, I don't feel old enough or ready, but I'm 21 now and supposed to feel like a man, so maybe I'll feel better afterwards.'

'I wonder if Giuseppe's nervous too?'

'I'm not sure he's ever been nervous. You know what he's like! Now, are you feeling strong?'

'Why?'

Removing three large crabs from a big pot on the stove he handed her a small hammer and a hook and showed her how to rip the claws and legs off to retrieve the sweet meat from the shells. Gabriella found it to be hard work, but eventually got the knack of hooking the meat out.

'I learnt to do this with Nonna. It's fiddly but so worth it for the flavour. Put the crabmeat in this bowl, and can you cut me up a chilli pepper, please?' Corrado handed her a knife.

'Into tiny slices?'

'Yes. Make sure you wash your hands properly afterwards, though. Once I forgot and rubbed my eye. It was agony. It watered for ages.'

'Shall I put the chilli in the crabmeat now?'

'Mix it in and add some lemon juice and seasoning.' He passed the pepper mill over to her. 'Excellent. Well done. We'll mix this with the pasta once it's dry and we've made it into spaghetti. Are you enjoying doing all this?'

'I love to cook. One day I'm going to work with you in the *osteria*.'

'At this rate you'll be taking over and running it. I'll be redundant. I'll sit at a table all day with my feet up, waiting for you to bring me food. Once you've finished school, of course.'

Laughing, Gabriella shoved him.

'Lazy!'

'The last thing we have to do is prepare the porchetta. I hope you're good at tying knots.'

A side of pork was hanging in the pantry. Corrado hauled it on to the table, then began sharpening a large knife. Gabriella had to stop herself from shuddering at the sight of the pig's staring eyes. This was her real test. She always felt slightly odd around dead animals, like the time she had found a dead chicken and Papa had asked her to help pluck it for soup. She knew that if she wanted to be a good cook and impress Corrado she had to overcome this problem, so she smiled brightly.

'What can I do now?'

'Camilo has boned this pig, but here are the heart, lungs and liver.' He handed them to her in a bowl. 'Do you want to cut them up?'

Determined not to let him know how she was feeling, she steeled herself. Then, ignoring the smell and taking a deep breath, she picked up the bloody heart and cut into it.

'When was the first time you made this? Was it with Nonna, too?'

'Yes. We only have it on occasionally, as it is such a speciality. Are you all right to carry on cutting all that up while I prepare the zucchini flowers?'

'What are we going to do with this once I've finished?'

'You have to persuade the flavour to come out by sizzling it in salt, pepper and good olive oil, the one we got from Abramo, with garlic and rosemary. Oh, and a bay leaf, too.' Corrado carefully washed the large orange flowers and laid them to dry before making the batter from flour mixed with vivid green parsley, thyme and cold water. 'That has to stay cool for later. Now you can heat the pan to fry your bits up.'

As they stood side by side, cooking together, Gabriella looked up at him.

'You know last night you said you want to go to London? Did you mean it?'

'It is something I've always wanted to do, yes. Ever since Nonno told me all about his adventures.'

'Where did he go?'

'Paris, in France. He said they make the most wonderful bread there, and he went up the Eiffel Tower, right to the top. He said that you can see for miles and miles. He brought back a postcard with a picture of it. I've got it somewhere up in the attic in my scrap book. I'll show you sometime.'

'I'd like that. But it's London you'd really like to see, isn't it?'

'I want to see Westminster Abbey. It's huge and very beautiful. I'd also like to go to Buckingham Palace, where the King of England lives. There are special soldiers outside all the time. Nonno said they wear funny black hats called busbies and people go and watch the changing of the guard. The soldiers never smile. It's a very serious business.'

'Do you think you'll ever go?'

Smiling sadly, Corrado shrugged his shoulders. 'Who knows?'

'If you do can I come and visit you?'

'Definitely. You can come and cook in my *osteria*. We'll show the English people how to eat, won't we?' He nudged her until she laughed.

'Now we have to prepare this pig. Here.' He passed her a large jar of coarse salt. 'You need to rub this all over the skin to make it crackle up.'

Tentatively Gabriella began to pat the pig's skin.

'Look. Like this.' Corrado took her hands and made them push into the pig. 'Do it the same way you kneaded the pasta dough. Properly massage it in. We want to enjoy this porchetta and make the most of him. He had a happy life roaming the hills and now we will have a happy time eating him. You have to make him fall in love with you, and you have to fall in love with him.'

Ignoring her protesting muscles, Gabriella got stuck in and found that she was enjoying the rough texture of the salt as she worked it all over the pig's body.

Corrado nodded his approval. 'That's better.'

'Are we going to stuff it now?'

'We are. If I hold the legs open, you spoon it all in. Don't forget we need to put in some lemon slices.'

They were wrestling with the string, getting it all knotted correctly, as Giverny sailed in and planted a kiss on both their cheeks.' Looks like you've been very busy. The smell of all this cooking got me up.'

'Gabriella is a wonderful cook. You should be proud of her.'

'I am.' Giverny smiled.

'Nonna would be proud of you too.' Corrado smiled and his niece beamed back at him.

LONDON

Hampstead Heath was full of life. Three boys in long shorts and flat caps led three donkeys topped with three sisters in white dresses. Each girl had a different coloured ribbon in her blonde curls and squealed with delight as the oblivious donkeys plodded on. Margaret watched them walk past a couple talking to an ice cream seller. The ice-cream man was standing in front of his black bicycle. Doffing his cap, he rolled up his shirt sleeves and loosened his tie as the sun beat down. The lady, wearing a lemon-coloured dress, put up her matching parasol as her companion offered her his arm with a look of adoration. Margaret stared wistfully at them. They talked about the weather before moving on, enjoying their ices. Plonking her floppy straw hat trimmed with white silk roses back on, Margaret quickly called to the ice cream man, who had started to push his bicycle towards the pond. 'I say, those look so tempting. Can I have one, please?'

'Yes Ma'am, of course.'

Taking her cone, she returned to her spot under the trees. The coldness made her lips tingle and she had to lick the side to stop a creamy dribble escaping on to her glove. A small boy launched his toy yacht into the pond, where it wobbled for a second before righting itself and floating away, its red sail proudly puffed out. A gentle wind rippled the water, making its reflection of the trees tremble. Margaret's favourite oak tree was in full leaf and formed a sunshade above her as she sat and watched the heath walkers, sometimes making up imaginary lives for them as she looked up from writing poetry. The balmy weather was not the only thing that had driven her outside: her loneliness was weighing on her like a yoke. Leslie had started spending every evening at his club after coming home for dinner. Confused, she was still trying to make sense of what he had said to her the previous day. He had come back from work in a strange mood. He had been drunk as usual and had again brought her new shoes. However, instead of being brusque, he had talked softly to her, the way he had at the very beginning of their relationship. Normally he was not exactly unpleasant, but their lack of intimacy stood between them like an invisible glass screen. It was impenetrable.

Each day the gap widened, until it was becoming an unbridgeable chasm. He refused to talk about their relationship and got angry if she raised the subject. But last night, for some reason, he hadn't been like that. Instead Margaret had been amazed when he'd kissed her and produced a dozen red roses from behind his back.

'I'm sorry. I've been so preoccupied recently. These are for you.'

Blissful was the only way she could describe the start of the evening. They had kissed like lovers. Hard passionate kisses that had made her body want to become one with his. He had behaved like a different man until near the end. Shivering, she remembered how he had picked her up and nuzzled her neck as they headed towards the bedroom. Suddenly, after placing her on the bed, he had stared round the room and his expression had changed to one of panic. Then he had broken down and cried. Margaret had held him to her until his shuddering sobs had subsided. Her hopes and her desire for him had faded, the way the sun dims as black rain clouds drift across it. His words, thick with tears, had tumbled out in a manic way, almost as if he had been drugged.

'Today,' he had looked up at Margaret without really seeing her, his eyes shining intensely, 'today it would have been my mother's birthday. Did I ever tell you about her?' Shaking her head, she stroked his shoulder.

'This was her room. She was the most beautiful woman I've ever seen. She was kind to everyone, too. My favourite part of the day was when Nanny would take me to see Mother after my bath and she would sit me on her knee and tell me stories. She was always wearing silk dresses that rustled as she moved. Her hands were lily white, without a blemish, and decorated with rings, the opposite to Nanny's, which were rough, calloused and misshapen with arthritis. Mother smelt of flowers all the time - flowers mixed with her face powder. Her eyes were cornflower blue and full of light. I never once saw her without perfect make-up and her hair coiffed.

'I longed to spend more time with her, but my father, a traditional man, wouldn't hear of it. I heard them arguing one night when I was about eight years old. They argued a lot. His voice was so harsh that I wanted to go and yell at him myself and tell him to stop shouting at Mother like that. She didn't deserve it. But I didn't dare confront him. He was a terrifying figure - a large man with a florid face and a permanent frown. I heard a scuffle and then a muffled scream before quietness descended on the house like a thick blanket. I sat up in bed, wondering why she had cried out, my heart seething with hatred for my father, wondering what to do.

After a short while my door had opened quietly and the silhouette of my mother filled the doorway. With the light behind her she looked like an angel.

"Are you awake, Leslie?" she whispered.

"Yes," I whispered back, and she gently closed the door before stealing across the floor, silent as a thief. I noticed her shoes as she stepped through the pool of light where the curtains were slightly open. They were silver and sparkly in the moonlight, perfect just like her. Pulling back my cover, she laid down beside me. I inhaled her scent and cuddled into her, wanting to warm her. I hoped she'd stay forever. As she kissed me on the forehead I felt a tear trickle down my neck. Studying her face in the dim light I saw she had a cut lip.

"Why did father hurt you?" My voice shook and I clenched my fists.

"Don't worry, darling. I'm fine." She smiled down at me crookedly, her lip swelling.

"Why are you still wearing your shoes?"

"In case I have to run away." She sighed.

I began to cry and begged her never to leave me, so she removed her shoes, tucking them under the bed, and stroked my hair with her soft hands and soothed me until I was almost asleep.

Then a crashing noise downstairs jolted me upright. Startled, I thought I had just fallen out of a tree in my dream. My mother stiffened next to me as the noise intensified and my father crashed into the room, his face incandescent with rage. Yelling obscenities at her, he pulled her from the bed. We were all screaming, but none of the servants dared intervene; they'd felt the rough side of his tongue before. Pushing her out into the hallway, he slammed my door. I leapt out of bed and wrenched it open to see Mother lying in a heap at the bottom of the stairs. My father stood at the top, shaking like a man possessed.

"No. Lydia. Wake up. Wake up now. I'm sorry you slipped. I didn't mean …" he muttered. Then he turned and saw me and hung his head.

"Come here." He beckoned me to him. In a daze, I walked over and to my astonishment he pulled me into his arms and held me tight as the tears coursed down his face and wetted my pyjamas.'

Margaret thought back to the way Leslie had looked into her eyes. His glazed expression had made her doubt he was even aware who he was talking to, but he had continued his story.

'That was the last time he ever touched me. I think he hated me for looking like her. I realise now that I must have made him feel guilty every day. He remarried quite quickly, and I was sent away to school and never allowed to mention my mother. Once I got upset, and he beat me so harshly I thought he'd kill me, too. His eyes were black with rage. He was out of control - like a vicious dog. I used to cry alone in my room. I still had her shoes - the ones she left under my bed. I hid them and would take them out secretly and stroke them whenever I felt sad about her.'

 Margaret hadn't known what to say.

   'That is such a sad story, I was totally unaware.'

   'I know. I've never told anyone before. I don't know why I've told you tonight.'

   Falling asleep in his arms, Margaret had felt some hope for their future, but she hadn't understood just how damaged he was. The next morning he had been worse than ever. Cold, and snapping at her over the slightest thing. She was baffled and had no idea what to do.

THE FESTIVAL OF THE MADONNA

The town perched vertiginously on the golden hill. It was shrouded in mist, like a beautiful bride hidden beneath a veil. Villagers making their way up to the square called to one another as the Madonna sat in the church waiting, her blue robe looking as if it was rippling around her, even though it was carved from stone. Crowned, serene, waiting for her moment, her pale moon-like face made her blue eyes stand out like sapphires as she gazed down at baby Jesus smiling contentedly in her arms. Outside, the residents, all wearing their smartest clothes, began making preparations. The men and boys wore suits and ties, the women wore navy dresses in reverence to Our Lady, and the girls were in white to signify their purity. The older contingent had settled down in places where they could get a good view and talk to one another. The air was thick with chatter and excitement. Children reacted by chasing one another round and round and getting in the way. The men shouted at them as they hauled tables and chairs into the middle of the piazza.

Women poured glass after glass of ice-cold *liqueur al limone* from the stone jugs lined up on the tables, and passed them round the waiting crowd, making sure all was well. Children drank lemonade to quench their thirst, all made with the sweet lemons grown in the grove on Ricardo and Giverny's farm.

Giverny and Gabriella walked through the side street to the piazza and stared up at the balconies, where strings of washing had been replaced with intricate arrangements of flowers and silk banners depicting the Madonna and child. Except for one balcony - where the Madonna's orange blouse and red skirt clashed with magenta geraniums - the colours mingled beautifully, perfectly illustrating the warmth and depth of the Italian people.

'Look at that one,' Gabriella pointed and waved at Signora Pellini, who had a face as lined as a ball of paper screwed up ready to throw in a dustbin. Waving back, Signora Pellini smiled, showing her one remaining tooth. Her balcony was decorated with dozens of pots of fuchsias - tiny pink and purple ballerinas pirouetting in the breeze.

'Where's Uncle Corrado?' Gabriella turned to her mother.
'He'll be getting ready with the others. Father Antonio prays with them before they leave the church.
I bet he's feeling quite nervous now.' Giverny squeezed her daughter's hand. 'Come on, let's get a good spot.'
People waited all along the five wide steps that led up to the

thick panelled door of the church, waiting for the icon bearers to appear. Inside, the rising sun hit the stained-glass windows, creating rainbow-coloured pools on the tiled floor. The aisle was long and wide and led to the splendid ornate altar where, above the table covered in rich cloths, long white tapered candles burned in golden candlesticks. The centrepiece, a painting of the Virgin Mary and Baby Jesus, was guarded by two angels with gold carved wings. Fragrant pink roses and gypsophila were intertwined amidst the candles, and the aroma of incense filled the air like an invisible cloud. The long wooden pews were worn with use, having been sat on by Civita residents and their forebears for centuries. Corrado looked around him. He always felt safe here. The grey stone font to his left was in constant use; his grandfather, his father, his brother and himself had all been baptised there as well as his nephews and niece. The sense of history comforted him, and he remembered Giverny and Ricardo's wedding; they had stood at the altar and been so happy as Father Antonio blessed their union.

Then he thought of his father being carried up the aisle in an open casket, followed a few years later by his mother. Clenching his fists, he suddenly became aware of the priest speaking and joining him and Giuseppe standing near the entrance. They circumnavigated the icon with their eyes closed as Father Antonio spoke in his low voice.

'You two have been chosen today as a mark of your maturity. You are crossing a threshold and becoming men. Now you are 21 you are both privileged to be given this opportunity to represent your families and lift Our Lady. God bless you.'

Taking deep breaths, Corrado tried to calm himself down. He thought of his parents, particularly his mama. She had been there when Ricardo had come of age, and he wished so much that she still was now. Stifling the guilt he felt about his longing to leave Civita, he cleared his thoughts. He opened his eyes as the priest fell silent. He and Giuseppe crossed themselves before moving into position, one holding each side of the throne, and hoisted the cold stone up on to their shoulders. Giuseppe looked at Corrado. Smiling nervously, he loosened his tie slightly as they left the gloom and followed the priest through the solid oak door. Blinking in the glare of the sun they walked sedately down the wide terracotta steps. Corrado's hands shook, but his face was a mask as they made their way through the pathway lined with villagers. Everyone was cheering and throwing dried rose petals scented with oils, and the air was filled with a heady perfume. The Virgin Mary gazed down beatifically, and the women began weeping and wringing their hands, forming a procession that followed the statue through the piazza and along small cobbled streets where creamy blossoms were thrown from the balconies above.

Clutching tightly on to Giverny's hand, glancing at her mother's face, Gabriella saw tears trickle through her thick lashes. The crowd grew denser and voices became louder as the streets narrowed. From above, the crowds looked like water, filling every aperture as they were swept along in a frenzy of wailing. The sound began as a low hum before rising to a crescendo and ebbing and flowing in waves. The sun reflected off Mary's gilt crown; blossoms fell into the crowd like snowflakes before they were trodden underfoot, turning the cobbles as slippery as ice. Gabriella was relieved when the Madonna reached her destination, and proudly watched her Uncle Corrado place his precious load down on the church steps. He looked so smart with his gleaming white shirt under his grey suit.

Just above his collar she could see the glint of the chain that held his gold crucifix, the one that he never took off. Nonna had given it to him for Christmas, just before she died.

Gabriella watched as her father embraced Corrado in a great bear hug. Everyone congratulated the young men, shaking their hands and clapping them on the back to cheers of 'bravo' and *'ben fatto!'* An orderly queue formed as one by one the crowd members knelt before the statue, crossed themselves and said a prayer before kissing her cold hand. Gabriella gazed wide-eyed at Camillo, the butcher, as tears dripped down his nose and disappeared into his bristly moustache. Everyone in the line was weeping; the crying was so unified it was as if it was controlled by an invisible conductor. It puzzled Gabriella that the people waiting were sobbing, yet as soon as they got up from their knees they seemed perfectly happy again and walked off in small groups to drink, eat and gossip. She followed her mother as she knelt and prayed soundlessly. Wondering what she was asking for, Gabriella sank to the flagged floor too, feeling its hardness press into her knees. Closing her eyes, she begged the Madonna to look after her family and help her to be good. Giverny hauled her daughter to her feet and smiled down at her, thinking how pretty she looked in her long white dress.

'Come on! Let's go and find the others. I want to give Corrado a hug.'

The tables filled with lemon sweets and puddings were surrounded by hungry children like a flock of sparrows at a bird table. Gabriella joined her cousin, Emilia as she waited in line for some lemonade.

'Did your mama cry?' Emilia took a long draught of lemonade and shivered at its coldness.

'Yes,' said Gabriella, 'everyone did, it seemed like. Did you?'

Emilia shook her head. 'You?'

'No, I think it's something you just do when you're grown up.'

Giverny and Ricardo stood enjoying their icy lemon liqueurs with Camillo and Lucretia.

'What an honour! Corrado, an icon bearer! He's finally grown up, and he's so handsome now,' Lucretia dabbed at the corner of her eye with a white lace handkerchief and sniffed delicately. 'Such a beautiful day.'

Giverny smiled and nodded. 'I know, we are very proud of him. Are you looking forward to coming up to the farm later for the party?'

'*Si*. I can't wait. This is one of my favourite days of the year.'

Children chased one another around and hid beneath the tables while the brightly coloured flower garlands adorning the shops and houses fluttered above them like bunting. After the final believers had said their prayers, the icon bearers shouldered Mary and took her back to the church amidst cheers and wild applause. Once she was gone the atmosphere changed; a calmness and sense of satisfaction descended on the villagers. Conversation and laughter filled the piazza before everyone began heading home for a siesta so they would be ready for the evening revelries ahead. Giverny and Ricardo rounded up the twins, dragging them away from their game of football, and Gabriella and Corrado followed them up the hill.

'See you later,' Giuseppe called to his friends.

'Yes, it should be a good night, *ciao*.' Corrado put his arm round Gabriella and squeezed her shoulder. 'What have you got there?'

Gabriella held up a lemon bun covered in sugar and offered it to Corrado.

'*Grazie*, I'll have a bite, mmm.'

She had one too and they walked home in companionable silence.

MARGARET

29th June 1927

An imposter. That's what I feel like. This house is so big and draughty, yet somehow empty. I don't mean from a lack of furniture. Initially when we arrived after the wedding and I walked up those sweeping steps the first thing that struck me was its sense of opulence. It's filled with beautiful things and stands on Bishops Avenue, one of the most prestigious streets in London. I just don't belong here. It has a shroud of sadness hanging over it like a thin layer of dust. The exception is the morning room. It's small and sunny with an oak writing desk, and there's a chaise longue under a window that looks out over a rose garden. I think it was his mother's room as it's different to the others, and beautifully done out with a tiny pink apple-blossom pattern on the wallpaper and chintz curtains. But even that has a desolate feel to it. I suppose it's because I know about his mother dying here. It feels unloved and heartless. And I feel as if I'm being watched all the time. Not long after we married, I wanted to see Leslie's room. I tried the door, but it was locked. Suddenly, Andrews, the butler, seemed to come out of nowhere, and he asked if he could help me. I made an excuse, but I don't feel as if this is a home at all.

It's like the staff know I don't belong and they resent me. When they lined up to meet me they were polite, but I could tell the housekeeper hated me on sight. She looked at me as if she thought I was not good enough. The only one I like is the gardener, Ted. He always stops and chats to me when I venture outside. He's told me he's been here for more than forty years and you can tell he takes a pride in the gardens. They're beautiful. The box hedges surrounding the house are perfect, with not one twig out of place, and he tends the roses so fondly, like they're his babies, talking to them softly as he deadheads them. When Andrews had gone back downstairs I thought I'd explore some of the other rooms. I know I shouldn't have, but I felt I had to tiptoe so no one could hear me. At the end of the long passage two doors down from mine I found a heavy door and opened it and crept inside, shutting it behind me. The brocade curtains with their gold and brown spiral pattern were shut. They felt heavy as I opened them and stared around the room. A table in the corner held a toy yacht with blistered paint and a threadbare teddy bear. A photograph of Leslie as a small boy stood in a frame. He was proudly wearing his school uniform with his cap slightly lopsided. It reminded me of the photograph downstairs. Except in this one I noticed, as I picked it up and blew the dust off, he was smiling from ear to ear obviously looking forward to starting school. Picking up the forlorn bear I sat on the high bed and hugged it picturing Leslie doing the same as a *plan had formed in my mind. We could have a baby. This room is perfect.*

I imagined a crib in the corner and toys and books and tiny clothes and Leslie and I singing lullabies as we looked down at our child sleeping peacefully.

Flicking back through the pages she cringed remembering how she tried to seduce Leslie hoping they could have a baby. Her advances were ignored. She had never felt more rejected before that day.

12th June 1927

I have been deceived. I fell for all that nonsense about marriage making you feel complete as a woman. I bought into the idea that it was my duty to marry and have children.

Did I really believe that? Or was it just my parents' ideals? It's not fair. Leslie's life is exactly the same as before we married. Better for having me in it, in fact. But, I have become a worthless ornament, on a different type of shelf. My life is empty. I no longer work or feel fulfilled. I hate being a woman and subservient. I wish I could do something different with my life I want to change things like the Suffragettes have. I wish I had Emily Davison's courage. She died for her beliefs. Instead I've become nothing. I don't know who I am anymore. Maybe it was that day in Hyde Park, when I was little, about seven or eight, that changed my trajectory…

THE PARTY
ITALY

The creamy coloured tent on the hillside, stood out like a sandcastle on a beach in the late afternoon sunshine, and the bright bunting fluttered in the breeze, beckoning to the groups of villagers zigzagging up the hill, clothed in their Sunday best. The cows in the field next to the path continued to chew the cud, watching nonchalantly as guests pushed prams, bath chairs, and even some handcarts to carry the small members of their families home later. As the early birds arrived outside the tent, a few notes could be heard from the band getting ready and tuning up.

'Where's Piero? His accordion's here but he's not.' Ricco, fingered his violin, placing it under his chin, he swept his bow back and forth a few times, issuing quavering notes.

'Probably having another quick drink,' laughed Alfonso, polishing his flute until it shone. 'We'll have to keep an eye on him after last year when he gave Giuseppe a run for his money and tried to drink him under the table with that punch.'

'I know he couldn't play and fell asleep outside. I was looking for him for ages.'

The tent was set up with a small stage for the musicians at one end; benches and tables were placed around the edge leaving an open space in the middle in anticipation of wild dancing far into the night. Gabriella and her cousin, Emilia, were in there working hard, putting the finishing touches to the long trestle tables laid with milk-white starched cloths as they stood waiting to be laden with food. As well as plates and glasses each table boasted a silver candelabra housing three long tapered red candles and a vase of roses to match, their scent clinging delicately in the air filling the tent. Giverny clapped as she walked in.

'Girls, well done, you've arranged the flowers so well, I'm proud of you both.' With tears in her eyes, she bent down to smell a ruby red bloom. 'Mmmm, *delizioso*, Nonna would be proud too,' before wrapping the girls in a warm embrace. Outside, the piglet was golden brown as it slowly turned above the embers of a small fire made from wood chips cut from lemon branches. The air began to fill with the mouth-watering smell of the *porchetta*, the sizzling sound as its flesh was seared, as well as the voices of the party goers flooding into the farm. Ricardo and Abramo, stood by the gate greeting the guests.

'Ah, Camillo, *grazie mille* for the stunning meat my friend, that smell!' Ricardo pumped the butcher's hand before turning to Lucretia, his wife, and kissing her on both cheeks.

'*Benvenuto*, I must say you are looking very pretty today.' Lucretia blushed, laughed and rounded up her boys who were chasing each other around.

'Come on you two.'

'*Ciao* Mario. *Grazie* that is very kind,' Abramo took the proffered bottle of wine and scrutinised the label. 'One of yours I see, last years?'

'It is. It was a good year. I'm really looking forward to Corrado's food. The smell of that porchetta got me up the hill. Phew!' He removed his hat and used his forearm to wipe his sweaty brow.

'My brother has surpassed himself this year just wait and see what's to come.' Ricardo winked, slapped his friend on the back, kissed his wife, Chloe, on both cheeks and pointed. 'Help yourself to drinks up in the tent. Where are the angels?'

'They're on their way.'

Three blonde boys aged nine, ten and eleven hurtled past them up the hill, laughing.

'*Ciao* Ricardo.' They shouted.

'No climbing trees today d'you hear?' Ricardo called to their backs.

Their nickname was a standing joke as they were the naughtiest boys around. As a result of their mother's French heritage, they were fair haired and looked angelic when they were little, so she had named them after three of the archangels: Raphael, Gabriel and Michael. They weren't bad boys; however, they were always getting into scrapes and were like catnip to Alfredo and Tomaso. Tree climbing was now banned as the last time they'd gone out together, all five of them up to the lemon grove, Tomaso had fallen out of a tree and broken his arm.

Giovanni trundled up the hill next, in a cart led by his old black donkey. Beside him sat his large wife Carlotta and in the back laughing and holding down flagons of their Papa's deadly punch were their four daughters, Agnesa, Allesandra, Alonza and Allegra, four pretty girls aged between seventeen and twenty-two who had yet to concede to their mother's figure.

'Welcome, to you all.' Ricardo patted the donkey on the neck and gave his soft ears a rub.

'*Ciao*, we've got the punch, the girls are holding it to keep it safe.' Giovanni pointed behind him.

'We can always rely on you, can't we?' said Ricardo. 'Put it in the tent for later.'

Giovanni waved in reply as Ricardo turned to Abramo and grimaced.

'No one's got the heart to tell him it's like firewater and gives the worst headache ever.'

'Oh well. At least it gets the party going.' Abramo made them both chuckle.

Corrado was up in the farmhouse putting the finishing touches to the food. The aromas wafting from the kitchen promised a feast. He thought back to Gabriella helping him earlier in the day. She was a natural cook; working hard for hours without complaining. She had been brilliant at helping him stuff the piglet with rosemary, garlic and sage holding the skin taut while he tied the knots to hold it together, she did everything he told her and asked so many questions. She definitely had the family gift. He looked around the kitchen, dipping a spoon into his fish sauce before pursing his lips, blowing on the spoon and tasting.

'A touch more pepper, I think.' After correcting the seasoning Corrado removed his food stained apron and was sitting down with a glass of red wine swishing it around, making a whirlpool, before taking a sip and enjoying the fruitiness wash over his tongue, as Giverny flew into the room carrying a huge tray of rattling glasses.

'Whoa, slow down.' Corrado made a space and took the glasses from her.

'I've still got so much to do though everyone's arriving and...'

Corrado held out his hands.

'Right, stop for a minute, let me help you, what's left to do?'

'These glasses have to go out and all the plates and cutlery.' Giverny sighed.

'Sit.' Corrado pushed his sister-in-law into a seat and poured her a glass of wine ignoring her protests. 'I'll sort those out, you need to relax, all the people arriving are our friends, everything's under control, now take a sip and--'

Eduardo pushed open the door to the steamy kitchen followed by Marcello.

'Mmm smells good in here too. Mama sent us to see if we can help.'

Corrado smiled. 'Just in time. Yes please.' He piled them up with trays and nodded at Giverny, 'see, it's all fine, put your gloves on, drink up and let's party!' Placing a sunhat decorated with wild cornflowers on her head he passed her white gloves to put on, before linking arms with her and leading her out into the sunshine into a crowd of friends.

'Giverny,' waved Isabella, walking over and giving her friend a resounding kiss on each cheek, before taking in her new dress; a navy-blue summer frock decorated with white daisies. 'You look wonderful.'

'Thank you, so do you, so good to see you, have you got a drink? I love your dress too, red really suits you with your dark hair.'

Next, she greeted Vincenzo and his wife Veronica.

'Mwah, mwah,' kissing them both she stood back to admire Veronica's frock. Stunning. It was peacock blue silk finished with beaded tassels. Her hat was like a tight-fitting bowl covering her black corkscrew ringlets that just peeped out of the bottom, with four large blue flowers fashioned from silk decorating the side. 'Have you been shopping again?' Giverny questioned her friend who laughed and nodded. Her husband pulled at his wife's arm.

'Come on. I want to say hello to Ricardo. *Ciao* Giverny.'

Vincenzo Trapani was a councillor with a problem and a reputation. Anyone who needed a law to be bypassed, such as getting a license for their business, or wanted to get planning permission would visit Vinnie, as he was known to his friends, and play an intricate game of bribery chess. Vinnie's problem was his beautiful wife who had very expensive tastes and tried to spend as much time shopping as she could.

While they were courting, he had constantly showered Veronica with expensive gifts while he worked overtime. Utterly blinded by her tawny skin, large golden eyes like a deer set in her heart shaped face, he loved to buy her heels to show off her long legs. She was always perfectly made up. Rumour had it that even Vinnie had never seen her bare faced, because she went to bed with a full face on and always rose before him to fix it before he woke. Shouting obscenities about their mothers he pretended to get angry when other men stared at her, gesticulating wildly at them but secretly it made him feel proud, like a real man, and a lucky one at that.

Once they were married, he realised continually working extra hours was no longer feasible and having quickly worked his way up through the council ranks he devised this scheme to keep his wife in the manner she had become accustomed. Those who needed his help would begin the game by suggesting a ridiculously small amount of money, say 2000 lire. Vinnie would laugh and look hurt.

'Don't you think my help's worth more than that?' The other party would agree and offer more and again Vinnie would frown and hold his hands up in despair. 'I don't think you really want my help.' Like dancers twirling around during an elaborate foxtrot they continued in this manner for several hours, until eventually Vinnie would grasp his opponent's hand and shake it hard before pouring them both a large glass of grappa, and the deal would be done.

Floating around, in their pretty dresses, like butterflies in a meadow, the women chatted at the start of the party. The men sat in the tent and made bets on the arm-wrestling competition going on, while their children played tag, darting in and out of the tent and groups of people tirelessly like tadpoles playing hide and seek in a pond full of reeds. Camillo, the butcher, sat opposite Abramo; both men burly and fond of their food, scarlet in the face - adversaries - gripping hands with a steely look in their eyes.

'2000 lire on Camillo,' Giuseppe placed his money on the table with a flourish, 'anyone?'

'I'll say 2500 on Abramo. Come on, my friend.' Mario clapped Abramo on the back. Sweat was pouring down their faces as they sat there like crabs locked in a battle to the death. The onlookers multiplied, along with the mound of money, as the bets came flooding in thick and fast. Alfredo, Tomaso and Marcello came in to find out what all the shouting was about; they couldn't see, so they dropped to the grassy floor and crawled between the legs of the excited crowd, popping up in front of the table surprising everyone including the wrestlers.

Abramo lost concentration for a second and Camillo took full advantage, his eyes bulged as his large hairy hand began to push down towards the table, until Marcello called out.

'Come on Papa.'

'*Si*, come on Uncle,' shouted the twins.

Their support reversed the momentum and Abramo finding an inner reserve of strength let out a roar as he took control and flipped his hand over slamming Camillo's down on the table. The crowd erupted, there was lots of slapping on the back and joviality as the money was shared out by the victors. Mario winked as he gave the boys some of his takings.

'I couldn't have done it without you three turning up at the last minute. *Grazie.*'

Laughing the three boys ran off to tell their friends, narrowly missing Corrado entering on their way out. 'Watch where you're going you lot,' he called after their receding backs. Giuseppe spotted Corrado, his old friend, and beckoned him over, passing him a glass of wine, he clinked the glasses together.

'Here's to the cook. *Salute!*'

Corrado laughed and took a long swig, before smacking his lips together and nodding.

'What's been going on in here, I heard lots of noise?'

'You missed a great spectacle my friend, Abramo beat Camillo in an arm wrestle. They were tussling for ages and at the end those three little monkeys crawled under the table, popped out and started cheering for Abramo. That was the decider. It broke Camillo's concentration and he lost.'

Corrado laughed. 'How are the plans coming on?' Are we still going in August?'

'Yes, although on days like this, I love living here.'

'Did you feel guilty today when we were in the church with Father Antonio?'

'Yes but, I put it to the back of my mind. I gather you did then?'

'I kept seeing Nonna's face and then Mama's and felt like I'll be letting everyone down-'

'They're not here and you've got to think about yourself, what will make you happy.'

'I know, I feel the same, but I still want to go.'

'Me too.' He raised his glass. 'To London.'

'To London.'

Outside, Ricardo made an announcement through the loud hailer.

'*Signore et signori*, if you could walk over to the meadow, it is time for the Beauty Contest.'

Ripples ran through the crowd as they began making their way over to the next field where a ring had been created and Giverny stood talking to Giuseppe's father, Luigi, who farmed the nearby land. The two families were old friends and he had been asked to judge. Gabriella and her brothers rushed up to stand in the ring with some other children from the village.

'Welcome to the beauty contest. I see we've got quite a few entrants here. I'd like to thank Luigi for doing us the honour of judging, can we give him a round of applause? So, Luigi what is it you're looking for we know you're an expert?'

'*Grazie* for having me, you can pay me in your wonderful liquer al limone later!' Everyone laughed and clapped again. 'I'm looking for bright eyes, a healthy comb, good legs and an all-round friendly demeanour. Let's get started.'

One by one the chickens were proffered up like feathered sacrifices to be inspected, held and stroked. Only one disgraced herself, after taking offence at Luigi inspecting her legs, she was disqualified for pecking the judge, the rest seemed to quite enjoy the experience, preening and showing off their glossy wings. Gabriella's chicken was special: small with greenish feathers, the colour of the dragonflies that buzzed busily by the river and never seemed to tire. Luigi picked her up and gently stroked her glossy feathers.

'What's her name?'

'Sofia,' said Gabriella proudly.

'She is a very good specimen and believe me I have seen a lot of chickens in my time, her comb is perfect, the colour of tomatoes and her eyes are sparkly. I can tell she is very tame she doesn't seem to mind me handling her.'

'That's because her mother died and I hatched her out. I was the first thing she saw when she came out of the egg and she thinks I'm her mama.' Gabriella put the chicken under her arm as if it were a wing and the crowd laughed.

'Well I think that decides it, this is the winner, Sofia, and her mother hen, Gabriella.' Luigi handed Gabriella a red ribbon which she attached to her white dress and matched the rose in her dark curls. Ricardo and Giverny looked on proudly at their beaming daughter as she was applauded loudly.

'Second is Benito, the cockerel, and Andrea-' the rest of his speech was drowned out by Camillo.

'*Urra! Urra!* My boy has won! Now I will forgive that bird for waking me so early in the mornings.'

'Last, but not least is this one.' Luigi pointed to a plump hen with lily white feathers and a scarlet comb, owned by Tomaso and Alfredo. 'Because as well as being beautiful she is a showoff look!' He held up his hand to show the crowd a perfectly shaped white egg without a blemish. Everyone laughed and Tomaso and Alfredo grinned from ear to ear.

'Not everyone can be a winner, and it seems our hosts have swept the board this year, but all those who didn't win don't be downhearted because over on the table is your consolation

prize.' Luigi pointed to a pile of lemon biscuits that stood proudly as the centre piece, glowing in the last late sun rays. With a cheer, the children ran over and devoured them like a swarm of locusts, within three minutes they were a distant memory and all that remained were a few crumbs.
Ricardo hugged Luigi.

'Thank you for judging and especially for making my children very happy, let's go and find you a drink, I believe I owe you several.'

LA TONNA 600AD

ITALY

'"Whoa!" He laid almost horizontal on the donkey's back to try to slow it down. Adjacent to him the crowd became a blur as they cheered and whistled. Continuing to hurtle around the makeshift track his life flashed before him like a kaleidoscope.

Earlier in the day Danilo Toscani was feeling confident as he fed his faithful brown steed, Diego, his oats with a little something extra. Initially, he wasn't sure how it would turn out but from what he'd heard he had a hunch. While walking in the hills surrounding Civita, he had heard voices in the distance. He had always been a nosy boy. His mother had predicted that one day this would be his downfall. Despite knowing it was wrong, he couldn't resist creeping up quietly and hiding behind a tree, eavesdropping. Gabriele Hugentobler was sitting under the largest lemon tree with his grandson telling him a secret. What Danilo learnt that day he hugged to himself and for once didn't pass it on or gossip to anyone.

As a consequence of his penchant for gossip, Danilo was not particularly popular. This annoyed him because his greatest desire was to take part in *La Tonna*. This was a traditional race held twice yearly in June and September. Chosen by the people, the riders represented families and *contradas*, areas of Civita and Bagnoregio. It was a matter of pride and a huge amount of money changed hands and was awarded to the winner so only the best riders and fastest donkeys were chosen. Danilo had been practicing and practicing every day ready for the trials for the past three years and never been selected. This year he decided would be different. Hatching a plan after hearing Gabriele's secret, he played back the words humming around in his head.

"What I'm about to tell you is a secret about this lemon tree we're sitting under that you must promise to keep. It's imperative that you understand its power."

"I promise."

"This tree produces lemons like no other. They have been used to cure the dying and heal the sick. They induce strength in those who eat them, both physically and spiritually; however, they must be used wisely and never ever for personal gain."

That night Danilo had stolen up to the tree serenaded by crickets and checking he hadn't been seen he filled a bag with lemons. There was eight weeks until the race and four weeks until the trials. Every day he ate three lemons and began to notice himself feeling fitter and less sluggish. A healthy glow surrounded him and consequently, girls were staring to take more interest in him. It was then he came up with his master plan to feed the lemons to Diego, his donkey.

On the day of the trials he sat on Diego waiting for his turn. Wiping the back of his neck with his handkerchief he twitched. The sun was relentless; he felt as if every sinew in both his body and Diego's were taut, stretched like the skin on a drum. Finally, it was their turn and as they flew round the track faster than any of the others Danilo knew he'd made it. People buying him drinks, clapping him on the back, saying Diego was a wonder and as fast as a horse was a new experience that he wanted to be repeated. Continuing to eat the lemons and add the juice into Diego's oats he started to love life. He got a girlfriend, Maria, who adored him, but he didn't tell her his secret as she fussed over him and cooked him dinner hoping he would propose to her.

Danilo woke with a start from a nightmare as the day of the race dawned. In his dream he was in the piazza ready to race but he couldn't move. Diego was rooted to the ground and the crowds were jeering at him calling out: "*falso, falso!*" He looked around him trying to catch his breath as he realised he was in bed. Excitement replaced his fear and he leapt out of bed to get ready.

The plaza was full of anticipation. The sandy buildings seemed to quiver with excitement as their balconies were decorated with large banners. Each flag represented the *contrada* and rider and there were twelve in all. Danilo's flag was black and red and fluttered proudly in the breeze. Residents shouted to one another as they opened their shutters and doors. Tables were laid out across the church steps topped with plates full of hard crumbly cheese, salty cured meats and long golden loaves of bread, warm from the baker's oven. Everyone from Civita and Bagnoregio looked forward to this. Those from Bagnoregio began wending their way up the track to the piazza waving to their friends and chivvying their children, until it was time for the race. The crowd watching was dense; people were perched on shoulders, sitting in stairwells and leaning from their windows and balconies to get a good view.

The twelve donkeys stood in a line as Father Domenico lifted his arms and blessed them all. The race worked on a course of elimination. Two riders and their steeds ran around the square three times battling it out and the one that wins stays on. Each race had bets put on it and the winner would receive a percentage at the end. The air was thick with shouts of people exchanging money, cheering on their *contrada's* rider and yelling derisory remarks at their rivals using colourful language that Father Domenico ignored.

Jostling with his opponent Danilo took his place. Wearing a look of grim determination, he barely noticed Maria kissing him and begging him to be careful. He had a feeling that this was his moment. After this everything was going to change. It was his destiny to win and be rich. He couldn't wait to start. Diego galloped around the track easily outstripping his opponent. Despite his coat being black with sweat he was pawing the ground waiting to race again. The cheers and slaps on his back still rang in his ears as he won again and again. Eventually it was the last race. He was against Matteo, the blacksmith. A large man who had been riding since he was a baby. He had won for the past five years and had an air of confidence that infuriated Danilo.

Matteo's family and supporters were the loudest shouting: "*Sempre un vincitore*! Always a winner!" and "*Campione per sempre!* Champion forever!"

The bell rang to start the last race. Danilo's felt his heart was hammering louder than the donkeys' hooves clattering across the cobbles. Matteo took the lead as the crowds screamed until Danilo forced his way through the gap urging Diego on.

"Come on! Come on! This is our destiny come on!" He shrieked as Diego took off. Lying back with the bridle pulling as hard as he could made no difference. Matteo won. Instead of riotous celebrations, the crowd became silent as Diego broke free from the track. Danilo's screams echoed around the hillside and his arms and legs were flailing as the donkey careered out of the plaza and down the steep hill. Realising he couldn't control the donkey Danilo saw his chance. Flinging himself from Diego's back he landed with a heavy thud headfirst deep into a thicket of gorse. Scratched everywhere, he felt as if the bushes had taken out little swords and stabbed him repeatedly. The last time he saw Diego he was still galloping as fast as a horse with a cloud of dust chasing him.

Removing himself from the gorse was as painful as landing in it. The branches seemed to clutch at him and embrace him as he screamed at them to let him go. Red rivulets began trickling down his face, legs and arms as the cuts deepened. Making a last concerted effort he finally broke free and fell down in the scrub grass panting and weeping.

Diego was never seen again. Danilo went home with his tail between his legs annoyed at being the brunt of everyone's jokes instead of the hero he felt he should have been. The following day he picked some lemons hoping that through eating them the deep scratches on his face would heal and not scar. He cut the lemon into quarters and pursed his lips around it expecting the sweet taste to comfort him as before. Instead he spat it out in disgust having never tasted anything so sour in his life. Utterly unpalatable. One side of Danilo's face was deeply scarred; consequently, Maria got sick of his self-pity and married someone else. Danilo gave up trying to be a jockey in the races and initially went back to his old ways enjoying listening behind doors and creeping around in the hope of hearing juicy titbits about other people which he could whisper in willing ears.

However, this did not last long because every time he said something about someone, he would get the taste of the sour lemon in his mouth and the deep scar on his cheek would begin to smart as if it had never healed. Eventually he changed his ways.'

MARGARET

Blustery, was how the weather could be described on that day in October 1913, as Margaret remembered it. She had written it down in her journal, so she would always remember it.

A sea of long dresses, women wearing purple, green and white, matched the colours of the banners bearing slogans demanding women get the vote and parasols blowing inside out were all mixed up with the falling fiery leaves. Most memorable was the atmosphere. Thrilling. Palpable. Change was in the air. A wave was swelling which would alter the world as we knew it forever. Police officers milled about holding large dogs on chains and scowling as a woman stood up on the bandstand and orated.

'That's her, look, Emmeline Pankhurst.' My mother took my hand so we could move closer and hear what she was saying.

'The time is now. I have recently been to America and delivered a speech – a speech I am here today to repeat to you.'

The throng moved forward as one. Banners flapped in the breeze and women excitedly stood shoulder to shoulder in silence. Aware of an air of anticipation as I stood among them, the scent of lavender from the lady next to me wafted on the wind.

. *Young and pretty she wore a lilac dress and a white wide brimmed hat decorated with silk roses. Turning, she smiled at me with warm brown eyes before turning her gaze to the bandstand as the speech began. Snippets are all I can remember from her speech and the majority of those I didn't understand at the time.*

"Today, I want to honour our friend and sister, Emily Wilding Davison. We must fight for our right to have our say in order that she did not die in vain. I am not only here as a soldier temporarily absent from the field of battle. I am here – and that, I think, is the strangest part of my coming – I am here as a person who, according to the law courts of my country, it has been decided, is of no value to the community at all."

A deafening wave of applause echoed around the park and a stampede ensued as she threw leaflets into the crowd like confetti. I looked at her and wondered why what she was saying was so important. She looked ordinary enough. Like a grandmother with her hair up and her high-necked green dress. It was her eyes I found the most interesting. Brown but not warm like the young girl who had smiled at me. Cold. She didn't smile once during her address or afterwards as her hand was shaken and she was praised for her tenacity. Suddenly my eyes were torn from her face as my mother pushed me away from the bandstand. Turning I saw a crowd of men forging their way forward, the way they were splitting the crowd reminded me of the Bible story with Moses and the Red Sea.

Ripping down banners in their path they roughly pushed women aside. Their aim was to reach the woman who stood like a statue unflinching, those cold brown eyes never wavering, surveying them as they forged forward.

REMEMBERING ANCESTRY

Carefully walking with Gabriella across the dewy grass, Giverny balanced her *secondi*, the platter of *porchetta*. Clear, the indigo sky was embroidered with silver stars, cradling a crescent moon.

'What a perfect night for the party,' said Giverny. 'Look at all those stars.'

'It looks like there are millions,' said Gabriella.

'My mama always said they're our loved ones watching over us.'

'Do you think Nonna's watching us now?'

'I like to think so.' Giverny smiled at her daughter. 'Come on.'

Entering the tent, they heard loud roars of laughter from a corner. The tables were full of smiling guests, eating, drinking and chatting by candlelight. This is what makes all the work worthwhile thought Giverny. Ricardo jumped up and relieved her of the tray, before kissing her.

'Well done.'

Giverny smiled. 'Everyone looks like they're having fun. I think we're about ready to eat.' Taking her place next to him at the table she sat down. Ricardo picked up a glass tapping it with a spoon before clearing his throat as the chatter subsided.

'Ladies and gentlemen, could I have your attention for a moment please? Thank you. I just want to make sure everyone has a glass of liquer al limoni, my wife's speciality, and secret recipe made from our lemon grove, before I make a toast. There are jugs on each table please help yourselves.' Pausing for a moment he waited while Camillo picked up one of the large stone jugs and filled up the glasses on his table. *'Grazie.'* Turning to his neighbours with a chuckle he said 'I wonder how many babies will come from drinking this tonight. You know there's always at least one born exactly nine months from today.' When the laughing had dissipated Ricardo continued. 'We are very glad to welcome you here as our guests today. I'm sure you'll agree that the festival this morning was a beautiful experience, we are especially proud of Corrado and Giuseppe who came of age today, carrying Our Lady. I'm certain I wasn't the only one with a tear in my eye, and I know that although their relatives were not here to see them, I'm sure they were looking down and smiling, eh Luigi?'

Luigi nodded, and a murmur of assent rippled around the tent. Ricardo paused to take a sip of his drink, enjoying the combination of warming acidic sweetness. 'I also want to remind you why we have this celebration afterwards. Our ancestors who farmed this land many years ago began the tradition that developed from a terrible experience. Corrado will tell you the story that happened in 1725 and has been passed down for almost two hundred years, through telling it we keep their memory alive, in years to come I expect my children to tell it too.'

Corrado stood and cleared his throat.

'The fire engulfed the great house sending black smoke billowing into the sky, obscuring the moon and stars. Having seen the dancing flames, the villagers raced up the hill to help. Forming a line that started at the pump they passed buckets along quickly, their hair sodden with sweat as they fought the ferocious heat. Their blackened faces and hands made them look identical as they worked fast and without stopping, yet still the house was indefatigably consumed bit by bit. The Contessa stood near the courtyard holding her crying children; all were tinged orange with black shadows playing across them as the fire danced tirelessly like a demon. Inside, the Conte ran through the burning halls and up the sweeping staircase screaming the name of his son.

"Gennaro, Gennaro where are you?" Wrenching open a door he forced his way through the thick smoke as it tried to repel him. Rubbing his hand across his streaming eyes he squinted searching the room until he saw the small boy cowering in the corner by the

*window his dark eyes wide with terror at the flames before him. His
father ran through them to him and quickly ripped down one of the
long mustard coloured curtains.*

*"I'm here, I've got you." Picking up his son, he wrapped him in
the curtain completely so his face and head were covered, and the
Conte hurled himself back through the flames which were spreading
fast and licking at the top of the staircase. Flying down the stairs he
ran out of the house as the upstairs window to the room they had
escaped from exploded. Flinging Gennaro into his wife's waiting
arms he joined the front of the human chain becoming indiscernible
from the peasants as he feverishly poured the water on to the fire.
The fire built and grew roaring into a ferocious dragon, until
stunned as he realised the futility of pouring water onto this
monster, the Conte sank to his knees and cried. "It has won, stop
now, there is no hope." The fire's reflection burnt in his eyes as he
turned away and put down the bucket; a broken man, his opulent
clothes charred and in holes and his hands blistered and burnt. The
Contessa ran to him and cradled him in her arms. Together they
watched, surrounded by their children, as the walls crumbled.
The intensity of the heat became unbearable as the wind changed
direction, sparks flew over all the spectators watching the flames
devouring their possessions, memories and the life they had known.'*
Corrado cleared his throat and drank some of his lemon
liquer.

'After their house was destroyed in this fire, they were left homeless without any belongings. Prior to this on the day of the festival of the Madonna, they would make all types of cakes and sweet things from the lemons on their farm and bring them down to share with the poor people in the village, they were always generous and looked after those who were in need. The villagers now had an opportunity to repay them for their kindness. They took them in, clothed and fed them and helped them to rebuild their house and lives.

We now live in the house they built and this party is testament to the resilience of the Italian people and their ability to overcome difficulties in life. As we all know, ever since then a feast has been held in memory as a celebration of unity, to show how much can be achieved when a community is strong and the people belonging to it work side by side.' His speech was drowned out by an eruption of applause so deafening that no one heard a car pulling into the drive and the door slam.

MARGARET

Reaching her they leapt on to the bandstand. The ringleader who held a bottle of beer in his hand hissed in her face.

'You'll never win. You think you're as good as a man but look at you.' He sneered.

Emmeline looked at him with disgust and he pushed her hard.

I didn't really see what happened next it all happened so quickly. The bandstand became a blur of people scuffling. The women in the crowd had leaped to their leader's defence; using their parasols as weapons there was pandemonium. Mother dragged me towards the big black gates. The last glimpse I had was of the police going in with the dogs. I shuddered and rushed away to the safety of home.

'What was all that about Mother?'

'They believe that women should be allowed to vote and make decisions about things just like men can.'

'Why were those men attacking them?'

'Because they believe women are too weak, too stupid to know anything about politics.'

'Who was the person she talked about who died?'

'Emily Davison. She was demonstrating at the races and she fell under the king's horse.'

'That's terrible!'

'A dreadful business. But it made people talk about us getting the vote which is what she wanted more than anything. She died a martyr for our cause and that's why we have to keep on fighting and agitating and having conversations about it.'

'So you agree with them?'

'Wholeheartedly.' She turned to me with a serious look in her eye. 'But don't tell your father where we went. He'll be angry as he hates the Suffragettes.' She stopped me and put her hands on my shoulders. Her eyes were full of passion. 'What just happened there was very important, we just witnessed history in the making. This can be our secret.' She put her finger to her lips then to mine; excited to have this bond with her - it made me feel special. I nodded then and have always kept it a secret to this day.

The only time she mentioned it again was five years later after the war. She took me to one side and her eyes shone as she whispered to me that it had finally happened. 'Now I can vote Margaret, thanks to the Suffragettes. I hope that soon you will be able to as well.'

I feel sad at how much Mother has changed now. Worn down by Father and the expectations put upon her. I still find it hard to believe that in all that time still only some women have the right to vote. It's taking so long. Nearly fifteen years on from when I went to that rally, but there is talk that it will all change soon. Even if all women get the vote there's still a long way to go. Memories of the day made Margaret put pen to paper.

Chained

Chained
To your ideals
And the railings
For us.
The new
Generation
Of women
Demanding
That we have
Choices
Voices
And rights
To be seen
Not as the
Weaker sex
But strong.
Strong enough
To take men's
Place during
The Great War
Not to be
Returned
To nothing.
To be free
Like birds
To fly
To spread
Our wings
And sing.

THE UNINVITED GUEST
ITALY

Ricardo's smile froze as Nicolai loomed in the doorway of the tent. Wearing black from top to toe, and a sneer, he sauntered in and took centre stage. A stony silence fell as the clapping subsided and he picked up a bottle of red wine and leisurely poured himself a glass.

'Well what a reception. *Grazie.* So good to see you all here.' Picking up a knife he stabbed a piece of meat from the platter, put it into his mouth and chewed slowly, the crackling crunching between his teeth punctuating the silence. 'Mmm, very tasty, compliments to the chef.' He nodded at Corrado, who stiffened and lurched towards him. Ricardo put a hand on his brother's arm and gave him a look. Nicolai took a long swig of wine and smacked his lips together before holding up his glass. '*Salute!* My invitation to your party seems to have got lost, but I knew I'd be welcome anyway.' Still and silent the guests sat like rabbits hypnotised by an acrobatic stoat, as he headed towards the door. Corrado's heart was pumping with fury, his mouth a grim line. Nicolai began walking out before turning in the doorway at a table filled with wine bottles and glasses.

Slowly using his index finger, he put it to the neck of the open bottle and pushed hard knocking it over like a skittle. 'Oops! *Mi dispiace.*' As he left his laugh rang out and the scarlet liquid glugged from the bottle covering the white tablecloth like blood pumping from an artery. Corrado leapt to his feet and Ricardo grabbed his arm in a vice-like grip, aware of his brother's volcanic anger.

'Leave him!' He commanded.

Luigi stood up shakily with tears in his eyes.

'My apologies for my son-in-law, I am so ashamed to call him a part of my family.'

'He's not part of our family.' Giuseppe shouted, jumping up from his seat. 'He's just married to my sister. How could he do that? And what does Roberta see in him?' Giuseppe's words escaped him, and he hung his head.

Bella and Giverny mopped up the tablecloth as Ricardo stood.

'I will not let him ruin tonight, come on ladies,' he beckoned them back to their seats. 'I want everyone to refill their glasses and I will finish my speech, so we can eat. Please be upstanding as we remember those who couldn't be with us today and I would like to propose a toast to friends and family.' The guests raised a sea of glasses and 'to friends and family' was repeated around the tent. Ricardo remained standing and blessed the food:

'Gesù, grazie per il cibo che ci dai e provvedi per chi non ne ha. Amen.'

Crossing themselves everyone repeated Amen before a wave of chatter arose as the villagers began discussing Nicolai. Giverny and Guilia began taking round the primo, steaming bowls of spaghetti flavoured with crab, lemon and pepper, and dishing out the food to their grateful guests. When Giverny reached Luigi, he sat with downcast eyes, she squeezed his arm.

'Come on have some food, I'm sorry we didn't invite them, you know I love Roberta, but I heard she's been quite poorly while she's been expecting and--'

'It's not your fault Giverny, none of us want him here, he's upsetting everyone, I don't know what to do.' Luigi shrugged his shoulders and let out a deep sigh.

'There's nothing you can do now, except try and forget about it and enjoy the party, once we've eaten it will be time to dance.' Giverny piled his plate up and moved on.

MARGARET

19th July 1927

The trouble is, I love to learn and writing is my passion. Why can't I have both? I still dream of being an author one day. Once I started work, I felt as if I was making a difference and doing something worthwhile - finding who I was - blossoming. I kept learning all the time, and entering writing competitions, pushing doors. I felt like a rambling rose tentatively producing blooms and enjoying the sun on my stems, until Leslie entered my life like a reluctant gardener. Suddenly all that mattered was what everyone else thought and wanted, it was as if adjacent to my rose bush, thick ivy began sprouting from different apertures and angles, surrounding me. It manifested itself in my father's joy that I would finally be off his hands, as he had obviously thought no one would want me and I'd be on the shelf for ever. It manifested itself in my mother, and all the other married women organising the wedding; it was like suddenly becoming part of a strange cult, where I lost my identity and give myself up for evermore. My wrists felt as if they had invisible manacles fastening them, my mouth a gag, my growth was being choked in all directions and I did nothing to stop it, nothing at all.

Momentarily, I thought about calling it off with Leslie, but the guilt I felt relating to the suffering I would cause my family, not to mention the shame and disappointment stopped me. I saw their faces. I doubted their love. Was it conditional? Would they only love me if I fitted in to their plan? Yet still I convinced myself everything would be all right.

ITALY

Gloom had settled on the party like a heavy cloak and conversations were muted. Giovanni beckoned to his girls.

'Now is the time to cheer us all up. Fetch the punch and pour everyone a drink.'

The four sisters stood in front of the tables filling glasses, looking like fallen angels pouring the home-made punch with their dazzling smiles, beautiful white dresses and flowers in their hair.

'*Grazie*, Allegra,' said Vito. Once she had moved on to the next table, he took a cautious sip, coughed and whispered to his wife, 'at least if I go blind, I'll never have to see that bastardo Nicolai again!'

Once everyone had a drink Giovanni stood glass raised.

'I want to take this opportunity to thank our hosts for their wonderful hospitality and echo Ricardo's words earlier. Today, the festival was beautiful; we are very fortunate to have such good friends and families, I make this punch every year to honour my father, he would be proud to see us all here drinking it God rest his soul,' he crossed himself. *'Salute!'* They all joined him in the toast. The secondo was passed round next. Plates of porchetta with fried zucchini flowers stuffed with ricotta. The crunch of the salty crackling contrasting perfectly with the soft creamy cheese filling. The punch had done its job, and everyone was looking happier. Ricardo and Corrado were in heated discussion at the table.

'Why didn't you let me throw him out?' Corrado glared at his brother.

'It would have made things much worse and there would have been a big fight and-'

'And I would have won.' Corrado bristled.

'Maybe you would have today little brother, but what about tomorrow and the day after and the day after that? That wouldn't have been the end of it and the party would have been ruined.' Ricardo slapped his brother on the back. 'Come on have some more punch and cheer up! *Salute!*' Clinking glasses, they knocked back their drinks laughing at the identical faces of disgust they both pulled, as the band made their way to the stage. Piero fingered the accordion and Ricco and Alfonzo joined in playing an old Tuscan folk song with Adriana and Rosetta, the old twin sisters, accompanying them in their quavery voices, while the golden lemon tart was served and enjoyed by all.

Gabriella and Emilia sneaked under a table with second helpings and emptied their bowls quickly without talking.

'That tastes so good,' said Emilia, 'I wish Uncle Corrado lived with us.'

'What do you mean? It wasn't just him, I helped make that you know.'

'Maybe you can come and live with us then.'
They both laughed.

'I'm so full now-' Gabriella put down her bowl and wiped her mouth, watching as the dancing began.

The minute the four beautiful sisters stood in a line there was a scuffle as Mario, Vito, Maura and Giuseppe tried to stand opposite Allegra. Mario won smiling triumphantly. The girls held out their hands and curtsied as the boys twisted and turned around them, clapping in time to the music. Ricco stroked his bow across the strings faster and faster and Alfonzo kept time with his flute as the dancers clasped hands and the girls were twirled and twirled until they were dizzy. Onlookers stood around in a circle clapping and chanting and cheering on the youngsters. Giuseppe was in his element bounding in the air and performing acrobatic leaps. The music swelled into an exciting crescendo before stopping abruptly. Suddenly the boys all fell to their knees and the girls allowed them to kiss their hands before curtseying again.

Spotting Corrado in the crowd, Giuseppe ran over to him grabbing him by the arm.

'Let's have a drink. Come on.' Dragging him outside he produced a bottle of grappa with two small glasses.

'To us!'

'To us' Corrado echoed his words and gulped down it down in one. Giuseppe quickly refilled their glasses.

'How many of these parties do you think we've been to now?'

'Lost count, but I s'pose one a year at least.' Corrado shrugged.

'Not for much longer. *Salute!*'

Clanking glasses they headed back into the tent where Giuseppe spotted Viviana and her mother chatting to Giverny. She wore a lilac dress that accentuated all her curves. Her black hair tapering off into long braids gleamed in the candlelight. Taking his chance and smoothing his hair he sashayed over to ask her to dance and she accepted with a smile. Moving slowly around the floor as Ricco played an old folk ballad about families and their stories Giuseppe whispered into her ear. Suddenly her boyfriend, Antonio, appeared behind them; Giuseppe didn't notice him watching them and pulled her close putting his lips to hers.

A noise like gunshot echoed around the tent as Viviana slapped Giuseppe on his cheek. While he was still reeling, Antonio grabbed Giuseppe by the front of his shirt and propelled him backwards into a table full of glasses that smashed making the women scream. Punctuating his punches with threats and curses he lost control until Abramo pulled him off and pushed him out of the tent. Viviana followed admonishing him.

'Why did you have to do that eh? Do you think I need *you* to fight my battles? No! I don't and now we have to leave the party. The party I've been looking forward to for weeks and--' she stood in front of him, hands on her hips, stopping him from stalking down the hill. 'In fact, you know what? I'm not going. You can. I'm staying. We're finished.' Tossing her head, she turned on her heel and back into the tent as Antonio went home. Corrado pulled Giuseppe to his feet and handed him a glass.

'You never learn, do you?'

MARGARET

30th May 1927

My dreams of running a home have been thwarted by the evil Mrs. Jarvis, Leslie's housekeeper. Having looked after him, as a bachelor, she seems to have taken it as a personal affront that he has found a wife and changed the order of things, and as my punishment, she undermines me at every turn. Not overtly so that Leslie can see, subtly when he's around. At the beginning Leslie asked me to instruct Mrs Jarvis and choose the food for dinner for the week. She got the orders wrong on purpose and blamed me, making me look incompetent, which made Leslie laugh and call me a silly girl, which I found most patronising. It seems I have become utterly useless. I'm meant to sit at home and do nothing. I have to write all this down as I can't talk to anyone; I feel so alone. Leslie told me he didn't want me to work once we were married, he said if I carried on it would make it look as if he couldn't provide for his new bride. I said I'd keep in touch with Daphne - we'd still have book club but it's not the same. I feel like an outsider now. I can't bear going home to see my parents as they have no idea about my life, in fact I feel a bubbling anger inside me, like I'm a volcano full of lava about to erupt, which I have to keep under control.

I want to scream at them. I want to ask Father why he sent me to school and gave me an education, allowed me to be taught to question and wonder and not just accept, because all he's done is trapped me in a loveless marriage, where I'm not allowed to think or have an opinion or even do my writing, even that has become an act of subterfuge. Leslie came home from work the other day when I was scribbling away furiously in the middle of a poem and asked if I didn't have anything better to do than silly girlish story writing. Crushed. That's how I feel with no functionality, as a consequence of those around me who ostensibly appear to love me, controlling me and leaving me; me with an enquiring mind; me who lives to learn with nothing to do except brood.

I thought we'd go to lots of dinner parties and the theatre, but every time we get an invitation Leslie doesn't want to go and makes an excuse and I can't go alone as it would look odd. All he wants to do is come home, eat dinner, drink and read the newspaper. He looks bored whenever I try to talk to him and he's dismissive of my opinions. He's so different to when we first met as then he listened to me and took an interest in what I was saying. The two things keeping me going are my writing and music. The only time I go out is to my knitting circle. If I didn't have Caroline to talk to I don't know what I'd do. My only solace is after Mrs Jarvis leaves at two o'clock, I put on my favourite songs and dance and dream that things will change.

9th June 1927

I can't bear this loneliness. Leslie is so distant. All he does is buy me shoes. Today I opened the cupboard and stared up at a mountain of boxes, there's barely any more room, I feel as if they're going to topple down on me as I open the door, and still he brings more. But he doesn't love me. I don't understand. He drinks too much and always falls asleep. Why doesn't he want to make love to me? He seems to find me repulsive unless I'm wearing a pair of shoes that he's given me and even then he just strokes my feet. We've been married a month now and nothing has happened. I can't talk to anyone about this. To the outside world I appear to have the perfect marriage, a beautiful house, a new car, but none of that means anything without love. When we're in public Leslie is so attentive but at home he drinks whisky and ignores me. I seem to make him so angry he won't talk to me. I feel so alone. I just don't understand. Why did he marry me?

The final word was blurred with tear stains.

Yet, it's my own fault, I can't believe I've been so stupid. I allowed myself to be pushed and pulled. I became as malleable as bread dough. Before I knew it, I was married to a man I despised, and I have become invisible. I no longer have opinions, or a family in the same way I had. Instead, a whole heap of impossible expectations to live up to.

Stinging with tears again, she wiped her eyes and shook her

head and thought about going out later that afternoon to her knitting circle. Encouraged by her mother to take part, she and around ten women met up every week to drink tea, chat and make clothes for the Salvation Army to distribute to the poor. She was good friends with a few of them, particularly Julia and Harriet, who were sisters and the daughters of a friend of Margaret's mother, so she had known them for years.

However, Caroline was her favourite as they had something in common; she loved jazz and dancing too. Tall, blonde and vivacious, nothing ever seemed to get her down. The type of woman that men couldn't help but stare at as she walked down the street. She lived in the London flat belonging to her parents in Golders Green, while they lived on their country estate, and despite having a string of admirers was not interested in getting married. Once she had come to Margaret's house and they had spent the afternoon chatting listening to songs and dancing wildly before laughing and falling into chairs to listen to one of Margaret's favourites: *Exactly like You*. It was that day she had first found out that her friend had a beautiful voice as she sang along to the lyrics: *'She knew just around the corner was somebody exactly like you.'* Her deep, smoky tone leant itself perfectly to jazz. During a heart to heart Margaret asked her what she wanted from life.

'I want to be free.'

'What do you mean?'

'Well, I know that once I get married and have children I'll have to live my life for everyone else. I'll have to put my husband and children first, but I'm too selfish.'

'What about your parents? What do they say?'

'Oh, they're always trying to introduce me to some rich bore, but I refuse to give in. I want to travel the world and be a professional singer. They don't know that though. They think it a tawdry profession.'

'Freedom. Let's drink to that.' Margaret poured them both a gin and tonic. 'Cheers!'

'What about you? Are you planning on having a family?' Margaret sighed and almost confided her desperate inner thoughts but changed her mind. 'Yes, I'm looking forward to it.' She said before changing the subject.

Later Margaret had poured herself another drink and danced alone losing track of time considering what Caroline had said when she was interrupted by Leslie coming in. He slammed the door, stormed over and turned the music off.

'What are you doing?' Margaret glared at him.

'Haven't you got anything better to do?'

Leslie's disgust riled her. 'I'm dancing Leslie, dancing. It's not illegal you know.

It's still my body and I can dance if I want to. You don't own me. When we got married, I agreed to obey you but I'm not a nun although marrying you is like taking a vow of chastity isn't it?' She spat the final words like a wild cat.

Puce he turned stalking stiffly out as Margaret sank down on the chair shaking after hearing the front door slam.

Spending time with Caroline meant Leslie was forgotten. Margaret felt like a different person and hoped her strength would rub off on her; however, she felt like a fraud and was sick of pretending to be happy. Visiting her mother and sister, Jeanie, was the worst. So much so she was starting to avoid it so she didn't have to keep answering their questions about when she was going to have a baby. Fat chance of that! Fuming she wrote out the poem that had been floating around inside her head. After many crossings out she smiled grimly at the result and wrote it in full in her journal.

New Shoes

His eyes, piercing
And cold, observe her
Hands giving her away
As she removes the lid.
Unwrapping the crisp
Tissue paper and
Kneeling before her
He takes out a shoe
And she becomes a

Reticent Cinderella.

ROBERTA

ITALY

Side on in front of the mirror her large bump monopolised the reflection. Sighing, her gaze moved upwards, noting a tear streaked face, and a large red swelling under her right eye. A beauty with high cheek bones, full lips concealing beautiful white teeth, and eyes the colour of honey - her crowning glory was her hair, dark brown, poker straight and long enough for her to sit on. As the baby shifted inside her, she rubbed her belly imagining it stretching out a little leg in a bid to get more comfortable in its ever more restricted space. It had kicked her hard earlier when Nicolai was shouting, sensing her fear… how could her husband have turned into such a stranger? Mimi, her dog, pushed a wet nose into her hand. Roberta stroked her velvety ears while looking around the familiar room; the cardigan she was making for the baby, lay on the windowsill, still attached to the knitting needles stuffed into the large white ball of wool like a fluffy cloud, the double bed, where they had made love and created their baby, covered in the blue and white patchwork quilt made by her mother for them as a wedding gift.

Roberta's insides lurched as she thought of her mother, the longing she felt to talk to her, and the sadness, seemed as if they would never leave her. It was after she left that everything began to go wrong. Before that, she had no idea that her mother was so unhappy. She presumed she must have been miserable as she had been having an affair with a married man in Bagnoregio and they had run off together. She sent a letter, but it didn't explain how she could split their family like that and break her husband's heart. He went to pieces and the responsibility weighed heavily on Roberta as she tried to comfort her papa, while desperately sad herself.

Nicolai was so jealous of me looking after him, he couldn't bear it that he wasn't the centre of my world. I can't understand how, when I needed him so desperately, he could turn so cold. I wanted to talk to him about how I was feeling about Mama going but he wasn't interested, he called her a whore and refused to listen to me. It was then that everything changed, he began going out a lot and made new friends, ones I don't trust, they've changed him into a different man. Now he is a fascist and menaces those who were once his friends for money, in the name of Mussolini and the Cause, so no one trusts him. Roberta shuddered as she thought back to him coming home drunk a few months before.

Exhausted. In bed - tired out after suffering morning sickness that lasted all day - she was almost asleep when he stalked in loudly waking her up. Stripping off his clothes he got straight into bed and wrapped his arms around her. Wincing at the grappa fumes that filled her nostrils, Roberta tried hard not to retch. Nicolai was oblivious, his rough hands all over her made her stiffen.

'I'm sorry darling I'm not well.'

Ignoring her he kissed her hard on the mouth, his whiskery face scratching her soft skin, she kissed him back, but then pushed him away and shook her head.

'I can't tonight.'

Nicolai's face turned almost black with rage as he hissed at Roberta, pinning her down.

'You are my wife and if I want you I will have you do you understand?' Roberta had no chance to reply as he roughly pushed himself inside her. She let her mind go blank as she waited for him to finish. He rolled off her and fell asleep snoring loudly by her side, as she wept silently for her mother. She returned to the present as the baby wriggled inside her, she rubbed the tiny foot she could feel and smiled as she remembered the love she had felt for Nicolai. She had been brimming with hope. He had adored her. Everything was just perfect, they seemed to have a charmed life. When they were courting he would take her on long walks with Mimi, where they would lie in meadows full of dancing, bright butterflies drinking nectar, flitting between the flowers whose scent intoxicated them deepening their love. He picked wild cornflowers, putting them in her hair and told her she was beautiful. Yet now, his eyes once soft and full of love for her, had turned wintry. He had inherited his thin lips from his mother, Claudia, as well as his attitude. The youngest of four boys, when his father died, his mother transferred all her affection to her young son, spoiling him. He was the only one left at home now, when they had married Nicolai explained to Roberta that they had to live with Claudia. Holding her hands he had looked into his wife's eyes.

'I can't leave her. It would break her heart to be left all alone.'

Roberta had tried to win her mother in law's affection to no avail, nothing she did was ever good enough. Tonight, Claudia had stooped to a new low; she had walked into their room as Roberta had confronted Nicolai about the affair he was having with that whore down in the village.

'Your place is here with me and our baby. And you want to be with her. I just don't-' Roberta's voice was raised and full of passion, but Nicolai drowned her out shouting

'You don't want me. I can see it in your eyes all you do is cry like a baby and-'

'That's not true,' Roberta stood up, her face flushed, as she defended herself, 'when my mama died you didn't help me, all you did was go out and get drunk, what sort of a father are you going to make?'

Towering over his wife Nicolai's eyes flashed.

'You dare to criticise me-'

'Yes. I do.' She shouted. 'I don't know you anymore. You're not the man I married. He was warm and caring and not drunk all the time and-'

Claudia entered the room at the same time as Nicolai's fist collided with Roberta's cheek bone. Mimi growled at Nicolai, who kicked her sending her yelping across the room; Roberta gave her mother in law a desperate imploring look, hoping that as a woman and a mother she would for once take her side. Her face crumpled as Claudia gave her a stony look and walked out closing the door quietly behind her.

Roberta touched her bruise and winced as she searched her heart to find a shred of love left for her husband. Coming to the dull realisation that if her love for Nicolai was equated to layers of clothing, she was stripped naked. Before this evening, she had still felt an inkling of hope that when the baby was born things would come right between them and he would look at her with love in his eyes once more instead of regarding her as if she was a black beetle he'd like to tread on.

'Come on Mimi.' She patted the bed for the dog to lie beside her. 'It feels like you're my only friend now.' Curled up with her Roberta remembered the first time she'd seen her. It had been her thirteenth birthday. Mama told her to close her eyes and took her hand as she led her out of the back door. When she opened them, there sat the tiniest black labrador she'd ever seen. Her big brown eyes melted her new owner's heart making Roberta squeal and scoop her up. Inseparable from that day forward, one of the best parts of both their days was going on long walks in the hills that flanked the farm. Mimi would chase rabbits and the sticks Roberta threw for her, before lying down and panting loudly with her pink tongue lolling.

HAMPSTEAD HEATH

Shifting her position on the grass, taking off her hat and smoothing down her hair Margaret gazed at a saffron coloured leaf that had just blown from the oak tree above her. Watching it fascinated as it danced lonely in the breeze; twisting and turning waltzing all alone, searching for another to share the euphoria before it laid down to rest. Several times it almost reached the grass before appearing to fight and whipping itself from the ground in a frenzy refusing to join the others on the ground. The sound of a bicycle bell made Margaret look up as two men in straw boaters whizzed past narrowly missing a lady with a pram who tutted at them and shook her head before continuing along the path next to the water. Twirling like a spinning top Margaret caught the leaf in her hands and slipped it between the leaves of her notebook to press it. The leaf inspired her, it wasn't just lying down waiting to give itself to the elements and become mulch it wanted to continue with its life. Regarding this as a sign Margaret made a wish.

REVENGE

The *osteria* was emptying out, Corrado was relieved to see that Nicolai and his cronies had gone. He had kept his promise that he would frequent the Osteria and they often refused to pay for their drinks. Looking over the shoulder of his two old friends' playing cards he shook his head.

'You're never going to win with that hand Alberto, you might as well go home now!' Laughing, he poured them another drink.

'You're right,' sighed Alberto and pushed the matchsticks in the middle of the table to Mario. 'You win!'

'*Salute!*' Draining their glasses, they got up to leave. Whistling softly to himself Corrado wiped the tables and blew out the candles, turning around in surprise as the door opened with a bang like a thunderclap. Normally such a sharp dresser, Giuseppe looked odd as he stood in the doorway. Corrado had never seen him wearing a suit and looking so dishevelled with his tie undone. His eyes were black and shiny with tears and his face looked as haggard as an old man's. Taking him by the arm Corrado led him to a chair.

'What's the matter?' Corrado put his arm around Giuseppe's shaking shoulder as his tears escaped. Pouring drinks for them both he waited for his friend to calm down. Giuseppe sniffed, wiped his eyes with the back of his hand and took a long drink before turning to his friend and releasing a torrent.

'I found some things out tonight. Things that change everything. You know my sister is married to Nicolai, I've never… well, we've never liked him, have we? But she fell in love and you know I tried to be happy for her. I've heard the rumours about him demanding money from everyone, he's got big connections with some nasty people who back him because he pays them for protection.'

Passing a cigarette to Giuseppe, Corrado lit his own from the candle on the table.

'He's started it with me recently, he keeps coming here and-'

'Exactly!' Giuseppe banged his fist on the table, stood up and began pacing between the tables, smoking fast.   'I went round to their house. She wouldn't see me at first, said she was ill but I went in her room and her face was a mess, bruised down one side. It all came out. He's brought shame on our family, by sleeping with the whore in Bagnoregio, you know, Pamela.

Corrado patted the chair and poured them another drink each.

'Right. We need to think of a way to talk to him.'

'There is no way.' Spat Giuseppe. 'He won't talk about it, he doesn't care; he holds all the cards.' His brown eyes darkened and he leaned into Corrado 'I hate him so much.' Leaning back in his chair he ran his fingers through his hair, still staring at Corrado who let out a long sigh and shook his head before placing it in his hands and rubbing his eyes.

'Poor Roberta.'

'I've got it all worked out, I'm going to confront him, but I need your help.'

'How? What do you mean?'

'He comes in here doesn't he?'

'Yes, sometimes, so?'

'I'll get him on his own when his flunkies aren't around.'

'What?' You can't do that don't be so stupid. There must be some other way.'

Standing up he glared at Corrado.

'I'll do it without your help then.' Slamming the door on his way out he sent tinkling reverberations through the glasses at the bar. Giuseppe couldn't get Nicolai out of his mind. Lying in bed, he kept playing scenarios over and over in his head.

Thinking about what he'd done was making him ill –

gnawing at him relentlessly like a hunger that could never be satisfied. He 'd seen him just the other day with his arm around Pamela, the woman he was seeing on the side. He hadn't even had the decency to look embarrassed; instead he'd just smiled ingratiatingly. Corrado described his smile perfectly – like a snarling dog. He'd heard the rumours of course but had ignored them thinking that was all they were until he'd seen it for himself.

Thinking back he remembered how happy Roberta used to be, always bubbly, always laughing. She was the kindest person he knew; always ready to help others and make him laugh when he was sad. As his older sister he looked up to her and when their mama left they became closer than ever. She'd seemed happy with Nicolai at first but gradually her sparkle was melting away. Her bright eyes looked dull and haunted. Until she found out she was having the baby and seemed the happiest he'd ever seen her; blossoming after the sickness as it had always been her dream to have a home of her own and have children. Although she had to put up with sharing it with her mother-in-law who constantly criticized her she didn't complain. Clenching his fists, Giuseppe thought about pummeling them into Nicolai's face the way he had to a boy at school two years older than him who had been mercilessly teasing Roberta. It had taken two people to pull him off and he had scared himself as he totally lost control and broke his nose. This time his anger was different. A slow burning blaze heating up inside him…

Her face with its large angry bruise swam into his mind; he remembered their conversation. He had grabbed her hand trying to make her leave but she shook it off.

'This is my home. I'm having his baby. I belong here.'

'Not if he's hitting you. He can't do this – I can't stand it. He's just such a-'

Shaking. He'd stood in front of her clenching his fists.

'I'll teach him. Who does he think he is? *Merda!*'

Roberta put a hand on his arm.

'Please calm down. I know what your temper's like and-'

He shrugged it off. 'Is this the first time he's done this?'

She had never been able to lie to him; her eyes said it all. He couldn't believe she started to defend him.

'It's only when he's had too much to drink.

'Coward!'

'Shush. His mama's in there. Please go. He'll be angry if he finds you here and he's coming back soon.'

'What? So you're not even allowed to see your family anymore?'

'Giuseppe,' she looked imploringly at him. 'Please just leave. I know you always want to protect me but I chose to marry him. I'm hoping he'll change once the baby comes.' She put a protective hand on her belly.

'And what if he doesn't? If he can hit you while you're pregnant he could hurt the baby, have you thought about that?'

She stiffened and went silent making him turn as Nicolai loomed in the doorway.

'Just go,' she hissed.

Exasperated Giuseppe walked stiffly past his brother-in-law who glared at him. All he wanted to do was hurt him in the way he's hurt his sister. As he left, he heard Nicolai ask why he was there. He forced himself to keep walking away. Out on the road he stumbled as his tears blinded him. At home he went into the barn and punched the wall repeatedly imagining it was Nicolai until his knuckles poured with blood. Then he got blind drunk on grappa.

Wrenching open the *osteria* door, a few nights later, Giuseppe startled Corrado for the second time that week, as he was washing glasses.

'Do you know what that stronzo's done now? Slurring, he leaned against the doorframe, taking off his hat and shaking the drips from it, 'Roberta confronted him.

You know about Pamela and do you know what he did?' He slammed his fist onto the counter. 'He hurt her, because he's not trying to hide it you know.' Giuseppe stopped in front of his friend and held his hands up. 'Can you believe that? And she's having his baby. I can't get it out of my mind. I've been drinking all day and I just-' He tailed off before turning and screaming at Corrado

'Where is he?'

'What?' Corrado shook his head.

'I know he was here. I'm going after him.'

Before Corrado could stop him, he was gone. Quickly putting down the glass he was washing and closing the door, he followed his friend.   The only sound that punctured the silence was the clicking of the man's heels as Giuseppe ran, following him down the deserted alleyway, silently picking his way through the rubbish that covered the cobbles. As the clouds obscured the moon, he was oblivious to the relentless rain and the stench of rotting food.

Swiftly he ran up behind Nicolai and grabbed him by the coat. Surprised, he turned as Giuseppe began yelling at him. They grappled for a moment and Nicolai pushed him away.

'What are you going to do little boy?' He sneered. 'You'll only make it worse for your precious sister.'

Seething. Giuseppe clenched his fist and swung at him. Nicolai saw it coming, blocked it and punched Giuseppe raining blows down on him. Giuseppe saw red. Pulling a knife from his coat he plunged the long blade into Nicolai's chest. Blood gushed out covering his expensive black suit, the man's eyes bulged with terror and disbelief, and he let out a cry before sinking to the ground, gasping. Giuseppe stood there panting as Corrado ran up behind him and roughly grabbed him by the arm. The man took a last shuddering breath before falling silent.

'What have you done?' Corrado pushed Giuseppe in front of him. 'Quick, move.' He spoke commandingly as they fled back to the osteria. Gasping for breath, Corrado opened the door and they hurried inside locking it behind them. Grabbing a towel, he wrapped the knife in it and Giuseppe flung himself onto a chair. Shaking, Corrado reached for a bottle and glasses and poured stiff measures into both. Giuseppe took a great slug and slammed his glass down.

He slammed his fist on the table shaking the glasses, his black eyes shone with fury. 'I had to make him pay for what he's done to my sister and our family.' Removing his hat, he wiped his wet face with his hand. Corrado let out a deep sigh, before sitting down and taking a gulp of grappa.

'Merda! What have you done? He's dead.'

'I didn't plan to kill him. I took the knife to threaten him and he laughed at me and threatened Roberta again. I just lost my head. But he deserved it. He's a fucking coward. He can't hurt her anymore now.'

'Yeah but this won't be the end, will it? His family won't leave it like that, his brothers will come back and use his fascist friends to bribe the police. Nicolai was probably already doing that. You know how it works round here. Everyone's going to know you hate him for what he's done to your family. And I was there and saw you do it. We have to get rid of that.' He pointed at the knife. They sat in silence for a moment as their breathing began to return to normal. Corrado tried to think calmly and come up with a plan.

'I'll take the knife and bury it somewhere in one of our fields. We need to go now before he's found. Go and wait by the bikes.'

Once Giuseppe had stolen back out into the rain, Corrado remembered them playing football and sitting together in class. He also thought about how many times he'd bailed him out when he'd been in trouble for fighting or not doing his homework but this... Corrado was about to lock the door, but as he looked around he came to the realisation that they would have to move fast and get away.

That this could be the last time he was in the *Osteria*. Swiftly collecting his belongings together, he wrapped his cooking knives in his apron remembering Nicolai's slumped bloody body and shuddered. Grimacing, he looked around the room.

It had happened so near to his *Osteria* that he as Giuseppe's best friend would also be under fire; he had a bad feeling that this was not the end, but just the beginning. Revenge was cyclical, never ending, surely when his body was discovered, Nicolai's family would be coming...

Slipping the knife beneath his coat, he looked left and right before running across the piazza, down the hill to where Giuseppe was waiting. As they pedalled off swiftly, Corrado's brain was whirring.

'We'll have to leave now instead of when we planned.'

'What? How? We can't...' Giuseppe hands were shaking as his adrenaline subsided.

'Look, Nicolai's family won't let this lie. They'll put two and two together and my friend that will be it for us.'
They rode in silence down the stony track.

'Go home and get your things together and wait for me, I'll get rid of this.' said Corrado.

Corrado needed to sit under the lemon tree and sort out his thoughts. Whenever something puzzled him he picked lemons. Pulling the knife from his coat, he picked up a large haversack and a fork from the barn and walked up the hill. The chirruping crickets comforted Corrado. They were always there. The rain had stopped. Turning over the wet earth near the wall that once housed his relatives, he dug a deep gully while the knife by his side glinted at him accusingly. A hooting owl frightened him, making him drop it into the hole, cover it and wipe his hands on the grass. After pulling some earth and twigs over it he sat under the tree, thinking about the things he would miss, his family and friends, everything that had been familiar to him since childhood. Focusing on the scent surrounding him and standing up he emptied his mind. Searching the tree for the biggest lemons, and an answer. Expertly feeling each one, a sense of excitement welled inside him. This was their chance to escape, they could go to London now. But, he argued with himself, what about his family? The lemon tree seemed to sigh and as he remembered Nonna telling him her stories he began to cry, letting out all the pain he had ever felt, all those close to him he had lost and the guilt he felt for leaving.

Gabriella's face swam into his thoughts. Once they were settled she could come and visit. Maybe there is a way. Perhaps I could come back when everything dies down. A wave of relief washed over him and he knelt and prayed before heading down to the farm to break the news to Ricardo and Giverny.

By morning they were gone. Giuseppe left a letter for his father and sister. He couldn't face them. Ricardo took them to *Porto di Civitavecchia* where they would be able to board a boat to France and then to England to pursue their dreams. They knew some people who had moved there in the last couple of years and intended to look them up. Ricardo and Corrado cried as they hugged.

'I don't know when we'll meet again but write and keep in touch.'

Giuseppe cried too as the realisation of what he'd done began to sink in. He felt terrible abandoning his family and was worried that they might be implicated by what he had done. Boarding the boat, the salty air filled Corrado's nostrils, the screaming gulls echoed around him and he prayed that one day he would see his family again.

Elena Baglione walked blearily to the door, opening it to let the cat out. Seeing it was raining it curled itself around her legs and miaowed plaintively.

'You don't want to go out in that,' she said rubbing his head and was about to shut the door again when something caught her eye. A red river ran between the cobbles and past her door. Suddenly she let out a scream that echoed around the alleyway and brought her husband, Benito, running. He found her pointing a wavering finger at Nicolai lying slumped in a pool of blood with his hat next to him. Elena fell down in a faint and had to have lavender smelling salts wafted under her nose. By the time she came round, a crowd had gathered.

The news spread far and wide like the ripples on the lake when small boys had competitions to see how far they could throw their pebbles in. Benito and Elena told their story over and over again as more people heard and hurried to the scene including Enrico, the local policeman. Gossip and speculation were rife.

Roberta and her mother-in-law found out at the same time. Enrico knocked on the door, removing his cap as Roberta let him in to the kitchen where they were having breakfast.

'Buongiornio. Please sit down. I have some bad news. I'm afraid Nicolai was found dead this morning.'

Claudia stared at him in disbelief before her hard eyes narrowed and her whole being crumpled; she held her head in her hands rocking back and forth whimpering Nicolai's name over and over.

Roberta sat impassive unable to process what she had just heard. The baby wriggling inside her brought her to her senses and she looked imploringly at Enrico, who was a family friend.

'How? What happened? I don't understand what's-'

The door burst open behind them and Nicolai's brothers stood scowling in the doorway. The eldest, Nunzio, rushed over to his mother and held her. The other, Vito, paced around the room and glared at Enrico.

'He was murdered. And you better find out by who.'

'What?' Roberta stood up.

'We don't know what happened yet. Of course we will be looking in to it. My colleagues are on their way from Orvieto.' Roberta began to cry low sobs that shook her body. Enrico put a hand on her shoulder.

'I'm sorry for your loss. For all your loss.' He turned to the others, 'we will find out who-'
A knock on the door interrupted him. Luigi walked in, a grave look on his face. Roberta rushed over to him and fell in his arms.

Come on get some things together, I'm taking you home.'

Back at home, Roberta sat in her old bedroom, the tears streaming down her face as she remembered what her father had told her.

At the farm, Gabriella found Giverny crying in the dairy.

'Mama, what's the matter?'

'Something terrible has happened. Nicolai is dead. And Corrado and Giuseppe have had to go away.'

'Where? I don't understand. Why?'

'We have to keep it a secret, but I think they're going to England. If anyone asks you have to say you don't know where they are and that you knew they were going.'

'Did they have something to do with him dying? I can't

believe Corrado would-'

'No. It's not Corrado. But if he stayed he would get the blame.'

Giverny hugged her daughter tightly. 'We've got to keep going and say we know nothing about it. It's really important. Do you understand?'

Gabriella nodded. 'So it was Giuseppe then?'

'Yes. He lost his temper and they had a fight. He was trying to protect Roberta. Don't say anything to your brothers or anyone. We have to carry on as normal.' Sighing she turned back to separating the curds for the cheese she was making. Gabriella went to her room trying to hold back the tears. Life without Corrado was no life at all to her.

Walking up the track to Luigi's farm, Ricardo slowed down. Dreading the moment to come as he thought about all the family had been through already, he took a deep breath and forced himself to forge forwards. Taking the letter from Giuseppe out of his pocket he knocked on the door. Luigi answered and invited him in. Roberta sat in the corner her face drawn and tear stained.

'I'm so sorry,' he said.

'Come and sit down.' Luigi moved some papers and motioned to a chair next to the table. 'We don't really know what's happened. It's all so unexpected and…' he tailed off and shook his head.

'I'm sorry to be the bearer of more bad news, but this might make things clearer.' He handed the envelope to Luigi.

Dear Papa and Roberta

I don't know how to write this. I've done something terrible. I was angry with Nicolai for what he's done to you, Roberta, and what he's done to our family. I went and saw him last night and we had a fight. I didn't mean to stab him. I'm so sorry for what I've done. I've made everything worse. I only took the knife to threaten him and it all happened so fast. I know what I've done is unforgivable, but I hope one day you will find it in your hearts to understand.

I am going away with Corrado to England and I hope that one day we will be reunited.

Giuseppe

Stunned. Luigi's face had turned ashen as he read the letter. He handed it to Roberta and sank down next to Ricardo and wept. Huge racking sobs.

'What has he done?' he wailed wringing his hands. Roberta put down the letter with trembling hands and went to her father putting her arms around him. 'Papa, it's all right. Shhh now.'

'They left first thing this morning. I don't really know what to say except you know where we are if you need us and if I were you I would burn that letter. People are going to put two and two together but if they're not here to stand trial what can be done? We're going to pretend it's a coincidence.'

'But surely no one will believe that?' Roberta shook her head.

'I know but it's all we've got. No one knows except you and us and we will say it was planned. Corrado had been talking about going for ages. I don't know what else we can do because I imagine Nicolai's brothers are going to come asking questions and soon, so will the police, so you need to have your story straight and ours must match up.'

'I can't believe this is happening.' Luigi spoke as a broken man.

'You know where we are if you need anything.' Ricardo squeezed Luigi's hand and hugged Roberta.

PART TWO

Top Flat,
24 High Street,
Hampstead,
London.
July 1927.

Dear Ricardo,

Sorry it has taken me so long to write. What did everyone say about us leaving? How are Luigi and Roberta?
Things are going well here in London. I have set up an osteria and Giuseppe and I have also bought a farm in Sussex, a couple of hours away. There is a large Italian community here in London, everyone is friendly and stick together, although we both miss family very much. I'm having lots of requests for my lemons which is good because I can barter with them for good quality flour to make pasta. The farm isn't huge but substantial enough. We've got a small herd of cows so we have milk and make cream and butter, but I really miss the buffalo. Mozzarella just isn't the same. We also have pigs, ducks, chickens, goats and a dog. Thank you for the lemons. The ones you can buy here are pitiful, small and wizened with no flavour. It's because of the weather. The one thing I dislike about living here is the rain and the cold, even in summer. I long to see the sun again. London is so drab and full of buildings; I miss the sky at home. Only small patches of it are visible among the church spires, chimneys and grey rooves. I've barely seen the moon for the insistent clouds bringing yet more drizzle. Actually, while I'm on the subject, the other thing I hate is English food. You should see what they eat. There's something called gravy, a disgusting brown liquid that they cover everything in, it's vile. Please write back with all your news. How are the little ones and Giverny? Give them all a hug from me and please send more lemons soon.

Corrado

Home
August 1927.

Dear Corrado

It's wonderful to hear from you, we're so proud of you for getting everything up and running so well. The children are fine although I know that Gabby misses you a lot, her face lit up when I said you had sent her love. It's strange you not being in the osteria, we are keeping it going although it's not the same without you and everyone keeps asking after you. Roberta had her baby, a little girl, Eva, she looks just like her. She's gone back home to her Papa. This is a good thing as I know they both miss Giuseppe and the new baby is a good distraction for them. When I gave him Giuseppe's letter and told him you'd left he turned grey, he looks so old now. To make matters worse, Nicolai's family are very suspicious about you two leaving and keep asking questions. As you can imagine, gossip here is rife. I told them moving to London was always your dream, everyone knows that and I said you managed to persuade your best friend to go too. I don't think they believe me but they're buying it for now. Although they've turned their attention to Luigi now, taking money from him and threatening him. Giverny has not been well, she's suffering from terrible headaches, so Isabella has moved in and started working for us full-time to give her a bit of time off, you know how hard she works. Hope there are enough lemons for now. I'm having a few problems sending them over as Salvo Baglio's nephew has stopped working at the docks. He's sorted it out this time as a favour but I'm not sure about next time. I hope we can all come and visit you one day.

Ricardo

LONDON

Plunging her car into Whitestone Pond, near Hampstead Heath, gave Margaret a terrible shock. A liver and white cocker spaniel ran in front of the wheels, forcing her to send the car speeding down the slope where it came to rest with a huge splash in the water. It was a crisp morning, the watery sun shone on to the fiery trees clinging to their last leaves under a pale blue sky. The street was virtually empty as Corrado mulled over the changes he wanted to make to his menu with the shipment of lemons coming from his brother back in Italy. Crunching through a leafy carpet he smiled and raised his hat absent-mindedly to a lady pushing a crying baby in a large black pram. Thoughts of lemons were chased from his mind as startled ducks, geese and gulls became a mewling flock and flew as one from the pond. A car had just driven in, a wave washing over its black bonnet and shining it like a military boot.

Pulling up his trousers, Corrado waded in until he stood shivering next to the driver's window. Inside, Margaret, head in her hands, turned as he motioned for her to open the window.

'Are you all right?' Corrado raised his hat and stared into wide amber eyes, full of panic.

'I…I think so. I feel like a frightful idiot, though, and I …' said Margaret, her gloved hands shaking as they gripped the steering wheel. 'Where's the dog? Did I hit …'

'He ran off over there.' Corrado smiled and nodded to the other side of the pond. 'He's all right. Not sure I can say the same for your car. Do you want to move over and I'll try and get it out for you?'

Nodding, Margaret obeyed like a child, shifted into the passenger seat as Corrado opened the door and slipped behind the wheel of the beautiful car, a brand-new Austin Seven. He could smell her tantalising scent mixed with the strong leather from the red seats as he started the car. The engine spluttered a little before roaring into life, enabling Corrado to reverse back on to the road. He stopped. Margaret's relief was palpable. She sighed loudly and stared at her rescuer's profile with approval as he started the car. He had a Roman nose and coffee-coloured eyes that matched his long coat and hat. He turned to Margaret, smiled and held out his hand.

'Corrado Hugen-Tobler. Very pleased to be of assistance.'

Margaret held out her hand shakily, and he took it, feeling the softness of her glove and wishing he could actually feel her skin beneath.

'Margaret Mallows. I'm so grateful. I'd never have got the car out without you.'

'In my country you would be Margarita, like the flower. You have a pretty name.'

Margaret smiled and Corrado noted her lips were rouged, that she had beautiful white teeth and that she spoke in clipped tones like the women who ate in his cafe. He guessed she was in her twenties, like him.

'You look cold. I think you need a coffee.' Corrado raised a black eyebrow.

'Um, yes, but where—?' Margaret pulled her fur coat around her, rubbed her arms and sighed.

'My café's just around the corner. Shall I drive?' Corrado interrupted her.

'If you don't mind.' She leant back as Corrado drove past the pond and turned into Hampstead High Street, stopping in front of a four-story red brick building. Between the large glass window and the green and white striped awning, there was a sign that read:

OSTERIA

'Here we are.' Corrado went around to the passenger side and held the door open for Margaret. As she got out, she saw his wet boots. Her hand flew to her mouth and she groaned.

'Oh no, I feel absolutely awful, I didn't mean to ruin your boots, I am frightfully sorry and…'

'They'll dry out in no time. Come and have a hot drink.' He took her arm and led her inside.

A younger Italian man with a striped blue and white apron stood behind the counter and laughed when he saw the puddles forming around Corrado's feet.

'Good day for a paddle!' he said.

Corrado laughed. 'Gianni, I need to change my boots, *per favore* can you make us coffee?'

It was the smell that hit Margaret initially: almonds, bread, onions, combined with the aroma of coffee beans roasting. It made her stomach murmur as she sat down and took in her surroundings. There were no other customers, but the tables were laid up ready with cutlery, glasses and red and white gingham cloths. Behind the long wooden counter, cups and plates were stacked beside tea and coffee pots, all red and white to match the tables. Bottles of alcohol sat on a higher shelf next to different sized glasses.

The walls were the colour of buttermilk; one had a poster advertising a jazz night, another a picture of a lemon tree, laden with fruit and clusters of white blossom. There was also a large map of Italy. On the wall opposite the window, the menu was written on a big blackboard. Below it was an unlit fire, paper and sticks laid ready. Two winged armchairs covered in burgundy velvet sat invitingly either side.

Corrado returned and expertly lit the fire, getting it roaring. Margaret watched him, admiring his slim shoulders and thick blue-black hair that broke in a wave over his forehead, like a raven's wing. Once Corrado was sitting opposite her in bare feet, with two cups of coffee between them, Margaret began to relax. She kept her coat and gloves on, although she removed her hat.

'I've never been here before. How long have you had this place?' Margaret picked up her cup and put it to her lips enjoying its warmth in her hands through her brown leather gloves.

'Ah, not that long. I came over from Italy. I had a place there before, but I had to leave.' A haunted look crossed Corrado's face as he remembered the bloody knife and the man slumped on the cobbles. He shook his head. 'I love London. All the bustle and the people and the music.'

'I gather you like jazz.'

'*Si, si.* Yes, in the evenings I play songs.'

'In here?'

He pointed at a gramophone.

'Oh!" She said, 'I've got one like that at home. I love jazz too.'

'Where do you live?' Corrado said.

'In Highgate…' something stopped Margaret from telling him about her husband, Leslie. 'Shepherd's Hill. What about you?'

'I live above the shop on the top floor.' He gestured upwards.

Placing her empty cup on the table Margaret put on her hat and straightened it ready to leave.

'I hope you'll come back here again, now you've found it?' Corrado smiled, and Margaret felt her stomach give a little lurch. She thought again of Leslie, and was about to say no, but changed her mind at the last second.

'That would be lovely. And thank you again for rescuing me.'

Lying in bed that night, Margaret crept into Corrado's mind like the intoxicating aroma of the lemon trees at home. He remembered her scent and her eyes and the way she looked so animated when she talked about her love of music.

His heart lifted when he thought back to her agreeing to come back to the osteria before his thoughts turned to home as he remembered how life used to be. He sighed as he thought about his family. Especially little Gabriella, recalling the day he'd taken her lemon picking.

ROBERTA AND MIMI

ITALY

Enjoying the September sun's warmth on the back of her neck, as she pushed the pram up the drive, Roberta thought about what to cook for dinner with the shopping she'd just bought. Either side of her tall cypress trees, like paintbrushes, formed an avenue and she dipped in and out of the shade their long shadows provided. Bother, she thought, I forgot the flour. The baby began to whimper because she was hungry.

'It's all right Eva, we're nearly there.'

Opening the gate she expected to see Mimi, her dog, charging down to greet them as she always did when she was left behind. Turning the corner, she stopped dead and screamed. Luigi, her father, drove up the drive behind her stopping as he saw his daughter sobbing with her hand over her mouth. As he got out of the car and ran over the baby started crying too.

'What's the matter?' he said.

Speechless, she pointed at the path where Mimi lay lifeless in a pool of blood where her throat had been slit.

'Holy Mother. Who's done this?' Luigi picked up the dog and walked to the barn.

Eva began to wail plaintively bringing Roberta back to her senses. Gripping the handle of the pram she pushed the baby past her father before hurrying into the house and feeding her while the tears gushed down her cheeks and on to Eva's little white dress. She was hugging her daughter tightly when Luigi came in.

'I'm sorry, bambina,' he said. 'I know who did this.'

'What?'

Luigi began to pace up and down.

'Your brother-in-law, Nunzio. He keeps coming round and shouting about Nicolai. I've been giving him money but now he's done this, I can't believe it.'

'Why didn't you tell me?'

He sat down next to her and held her hand.

'I didn't want to worry you. You've been so busy with the baby, and so unhappy. I thought he'd go away but he's obviously greedy like his brother.'

'I'm scared. What's he going to do next? What about Eva, we can't stay here what if he comes back with his brothers?'

'Get some things together we're going to Ricardo's, hurry up.'

He went and sorted out the animals, carried the bags to the car and drove to the farm across the valley. Giverny was gardening as the car drove up.

She stood up and shielded her eyes from the sun, waving as she spotted Luigi. The car stopped and Roberta flung herself into her friend's arms crying hysterically.

'What on earth's the matter?' said Giverny.

Ricardo came out of the house and helped Luigi with his bags.

'I'm sorry, but I didn't know where else to go.'

'Come in.' said Ricardo.

Giverny made everyone coffee and Luigi explained about what had been going on.

'It started just after Giuseppe and Corrado left. Nunzio turned up one day and started asking where they'd gone and accusing them of killing Nicolai.'

'He came round here too, not long after.' said Ricardo.

'What did he say to you?'

'The same as you I suppose. I told him that it was a coincidence that they both went at the same time. And that Corrado had always wanted to travel.'

'He came back again though didn't he?' said Giverny.

'Yes. But we've just said the same thing.' said Ricardo.

'I tried to tell him I don't know where he is. He knows he killed him. It's all such a mess.' said Luigi.

'And it's all my fault.' Roberta began to cry again.

Giverny put her arms around her.

'Sh, now, come on. We'll think of something.'

'You can stay here as long as you like.' said Ricardo.

'Thank you. What about the farm and all the animals?'

'We can sort them out for the moment until we find a solution.'

'I don't know that there is one. I know Giuseppe did this because of his sister's honour. But he's made everything much worse.' A tear trickled down Luigi's large nose which he quickly wiped away.

Later in bed that night, Giverny cuddled up to Ricardo.

'What are we going to do? I don't mind them being around but it's a worry. What if they come back here looking for them?' she said.

'I know. I can't believe they did that to her dog. *Bastardos.* They have no morals. She's had that dog for ten years and she was Nero's mother. It shows that they mean business they're obviously not going to back down.'

'This is a warning. They're going to have to leave, but where could they go?' she said.

'I don't know. I'm going to write to Corrado tomorrow. He already knows they've been sniffing around. Maybe they can go to England too.' Ricardo kissed his wife on the nose. 'Try not to worry too much darling and get some sleep.'

'Love you.'

'Love you too.'

THE BATH OF THE KING
766AD

'"He's coming, the King is coming," rippled sharply through the crowd like waves lapping on shingle. Magnificent. The wooden carriage, with green and gold curtains flanked by guards on horseback, wound its way up to Civita de Bagnorego. Pulled by two grey horses with white plumes, and shining bridles glinting in the sunlight, the driver stared straight ahead as he urged the horses along the stony road. As the procession got closer the people thronged together to get a closer look expecting the king to wave at his subjects; however, they were disappointed as the carriage swept past with the curtains firmly closed and proceeded up the hill making disgruntled peasants grumble amongst themselves.

"What's the point of a royal visit if you don't get to see him?"

"We've waited all afternoon too."

Wandering back to the jobs they had been neglecting, they muttered about taxes and manners.

The carriage turned to the right before entering the town and the guards got to work building the camp on the hillside.

Lavish, the tent took shape with brightly coloured silks in hues of mustard and juniper with amethyst velvet drapes and Turkish rugs covering the floor. Once they were settled, Desiderius, King of the Lombards, sat in his tent refusing to come out, despite the sunshine bathing the tents in honeyed light. Only his trusted manservant, Ernesto, was allowed into his inner sanctum. A tall man with stooped shoulders who tended to stroke his long grey beard and twiddle his hair, which fell in wisps around his ears like rain clouds, as he thought of solutions to the king's problems. He had looked after the king for his whole life since he was a small boy, when he had bathed his wounds after he fell from his horse and dried his tears. Then as he got older, allayed his master's fears about the kingdom. Now, beside himself as he saw his king's suffering and could do nothing to help. It was him who had enquired and discovered that the springs here had healing properties, and he was only too glad to be of use.

"Bring me the wise woman from Civita."

"Yes, my Lord." Pacing up and down as he waited, constantly staring at his reflection in the mirror he carried in his hand, the king wore a long dark beard as was the fashion

at the time and had kind brown eyes above a strong nose and determined mouth. His subjects were delighted to have such an attractive king and half the princesses in the land swooned over him until…

The day he had woken up with an itchy toe. He had never known anything so aggravating. During that day it spread to his foot which became covered in an angry scarlet rash which minute by minute began spreading to his whole body. It itched and itched, and nothing seemed to work to get rid of it. After trying copious balms, ointments and tinctures to no avail, he was fearful that he had been cursed by one of his enemies. Coming to Civita was a last resort, as now it had finally spread to his face. Here he had been told that there was a special place in the hills where a tributary spring that came from deep underground within the volcanic rock fed the stone baths there.

Hearing a noise outside he entered his bed chamber standing behind the curtains, peeping out so only his eyes could be seen, as Ernesto returned with a very old woman. She had no teeth and crevice-like wrinkles covering her face and hands. She wore the uniform of the peasant women - black from head to foot - with a headscarf covering her hair.

"Here is Signora Patrizia, my Lord." He bowed his head and left the tent.

"I have summoned you as your reputation for wisdom is renowned in these parts and I need your help."

Describing his affliction, the woman nodded and made strange clicking noises with her tongue. Finally, he told her his fears about being cursed.

"I will do my utmost to help you, King Desiderius. I need to go and prepare some medicine. Please wait for my return."

Wearily lying down the king scratched at his body until the skin began bleeding and shedding in agonizing strips. Feeling like a peeled vegetable, he prayed for relief and eventually fell into a restless sleep full of nightmares which terrified him. He dreamt he was being dragged into the jaws of hell by his ankles, he could feel the intense heat burning his body bit by bit as he was hauled in by two demons who snarled at him with slathering jowls. Waking up with a start he heard the old woman gently calling him. His bedclothes were wringing wet and the itching was overwhelming.

"I have come with a tincture, Lord."

"Thank you. What does it contain?"

"Herbs from these hills and spring water."

It smelt pungent-of rosemary and wild garlic. The king gulped it down, relieved that it tasted fairly pleasant compared to some of the treatments he had endured of late.

"How long will I have to wait?"

"Until tomorrow when I will return."

Tortured with itching and driven half mad he didn't sleep a wink. His attendants looked at each other as they heard his moans of despair wishing they could help him. He was a good man and a wise and fair king, they wanted him to recover as he had been suffering for more than two weeks by this time.

On the following day the wise woman came to find there was no improvement. Seeing the king's desperation, she scurried away racking her brains. Later she returned breathless with two remedies this time.

"I am sorry the tincture had no effect. Try this instead." She handed him a draught. And a package. "You must drink this. It is the first milk from a new mother. Her baby was born an hour ago. And you must rub these ashes all over your body, they are from the goat, sacrificed for the celebration of St Dominica a few days ago. This remedy has been known to cure sores on the skin in the past. After two hours, bathe in the stone bath. I have asked the attendants to prepare it for you." Rubbing the ashes into his skin was agony as touching anywhere on his raw body inflamed the rash and the incessant itching and bleeding continued relentlessly. Covering his face and body with embarrassment he walked to the baths. Commanding the attendants to leave him he sank into the cool water.

Feeling some relief for a few moments he looked around at the sandstone walls hewn out of the rock which circled the large round bath. Starting to feel some confidence in the old woman's medicine he began to whistle cheerfully much to the relief of those listening outside. However, the itching returned with a vengeance once he got out. Returning to his tent with a heavy heart he felt he was beginning to lose his mind.

Signora Patrizia felt that more was needed and worried that what she had prescribed would not work, so she hurried from her house in Civita to across the valley to see Padre Cecilio. A wizened bald man wearing a brown robe led her through to the beautiful gardens that surrounded the abbey where he lived - a crumbling sandstone building surrounded by fragrant flowerbeds filled with margaritas, roses and honeysuckle. Seated on some steps, next to lobelia falling from terracotta pots like small snowdrifts, she enjoyed the sound of birdsong and the scent of stocks and sweet peas filling the air and swimming towards them on the light breeze that carried up from the valley. Once he had heard her story and he understood her problem, he asked her to wait for a few moments and went back inside. He came out with three large thick-skinned lemons in his hands and gave them to her.

"This is to be a secret between us, you understand? I do not want the king to know where you got them from. Mix the lemon juice with a little honey and give it to him to drink. Also put some juice and honey into a bottle and tell him to spread this on his wounds. By tomorrow morning, I believe his skin will be healed. I will also pray for him."

Hastening back to the king's tent the old woman knew he had not been cured. The sound of moaning reached her ears as she crossed the tussocks of grass leading to the camp. Ernesto let her in where she found the king beside himself, almost delirious with the pain. Leaving instructions, she went home to wait. The king had to have help now to drink the liquid and to administer the balm. Although begging for death and refusing any treatment, Ernesto gently poured the honey and lemon on to his wounds and coaxed him to drink. Immediately he fell unconscious which terrified Ernesto as he thought he had killed him. Running away he disappeared to hide in the hills. King Desiderius slept all night as worried soldiers listened at his doorway to his laboured breathing. As the first light began to play across the silks surrounding his bedchamber shining them like polished jewels he awoke and rubbed his eyes looking around him unaware of his surroundings.

He had been dreaming he was at a banquet surrounded by sumptuous food, and there was lots of dancing and laughter. Putting a hand to his face he discovered it felt smooth and unblemished. Then he looked at his legs and feet to find clear skin. Shaking his head, he thought he must still be dreaming as there was no itching nor any sign of his affliction. Quickly he sat up and picked up the mirror to see that he was cured. The soldiers milling worriedly around outside looked at each other in surprise as they heard a loud laugh emerge from the tent. Delighted when the king appeared in his doorway and began to dance amongst them.

"I have been saved! Where is Ernesto and the wise woman?"

Ernesto was found cowering, crouched behind some bushes nearby, and brought before the king.

"I hear it was you that persuaded me to drink this medicine and you applied the balm with your own hands even though I begged you not to?"

The manservant gulped and nodded.

"I'm sorry I just wanted you to get well and..."

"I know. And I want to thank you for saving my life. I will reward you with riches - gold and jewels - and remove you from my service.

You will be free to live at the palace but no longer need serve me. You shall be known as the man who saved the King. And henceforth, Civita de Bagnorego shall be called Balneum Regis, the Bath of the King."

The old woman was given a trunk full of gold to thank her. Keeping her promise, when the king asked her what was in the draught she had given him she said it was just another of her old remedies and that it was the spring water that had made all the difference.

That evening the king held a party for all the residents, and in his speech apologised for hiding himself away, the villagers gladly gave their meat, fish and bread so that the royal cooks could produce the finest food and drink they had ever tasted. Charming everyone the king sat in splendour wearing a golden crown, a hand's length high. Encrusted with rubies it sat atop his long brown mane which rested on the shoulders of his velvet scarlet cloak entwined with silken threads of gold and clasped at his breast with a great sapphire. His musicians played, and everyone danced and celebrated because he was cured, and spoke of the wondrous spring that had been part of the healing process.'

ITALY

Home,
September 1927.

Dear Corrado

I have some bad news. Nicolai's brothers are constantly threatening Luigi and Roberta as they are convinced that Giuseppe did it. They keep going to their house and last time they killed Mimi, their dog. Roberta's heartbroken and terrified about what they might do next. She and Luigi are in hiding here at our place but we don't know how long we can keep them safe. They are going to have to move away and sell the farm, fortunately they have a buyer. I suggested they come to you, either that or they will go north to Bergamo where no one knows them. Can you please talk to Giuseppe and write back?

Ricardo

Waiting for a reply they settled into a routine at the farm; Eva was never short of attention with Gabriella around. She loved pushing her round the farm in her pram, singing songs to her while showing her the different animals, which gave Roberta and Giverny a chance to talk. Roberta hung the washing on the line in the sunshine, while Giverny pruned the rosebushes in the bed next to her, filling the air with a delicate scent as she brushed against the petals.

'She's such a good baby, very contented.' said Giverny.

'I know. I'm lucky.' Roberta sighed, 'but what sort of a life has she got? No father, no home.' Roberta bit her lip and blinked away the tears that were always threatening to fall. Giverny put the shears down, took the last nappy, hung it up and steered Roberta to the table near the rose garden.

'My mama always used to say there's no more satisfying sight than a line full of nappies flapping in the wind and being blanched by the sun. Have you even had a chance to talk to anyone about everything that's happened?'

'Not really, it all happened so quickly. Nicolai came home drunk. We had a huge row because I accused him of sleeping with the whore in Bagnoregio, you know, Pamela Vanore? To shut me up he hit me! Even though I was pregnant can you believe it?'

Giverny took her hand.

'That's terrible.'

'Well what's worse is that evil bitch of a mother of his was there and turned a blind eye. So Giuseppe came round and I wouldn't let him in. I didn't want him to see my face, you know what he's like. I knew he'd go and confront Nicolai. He kept on and on and wouldn't leave so in the end I opened the door.

Of course, he went mad as I'd predicted although I never thought he'd do what he did.' A fat tear rolled down her nose. 'I feel so confused. I'm angry with Giuseppe for killing Eva's papa. I know he did it because he loves me, but he's ruined everything.' She held her hands up in despair. 'And I know it's wrong, but a part of me still loves Nicolai. He used to love me too until he met his fascist friends. I thought having the baby would calm him down and he would fall in love with her and want to be with us all the time. But now...' she tailed off.

They sat in silence for a moment interrupted by the faint tones of Gabriella singing in the distance.

'It feels like it's just been one thing after another for Papa. First Mama leaving, then Giuseppe going and now this. He's not himself. I know he's trying to stay strong for me and the baby; but he doesn't want to leave the farm, he's lived there all his life. Going away isn't something he's ever thought about. I've been trying to persuade him that we should move to England too. He's accepted it as we have no choice, but he can barely speak any English. I've been teaching him but it's going to be very difficult although I know what's keeping him going is the thought of seeing Giuseppe and our family being back together again.'

'And what about you?' Giverny squeezed Roberta's arm.

'I'm all over the place. I want a new start for Eva because I'm scared of Nicolai's brothers, I can't relax. I keep looking over my shoulder all the time. I can't bear what they did to Mimi. I want to cry when I think of her lying there. I hate them so much. I'm petrified about the future. None of this was what I thought when I found out I was pregnant.'

Gabriella pushed the pram around the corner and put her finger to her lips.

'Sh. She's asleep.'

'Well done Gabby you've got the magic touch.' Roberta smiled as she peeped in at Eva.

'Right', said Giverny 'I need to sort the washing out upstairs.'

Humming to herself as she folded the clothes, fresh smelling from the line making each person a neat pile on the bed, Giverny's mind wandered. I hope those boys are behaving. She remembered how excited they'd been that morning to go with their father and Luigi to sell off the rest of his stock. Poor Luigi and Roberta having to leave, but at least they've had an offer on the farm, so their money will be sorted out before they go, Luigi was really worried about that. They were thinking of going to Bergamo, where Luigi had a cousin. Glancing out of the window at the valley stretching below she was certain it was a view she would never tire of; the silver, green, creamy hills undulating and falling in gentle folds. Civita rose up in the distance like a fairytale kingdom its gold bricked walls radiant in the sun's reflection. She could just make out a horse and cart snaking up the track to the square where Corrado's osteria was. She sighed. They all missed him but were pleased he seemed to be enjoying England. A large black car at the end of their drive caught her eye. She didn't recognize it and immediately felt uneasy. Standing at the top of the stairs she shouted down.

'Gabriella quickly hide the pram in the barn and get inside with the baby now!'

Giverny ran down and got everyone inside, including the dog before quickly locking the doors and ushering them upstairs.

'Keep away from the windows and don't make any noise. I think Nicolai's brothers are back.'

Giverny stood behind the curtain as the car swept through the gate and parked in their yard. Two men, one tall and one slightly shorter wearing identical hats and sunglasses, got out of the car and banged on the front door. Nero began barking frantically from his bed in the kitchen. The two men waited a moment before heading round to the back door.

'Do you think they're hiding them? That's what they're saying in Bagnoregio.' The shorter man said as he peered in at the kitchen window.

'You think they'd have got the message from last time with the dog.'

They both laughed making Roberta stiffen and clench her fists. Baby Eva let out a cry, her lip quivering as she began to stir making the tall man stop and listen. Roberta quickly put Eva to her breast and fed her. They all held their breath to see what they would do next. They banged on the back door loudly.

'We know you're in there.'

'And we know you're hiding them. They have to pay for my brother's death.'

'What shall we leave as a calling card this time?'

Hanging her head in her hands Giverny dreaded what they were going to do. Gabriella's terrified face looked up at her from the floor where she was hiding. Crouching down next to her daughter she hugged her whispering.

'It's all right. They'll be gone soon.'

The car engine started up breaking the silence in the room. Giverny waited until they were out of sight before breathing normally again and checking they'd definitely gone.

'You can come down now.'

Calling Nero, she opened the front door, went outside and gasped in horror. Every single rose had been decapitated. The surrounding ground decorated with a rainbow of petals and heads. Giverny's mouth set in a grim line a she thought about how upset Ricardo would be when he saw his mother's pride and joy destroyed. Gabriella and Roberta stood silently in shock.

'At least it wasn't an animal this time.' Giverny began to pick up the bruised petals feeling desperate as their perfume clung to the air for the last time. Remembering her mother in law's pride in her rose garden she welled up. Her head was beginning to pound again. It was happening more frequently now.

London

Dear Ricardo

Poor Luigi and Roberta please tell them we have a plan. Giuseppe is beside himself and wants them to come here and live on the farm. He asked me to thank you for helping them. Is there a way you can help them get to us? They will be safe here. The farm here is going quite well and there is room for them. Please write back and let us know as soon as possible We've done some research and think the best way is to drive to France and then get a ferry across it will be quicker than when we did it and easier with the baby. See what you think but please reassure them that they will be very welcome and write back quickly as Giuseppe is going out of his mind with worry. I have enclosed a letter for them from him detailing how to get here
.

Corrado

Dear Corrado

I sent this straight away. Luigi and Roberta have agreed. Please give Giuseppe the enclosed letter from them. They are so scared they're just relieved although Luigi especially is sad to leave the farm where he has lived all his life. I think you're right about driving through France and I have another idea too, one I know that you'll love. What about them bringing some buffalo calves for you to start a herd? I've got four young ones and Carlos and Manuela. You know enough about breeding to look after them. The problem is, I've looked into it and it would be difficult to get authority to do it but I could get false papers from Vincenzo Tripani, he owes me a favour anyway as I let him use the osteria as a venue for his wife's birthday. I'm going to drive the calves in a truck with Luigi and Roberta as far as Calais and then we'll put them on the ship where you can meet them with a truck your end and take them all back to the farm. I could also fill up a couple of trunks with the lemons we have stored. I'm afraid I have more bad news the tree is sick. Its leaves are brown and it's not producing any fruit, so I'm afraid that this is the last load I can send you. We are planning on leaving next week so there won't be time to write again. The ferry gets in to Dover at 5.00 pm on the10th of October.

Ricardo

LONDON

Stirring, Corrado was woken by the birds scraping the slates above his head as they hopped about on the roof, chattering like they were having a party. Looking out at the small square patch of grey he could see through his window he sighed thinking how much he missed the Italian sky, bright as a sapphire and vast by comparison. Yawning he stretched languorously like a cat.   He lived on the top floor of the red brick Victorian building, in the attic, under the eaves. Below in the garden, Mrs. Wilkins, his landlady, was hanging washing out in the yard below. Her grey bun looked like an empty bird's nest. She lived on the first floor; a thick-set woman with a permanently furrowed brow who spent her whole life complaining and snooping around, checking that he never brought anyone back to stay with him. She did this because initially, when he shared the room with Giuseppe, he had sneaked some of his lady friends silently past her room and up the stairs while Corrado was at the farm. She'd almost caught him several times and when she finally did, consequently evicted him. Several times a week it was the same.

Arriving at the top of the stairs, breathless and florid, she patted her hair and knocked on his door under the pretence of asking a question about the tenants who lived in the middle flat who she also disapproved of.

A young couple who went out drinking at the weekends. At closing time, they would roll home having the most spectacular arguments which continued up the stairs and into their flat with no thought for their neighbours. Like a doll, she was very beautiful, with long blonde hair and big blue eyes; it obviously drove her husband insane with jealousy because men would stare at her and he would accuse her of all sorts of things. Although she looked as innocent as an angel, she gave as good as she got and would scream at him like a fish wife. Abruptly, the screaming would stop to be replaced by equally noisy love-making as they made up. They never seemed embarrassed when they occasionally met Corrado on the stairs, smiling and passing the time of day as if nothing had happened. Sparsely furnished, Corrado's room was filled with a mish mash of rejects. A single iron bedstead and a rickety chest of drawers stood on one wall. The wardrobe was a patchwork of shiny and worn wood where it had been scratched and the layers of varnish had peeled away. Enormous, it took up most of the space. Living there was convenient as it was above the osteria and he and Giuseppe had invested a lot of money into the farm. Sighing, Corrado walked past the smiling photos of his family back home and went to the cracked sink and splashed cold water on his face. Margaret came laughing into his mind like an old friend. He saw her head tilted back, her eyes shining. He found she was on his mind constantly. She had begun making daily visits to the osteria which was making him feel very confused. Terrified of getting close to anyone again he was beginning to feel he was losing his mind having never felt like this about anyone before. Previously, all his spare time would be spent devising new recipes; but she had hijacked his thoughts and although he kept trying to stop himself, he surrendered gladly. Thinking of her was as delicious as freshly baked ciabatta. Dressing, he decided that today he would make her a lemon meringue pie. He took the stairs two at a time. Every day he made a new lemon recipe, ostensibly for all his customers, but secretly just for her. The only problem was they were getting increasingly popular and more and more women were coming every day, which made him feel awkward as they all wanted to chat to him, but he only had eyes for Margaret.

It did, however, make Giuseppe very happy as he would come every afternoon and attempt to seduce them all starting with the prettiest and working his way through. He didn't care that some of them were married. Corrado couldn't help but laugh at his astounding self-assurance.

Dressing carefully in a grey woollen pencil skirt and cream silk blouse Margaret fastened the ruby choker that her grandmother had given her. It was very beautiful and glowed against her pale skin. Finishing off the look with navy shoes she tied the ribbons that criss-crossed up her legs and topped her hair with a red beret. Squirting her neck with scent before putting on her coat and gloves she wondered what Corrado would cook for her today. Until meeting him she hadn't known that lemons could taste so good, having only really had them in her gin and tonic. Smiling she remembered how disparagingly Corrado spoke about the lemons English people used. Conjuring up a new lemon surprise every day - he was a magician - all the customers looked forward to trying them out. Since the debacle with her car, she had begun popping into the osteria every morning. It had been two weeks now and she found she had a spring in her step and looked forward to seeing him.

The last few nights while Leslie's snores reverberated round the room she had allowed Corrado to fill her mind, thinking about the little dimple in his chin and the way he spouted Italian and gesticulated wildly when he was talking to Gianni and other friends that came in. She found him fascinating; he made Leslie seem grey and staid by comparison.

Corrado whistled as he beat the egg whites. His pastry, with finely grated lemon zest in was baking blind in the oven and his lemon mixture was bubbling away filling the air with one of his favourite smells. Thinking about the lemon tree back home made him wish he could visit it. He felt a pang of sadness as he remembered Ricardo writing that it was sick. Almost overcome with excitement Margaret forced herself to feign an air of nonchalance as she opened the door. The smell of lemons made her smile brightly as she breezed in trying to stop her hands shaking. Corrado's heartbeat quickened as he looked up and saw her.

'Buongiornio.'

'Good morning.'

Margaret wanted him to talk Italian to her all day. They both found themselves tongue-tied and after an awkward few seconds talked at once.

'Looks like rain to- '

'What can I get-'

They burst out laughing.

'Would you like a coffee?'

'Yes please.'

As he deftly ground up the coffee beans she watched him through the steam, admiring his hands. He had the most beautiful nails milky cuticles - little half-moons - that shone against his brown skin. Guilt crept in unannounced as she imagined those hands touching her. Don't be ridiculous, you're married she told herself sternly. She always took *The Guardian* with her. Pretending to studiously read it gave her the opportunity to surreptitiously peer over the top of it and watch him quickly glancing away if their eyes met. She had no idea if he was attracted to her and she told herself even if he did what difference would it make?

Later in bed that night she couldn't sleep and found herself thinking about the way he'd looked at her and smiled in that lazy way of his. Looking away she'd pretended to be engrossed in an article about workers' rights thrilled to discover that when she glanced back he was still looking at her. Trawling back through every conversation they'd ever had, Margaret analysed each one. Even the ones about the weather. Does he really like me?

Shivering she remembered a smouldering glance he'd given her. Or did I imagine it? The thought of it made her blush. Despite knowing what she was doing was wrong she couldn't help herself; thinking about him was like getting into freshly laundered sheets after a long tiring day.

Lying in bed Corrado tried to figure out a way to see Margaret more. Uncertain whether she felt anything for him he was determined to find out, but doubts stole in. She's out of my league he thought. She's always friendly and polite but I don't know. He never knew what to say to her so he tried to let his food do the talking. Seeming to enjoy his lemony creations she was always very complimentary. They chatted easily about music too. He had felt an affinity with her until he asked about her life. A wary look glanced across her face and she closed up like an oyster. Knowing from experience that you have to sneak up on oysters so that they don't know you're coming, he decided to bide his time and not pry, although he felt sure she was hiding something. When he talked about food she seemed really interested and in the Italian community that he was part of. Explaining to her the way they bartered with food made her laugh and she had listened carefully when he talked about the lemons sent from home. Finally, he plucked up the courage and invited her to come to a party at the osteria and she had agreed. He clenched his fists hardly able to contain his excitement as he thought about her smiling and agreeing.

CORRADO'S PARTY

Margaret spent longer than usual getting ready. She had lied to Leslie about where she was going, telling him she was meeting up for drinks with an old-school friend. He didn't seem to care anyway, barely looking up from his paper, she was almost invisible to him now. They were living a lie and Margaret had no idea how to change her situation. Driving Leslie from her mind she hummed along to her favourite song before joining in with the chorus.

'Hitting the ceiling, hitting the ceiling
Breaking through to the sky...'

Twirling, she sprayed herself with perfume, inhaling the floral scent, before pulling on her silk stockings and opening the wardrobe door to find some shoes. Leslie still bought her a pair every week, even though she had stood up to him and started refusing to let him stroke her feet while she wore them. Feet and shoes were his obsession and in a perverse way how he showed her love. Yet how come then they still hadn't consummated their marriage?

Margaret gazed up at the mountain of boxes that stood from floor to ceiling and feeling slightly sick. She quickly chose a pair near the bottom and eased the box out. At the last moment, her hand slipped and the pile wobbled causing an avalanche as the shoes fell out of the boxes all around her.

'Damn and blast.' Tears sprang to her eyes as she drowned in shoes. Wearily she paired them up and restacked them. What am I doing? I must be mad going to a party full of people I don't know, my whole life seems to be based on lies these days. Her mother's face swam into her head; her words were well meaning, but…

'Darling are you all right? You haven't seemed yourself the last few times you've been over. Is there something the matter?' Her eyes searched her daughter's face. Margaret's eyes had filled with tears and she longed to let it all out, her emotions welled up, threatening to burst out - a firework of frustration and disappointment - but instead she bit her lip and forced back the tears.

'I'm absolutely fine Mother, maybe a bit tired that's all.'

'It's just that I thought you might be having a baby, is that why you're so tired?' She smiled conspiratorially. Margaret's stomach churned as she forced a smile.

'No Mother, not yet, but I promise you'll be the first to know.'

On the way home from her parents' house, she imagined telling her mother about Leslie. Not the man they knew who exuded charm and told witty stories at dinner. The other Leslie, the one who seemed to take perverse pleasure in psychologically breaking her down. Margaret felt so confused, torn between feeling pity for him and hating him. The feeling that she couldn't win combined with being sad all the time, was what made her agree to go to the party. She wanted to feel young and carefree for once.

Staring at her reflection in the full-length mirror she smiled, pleased with her dress; sage-green silk to the knee that clung to all her curves, with a ruched bodice sprinkled with silver beads. As it was sleeveless with an open back, she covered her shoulders with a white fur tippet, before completing her look with cherry red lipstick and elbow length silk gloves that matched her dress.

Whistling, Corrado began preparing the ingredients for the party. Gianni put a note on the door.

Closed for Private Party

Together they moved the tables to one side and created a small dance floor. Corrado put on some music while Gianni lit the candles.

'So', said Gianni, 'what's on the menu?'

'*Spuntini*, lots of snacks.'

'Mmm, and who's coming?' Gianni screwed up some newspaper and laid it in the fire.

'You, Leonora, Luca, Manuel, Salvotore, Arianna and Sofia, oh and Margaret.'

'I didn't know you'd invited her.'

'That day I helped her, she told me she loves jazz, so I thought why not? Corrado, shrugged his shoulders and straightened a tablecloth as he walked out to the kitchen.

What Corrado didn't tell Gianni was that while he was talking to Margaret the other day in the osteria, he had been frantically trying to think of how to see her again and when they'd talked about their shared love of music, he'd concocted the idea of a party on the spot. He realised that he didn't know anything about her; their chats had always been so brief, he was really looking forward to getting to know her, as he had never met such a beautiful woman.

Quelling the butterflies in her stomach Margaret parked her car and checked her lipstick in the mirror. Wondering what his friends would be like she almost started the car again before forcing herself to get out and start walking. Taking a deep breath, she opened the osteria door and walked in. The air was filled with music, chattering and the smell of food, instantly Corrado was at her side beaming.

'Hello.' He kissed her on both cheeks and she caught a whiff of his musky scent. Taking her arm, he guided her to a table.

'Would you like a drink?'

'That would be lovely. Thank you.'

'Try this.' Corrado picked up an elegant cut-glass decanter and removed the tear drop shaped stopper.

'What is it?' said Margaret.

'A special family recipe. Our liquer al limoni,' said Corrado picking up a tiny glass and filling it to the brim, 'and you have to drink it the Italian way, down in one.' Handing her a glass before filling one for himself he chinked their glasses together.

'*Evviva!*'

Tipping back her head back Margaret swallowed.

'Delicious.' She gasped as the yellow liquid travelled down her throat and warmed her all over. 'Thank you.'

'*Prego*' replied Corrado with a smile.

Gianni and his girlfriend walked over, he held out his hand to Margaret.

'Hello again', he smiled and shook her hand, 'this is my girlfriend Leonora.'

Leonora shocked Margaret slightly by kissing her on both cheeks rather than the hand shake she had been expecting.

'I won't be long.' Corrado left them talking, as he changed the music. Putting on one of his favourite songs he observed Margaret from across the room enjoying the way her eyes shone in the candlelight. Admiring the silver comb that held back her wavy chestnut hair he drank her in from head to foot, so he could picture her later. At her throat, she wore a delicate chain with a miniature silver bird in a cage and matching earrings that sparkled, like her, in the dim light. Mesmerised he watched her throw her head back laughing at something Gianni had said and felt jealous. Gianni and Leonora began talking to Manuel, and Margaret gazed out of the window. Corrado felt a thrill of pleasure as he realised that she was singing along to the music. He strode towards her.

'Dance?'

Margaret nodded and Corrado took her in his arms.

'You look beautiful in that dress' said Corrado.

'Thank you.' Margaret blushed slightly.

'You look rather dapper too.'

Corrado smiled. He had taken great care with his outfit that evening, deciding on a crisp white shirt, and black trousers. He wanted to look like he hadn't tried too hard, so he didn't cover his braces with a waistcoat and left his collar undone.

A new song started and Corrado sang softly.

'I may be wrong but I think you're wonderful.' He smiled down at Margaret.

'We seem to have the same taste in music!' Margaret laughed. She loved his accent; the way he spoke English in a sing-song voice and made the words sound exotic.

Beside them the other couples drifted around the floor.

'In a moment, I want you to meet the rest of my friends and then you must excuse me while I serve the food.' The song came to an end and Corrado steered Margaret to a table full of decanters, bottles and glasses.

'Another liquer? Or perhaps a glass of Prosecco, the Italian answer to Champagne. I had to swap a lot of lemons for this. Would you like some?'

'Yes please. All that dancing has made me thirsty.' She watched as Corrado deftly popped the corks on two bottles, and everyone cheered. He handed around glasses and introduced Margaret to the rest of the party. She was just discussing her favourite hat shop with Arianna when Corrado reappeared with a tray holding several small red plates. As the guests helped themselves, and sat down, Corrado brought a plate over and put it on the table. Pulling out a chair for Margaret he sat down opposite her.

'In my country, we call this *spuntini*, in yours I think it is bites maybe? No need for knives and forks we use our fingers, *si?*' The plate was unlike Margaret had ever seen before. Leslie was a traditional man, if he was a colour he would be beige, whose idea of food matched his personality perfectly. Intrigued by the bluish black shells with pearly insides that looked like small boats floating on a red lake, Corrado showed her what to do.

'You have to open your mouth and tip your head back. Eat it at once like an oyster.'

Placing the mussel shell to her lips he watched as she tipped her head right back and emptied the contents into her mouth. Nodding her approval as she chewed.

'That's frightfully tasty. What's in it?'

'It's so simple, breadcrumbs, tomatoes, mussels and parsley.'

Margaret loved the way he pronounced English words. He sounded so different to the other men she knew who all sounded terribly prim and proper.

Next, on a fork he fed her arancini.

'My goodness! That's even better, what is it?' •

'Taleggio cheese and risotto.' Corrado was beaming at her obvious pleasure in eating his food.

'Ready for more?' Corrado placed a tiny triangle of toast topped with pate into her open mouth which he wished he could kiss. 'This is a speciality of Tuscany, where I come from. Crostini Toscani. You like?'

'Very much so, thank you.' Flustered, Margaret took a long sip of Prosecco enjoying the sensation of the bubbles tickling her tongue as the flavour fused with the food she had just eaten. Removing her tippet, she placed it behind her on the chair.

'Did you say that was cheese and risotto?' Margaret dabbed at her lipstick with a napkin.

'Yes, taleggio have you tried it before?'

'No.' Margaret shook her head 'it's so different to our cheese.'

'In my country arancini is traditionally made from mozzarella cheese, made from buffalo milk. But taleggio is made from cow's milk. I made it on my farm in Sussex, we produce a lot of our own food.'

'That's interesting. Do you go there much?' Margaret took a cigarette from her case and offered one to Corrado before placing hers in a long black holder. Corrado lit them both and refilled their glasses as they smiled at each other through the smoke haze. 'Thank you.'

'*Prego.* Around once a week I suppose. I miss it as I was brought up on a farm. I'm not really used to living in the city, although I do like it here, the excitement and the music of course.'

'I know I love living in London but sometimes it's nice to go to the countryside and get away from it all.'

'Would you like to come with me sometime? Like I said I go there every week and it would be nice to have some company.'

Margaret smiled and nodded.

'Yes. I'd like that, to do something different for a change.'

They were interrupted by Arianna coming up behind Corrado and kissing him on both cheeks.

'*Grazie, Corrado per una bella festa.* Lovely to meet you Margaret, see you again.' Tossing her long dark hair over her shoulder, she gave a big smile and left.

'Goodbye,' called Margaret. 'I ought to be going too.'

Corrado stood up and pulled out her chair before helping her into her cape. Margaret waved goodbye to the rest of the party as they called back.

'*Ciao bella.*'

Out in the fresh air, Margaret tottered on her heels giving Corrado the excuse to hold onto her arm. Their footfall the only sound as the sailing clouds massed and divided turning the rooftops and black railings silver. The wind gusting rustled through the branches of the trees and pushed them along as leaves fluttered and fell like red and yellow confetti. Margaret's eye was caught by a lit shop window selling shoes. Abruptly she turned away. Slipping between darkness and pools of brightness as the streetlights lit their way Margaret enjoyed the warmth of Corrado's arm as they crossed the road.

'Here's my car.' Margaret pointed. 'And this time it's not underwater!'
They both laughed and Corrado turned towards Margaret and gently kissed her cold lips. Taken aback, she reciprocated, revelling in his taste and the heat from his mouth before pulling away.

'I'm sorry. I can't. I should have told you I'm married.' Margaret turned away, as Leslie's face loomed large in her mind and quickly got in the car driving away without looking back; if she had, she would have seen Corrado staring at her retreating car, before sighing heavily and slowly trudging back to the party.

Only Gianni was left tidying away the glasses and getting the room ready for the next day.

'*Ciao*, I found this.' Gianni held up a cigarette case. 'Is it Margaret's?'

'Yes. She was in a rush to leave and must have forgotten it.'

'You two seemed to be getting on well. Maybe she'll pop in and pick it up sometime.' Gianni carried on sweeping the floor.

Corrado sighed gloomily.

'Maybe. I can't take it back to her I don't know where she lives.'

Driving home, Margaret's emotions jostled with one another each one elbowing itself to the front of the queue. The fun of the evening began to diminish; overridden by guilt because she had deceived Leslie, and Corrado for that matter. She felt like Alice down the rabbit hole. What's happening to me? How is it something that feels so right, like when he kissed me, can be so wrong? Margaret stood outside the house she shared with Leslie contemplating the kiss. Her lips felt beautifully bruised and she was light headed as she remembered Corrado's scent.

Admiring the silver stripes on the path between the trees, everything felt bright and magical. She didn't want to go into her lonely bed and cold husband; instead she wanted to revel in this moment. Opening her bag to take out a cigarette she realised she must have left them at the party.

'Damn!'

Suddenly the road seemed to dim as she slowly walked up the steps.

*

All that week she thought about Corrado wanting to see him again, and knowing she had to get her cigarette case back as it was a present given to her when she left the school. She remembered her leaving day. Mainly because she had been so happy as she was moving on to a new chapter in her life. Miss Osborne had shaken her hand and given it to her with a card signed by all the staff saying Good Luck in silver writing. She had been touched by their messages, and the gift, as it was incredibly beautiful - made from tortoiseshell – the tawny parts of the shell glowed as the light played over it and it had an M embossed on it. Now look at me, she thought. In an unhappy marriage being kissed by an Italian I barely know, what a mess! I'm going to have to go to the osteria but it will be so embarrassing.

Making up her mind the following day, she pulled her hat firmly down over her ears and walked out of the house before she could change her mind. Driving down Hampstead High Street she rehearsed what she was going to say.

'Hello. I'm frightfully sorry about what happened, and-'
I could just pretend nothing happened. But I can't. I hope I don't blush. She sighed waspishly. Maybe I'll do it tomorrow.

'No. Do it now.' She talked herself into it.

Unaware of the drops of rain spattering the windscreen as she parked the car, Margaret tried to concentrate on staying calm as she was filled with a mixture of jangling nerves combined with great excitement about seeing him again. Walking up the road, a picture of their kiss floated into her mind, she hastily batted it away like a fly. Bracing herself she pushed open the door and came face to face with Corrado. Margaret looked him in the eye, her cheeks burning and said.

'I say. I want to apologise for what happened after the party. I should have told you it's just..'

'I see.' He nodded stiffly, unsmiling and went behind the counter and handed her the case.

'Thank you. Goodbye.' Margaret turned on her heel and left with her face on fire.

That's it. He hates me now. I'm never coming back here again, I'm so embarrassed.

Corrado went into the kitchen his mouth a grim line muttering. 'Love. All it does is make people unhappy. I thought I'd learnt my lesson back home. The only person you can rely on is yourself and don't ever forget it.' Taking his frustration out on a fly buzzing aimlessly at the window he killed it by flicking it with an apron which he threw across the room before wearily returning to kneading his pasta.

THE JAZZ CLUB

Recklessness surged through Margaret, a forbidden thrill, as they glided into the smoke-filled club and stood at the top of the steps surveying the room. Caroline had persuaded her to come and she looked as fabulous as ever; however, Margaret had pulled out all the stops for the occasion: her new black velvet dress and high heels with black bows made her feel the night was hers. Last week walking home, after knitting, Caroline had linked arms with her.

'I've got some good news and some bad news. Which do you want first?'

'Oh! The good news.' said Margaret.
Caroline's eyes shone. 'Do you want to do something really wild?'

'What do you mean?'

'My brother has got me two tickets for Billie's, the jazz club in Soho.'

'What?' Margaret wheeled on her friend. 'Really?'

'He knows someone who works there, so will you come?'

'I'd love to, but isn't it a bit risqué us going alone?'

'So? You only live once!'

'When?'

'Tomorrow night.'

'What's the bad news?'

'I'm leaving.'

'What? When?'

'Next week. I've got a job on a cruise ship singing.'

'Oh!' Margaret tried hard to hide her emotions. 'That's wonderful, I'm so pleased for you.'

Dressed in dinner suits and bowties the band infected the air with their enthusiasm moving as one in time to the beat like tap dancers, their shiny shoes pounding the wooden boards of the stage. The saxophonist caught her eye. He had cocoa skin, slicked back hair, a thin moustache and an expression of pure joy. She giggled as his eyebrows - two hairy caterpillars -seemed to be members of the band. He tipped his head back and they jumped around in all different directions as he commandeered the keys of the beautiful brass instrument with flying fingers. Gleaming in the dim light, it seemed to sing just to her. Quavering notes beckoned her in and searched her soul as if she were standing at the gateway to heaven; however, virtuous was not how she was feeling.

'Let's get a table.' Caroline shouted in her ear.

Following her, Margaret drank in the atmosphere. The music

made her whole body vibrate and they had to squash past people to get near to the bar where tables circled above the dance floor. Sitting down a waiter appeared with a smile and a menu.

'Cocktails?' said Caroline.

It was difficult to talk as it was so loud. Margaret took in her surroundings smiling inside as she thought how angry Leslie would be if he knew she was there. Caroline nudged her and pointed at a couple kissing.

'I love Soho, so Bohemian!'

Margaret laughed and then stopped shocked, as the couple broke apart and she realised it was two men.

'That's illegal!'

'So are a lot of things, but they still happen.' said Caroline, laughing at Margaret. The floor below them was jumping; Margaret was fascinated by the dancing – wild and free – the whole floor pulsed with an invisible energy led by the musicians. She studied the band, the pied pipers leading the rhythm. The trumpeter wore large, round, black spectacles and he was laughing at the drummer, his sticks a blur as he kept time, and then she saw him.

Corrado was standing next to an extremely good-looking Italian man. Stunned, she watched as they shouted 'Cheers!' and smashed their glasses together before downing their drinks in one. Weaving up the stairs towards the bar Corrado looked a little worse for wear. Putting her head down she rummaged for something in her bag as he walked past. Last time they'd met he had looked at her like he hated her, as if she were a slug he'd stepped on wearing new shoes. She didn't want him to look at her like that again. Glancing up she was relieved to see he was at the bar, but suddenly he turned and looked straight at her. Smiling weakly, she was rewarded with a beam before he bounded over and kissed her on both cheeks.

'Margarita, how are you?'

'I'm very well thank you. This is my friend Caroline.' Turning he shook Caroline's hand who had been watching on with a smile. His friend appeared and Corrado did the introductions.

'This is my friend, Giuseppe, this is Margaret and Caroline.'

Giuseppe kissed both their hands his lips lingering a little too long on Caroline's. 'Very pleased to meet you.' He said staring into her eyes.

'It's his birthday so we're celebrating. We've been celebrating all day.'

'Happy birthday. Many happy returns.' They all clinked glasses.

'Thank you. Would you like to dance?' He offered his hand to Caroline.

'I can't really say no as it's your birthday.' Laughing she allowed him to lead her off.

'Would you like a cigarette?' Margaret offered him her case and immediately kicked herself as she remembered picking it up from the Osteria.

'Thank you.' He lit them and blew a perfect smoke ring before picking up the case and examining it

'It's very beautiful.'

'It was a present when I left work.'

'Where was that?'

'I was an English teacher in Camden. I left when I got married as my husband didn't want me to work anymore.' Corrado noticed the cloud that glanced across her face and tactfully changed the subject.

'What do you think of the music?'

'It's so exciting being here. I love it, I only found out we were coming yesterday.
Caroline's brother got us tickets. I've never been anywhere like this before. In fact, I hardly ever go out.' She stopped as she realised she was babbling. She looked at him and noticed he had a slightly wild look in his eye.

'Let me get you a drink.'

Returning he put her gin and tonic on the table and took a lemon and a penknife from his pocket before cutting thick juicy slices and placing them in her drink where they landed with a plop.

'Now that's a lemon. Not like the ones they have behind the bar.' He sniffed and watched her take a sip.

'Dance?'

Throwing off her inhibitions she followed him down the stairs and onto the crowded dance floor. The smell of sweat mingling with a variety of different scents worn by the dancing throng excited her. Caroline waved at her and Corrado took her in his arms. Galvanised as his hands grasped her waist, she let herself go and entered a new world. Looking back, she decided that was the moment she fell in love with him. She didn't realise at the time, but he had captured her heart and taken her to a place she had never been, somewhere magical so she felt like a character in a fairytale. They became one as the band turned up the tempo, whirling and laughing.

'I've had an idea. Would you like to come and visit the farm with me next week?'

Still caught in the magical moment she answered without thinking. 'That would be fun. Which day?'

'I was thinking Thursday. Are you free?'

'Yes. That would be lovely. Thank you.'

'Come to the Osteria at about 9.30? We'll drive down and I'll cook for you and you can stay over too, there's plenty of room so we can have a whole evening.'

'See you then.'

Wending their way home, Caroline and Margaret laughed and joked as they discussed the night. Margaret was staying the night with her friend, although she had told Leslie she was going to her sister's. Caroline let them in and got more drinks as they settled on the long cream sofa. Taking off her shoes Margaret sighed.

'My feet are aching from all that dancing, but it was so much fun. Thank you for taking me.'

'Pleasure. Now are you going to spill the beans? How do you know those two Italians?'

'It's a long story.'

'You are a dark horse, come on then I'm all ears.'

'It all started when I nearly ran a dog over.'

Caroline listened enrapt as she told her the whole saga and squeezed her arm at the end when she explained how hopeless it all was.

'Leslie and I don't love one other, we should never have got married and now I'm stuck with him forever. Corrado seems to care about me and I've got feelings for him, but I'm trapped and there's no way out.'

'And you're going to go to Sussex with Corrado next week anyway?'

'Yes. I know we can only be friends of course but I just want to see him. He's so lovely.'

'I see. Just be careful you don't get hurt.'

In the morning as she was leaving she hugged her friend.

'I'm really going to miss you. I'm happy for you following your dream but having fun with you is what made my life bearable. I hate being married. I wish I could be free too.'

'I almost forgot. I've got something for you.' Caroline picked up a package wrapped in brown paper from the hall table. 'Some of my favourite books. I want you to have them and I hope in time you'll find some happiness. I'll send you postcards and when I come back we can meet up. Look after yourself and keep your chin up.' She hugged Margaret. 'Goodbye.'

'Goodbye and good luck.'

TRIP TO SUSSEX

Whistling to himself Corrado cleaned out his truck. Hungover, the morning after the night at the club, he had regretted inviting Margaret. Now she was coming he was on edge. Terrified of opening himself up to getting hurt. Helpless. She constantly occupied his thoughts and he wanted to know everything about her. Dying to see her again. Meeting that night had cemented his feelings; however, he knew he had to be careful not to overstep the mark and let his curiosity get the better of him.

I must find out about her husband. They can't be very happy as she's always alone and doesn't mention him. I want to find out what's going on and what he's like, he thought, as he went back inside to get changed and wait for her.

Margaret's hand shook as she applied lipstick that matched her pillar box red umbrella. Straightening her hat, she waltzed out of the door and down the steps into a squally rain shower. Humming to herself she skirted the puddles between the broken cracks in the pavement.

The wind snatched at her umbrella mischievously, trying to get underneath it and turn it inside out. Ploughing on regardless, she refused to allow this, and the leaden sky, to dampen her spirits. Excitement bubbled inside her like a volcano threatening to erupt- she felt daring and frivolous as she walked to meet Corrado through the sodden streets. Nearing Hampstead High Street, she stopped opposite the osteria, waiting to cross as a tram and a bus formed a wall in front of her. She smiled at the irony of the poster on the side of the number 35: a picture of a palm tree on a hot desert island advertising PALMOLIVE SOAP in red letters. Below, the raindrops chased one another in rivulets down the windows blurring the passengers' faces so Margaret couldn't see their expressions, as if an artist had been unhappy with what he'd drawn and partly erased them. The advert on the front of the bus was more apt thought Margaret, reading OAKEY'S WELLINGTON BOOT POLISH. Glancing behind her she saw a woman wearing a fur coat sheltering inside the butcher's, next to a huge pale pink pig carcass hanging in the window. In her hand was the lead of a white poodle, wearing a green tartan coat, and her voice droned loudly above the traffic as she told the butcher all about the party she was planning. Margaret noticed that her carmine lipstick was bleeding into the creases around her mouth and tried to imagine the woman without white hair, when she was young, musing on how fleeting beauty was, outer beauty anyway.

The wind gripped Margaret's hat making her turn around and clutch it tightly with her free hand while grasping the umbrella that was also threatening to blow away. The bus had been replaced by a horse and cart, the horse's chestnut coat looked almost black with rain and Margaret caught a whiff of wet earth and hay mixed with sweat as he trotted past. The woman's lipstick and Margaret's umbrella were the only patches of brightness; even the rusty coloured brick buildings lining the street, that took on a fiery glow in the fading sunlight, looked dull and subdued because of the rain. Feeling sorry for the three ragged beggar children standing together under an archway Margaret fished in her purse for a penny for each of them and smiled at the fruit and vegetable stall holder near Corrado's place huddled beneath his white awning glaring up at the glowering sky because the streets were almost deserted. Looking left and right before carefully crossing the road and making sure her heels didn't catch in the criss-crossing tram tracks that snaked in swirling patterns along the road below, she greeted Corrado with a smile.

'Hello.'

Corrado came out and opened the passenger door for her.

'*Buongournio.*'

Shaking her umbrella to get rid of the drops she put it in the back as Corrado started the engine.

'Lovely weather for ducks!' said Margaret.

'How *do* you English stand it? Everything's so grey.'

'We're very stoic about it you know, it's part of our make-up. And actually, it's a good thing as it gives us something to talk about.'
Corrado laughed.

'And,' she continued 'I bet Italians don't walk around saying weather related sayings. It would get boring as it's always sunny.'

'Not always, but a lot more than here.'

'I suppose you really miss Italy, don't you?'

'*Si*. I miss my family the most.'

'Tell me about them.'

'Well, my parents are dead, my father died in 1920, and my mother passed quite recently.'

'I'm awfully sorry.' Said Margaret.

'I have an older brother, Ricardo, he's married to Giverny and they have three children. Gabriella, who is thirteen, and twin boys, Alfredo and Tomaso, who are ten. They live on our family farm on the borders of Tuscany and Umbria.'

'How did you learn to speak English so well?'

'My father was a Professor of Languages and travelled a

lot, so he taught us from a young age, before he took over the family farm. And our village school is run by sisters from the Abbey, one of them, Sister Anne, was English.'

'Ah, I see. I wondered, because although you've got an accent you don't speak in the same way as some of your friends.'

'What do you mean?'

'Take Manuel who I met at the party. He puts an a on the ends of his words. So, he'll say "woulda you like a drinka?" You don't do that.'

'That's because Sister Anne was very strict and made us practise endlessly, it felt like, but I'm pleased now as I knew I always wanted to come here.'

'Well I'm glad you did.'

It was out of her mouth before she had a chance to stop it. Margaret blushed and looked out of the window. Corrado smiled to himself, thinking how attractive she looked with flushed cheeks.

'So, what about you? Does your husband know you're coming away with a strange foreigner?'

Margaret looked uncomfortable.

'No. He thinks I'm staying at my cousin's in Devon.'

'Devon? I've heard it's supposed to be very nice there.'

'It is. Look, I couldn't tell him. Not that I think he'll be that bothered.' She said sadly.

Chatting away, they barely noticed that gradually, the bustling London streets had given way to leafy lanes and the rain had stopped.

'So, Giuseppe's at the farm? I didn't get much chance to talk to him the other night, what's he like?'

'Giuseppe? He's a peacock! Hot blooded and hot headed. I can't imagine him ever settling down. He loves women too much. None of the girls in our village will have anything to do with him. He's got a reputation. But to me, he's my best friend we've known each other all our lives. Sat in class together, got into trouble and fights together, fought each other, played football for the school team. He's going back up to town later, he came down to get some cheese to sell.'

'He seemed to quite like Caroline. Did you always plan to move away together?'

Corrado frowned and shifted in his seat.

'Yes and no. It all happened quite suddenly. Look we're here.'

They turned into a driveway bordered with wooden fencing. On the gate Margaret noticed it said Horseshoes Farm. It made her smile as it had been constructed from old horseshoes, manipulated into the letters. They drove up to a long, low white farmhouse, with small diamond paned windows crowned with a honey coloured thatched roof. To the left-hand side stood a circular building with small terracotta tiles, each one overlaid across the next, and covered in thick strands of ivy. On the top was an iron weathervane with a cockerel, pointing eastwards. The wooden front door opened and out rushed a collie dog barking wildly followed by Giuseppe wiping his hands. Corrado opened Margaret's door and then crouched down giving the dog a big fuss as it gambolled around his legs.

'Yes. Yes, hello Bella. Have you missed me eh?'

After he and Corrado kissed on both cheeks Giuseppe turned to Margaret and pressed her hand to his lips while looking at her with laughing brown eyes.

'*Buongiornio*. The beautiful Margaret. *Very* pleased to see you again.'

'Thank you.' Margaret blushed and followed them into the hallway past a settle and an oak stand filled with walking sticks, umbrellas and a shepherd's crook into a large airy kitchen. The warmth from a gleaming creamy coloured range filled the kitchen.

'Would you like a drink?'

'That would be lovely. Thank you.' Said Margaret Corrado put the kettle on top of the range.

'What do you think of our oven?'

'It's very nice.'

'It's brand new, an Aga, when the engineer fitted it he said that only three hundred people in the country have got one. Although he said everyone's beginning to catch on now. I wanted to get the best and I've barely used it, so I'm looking forward to cooking for you tonight.'

'How lovely, I can't wait. The food you cooked at the party was incredible.'

Returning with a small white jug filled with creamy milk and some cups and saucers with a leafy green pattern decorating the rims Corrado made tea for her. While the two friends discussed the farm and talked business, Margaret sat at the long wooden table, sipping her drink and looked around her. Returning with a small white jug filled with creamy milk and some cups and saucers with a leafy green pattern decorating the rims Corrado made tea for her. While the two friends discussed the farm and talked business, Margaret sat at the long wooden table, sipping her drink and taking in her surroundings. Above the new oven, wooden boards formed a slatted structure draped with drying bunches of green herbs. From the black beam crossing the ceiling drooped a brace of stuffed pheasants; the royal blue of their heads, and the red spectacles circling open, unseeing eyes stood out against the white ceiling. Under the table she felt a wet nose nudge her hand, asking for a fuss. Margaret smiled and stroked Bella's wiry coat.

'Right. I'm off. Hope you enjoy your stay and I'll see you soon.' Said Giuseppe.

'One moment Margaret, I just need to get something.' Corrado headed out with his friend.

Nervous and excited, Margaret felt reckless as if she had been let out on parole. All her days drifted into one at home doing the same old thing, this was something completely different and she couldn't wait to be alone with Corrado.

Eager to see the animals, even the rain drizzling again so the farmyard was oozing with thick fudge coloured mud didn't dampen her enthusiasm. A bedraggled white hen clucked at them miserably as it stood sheltering beneath a lavender bush.

'It's a good thing you wore sensible clothes, I forgot to say how muddy it gets. I like your outfit by the way.'

'Thank you.'

Margaret didn't add that she had bought it for this very occasion. It wasn't often that she wore trousers but when she'd spotted this pale green tweed suit she thought it would be perfect for this trip, glad now she'd also bought an olive-green hat with a wide brim to match; she already had the boots which she wore in the winter for her walks on the heath.

Corrado led her to a field full of cinnamon coloured cows who looked curiously at the visitors momentarily before continuing to eat the wet, silvery grass.

'When we got the farm, we bought it as a going concern with all the animals. We have a manager and his wife who work for us. We make our own butter, cheese and honey.'

'I remember you saying at the party you make Italian cheese.'

'Yes, we sell it up in London. That's where Giuseppe's going to meet some prospective buyers.'

'I can see why he's a hit with the ladies!' They both laughed.

Walking back through the yard, Corrado picked up a bucket and filled it with feed from the barn before taking Margaret down a narrow lane. He accidentally brushed his shoulder against hers and apologised. Margaret hoped he'd do it again. A chorus of loud bleating brought her back to the present.

'The sheep and goats don't need an introduction!'

A crowd of shaggy brown goats came clamouring forwards their curled horns butting one another trying to get to the bucket. Corrado opened the gate and pushed them back so he could pour their feed into the trough.

'The pigs are further away as they smell so bad, but there's one more thing I want you to see.' He led her to the circular building and opened the door using a large key. 'We really wanted one of these, so we can smoke and dry our meat.' Gazing upwards Margaret was surprised to see large brown ham haunches drying on huge silver hooks alongside pink blotchy salami parcels in string bags. The animal aroma was strong – evocative – combined with being in such a confined space with Corrado.

'Was this what it was built for?'

'No. It was made to dry hops in for making beer, but I saw the potential and we think it will work, although it's an experiment. Back home we use wild boar but here we are using English pork, so we have no idea what it will taste like. We're using the same recipes to make the sausages and prosciutto.' He pointed up to some long rectangular pieces of meat, flattened in a vice made from planks of wood.

'Is that bacon?'

'Similar but much better. We have to wait the drying takes a long time so…' he shrugged. 'Now, let's get in out of the rain, I can show you your room and think about what I'm cooking.'

Sinking down on the single bed, Margaret looked around. The whitewashed walls contrasted starkly with the dark floorboards that she'd almost slipped over on when walking in her stockinged feet. The bed stood against one wall covered with a lilac candlewick blanket. A small fire crackled cheerfully in the grate, below a wooden clock on the mantelpiece. It was obviously a spare room as it was sparsely furnished with just a wardrobe and chest of drawers. In the corner a cracked china jug and bowl patterned with sprigs of pink roses stood on a washstand.

Feeling risqué she shook out her dress enchanted by the silver beads shimmering in the light and making a noise like waves gently washing onto shingle. It was new. Expensive. The bodice was the shade of ripe plums and the knee length skirt was made from the beads. Finishing her look with silver shoes she applied lipstick and a squirt of perfume.

Following her nose, Margaret headed back down to the kitchen and opened the door to the strains of a trumpet from the jazz he'd put on. The kitchen was cozy; candles illuminated the raindrops that continued to patter at the windows making each one glow like a tiny seed pearl. Corrado was in full swing making pastry, while on the range, pans sizzled and spluttered like mini fireworks going off.

'Smells delicious,' she said.
He handed her a glass of deep red wine that matched her dress, clinked his glass with hers and looked her up and down.

'Bellisima. Cheers!'

'Cheers. Thank you.'

'You look very beautiful. I'm planning on making a feast, but it will take some time, so I hope you don't mind me working while we talk?'

'Thank you. Not at all. What are you making?'

'To start with, ravioli, then *osso buco*, one of my family's favourites, followed by lemon tart.'

'Goodness that sounds wonderful, but a lot of work for you.'

'Cooking is not work for me. I enjoy it. I've already made the pastry for the tart and now I have to get the *osso buco* cooking as it has to braise for a long time to make the meat really soft.'

'What is *osso buco*?'

'It's a bit like a stew I think the English call it, but very different. Now it's your turn. Tell me about your family.' Margaret took a sip of her wine.

'Right. I'm the middle one of three sisters, Jeanie is the eldest and Win is younger. Jeanie's married to Jim and they live near my parents and Win who live in Hendon. Before I got married I was an English teacher and taught in a school in Camden. Now I'm married I don't work anymore, although I miss it dreadfully.'

'Why did you have to stop working because you got married?'

'My husband's quite old-fashioned and feels me working will make it appear that he can't provide for me.'

'I see.' Corrrado frowned, confused.

Rapt, she watched as he added chopped carrots and celery to onion and garlic, already sizzling in the pan. Quickly ripping rosemary from a stalk, he added it, before chopping up tomatoes so rapidly Margaret feared for his fingers.

'I know,' said Margaret 'the thing is I've made a huge mistake marrying him.' She took a swig of wine. 'I got swept away when my father introduced us and now I'm beginning to realise that we don't have anything in common.'

Corrado took two oblong pieces of deep red meat and dusted them with flour, salt and pepper and placed them in the pan too. Immediately the room was full of the most wonderful aroma.

'That smells better than Christmas,' she said.

'It's got to cook for a while. Now I'm going to make the ravioli.'

Fascinated, Margaret observed him as he poured a huge mound of flour onto the table and made a well in the middle, so it looked like a volcano. He began to add beaten eggs to it gradually, constantly mixing and always retaining the sides until it finally collapsed in on itself and he brought it together into a dough before kneading it. Margaret enjoyed the way his muscles flexed as he caressed it into submission.

'How did you learn to cook?'

'My mama taught me. She was always in the kitchen. She never stopped making food, it's how she showed us she loved us.'

'She must have been a strong woman that looks like heavy work.'

Corrado laughed.

'She was. So, English is the subject you teach?'

'Yes, I love reading. What about you, have you read many English books?'

'I've read some. At school we had to read and out loud to improve our pronunciation. Sister Anne is a big fan of Charles Dickens. Do you like him?'

'I like *A Christmas Carol*.'

'I read that a while ago, now I'm reading *David Copperfield*.'

'I seem to remember that for animals with strange behaviour; a donkey and a naughty dog.'

'I thought that all the English people I met would be like that, have no manners and let their dogs sit at the table while they ate.'

He was pleased to see Margaret's face blossom into a laugh as she realised he was teasing her.

'Well I thought that Italian men spend their whole time pinching girl's bottoms!'

Corrado laughed loudly.

'That's more Giuseppe's style than mine. Although all Italian men appreciate beautiful women, some of us are slightly subtler.'

'Anyway,' said Corrado, 'I've made a bet with Gianni that I can read every single Dickens novel by his birthday.'

'When's that?'

'April the 16th.'

'So how many have you got to go?'

'About six. I'm going to do it and win the bet.'

'The thing with Dickens is that they're rather long. He uses several words when he could use one or two.'

'Yes. I've noticed that.'

'It's because his books were serialised initially and he used to get paid by the word.'

'I see. I thought it was a bit odd.'

'Mind you if you love a book, and can't put it down, the longer the better. And he was an important activist. Through his writing he highlighted the class divide and issues for the poor.'

'Which books do you recommend to your students?'

'We have set texts to study.'

'So, which book would you recommend to me? What about your favourite.'

Screwing up her nose Margaret thought while Corrado deftly chopped sage leaves, their strong scent mingling with the meat bubbling away.

'That's difficult. Do you want me to tell you my favourite book or think of one I think you'll enjoy?'

'Your favourite.'

'It would have to be *Pride and Prejudice* by Jane Austen then. I can lend it to you if you like, but I don't think you'll have time if you want to beat Gianni.'

'I'll make time. I'm a fast reader'

Sipping her wine Margaret found she was enjoying herself. Corrado rolled out the pasta on the table in two long strips. He began to mix ingredients together.

'What's going in the ravioli?'

'Two of our cheeses, parmesan and *caciotta*. The *caciotta* is made from sheep's milk. Then some milk, eggs, pepper, nutmeg and marjoram.'

He placed spoonfuls of the mixture at intervals along one of the sheets leaving gaps between before placing the other sheet over the top and using a cutter produced perfect little parcels. He reminded Margaret of a potter, the way his fingers skillfully shaped them and put them onto a board.

'So, where did you go to university?' said Corrado.

'I didn't. I went to a teacher training college called Whitelands, in Chelsea, for three years to get my certificate. It was hard work but really fun, especially in spring and summer as we used to play tennis and have the May Ball.'

'What happens at the May Ball?'

'Maypole dancing and the May Queen presentation. Then dancing in the evening.'

'We have Maypole dancing in my country too.'

'Really? I thought it was an old English tradition.'

'In Italy, we celebrate *Calendimaggio,* the evening before. There is a love song contest and the Maypole dancing. Afterwards, a competition to see who can climb up the slippery pole and reach the prizes of money, cheese, ham and salami hanging from the top. Giuseppe's won that before.'

'How funny putting meat prizes on top. It's a bit different to ours. In my final year, we had a special May Day where there was a secret ballot, so we could cast a vote for the May Queen. I can remember it like it was yesterday. The Bishop of London came to preside over the chapel service before. We wore white and had our hair back, in buns like ballerinas. We walked in a procession with everyone watching around the college gardens.

They were very beautiful full of poppy and lily filled flower beds, and when we went beneath the apple and hawthorn trees their blossom wafted down on us like confetti. The flowers smelled so strong, they seemed to be vying with one another to attract the bees and butterflies going about their business oblivious to our parade.

Afterwards a reporter from *The Times* took photographs and interviewed some of the girls while we waited in the hall. It looked so beautiful; the ceiling above us was decorated with garlands of greenery and the green curtains behind the stage with clusters of May blossom, pink and frothy as organza. It was such a beautiful day. The windows were open and I remember being so hot and uncomfortable as we sat for ages on rock hard benches waiting to hear the result. I voted for a girl called Amelia, and she won.' Margaret stopped suddenly. 'Sorry I've just rabbited on for ages. Father's always telling me I talk too much.'

'Not at all.' Corrado didn't say that he found her more attractive when she talked without any inhibitions.

'Tell me more about yours,' said Margaret.

'Well, we have a great feast and everyone parades around the streets carrying silk banners. Do you eat at yours?'

'Yes, but the food wasn't very good at the college.'

'Well I hope you're hungry as the *primo* is almost ready.'

Margaret's mouth began to water as he dished out ravioli onto dark blue plates and finished them with a trickle of sage butter and some thin flakes of parmesan.

'*Ecco.*' He put the plate in front of her.

'Thank you very much for this, it looks and smells absolutely wonderful.'

Corrado watched her anxiously. She didn't speak, only smiled, until each bit had gone including every drip of the butter.

'I have no words to describe how much I enjoyed that, thank you so much. Now tell me some more about Italy, I think you said you had an osteria there?'.

'I did. In a place called Civita, it's near Lake Bolsena which is very beautiful. Civita and the next village, Bagnoregio used to be joined but the land between was devoured by earthquakes. We live in a valley nearby, but our family have owned a house there forever. The only way in or out is a long, narrow footbridge, not wide enough for cars, the only transport is donkeys, carts and bicycles. Would you like some more wine?' Corrado smiled.

'Yes please.'

'The centrepiece of the square is the church where we go to mass. Do you go to church?'

'Sometimes. At Christmas and Easter.'

'As Catholics, the church is a big part of our lives in Italy, we celebrate saints' days with processions and feasts it's an important part of our culture.'

'I've read about that, it must be an amazing spectacle. I'd love to see it.'

'It is,' said Corrado wistfully. 'Maybe you will one day.'

ITALY

932AD

'Engorged. He looked down in horror.

"What's the matter?" Sabina sat up ripping off her blindfold and he jerked away so she couldn't see what had happened to him.

The moonlight stabbing through the gap in the curtains illuminated her taut flat stomach and the triangular thatch of hair crowning her long legs made his swelling increase.

From the moment Lorenzo was born women cooed over him. He learnt to flirt before he could walk; fluttering his eyelashes so long they would make a buffalo proud. With his big brown eyes and dark hair, he grew into a very handsome young man and used his looks to his full advantage. Baking and being a gigolo were his specialities in equal measure. Spoilt dreadfully; particularly by his aunty who had no children and was blinded by his beauty. He was her only heir and she entrusted him to the lemon tree's secrets at a young age. Too young.

When he lost both his parents in a tragic accident she took him in to her home in Bagnoregio. He inherited the bakery in the piazza in Civita from his father as well as his flair for cooking and as he got older decided to move in to the rooms above the shop soon realising that this was a great benefit especially after hearing of the tree's capabilities. However, he was hiding a secret.

Coy and nonchalant was how he behaved about his cooking; however, once he began using the lemons he began to understand the true power of the fruit. Due to its aphrodisiac effects he had a constant stream of women hanging around him like a cloud of gnats. Every woman, married or not who ate one of his lemon creations fell at his feet. Sabina, the butcher's wife was no exception. Biting into a slice of his lemon drizzle cake, her eyes shone with lust. Smiling to himself, Lorenzo mouthed to her: "meet me upstairs later."

Excited by his latest acquisition he prepared his bedroom. The secret he was hiding was that he wasn't very well endowed. Therefore, to compensate he became incredibly skillful with his fingers and tongue to make up for his lack of girth and length; but it had always irked him so to make him feel more of a man he started playing a dangerous game. Having seven women on the go was exhausting and he had to remember not to call them by name in case he made a mistake. Each of the women thought they were the only one and he always said that they had to keep their affair secret as his aunt wouldn't like it. They hugged it tightly to themselves as Lorenzo had the knack of making a woman feel like a queen and the most important person in the world while he was loving her. When they knocked on the door, he always started the evening the same way by blindfolding her and making her vulnerable. He pretended it was a game; however, in reality, it was to hide his manhood and also because he had recently realised that if he rubbed it with honey and lemon it grew by two inches. It had to be done once he was already aroused or it wouldn't work. He'd tried. So to ensure that Sabina didn't see he gently placed the blindfold, a red silk scarf over her eyes and told her to trust him. When they knocked on the door, he always started the evening the same way by blindfolding her and making her vulnerable. He pretended it was a game; however, in reality, it was to hide his manhood and also because he had recently realised that if he rubbed it with honey and lemon it grew by two inches. It had to be done once he was already aroused or it wouldn't work. He'd tried.

So to ensure that Sabina didn't see he gently placed the blindfold, a red silk scarf over her eyes and told her to trust him. She felt for his hand as he led her upstairs and guided her to the bed. Reverently undressing her he became aroused at seeing her naked breasts with puckered nipples peeking shyly out from the long sheet of hair that fell to her waist. Quickly he undressed and began to rub himself waiting for the effect until he screamed in agony. It was swelling and swelling without stopping. Lemon shaped and knobbly it looked deformed and the pain was excruciating. He felt as if he was bursting at the seams like an over-stuffed pepper.

Sabina screamed too when she saw it and ran away, trailing her clothes, straight into her husband brandishing a carving knife. Shoving her away he stormed into the bedroom stopping short in disgust at the sight of the snivelling man lying on the bed. He put the knife to Lorenzo's throat and spoke in a low menacing tone.

"If you ever, ever touch my wife again you'll wish you'd never been born, do you understand?"
Suddenly catching sight of Lorenzo's swollen appendage, he recoiled in horror backing out of the door and pushing his wife before him into the square. Falling to his knees and praying, Lorenzo begged for mercy and swore that he would do anything to negate what was happening to him.

"I promise to never have sex again or use the lemons." He whimpered. Several hours later, he began to feel some relief as the swelling diminished. Mortified he packed some things and left a note for his aunt after putting up the closed sign on the door.

For the rest of his life he kept his promise and so as not to risk temptation lived as a hermit up in the hills. Taking over an old shepherd's hut he lived simply eating berries and mushrooms that he foraged never setting eyes on another soul until one day, when he was an old man, he was sitting by his fire and saw a figure approaching in the distance. Shielding his eyes he stood and saw that it was a tall man with a beard. His hair was just beginning to grey at the sides; but he looked smart and healthy making Lorenzo ashamed of his own appearance with his long straggily beard and thick matted hair that almost reached his knees.

The man waved and called out to him.

"Buongiornio. Is your name Lorenzo?"

"Who's asking?" He replied gruffly.

"My name is Giorgio and I come from Bagnoregio. I have something I need to ask you."

"I am. Sit down." He motioned to a log on the other side of the fire. "What do you want?"

"My mother's name is Estella Cavalli, or rather was."

"And, what has that to do with me?"

"I was hoping you could tell me." He handed Lorenzo a letter.

Realisation dawned as he read the letter. Estella and he had been having an affair just before he left and according to the letter this man sat in front of him was his son.

"So you see," said Giorgio, "it appears that you are my papa. I only found out once she had passed away and I received this letter."

"What do you want?"

"Nothing. I just wanted to meet you."

Having had no company for so long, Lorenzo found he enjoyed chatting with the man and when he got up to take his leave felt a sense of sadness.

"I'm sorry that I haven't been a father to you Giorgio, but if you would like to visit again I would be glad of your company." He took his hand and squeezed it.

"Thank you. I will come back and see you."

Giorgio visited frequently and Lorenzo grew to love and trust him implicitly. Eventually when he was near death, despite his shame, Lorenzo confessed about the lemons to his son and asked his forgiveness which was granted. Then he made him the keeper of the lemon tree stories.'

ITALY

Although the trees had turned from deep green to bronze, gold and crimson, the sky stayed blue and the air was stifling until the wind changed. It became a sheepdog driving the clouds forwards like a flock of black sheep. Nero hid under the table, the rising heat became unbearable as Roberta and Giverny rushed around packing, the sweat dripping off them in large beads. Finally, the storm came. It was as if Jupiter had entered the valley riding on his eagle hurling lightning bolts when the first great flash tore the sultry sky in two and the thunder ricocheted around like opposing bullets in a shoot-out. The clouds exploded. The pond turned into a stage, raindrops dancing across it, like a thousand ballerinas and Luigi and Ricardo were soaked within seconds as they ran indoors for shelter past the fading flowers being pummeled by the deluge. Afterwards, everyone had to help separate the two full grown buffalo and the calves ready for the trip that night. They put on their boots that soon glistened like peeled grapes, and enjoyed the cool air blowing as they walked past dripping trees and lizards venturing out to check the weather from the holes in the stone walls.

The wet, shiny buffalo sensed danger and instinctively stood close together as a herd.

'Right,' said Ricardo 'this could be tricky, especially with the bulls. I'm going to lead them off over there and then you can catch the calves.'

The twins and Gabriella were in place at one side of the field to form a barrier as Luigi and Giverny put halters on the male and female calves. Luigi sidled up to the large bull.

'Be careful with Carlos.' Giverny deftly fastened the halter on Manuela, who grunted indignantly. 'You know what he's like.'

He wasn't quick enough, so the bull sidestepped him. Luigi made a determined lunge and caught him. Carlos panicked, put his head down and galloped off with Luigi hanging on to the rope. Stopping suddenly, he changed direction making Luigi trip over but grimly hang on as he was dragged across the field. The twins were leaning on one another crying with laughter. Eventually Carlos stopped and Luigi stood up, completely covered in mud and brushed himself down, making everyone laugh.

'See, that's how it's done!'

The mother buffalo began to low and swish her horns. The calves shook their heads anxiously and cried. Then Carlos slipped his halter and careered off down the hill.

 Tomaso quickly headed him off by waving his arms and shouting. The noise was deafening as Ricardo ran and caught him and they hurriedly led them out of the field.

'Careful. Come here out of the way now.' Giverny waved at the children who quickly moved towards her and out of the gate. Desperate, the mother buffalo made an anguished sound, like a strangled cat, which was unrelenting all the way back to the house. This intensified as she watched her babies being led away before losing sight of them. The truck was ready with the ramp down. Luigi led Carlos up. As he pulled the second one it began backing away into the others behind who reared up.

'Easy now.' He kept talking softly to the calf until eventually six buffalo were loaded into the open pen in the back of the truck, their heads poking out of the top with the little ones still crying. Gabriella was distraught.

'Mama, they're so sad. Poor things.' She said.

'I know,' said Giverny. 'But we can't keep them all. And if they weren't going to Uncle Corrado we'd have to sell them. It's horrible, but they'll get over it soon, don't worry. Right, bedtime for you three say goodnight and go and get ready.'

'Good night.' The twins trooped inside and upstairs. Gabriella hugged her mother.

'I'm glad I'm not a baby buffalo.'

Giverny laughed. 'Sometimes you're as noisy as one. Now you need to say goodbye to Luigi and Roberta and the baby because they're leaving later during the night.'

SUSSEX

There were no awkward silences as they found out about each other's interests and pasts. Margaret didn't tell him anymore about Leslie and although Corrado didn't tell her the real reason he had left home, he confided in her about Giuseppe's family coming from Italy, but not the whole story about why they had to leave. She enjoyed the way he was so animated as he told her about the buffalo and his plans.

'I have to come back here in two days and drive to Dover to pick them up. Giuseppe is so excited to see them again and he hasn't met his baby niece yet.'

'That will be lovely for them to be all together again.'

'It's going to be tricky getting the buffalo over. My brother has had to get false papers for them as you can't really move livestock, so I devised a plan which I hope is going to work. I came up with it when I was walking past the zoo. I've had a letter written that says we are transporting them there.' Margaret laughed.

'How did you do that?'

'My friend, Claudio works there; I got him to get the proper headed paper they use and write an official looking letter. I'm a bit nervous, but fingers crossed.'

'And toes!' said Margaret.

The *osso buco* melted in her mouth and the lemon tart made her feel giddy. She so wanted to be kissed by Corrado again and had to force herself to go to her room before completely losing her resolve. Margaret sat on the bed in the farmhouse wide awake. All she could think about was him being somewhere along the landing. Every fibre in her body wanted to throw the doors open of each room until she found him and beg him to hold her and kiss her like he had before. Shaking herself she tried to calm her breathing. She felt drunk, not just on the wine but on life, by being in this place and feeling free. Reluctantly she forced herself to get under the covers shivering at the coldness of the white cotton sheets. Corrado shut his bedroom door and slowly undressed. Picking up the photograph of his family he remembered the day it was taken. They had been for a picnic up near the lemon grove, everyone was smiling and laughing without any idea then that they would be separated in this way. He wanted them to meet Margaret, he felt sure she and Giverny would get on.

Sighing he got into bed and picked up his book, but instead of taking in the words he thought of Margaret in the room next door, so near yet untouchable. Picturing her sparkling eyes, her pale skin and the way she laughed. Why does she have to be married to someone else?

Margaret fell asleep eventually, but even then Corrado stole into her dreams like a thief in the night. She dreamt she was with him in Italy at a big celebration. They were laughing and joking and had just turned a corner when she saw Leslie in front of her. He grabbed her arm and pulled her away from the crowd. As she looked back Corrado was staring at her reproachfully. Waking with a jolt, the room was pitch black. It took a few seconds to get her bearings and remember where she was. The clock ticking was the only sound as she lay back down and shivered.

What am I doing here? All her laissez-faire feelings from earlier were replaced by a feeling of hopelessness. Why did I come? Leslie's face loomed large in her mind. I'm not doing anything wrong just spending time with a friend she told herself, trying to appease her conscience which kept telling her that she wanted him to be so much more than that. The panic began to rise from her stomach and flood her brain. How can I be so selfish? I'm married and I'm stringing Corrado along. I vowed I wouldn't do this after the party. But it was him who said he just wants to be friends she reasoned. We're both saying that but it's not really what we want. I'll have to be honest with him and tell him I can't see him anymore once we get back. Falling back into a restless sleep she woke up with a heavy head.

Glimmers of sunlight were fighting the clouds for space in the sky as she dragged her clothes on and went downstairs to be greeted by a plump, smiling woman with a grey bun wearing a blue apron with a teapot in her hand.

'Good morning, you must be Margaret.'

'Oh, hello.' Margaret held out her hand and shook the chubby warm fingers lightly.

'You sit down and I'll make you a nice cup of tea, dear. Corrado's seeing to the animals, he won't be long.'

'Thank you,' said Margaret weakly and sank down at the table.

The tea revived her and she found herself chatting to the housekeeper whose cheerful air was infectious, as she bustled around the kitchen, despite the dread Margaret felt about the conversation she was planning for the trip home. Corrado strode into the room and beamed when he saw her sitting there.

'Good morning. How did you sleep?'

'Well, thank you.'

'I see you've met Mrs. Jones. What about some breakfast?'

'It's just coming.' Mrs. Jones put a plate with a speckled, brown boiled egg in a white egg cup in front of her, surrounded by soldiers of toast. Then she brought a silver holder full of toast triangles to the table, a dish of golden butter, a jar of orange marmalade and a pot of thick honey.

'I hope you're hungry,' said Corrado. 'The eggs are from our hens, and you must try both the marmalade, because Mrs. Roberts made it, and the honey as it's from our bees.' Margaret carefully peeled the top from her egg and removed the white with her spoon before dipping a soldier into the yolk where it dribbled down the side.

'This is frightfully tasty. The yolk's so yellow.'

'That's from the corn we feed the chickens. I'm going to take some eggs back with me to make pasta. That comes out really yellow too.'

'This is delicious.' Margaret smiled at the housekeeper as she tasted the marmalade.

'Thank you. I won a prize for that at the village show this year.'

'I can see why.'

'What time do you want to head back?' asked Corrado.

'I suppose quite soon.' Said Margaret.

'Right, I'll finish up here if you want to get ready.' Margaret got in the car working out what she was going to say. Corrado looked at her profile and wondered what was wrong as she looked so deflated.

'Are you all right?'

'Yes.'

'You seem a bit quiet.'

'I know I'm sorry it's just… I feel terribly guilty. I had such a lovely time last night but I'm a married woman and I shouldn't have come. It's not fair on Leslie or you or me for that matter.' She stared out of the window as they flew past stone walls and fields of cows.

'I know that you're married. And I know we can only be friends. I promise I won't ask any more of you than that. Although,' he faltered, 'I don't know if I should say this, but I'm afraid I have feelings for you. So, if you should ever decide that you like me too and want to take this further you know where to find me.'

Blushing, Margaret turned to look out of the window, so he couldn't see her face. Inside she felt delight bubbling inside her, but she forced herself to quash it and answered stiffly.

'Thank you. I do have feelings for you too and unfortunately, that's why we can't see each other anymore. I'm very sorry.'

The rest of the journey was spent in silence as they were both lost in thought. Corrado was kicking himself again for being too forward like the night he'd kissed her. He couldn't understand it, as they'd eaten the lemons on both of those nights. Margaret was wrapped in misery as she thought about the life she was returning to, a grey, empty life that no longer had Corrado in it.

ITALY

The waxing moon illuminated the yard as they packed up the truck, giving everything a silvery ethereal tinge. Ricardo lifted the large wooden trunks into the back with the calves. The rest of the luggage was strapped to the roof. Giverny was surprised that her children managed to sleep through the departure; the two smallest buffalo stood in the back of the pick-up truck sounded like miaowing kittens answering their mother's cries from the fields behind the house. Carlos and Manuela snorted indignantly; Eva was also crying with disgust at being taken from her warm bed and Roberta was crying as she said goodbye. You couldn't even hear the cricket chorus which normally filled the night.

'Don't forget to write and let me know how you are.' Said Giverny as she hugged Roberta.

'I will and I'll remember to give Corrado a kiss from you too. Thank you for looking after us. Promise you'll come and visit soon?' said Roberta tearfully.

'Yes. I'd love to. Goodbye Luigi.' She hugged him and went round to kiss Ricardo through the open window.

'I'll see you in a couple of days,' he said.

'Drive carefully.' She shouted, holding her hands up at the cacophony of sound. And laughed at the spectacle of the overloaded van full of buffalo standing in the back.

'So much for making a quiet get away. Bye, love you.'

As the silver road ribboned in front of them taking them to their new life, the silence inside the car was punctuated by the buffalo in the back and Roberta sniffing as she tried to stop the tears flowing onto Eva who was snuffling in her lap. At the turning to their farm they stared up the lane.

'Not much to show for a whole life's work is it, a few trunks and suitcases.' Said Luigi.

Roberta squeezed his arm. 'We're going to see Giuseppe again and we didn't think that would happen.'

'I know. But I've spent my whole life there with your mama, the memories are all from that house.' He said.

'At least now we'll be safe.'

They slept while Ricardo drove all night. He found himself getting drowsy and opened his window to let in some breeze. Suddenly a bellow in his ear and a great horned head appearing in the window jolted him awake making him jump.

'Whoa Carlos, you scared the life out of me.' He rubbed the buffalo's shaggy chin and pushed his head back out of the window.

Roberta woke up as they bumped along the stony roads until it got light before stopping for a breakfast at the edge of a field next to the road. Giverny had packed them up enough food to last until they reached Calais. The sun was rising above the French hills and a farmer waved as he drove a cart pulled by an old grey donkey past them. The field was full of stubble after the harvest. Sat in silence they enjoyed the feel of the climbing sun on their backs and faces as well as the taste of the pastries Giverny had made them. Buttercup yellow and sweet, little flakes fell into their laps as they bit into the soft lemon curd parcels.

'Mmm these are delicious.' Said Roberta

Luigi nodded.

'What time's the ferry?'

'We're making good time, it's at 2. It's 7 now so we've been driving for eight hours. I worked out it's around 15000 km and we've covered 9000 or so.' Said Ricardo.

'Let me do some driving now,' said Luigi. 'You've got to drive all the way back as well.'

'Thanks. I'm just going to give the buffalo some hay and water.'

'They've finally settled down. I hope they have back at the farm too.'

Falling asleep Ricardo thought about his brother, pleased that he'd got him some lemons. Although he had given him ones from the store. He and Giverny had gone to pick them. It had started out as a lovely evening, just the two of them walking up the hill hand in hand under a tangerine sky.

'Do you remember the first time I brought you up here?' he said.

'How could I forget. I think it was where we had our first kiss.'

Ricardo had pulled her to him and kissed her gently. 'I was falling for you then and I've never looked back.'

'Me neither. It seems crazy we've been together for so many years. So much has happened especially lately.'

'I know.'

Reaching the grove, they were shocked to find that the biggest lemon tree looked terrible. Its leaves were brown and curled up as if it was diseased and struggling to survive. And there were no lemons.

'I don't understand.' Ricardo stared up at it. 'I've never seen it like this, do you think it can be dying after all this time?'

'But why now?'

'I have no idea. We'll have to pick some from the other trees.'

Ricardo slept soundly until he was woken by Roberta gently shaking him.

'We're here.'

Huge. The port was filled with travellers rushing to and fro pushing trolleys piled up with trunks. Laughing – in jovial mood – excited to be going on holiday. Once their belongings were stacked in a large pile Ricardo and Luigi left Roberta and Eva in her pram with them while they found someone to help them unload the buffalo.

'Do you think Vincenzo's papers will work?' Luigi looked furtive.

'Not if you look shifty like that. Come on be confident, act normally.'

'*Scusi.*' Ricardo called out to a porter. 'Do you speak Italian?'

'*Si.* What do you need?'

'Help moving them.' He pointed to the buffalo behind him who were beginning to stamp and snort, fed up with being so enclosed.

'Ok I'll be back.'

Ricardo let down the ramp and led the four calves down tying them up to the railings at the bottom.

Luigi did the same with Manuela, coaxing her with some hay; she nuzzled her two calves, while Ricardo led Carlos down he rubbed his hairy head between his horns and talked gently to him.

'You've been nothing but trouble from the word go. Always escaping and turning up somewhere you shouldn't be. I'm going to miss you, boy. I don't suppose Giverny will though. The amount of times she found you in her vegetable garden with her carrots hanging out the side of your mouth.' He remembered his wife's face when she found him the first time and dragged him out back to the field scolding him all the way, while he walked indifferently beside her munching away as if he hadn't a care in the world.

'We are ready now sir.' The porter brought back help and the four of them led the buffalo onto the ship.

'I don't want any trouble from you do you hear?' Ricardo rubbed Carlos under the chin.
The buffalo tried to back away at first when they were led down the ramp and into a new container, but soon went inside when they saw the hay.

'*Grazie.*' Ricardo shook the porters' hands.

'Where are you taking them?'
Ricardo pointed to Luigi.

'He's taking them to the zoo in London.' He handed over the papers to the man who gave them a perfunctory glance.

'Ah. *Ciao.*'

'That was easier than I thought. Let's get Roberta and everything else on now.'

As they got in line at *Contrôle des Passeports* the family in front were speaking French. Roberta admired the woman's long fur coat and elegant shoes made from shiny tan leather with a stitched pattern at the sides. Her husband was handsome wearing a black and white pinstripe suit and holding their daughter's hand. She wore a fur coat a replica of her mother's and a navy-blue beret over her long fair plaits. Roberta felt a stab of jealousy and wished she was going on holiday like them and had a husband to help her bring up her daughter, instead of this whole mess they were running away from. At the counter, a swarthy Frenchman wearing a grey uniform with a peaked cap decorated with a gold leaf didn't smile as he scrutinised their papers. Roberta and Luigi waited anxiously for what seemed an eternity but eventually he waved them through where they said a tearful goodbye to Ricardo. They stood on deck as the ferry got up steam and moved slowly out into the ocean leaving black coal clouds in its wake. Ricardo waved them off and sighed as he got back into the car for the long drive home.

Roberta and Luigi stood next to the pram watching until the sea of fluttering white gloves and hats of the people left behind diminished. Soon, the mainland shrunk as they headed out into the channel and all around them was deep water. The grey clouds hanging heavy above them were reflected in the sea. The wind began to howl bringing a storm, so they went inside for shelter. Roberta had booked a cabin, so she could lie Eva down for a sleep. They were strictly single sex occupancy otherwise Roberta would have shared with her father. Instead she opened the door to find a dumpy woman, with white curls poking out from her bonnet, sitting on a bunk wearing a frown.

'*Buona sera.*' Said Roberta.

'Bon soir.' The woman spoke in a weak voice.

The ship rolled over a particularly large wave and Roberta almost fell over. The woman laid back on the bed panting and holding her stomach. Roberta gently put Eva down and covered her with a blanket before looking out of the porthole at the choppy waves and wondering what life would be like in England. I'm worried about Papa I know he didn't want to leave he feels like he's losing Mama all over again by leaving our home and the farm. Screwing shut her eyes she pictured her parents together before her mother had left. They were always laughing and joking when she was younger.

She had dreamed of having a relationship like theirs and still couldn't forgive her. When she met Nicolai, she thought he was the one. People had warned her, she remembered her mama voicing her doubts; but she hadn't heeded them thinking she could change him, especially once they had children.

A retching noise came from the woman in the next bed before a swamp of vomit filled the floor in the gap between the beds. Roberta felt nauseous herself as the smell assailed her nostrils. Looking at the French woman with a mixture of pity and disgust, she gave her a handkerchief and left, tiptoeing around the pool of sick, with Eva to find Luigi sitting on a bench under a shelter. Leaning against one another they fell into a fitful sleep. When Roberta awoke she could taste salt on her lips from the sea spray, terns wheeled above her and the shrieks of the peevish gulls were stolen by the wind. Standing up she pushed her hair back from her face and was surprised to see they were fast approaching land. The waves relentlessly crashing against the side of the barnacled boat, were splashing overboard onto the wooden planks bleached and weathered by the salty wind. Roberta wondered how the French woman in the cabin was bearing up. The rain slewed sideways into the pewter sea. In the distance, she saw opal white cliffs rising and disappearing into the clouds like impenetrable gates making the link between land and sea. Roberta wondered how the French woman in the cabin was bearing up. The rain slewed sideways into the pewter sea. In the distance, she saw opal white cliffs rising and disappearing into the clouds like impenetrable gates making the link between land and sea. A rat running past her made her jump and wake Eva up. Roberta held her close and shook he father awake.

'Papa, we're almost there.'

Watching silently as the landscape became more distinct they were just able to make out figures on the dock and screeching gulls perched on the rocky outcrops, as the boat turned from its course in the open sea and began hugging the shoreline. Shivering in the cold wind. Their first glimpse of England filled them with trepidation; it looked cold, grey and inhospitable as the boat docked.

'You take Eva and pretend you're alone, in case they stop me because of the buffalo like we agreed.'

'All right, but if there's a problem I'm not going anywhere without you.'

Roberta went and found the pram put Eva in it. The deck of the boat became a flurry of activity. Porters pushed trolleys loaded with trunks and suitcases.

Roberta stood next to theirs and smiled gratefully as a porter asked her if she would like him to transport her things. He stacked them adeptly and she pushed the pram behind him as he merged into the queue disembarking. Waiting with

Eva in the border control area she felt like an outsider. A couple sat opposite her were obviously on their honeymoon oblivious to anyone else as they whispered to one another. Next to her sat a large Spanish woman with several dark-haired children. One was grizzling and another two were arguing over a drink.

'Just share!' The woman sighed and gave Roberta a look of mother to mother making her feel proud to be in the club of parenthood. She smiled back at her and tucked Eva's blanket around her more tightly. Everyone was rushing around, talking in different languages – each person had a purpose – a place to get to. Roberta felt strangely excited and couldn't wait to see where she was going. At last they got through and Roberta waited outside for her brother with the rain stinging her eyes. She saw him first.   He sauntered across the road eyeing up any woman under the age of forty. He stroked his moustache and smiled at one; a sophisticated woman in a knee length beige coat. She frowned as she caught him staring at her legs.

Unabashed he turned his attentions to a lady hailing a taxi sweeping off his hat and giving her his most ingratiating smile before placing her bags in the car. He hasn't changed, laughed Roberta to herself. He was about to enter the border control building when she called out to him.

'Giuseppe!'

Turning his face creased into a grin and he ran over and picked her up in his arms. They were both crying and hugging each other. He looked in the pram.

'So this is my niece?'

Roberta nodded.

'Eva meet your Uncle Giuseppe.'

She began to whimper so Roberta picked her up and gave her to her brother, who cuddled her.

'She's so small and she looks like you. Where's Papa?'

'He's trying to sort out the buffalo.' She spoke in a low voice. 'He's worried that the papers won't stand up to inspection.'

'You stay inside out of the rain. Corrado's gone around the other side with the truck to find him, we'll get them all loaded up and then come and get you. It's so good to see you, we can talk properly once we get back.'

Luigi handed over the papers to the official. There were two lots, one faked by Corrado from the zoo and the others authorised by Vincenzo, the councillor. Ricardo had worked hard that night getting them from him, he hadn't been keen and had to pay over the odds. The official looked them over then said something in English to his colleague who also began reading them.

'Do you speak English?' The first man barked at Luigi. He shook his head. '*Italiano.*'

'That's no good we can't read these papers they're all written in Italian. Stay here.' He said to Luigi.
Luigi's heart was pounding as the first man walked over to another group of officials and showed them the papers. He watched as they shook their heads, and he wondered what to do. He didn't want to jeapordise Roberta and Eva coming to England by being associated with him he'd had a feeling there was going to be a problem and was glad that she'd got off separately. The man walked back towards him looking grim and speaking loudly and slowly.

'We are going to have to detain you for questioning about these animals. You will have to wait until we can find an interpreter.' Luigi looked puzzled, so the man took his arm, led him to a chair, pointed and said loudly 'sit!'
Corrado walked around the corner and saw Luigi being ordered into a seat. Instead of talking to him, he headed up to the desk.

'Excuse me I'm looking for a lost bag for my sister who's just arrived from Italy.'

'Lost luggage is over there.' The man jabbed his thumb towards a desk on the other side of the room.

'*Grazie*, I mean Thank you.' Said Corrado and was about to

walk off when the man stopped him.

'Are you Italian?'

'Yes.'

'Do you think you could read these papers for us it would save us an awful lot of bother?'

'Of course.'

Corrado ignored Luigi as he translated the papers to the two officials.

'Thank you very much,' he said to Corrado 'and could you tell him he's free to go too, he can't speak the lingo.'

Corrado smiled and went over to Luigi speaking swift Italian.

'*Ciao*. Pretend you don't know me and we should be out of here pronto.'

'*Grazie*. I need to get the buffalo though.'

'Right.'

Corrado spoke to the official.

'He says he needs help to get his buffalo off the ship and loaded up.'

'Tell him, if you don't mind that that's not my department and he'll have to find the cargo desk over there.' He pointed in the direction of some doors.

'Thank you. I'll tell him.'

'Walk off in the direction of those doors and wait for me I'll join you in five minutes.'

Luigi shook his hand and walked away clutching his papers relieved to see the red stamps on them authorising the buffalo to be unloaded. Around the corner, Giuseppe was waiting and he flung his arms around his father.

'Papa I'm so sorry for what I did and all the trouble I've caused. Sorry you've had to come here.'
Luigi cried and hugged his son.

'My boy, my boy.'
The rest was plain sailing, even Carlos did as he was told and walked docilely up the ramp into Corrado's truck. It was a tight squeeze with the trunks and pram, passengers and the buffalo. The trunks were strapped onto the roof and the buffalo had their heads poking out like before although they looked less than impressed with the weather and began lowing indignantly, refusing to stop all the way back to their new home.
Once they were unloaded, they kicked up their heels and careered around the paddock relishing the open space.

'They look a bit happier now,' said Luigi. 'That was a close one at the port. Phew! You played it well Corrado. Thank you.'
They watched until the buffalo calmed down and Manuela's calves began suckling.

'So, soon we can make real mozzarella, I can't wait. We've

already got the dairy sorted out for it, as we've been making it from our cow herd but it doesn't taste like the real thing.'

Inside Roberta looked around her new bedroom. Touched to see that they had tried to make it as homely as possible with a cheery fire in the grate and a crib for Eva with tiny sheets and pink blankets. Putting her in there she sat on the bed admiring the diamond work on the patchwork quilt in hues of pink and white. The room was wallpapered with a scheme of tiny pink roses and little blue flowers on a cream background. Giuseppe had transformed the room that Margaret had stayed in to make his sister happy by decorating it and buying bits and pieces. The oak washstand held a new bowl and pitcher decorated with purple pansies. Unpacking their things made her feel better and more at home immediately.

Putting the photograph of her parents next to her bed and checking the baby was sleeping she tiptoed downstairs leaving the door ajar so she would hear when she woke up.

The staircase was crooked so she had to watch her step, but she was pleasantly surprised when she looked out of the window half way down at the view. Despite the greyness of the sky, the landscape looked appealing and reminded her of home more than she expected. Fields of lush grass housing proud oak trees gave way to a river flanked with weeping willows who looked forlorn without their summer leaves.

Rising up behind were hills dotted with sheep and cows. Although she was sad she made up her mind to make the best of it and be strong for her father. She found him drinking coffee in the kitchen.

'You've got a nice place here. How did you find it?' said Luigi.

'When we first came over I found the Osteria in London and we lived above that for a while until Giuseppe got his own place. We always planned to get a farm and we didn't want to be too far from London, so we began looking round here,' said Corrado.

'We were lucky that this place came up just at the right time. The old man that owned it had died and his family wanted a quick sale, so we bought the lot, animals too. Tomorrow we'll show you round properly, you must be exhausted.' Said Giuseppe.

'Glad we're here at last,' said Roberta, 'have you met many people?'

'No, not really, Mrs. Jones, the housekeeper is a treasure though you'll meet her tomorrow.'

'Are there any other Italians?'

'Not here that I've seen, but in London there are. It's like our own community. We'll take you when you've settled in and you can meet our friends.'

'Everyone back home sends their love and one of the trunks is from Ricardo, filled with lemons.'

Corrado's eyes lit up.

'He said to tell you this is going to have to be the last lot as he can't get them across to you anymore, it's too risky. And I'm afraid there's bad news. He went up to pick you some lemons but the big tree is sick,' said Luigi.

'Yes he said that in his letter.' Corrado felt a surge of guilt washing over him.

'Its leaves are curled up and falling off like it's diseased and it's not producing any lemons.'

Corrado hoisted the trunk out into the barn where he stored the lemons and sat down sadly thinking about the tree.

ICE SKATING

LONDON

Margaret woke up alone, as usual, and with the dread of another miserable day crawling away at a snail's pace. Permanently swamped with negativity. After forcing herself to stop seeing Corrado she really missed him. Prior to the trip to Sussex, her days had been shaped by popping into the osteria and chatting, not just to Corrado, but Leonora and Gianni too. Now she felt empty again. Each day of loneliness merged into the next. It had happened gradually like the tide ebbing; her emotions became flotsam and jetsam strewn carelessly by Leslie's rejection of her and her parents' lack of love. The weather was freezing so she'd stopped going out and lay huddled in bed most days not bothering to dress. Margaret took out her journal and wearily turned to a clean page.

30th November 1927

I hate this house. It's nothing more than a beautiful prison. I barely leave my room now as I can't bear to see the servants with their knowing looks. Particularly Mrs Jarvis who walks around with a triumphant look on her face as if she's won a contest between us that

I never wanted to take part in. The others can hardly disguise their pity.

Leslie and I have been married more than six months now and we barely speak. I used to think he detested me but now I think I've worked it out. He obviously regrets marrying me. Perhaps he felt pushed into it by Father. Initially, our marriage seemed to have all the ingredients to work, like vinification needing grapes, sugar, yeast and the right conditions. Leslie seemed to be an intelligent, caring even jovial person. I believed I loved him. However, his serious issues around shoes and sex are the equivalent to a fruit fly blighting the wine and turning it sour making it utterly unpalatable. When we first got together, everyone kept congratulating me that I was marrying a man with money. They said that money makes life better. If you've got money you can make choices. That's simply not true though. In fact, money doesn't make you happy. Ironically, by marrying into money, I unwittingly removed my choices.

I veer between feeling pity for Leslie; now I know about his mother and what he went through during the war. I also feel enraged that he has left me in this place and is getting on with his life. I think he can't bear to speak to me or look at me because he dislikes himself and feels guilty. Maybe he thought he could sustain a marriage and keep up the façade; however, he didn't factor in how damaged he is. Maybe he didn't even realise until he was confronted with me every day. To think I thought we'd have children. I had designs on the room across the hall. I used to go in there when we were first married and plan where I'd put the cot and imagine it full of baby things. Now I feel bitter and wretched. I can't even write anymore. I've got no inspiration. I feel sad, lost and trapped. And the weather isn't helping.

Forcing herself to get up, she dressed. While eating her breakfast, she decided to go for a walk in the snow. The frosty air assailed her cheeks and she pushed her hands deeper into the white fur muffler that hung around her neck, concentrating on staying upright on the icy pavement. Walking briskly, her head began to clear as she headed towards Whitestone Pond following her ears until she found a band playing music and saw a crowd had gathered to ice skate.

As the band upped the tempo, the skaters danced and twirled faster and faster, dizzily scarring the ice with swirling patterns like childish scribbles. Margaret sat tapping her foot on a bench, the cold air escaping from her coral lips. Small clouds sailed across the weak sun which made the ice sparkle. The pond had been frozen solid for a week as it had turned into such a harsh winter. She remembered meeting Corrado here, back at the start of autumn, as she watched a couple skating, admiring their dancing to the band. The woman wore a smile under her crimson hat tied with a white ribbon, a fitted jacket in the same shade and a long black skirt. Holding her tightly in his arms, her partner was gazing at her with such a look of love it made Margaret sigh. Oblivious to the crowd ice skating around them, they threaded their way through with grace and poise, she extended one leg forming a beautiful angular shape. Seeing her reminded Margaret of her old jewellery box; the one she had loved when she was little. It had a key to wind it up and once the tinkly music began a ballerina would twirl with her arms in the air until the music stopped.

Sitting in the snowy scene Margaret felt as if she were in a snow globe trapped forever to be lonely and looking out at a world she could never inhabit and only dream about. Leslie had never looked at her like that with adoration. The only person who had was Corrado. The big bass drum boomed to keep time and the accordion player became more and more frenzied as the band fed off the dancers whirling around them. The trumpeter stood out. Margaret noted that he had an air of panache about him with his slate grey fedora and scarlet cravat at his neck. As he played the final note, the whole band swept their hats from their heads and took a bow so low that their long overcoats brushed the ice.

The cheers and clapping rose to a crescendo, Margaret joined in until a shadow blocked her view. Looking up she was astonished to see Corrado in front of her.

'Hello.' Corrado shouted above the din, sitting down with a huge beam.

'Oh, hello.' Margaret smiled and inside her stomach contorted.

'They smell good.' Corrado pointed to a stall selling roast chestnuts on the other side. 'Would you like to try some?'

As they strolled around the pond the band started up again, and a small boy whizzed past before falling over and laughing as he attempted to get back to his feet. A double decker bus advertising Pears Soap crept past a horse and cart whose owner had paused to enjoy the band for a few minutes. The carnival atmosphere was catching - making Margaret feel carefree. Meeting up with Corrado was like playing tennis and eating strawberries and cream on a sunny afternoon. As the band packed up, the squeals of the skating children followed them as they walked towards Hampstead Heath crunching on chestnuts.

'These are delicious. I wasn't sure, but they do taste as good as they smell.'

Nodding, Margaret buried her cold hands deeper into her fur muff and concentrated on walking.

'That band was capital.' said Margaret. 'I haven't listened to any music for ages.'

'I didn't catch it all but what I heard sounded good.'

'How are you?' Corrado gave Margaret a sideways look.

'I'm very well thank you and yourself?' she replied stiffly.

'I'm a lot better for seeing you.'

Margaret looked at the floor as they turned on to the heath. She wanted to tell him that she'd missed him desperately, but she couldn't, it wasn't fair. He didn't tell her that he'd been going for walks every day for weeks in the hope of bumping into her.

Hampstead Heath was transformed: there were sledges being pushed and pulled, skaters wheeling around the ponds, snowmen being built and snowball fights being won and lost all around them. The trees and plants were heavy with powdery snow and the pathways were covered in crisscrossing different size boot prints. Squeals of joy filled the air as Margaret and Corrado walked to find a quieter spot.

'This is my favourite tree.' Margaret stopped under a majestic old oak.'

'Why this one in particular?' Corrado looked up at it.

'I like to sit here in the summer and read.'

'Seems like a good spot. My favourite trees are the lemon ones back home on the farm. Are you still going to lend me your favourite book?'

'Well that depends on how your bet's going, who's winning at present?'

'I'm still confident I can do it. I'm reading *Great Expectations* now.'

'Ah, that's a good one. I love the beginning. He's a clever man, Dickens, the way he takes the reader from the huge desolate landscape to little Pip, which makes him seem all the smaller and more vulnerable.'

'Yes, his descriptions are beautiful. So, how are things at home?'

Sighing inside, Margaret made up her mind. Once she began talking about Leslie that would be it, he would forge an invisible wedge between them - become the elephant in the room - and her guilt would overpower her again like before when she felt she was drowning in it, wave after wave suffocating her. She pushed these thoughts away until they were shadowy and buried.

'There's not much to say really, except he's always at work so we don't see each other all that often.'

Corrado turned to Margaret and looked her in the eye.

'If you were my wife I wouldn't let you out of my sight.'

'So, what have you been up to?' said Margaret, blushing.

'I've been very busy. Giuseppe's papa and sister and niece have moved to the farm now.'

'Your plan worked then? '

'Yes. It was touch and go for a moment but now they're here settling in and so are the buffalo. Although I don't think any of them are enjoying the cold very much.'

Margaret shivered and buried her hands deeper into her muffler.

'I know it's absolutely freezing.'

'Shall we go somewhere warmer. Would you like a drink?'

'That sounds like a good idea, we could walk up to the Holly Bush. I expect they'll have a good fire?'

They hurried through the door of the large white building to get out of the cold. Corrado went to buy the drinks and Margaret chose a table with two leather armchairs in front of the roaring fire. Pulling out her chair she noticed the scuff marks on the polished, old oak floor from people's boots before sinking gratefully into it. The wooden fireplace was patterned with carvings of vine leaves and she wondered idly how long it had taken the carver to do. On the mantelpiece, one either end, sat two brass candlesticks hidden beneath rivulets of melted wax. She watched Corrado as he chatted easily with the barman. She loved that about him, he was so friendly, in fact all the Italians she had met were. Corrado sat opposite her and handed her a gin and tonic.

'I asked for lemon, but they've run out, although I think I might have one.' Like a conjuror, pulling a rabbit from a hat, he produced the biggest lemon Margaret had ever seen from his coat pocket and put it on the table.

'That's enormous!'

'I know,' said Corrado proudly 'it's from my farm back home. Smell it.' He put the lemon to her nose and she gasped at the strong scent that filled her nostrils. She felt exhilarated it was like the smell of the sun.

'It smells exotic.'

He took out his pen knife and deftly cut a slice before halving it and putting it in her glass.

'Thank you.' She took a sip and smiled. 'That tastes fabulous. I remember you putting some in my drink that night at the club.'

'In my book no drink is complete without a slice of lemon. You picked a good table by the fire, the cold's starting to get to me.'

'Tell me about Giuseppe's family.'

'They lived in the farm across the valley from us. Their mama ran off with another man not that long after my mama passed. Luigi, Giuseppe's father, turned into an old man after that, he's never been the same since.' said Corrado sadly shaking his head.

'Oh dear. What about his sister and niece?'

'Roberta was married to an idiot, but she's got a beautiful baby, Eva. She's such a sunny little thing, always smiling.'

'You said she was married, where's her husband now?' Corrado looked serious and took a sip of his drink as he thought for a moment.

'He died.'

'Oh no, that's awful. How?'

'Can I trust you Margaret?'

She looked a bit taken aback 'Er, yes of course, why?'

'If I tell you something, you must never tell anyone I've told you. You must promise me.'

'I promise.' she said.

Corrado swept his hair back nervously and took another sip of his drink.

'I don't know if I can, you might think badly of me.'

'You're scaring me now, whatever it is it can't be that terrible, can it?'

'All right. As I said we lived near one another and ours was a very tight knit community, a small village where everyone knows everyone else. Roberta married Nicolai, someone we've always known, although not particularly liked. Anyway, Roberta fell in love with him and straight after the wedding she got pregnant. He began to change for the worse. Fascism is something that is growing in Italy, pockets here and there. Mussolini is trying to unify the Italian people.

Nicolai fell in with some others who think like him and they started demanding money from people for protection saying it was for the cause. Obviously, people weren't happy, one friend of ours, Ciro, moved away because they began threatening his family. He tried it with me a few times. The thing is he's got heavies that do his dirty work for him and his brothers, he's the youngest, who look after him. When he and

Roberta married, his mother was so upset about him leaving that instead of getting their own house he decided they would stay with her. Would you like another drink?'

'No thank you.'

'She was jealous of Roberta and made life difficult for her, always taking her son's side even when it came out that he was sleeping with a prostitute.'

'That's dreadful.'

'It gets worse. One day, Roberta confronted him and he hit her, bruised all the side of her face. He didn't care that she was pregnant, and nor did his mother.'

'Poor girl.' said Margaret.

'Yes. And she's so lovely, funny and kind. She's the only one who can keep Giuseppe in check. She's always telling him off, being the older sister, but she absolutely adores him, and he feels the same about her. Which is where things get really bad. Giuseppe came into my osteria one evening, in a terrible state shouting about Nicolai, her husband. I couldn't understand what he was saying and by the time I ran after him, I found him standing over Nicolai in an alleyway. He'd killed him Margaret. They had a fight. He stabbed him with a knife.'

'Oh, my goodness!' Margaret's hand flew to her mouth.

'This is why you can never ever tell anyone I've told you, and definitely not Giuseppe.'

Margaret nodded, reeling.

'So we ran back to the Osteria, cycled back to my house and we left the following day. We had to. Everyone would have suspected Giuseppe but with him not there they had no proof.'

'They must have thought it was a coincidence though you both disappearing like that?'

'Of course. Accusations were thrown left right and centre but our families kept to the same story, saying that we'd already left by the time it happened. One good thing was that everyone had always known I'd wanted to travel, so for a little while things died down. Roberta moved back in with Luigi and had the baby, but then Nicolai's brothers started threatening them. They came home one day and found their dog had been killed.'

'What?'

'Yes. Roberta had had her for over ten years. It was brutal. They slit her throat. It was a message, to tell them that they mean business.'

'So that's why they've come here then?'

'Yes. They managed to get away with the help of my family. I need another drink now, please let me get you one.'

As he went back to the bar Margaret stared around at the pictures on the walls of stern Victorians in various poses, trying to take in what she'd just heard. She couldn't believe all that they'd been through. It made her problems seem trivial by comparison. Shivering, she held her hands out to warm on the fire. Corrado returned with the drinks, chopped some more lemon and took a deep breath.

'Do you think badly of me now?'

'No. You haven't done anything, except help your friend.'

'But I'm an accessory to murder…' he began.

Margaret put her hand on his arm and looked him square in the eye.

'I honestly don't think any differently about you. I do feel sorry for you, for all of you, what you've been through is inconceivable and thank you for confiding in me.'

'I'm so relieved. I haven't told anyone before. What about Giuseppe how do you feel about him?'

Margaret frowned. 'Well, he was obviously enormously provoked, but I just can't imagine him doing a thing like that. Anyway, I'll never tell him I know, so it makes no difference.'

'He's always been a firebrand; people used to say his temper would get him into trouble one day and they were right, but I never ever thought as spectacularly as this.'

'It's not something you could predict, circumstances like that.'

'I'm going to spend Christmas with them, which will be a bit like old times.'

'That's nice.'

'What about you, got any secrets to tell me?' Corrado laughed stopping suddenly as he saw the serious look on her face.

She took a deep breath. 'My husband doesn't love me. And I don't love him either.' she blurted out.

'Do you want to tell me why?'

Margaret took a swig of her drink. 'Yes,' she nodded. 'I think I do. He works with my father and he introduced us. Before I knew what was happening we were engaged. My father wants him to take over the business you see, so he can retire. I can't deny that I was a willing participant. Leslie seemed so charming, everyone kept telling me how lucky I was to have a rich man wanting to marry me. He's quite a bit older than me, in his late thirties and he seemed so mature and agreeable at the beginning. Once we got married the cracks started to show.'

'What happened?'

'Well it's difficult to talk about.' Blushing, she took another sip of her drink. 'The thing is nothing happened.'

Corrado looked puzzled.

Margaret looked at the floor and said in a flat voice.

'He's never…never touched me.' She continued to stare dolefully down at the floor, refusing to meet his eye. 'He's so cold towards me and he has these terrible nightmares from when he was an army officer during the war. He shouts and yells. I was really frightened the first time.

The only time after we were married he was really kind to me and I thought we were at a turning point was one night he came home from work and brought me flowers and was the man he seemed to be before we got married. Then he told me all about his mother dying. I remembered about it when you told me your story, his father threw her down the stairs and she broke her neck. After that I got frightfully confused because I felt sorry for him. But then he completely shut off from me and now we don't even speak really, he's even stopped buying me shoes thank goodness.'

'What do you mean stopped buying shoes?'

'I didn't mention that did I?' She spoke in a flat tone. 'I've got hundreds and hundreds of pairs of shoes, in a strange way that's how he tries to show love, but it's not love. He likes me to wear them, so he can stroke my feet.'

'Oh, I see.' Corrado looked baffled.

'Now, I've been awfully frank with you what do you think of me?'

'I could never think any less of you, Margarita,' he said softly. 'I don't know if you believed me when I told you that I'd fallen for you on the way back from Sussex. I can assure you I have never felt like this in my life before. I've been trying to fight it but it's impossible I have such strong feelings for you, so I don't understand him at all. I just think he's crazy.' He put his hand under her chin, leaned across the table and gently kissed her. Margaret stiffened initially then relaxed into the kiss, enjoying the warmth of his lips after the coldness of her drink. As he kissed her harder she could feel his desire mounting and it was as if all the anticipation of them touching again after that first kiss built into a crescendo inside her. Her lips were on fire, every single nerve in her body responded to the kiss. When he stopped, she felt dizzy and as he took her hand she felt as if she had been electrified.

'What are you going to do?'

'What do you mean?'

'About your husband.'

'Oh. I don't know. What can I do?'

'Leave him.'

'But where would I go?'

'Come and live with me.'

Margaret looked incredulous.

'But we're not married.'

'So?'

'But I thought you were a Catholic?'

'I am. And I'm already spending half my life in confession for coveting another man's wife.' He smiled at her. 'Look since everything that happened with Giuseppe I've got a different outlook on life. It doesn't mean I don't believe in God any more, I just believe things happen for a reason. I love you and you're unhappy in your marriage. Why don't you leave?'

'I can't. What would everyone say, my parents and-'

'Since coming to England and leaving all my family, I've realised you've only got one life. I can't go back to Italy, I might never see them again, but then I could die tomorrow. I want to die knowing I did what I could to be happy. And being with you makes me happy.' He kissed her again.

'I love being with you too, that's all that's kept me going the last few months, but it's hopeless.' A tear trickled down her cheek and Corrado wiped it away.

'Nothing is impossible, don't ever forget that.' Margaret gave him a weak smile.

'I really ought to be getting back.'

'I'll walk you back some of the way.'

As they walked it began to snow again. Lazy pirouetting flakes gave way to swirling flurries that dusted Corrado's black coat and stung their eyes.

 Margaret walked the rest of the way home slowly through the brown slush singing her favourite song, happier than she'd felt since the party and the kiss, especially when she remembered Corrado's parting words to her as he had kissed her goodbye.

'Don't forget. I believe that everything is possible. Let me be here for you, you know where I am. Please don't shut me out anymore.'

ROBERTA

SUSSEX

Incredibly homesick at first, Roberta worried about her father. He seemed to have aged considerably since arriving, although he was delighted to be with Giuseppe again and kept hugging him. She thought she would never get used to being there; however, during the last few weeks, she had slipped into life at the farm more easily than she had expected. They had been teaching their papa English words, making him practice and ask for things at the market. When he first started, he was nervous but slowly becoming more confident. Roberta made a rule that they would all only speak English during the day, to help him and because she wanted Eva to be bi-lingual, although they tended to lapse back in the evenings, whilst relaxing over dinner. Mrs. Jones had taken Roberta under her wing and invited her to a tea party so that she could meet some other mothers and babies. There she made a friend, Sarah, with a little boy, Edward, a similar age to Eva. Mrs. Jones had taken Roberta under her wing and invited her to a tea party so that she could meet some other mothers and babies.

There she made a friend, Sarah, with a little boy, Edward, a similar age to Eva. Pretty in a robust kind of way, strawberry blonde with kind blue eyes, she lived with her husband, David, on a dairy farm down the road, on the outskirts of the village.

Mrs. Jones had taken Roberta under her wing and invited her to a tea party so that she could meet some other mothers and babies. There she made a friend, Sarah, with a little boy, Edward, a similar age to Eva. Pretty in a robust kind of way, strawberry blonde with kind blue eyes, she lived with her husband, David, on a dairy farm down the road, on the outskirts of the village. Overwhelmed at how welcoming the villagers had been Roberta also felt a sense of relief that they no longer had to keep looking over their shoulders like back at home. Even beginning to feel quite happy until the bad news had come from back home.

Home 1927

Dear Corrado,

I can barely write this terrible news, Giverny has passed away. She had been complaining of headaches and Doctor Antonio said it was a blood clot in her brain. We are all beside ourselves. The twins have each other but I am worried about Gabriella. She never smiles anymore; it's hit her the hardest she doesn't talk about it but she's trying to take her Mama's place. She works tirelessly on the farm, keeps up with all her school work and cooks in the Osteria. She acts like a mother to the boys chivvying them along and cooking and cleaning. I can't stop her she doesn't ever speak about Giverny or how she's feeling, I don't know what to do. I miss you Corrado, we all do. Nicolai's family still keep asking where you've gone. They know you are something to do with his murder, I've told them it's impossible, but I think it would make it worse if you came back, although I know you would want to attend the funeral. Things are changing here. Enzo Farnezi went to market in Orvieto the other day and there was a rally for Mussolini's followers. They wore boots and marched through the town collecting outside the Dumo where men shouted through megaphones to encourage everyone to join the fascist regime. The worst thing was people seemed to believe what they were saying - that their way will make Italy a better place. It is a canker infesting our country and I will never submit. Maybe you are better off where you are. God bless you, brother.

Ricardo

ITALY

1927

Three of the four raven coloured horses stood sombrely between the shafts of the carriage, ornately decorated with black and gold plumes and tassels. The front horse on the left pawed the ground with its hoof, raring to go. Wearing a black top hat and suit, the coach driver clicked his tongue and deftly flicked his whip above their adorned heads urging them slowly towards the church. The road was lined with mourners who removed their hats as Gabriella and her brothers held hands and walked beside their father who was weeping silently, heading the procession of followers all dressed in black. The clicking of the horses' hooves on the cobbles broke the silence. As they turned towards the church, the bell tolled, welcoming Giverny on her final journey.

The air in the church was laced with the scent of lilies and Gabriella felt soothed by the singing. Above her stood a marble angel, its wings spread out protectively with a peaceful smile on its face. This comforted Gabriella as did the icon of Mary, dressed in blue as she always was, it had been her mother's favourite colour. Gabriella remembered her fingering her rosary beads and praying to the Virgin. She would be going to heaven to have a wonderful time, reunited with her family who had died. Standing in line behind her father while waiting to kiss her mother lying at the altar in her polished wooden box lined with white silk, Gabriella knew that Mama would look down and keep watch over them so she vowed then to make her proud.

Approaching her mother, she was aware of Ricardo stifling his sobs, her brothers behind her, her aunt and her family behind them. Giverny looked peaceful with her hands folded across her chest and her curls framing her face like a halo. Gabriella bent to kiss her cheek which felt as pale and cold as the stone baptismal font where Giverny had promised her babies to God, never dreaming that not so many years later they would be burying her.

The service was long and beautiful. Hail Mary's swelled through the church filling the rafters like breaking waves. Gabriella held her father's arm throughout, shed no tears and wore a look of grim determination. Afterwards, as they took the steep slope to the graveyard, Gabriella looked up at him.

'I am going to take Mama's place.'
Ricardo hugged her to his chest and stroked her silky black curls before taking her arm and allowing her to lead him down. Trying to hold back the tears. Beside himself with grief and hearing his only daughter speak so solemnly only made

him feel worse.

How am I going to bring up the children without her? Gabriella is almost a woman. This can't be happening to us. Guilia and Abramo had come to stay, but Gabriella had been the one who, in the lead up to today, had talked to the women who came with food as was customary when there is a bereavement. Aware that her father was struggling with the pleasantries of trying to be hospitable to their neighbours, she stepped in constantly reminding him of her mother. He missed Giverny desperately, socialising was her forte. She's so much better than me at this, he thought, I never know what to say. Thankfully, Gabriella's a chip off the old block.

Dimly aware of a sea of black flanking them, Gabriella refused to look up until they reached the gateway guarded by two stone angels twice as tall as her father with praying hands and unseeing eyes. The funeral party entered beneath their outstretched wings and began wending their way through the dead. Past the ornate mausoleum defended by a seraph that housed the important historical figures from the area to where the gravestones rose surrounding them; some crumbling, the stones covered with orange lichen obscuring the loving words once carved into them. Another inscribed with the words 'Sophia aged Six Returned to Heaven'. Others, grey and marble with newly etched names and messages each telling a different story of loss.

Feeling the cloudless blue sky was mocking her, Gabriella wished instead it was grey and cold to match her mood. Near to the stone wall sat a family talking and eating a picnic next to a grave. A father and his two daughters, who fell into a respectful silence as the procession snaked past and Gabriella realised this was a club her family now belonged to. Refusing to let her father see her sorrow, Gabriella only allowed her grief to manifest itself in her diary. Keeping it hidden so her father couldn't find it she poured out her feelings onto the pages.

Dear Ricardo,

I received your letter today. I can't believe Giverny's gone. She was such a wonderful wife and mother. I am so sorry for your loss, all our loss. You are fortunate to have such loving children and that you are a strong family. I miss you all too especially Gabriella. I have written her a separate letter please pass it on to her for me. I am sorry that I can't come home without causing more misery for our family. I am praying for you all. Stay strong brother and God bless you all.

Corrado

Sadness shrouded the farm. Every day they would talk about Giverny and wonder how they were coping back home. Corrado felt an enormous amount of guilt mixed with grief because he was unable to be there for his family. When they had received the news, they had gone to church to pray for their loved ones and to try to make some sort of sense of their loss. Corrado felt a familiar surge of anger, the same when their mama had died. He found himself standing in church, clenching his fists and asking God why? Why his family? So much sadness and cost. He threw himself into working hard at the osteria as it was nearly Christmas and there were lots of parties booked, but he was going back to Sussex for Christmas, needing to be with those who reminded him of home.

SUSSEX

With Christmas fast approaching, Roberta found herself invited to all sorts of events. The first was the Church Bazaar, an annual occasion always held the Saturday afternoon before Christmas, with a special tea for all the village children in the parish hall. Walking in, shyness overtook her. Clutching the tin with her cake in she stood by the wall and looked around her. The hall was very hot and crowded. A long low whitewashed building purposely built, Roberta read on a plaque on the wall, for the village by the villagers after the war. A place where weddings, christenings, wakes and jumble sales were held, the hall was the hub of the community - familiar with all the villagers - knowing them well but Roberta was a stranger as she listened to the mixture of conversations that confused her ears. She longed to be at home hearing her mother tongue instead. Thinking of Giverny made her well up. Suddenly, Mrs. Jones appeared at her side.

'Hello dear. Come through to the kitchen.'

Smiling gratefully and blinking back her tears she followed Mrs. Jones' broad back through the crowd past tables lined up along the walls and into the kitchen to a table full of blue and white china cups and saucers all waiting to be filled by the bustling ladies wearing aprons holding enormous brown tea pots. Another held plates full of slices of cake ready to feed the hungry throng. Roberta handed her tin over.

'I made a panettone, like we do at home at Christmas.' Mrs. Jones cut it into slices and tasted it.

'That's wonderful my dear, thank you. You must give me the recipe.'

Roberta beamed.

'I will. Have you seen Sarah?'

'She was serving the mulled wine earlier over there.'

'I'll go and say hello then.'

Long tables were laid with cloths of different colours and laden with things to buy. The first one Roberta came to had chutneys, jam and lemon curd for sale. Lids made from material with holly leaves and scarlet berries looked like little mob caps all tied up with red ribbon. There were boxes of shortbread, mince pies and Christmas yule logs decorated with snowy icing. Roberta loved lemon curd and toyed with buying some. Then she thought about the way Corrado laced his with liquore al limone and knew it would never match up, so she bought some raspberry jam instead.

Looming at the far end of the hall next to the stage, an enormous tree almost reached the ceiling. Its earthy scent wafted around as people brushed past it while gossiping and buying Christmas presents. Beautifully decorated it looked magical - ablaze with candles - and adorned with silver baubles and red ribbons. The vicar's wife was herding children onto the stage ready to sing. With their rosy cheeks they sang *Away in a Manger* like little angels. The next table was full of toys. Wooden trains and horses sat side by side with teddy bears and a small knitted white mouse with pink ears and nose. Roberta picked it up and underneath was a little rag doll. She had brown eyes and plaits, a tiny embroidered pink rosebud mouth and a forget-me-not-blue bonnet and dress. Roberta fell in love with her straight away and couldn't wait to give it to Eva for Christmas.

LONDON

Dread continually overtook her like a rainstorm she kept trying to outrun. She even dreamt about it. Exhausted from living a lie, the thought of having to spend Christmas day with her parents and Leslie made Margaret queasy. There was no way of getting out of it. So she had gone shopping to take her mind off it. While browsing in *Hats Off*, the shop she had discussed with Arianna at Corrado's party, a shiver of excitement overtook her as she remembered his kisses. He was her guilty pleasure now. The only time she felt happy was when her thoughts turned to him. It was still hopeless though, there was no way they could be together despite what he had said. The book shop caught her eye and she pushed open the door. It was her idea of heaven - a treasure trove - with books lining the walls from floor to ceiling. The man behind the counter was balding with round glasses. He looked up from his book and smiled. 'Can I help you?'

'Good morning. I'm just going to have a wander around if that's all right?'

'Help yourself and let me know if you need anything.'
Perusing the A section Margaret ran her finger across the shelf until she found what she was looking for. It had a green cover and the title *Pride and Prejudice by Jane Austen* embossed on the front. Perfect. She paid for the book and asked to borrow a pen writing an inscription inside.

Dear Corrado
Happy reading
With love
M.

Waiting while the man wrapped it in brown paper for her she decided to go and see Corrado as it had been a couple of days since their heart to heart at the pub.

Steamy, as she opened the door it smelled strongly of coffee and spices from the mulled wine they were serving. He was so pleased to see her, and touched that she'd got him a present, but it was very crowded that day with customers taking a break from their Christmas shopping, coming in laden with bags, that she felt a little in the way.

'I'm sorry we're so busy. If you want to sit down, I'll come and see you when I get a moment.'

It gave her a chance to watch him unobserved, as he served his customers and he and Gianni shared a joke speaking swiftly to one another in Italian. He kept catching her eye and smiling. Every time he tried to come over for a chat more people came in. She'd never known it so packed. In the end as she left he apologised and asked her to come back the following day instead.

'I can't tomorrow I'm visiting my sister, but I'll try and come before Christmas.' said Margaret.

'I'll look forward to it. And thank you again for this' He waved the package at her as a new surge of shoppers pushed past her to get in the door.

Sadly, she returned home, expecting the house to be empty, apart from the servants. Going upstairs to put her new clothes away in the bedroom she found herself rooted in the doorway of her room. Leslie stood in the middle, beside the bed, a huge pile of her shoes in front of him. Gaping boxes strewn across the floor made it look like there had been a robbery in a shoe shop. He slowly turned to Margaret with that look upon his face, the one she'd seen before when she wore the shoes he had bought her and stroked her feet. Looking down she realised his trousers were around his ankles. Pushing past him and trying not to trip over shoes, she dragged a suitcase from the wardrobe and flung clothes into it before marching down the hall and slamming the front door behind her. Shaking, she ran as bile rose in her mouth, the taste mirroring her disgust with her husband. Wrenching the car door open she screeched away stopping around the corner because her tears were blinding her. Turning the engine off she put her head in her hands and wept as she considered what to do. Deciding that going home to her parents was her only option, she fished her handkerchief from her bag, wiped her face, took a deep breath and drove straight there before she could change her mind.

Wondering how they would react as she drove through the familiar gates and pulled up outside, a wave of relief washed over her when she realised that father's car was not there. Determined to be honest and not continue with this whole façade any longer, she was desperately hoping that they would be understanding and support her. Falling into her mother's arms, she cried like the time she had fallen and scraped her knee as a little girl.

'There, there.' Verity, her mother, smoothed her hair.'Sh now and tell me all about it.'
They sat down together and Margaret gulped as she thought about how to begin.

'My marriage is a lie. Leslie's a liar and he doesn't love me.' Her tears flowed freely as she stared beseechingly at her mother, making no effort to wipe them away.

'What do you mean?'

'I mean he's got so many issues. I mean he's…. he's a pervert.' Margaret frowned at the floor.

Her mother looked a little embarrassed.

'Ah, I see. Well as a wife I'm afraid one has to put up with one's husband's bed habits and you never discuss it with anyone, ever.'

'But, I don't think you quite understand Mother we haven't…'

'Enough! I don't want to hear another word, think of all the benefits from getting married. You've got a nice home and a car and you don't have to worry about money, I know he's always buying you clothes and shoes and-'

'Yes, but those things are irrelevant if you don't feel loved. Father loves you, doesn't he? I can tell he does.'

Her mother's lip quivered before she snapped.

'There are things you don't know about your father; things I would never dream of telling you or anyone. When we first married I was naïve and believed he loved me and we would live happily ever after like in a fairy tale.' Stalking to the fireplace she poked the logs, reigniting the flames making them crackle as orange sparks flew up the chimney before standing up with her back to her daughter. Margaret stared at her mother's back, she was a tall angular woman and wore a long grey knitted dress. She turned around and Margaret saw she was upset because her nostrils flared as she tried to rein in the tears threatening to spill from her green eyes, before leaving the room.

Sniffing, Margaret gazed around the familiar room, at the French windows, spattered with rain that led out to the garden. She remembered playing hide and seek with her cousin, Alice, out in the bushes and trees as a child and having no cares. The walls, a shade of pale yellow that glowed on a sunny day, held imposing paintings of landscapes and ancestors - her grandmother, Katherine, stared down at her from above the mantelpiece - she had a strong face with large, liquid brown eyes like a deer. A half smile played on her lips as if she was thinking of a private joke, her auburn hair was piled high on her head with ringlets falling in waves around her pale shoulders as they emerged from a velvet, midnight blue dress. Margaret remembered how she had a knack of making whoever she was talking to feel like the most fortunate person alive. Entering the room her mother sat down by the piano. Her face was pallid as she stared out of the window and began speaking in a strange voice that Margaret had never heard before; a faraway, mesmerising monotone.

'When I married your father, I fell deeply in love with him, I was young and believed he felt the same until the first time,'

Verity bit her lip to stop it trembling, 'the first time I discovered he had slept with another woman.' She laughed mirthlessly. 'He didn't even try to deny it, just made out as if I was the problem. I felt like a carving knife had been plunged through my heart when I found out, stupidly I thought he'd say it was a mistake that wouldn't happen again and that he'd say sorry.' She stared into the dancing fire. 'You and Jeanie were babies then and I thought about my options, we had a blazing row and I told him I wanted to leave and take you two back to my mother's,' she nodded at the painting, 'but he told me not to be so ridiculous and that under no circumstances was I allowed to take you anywhere. And furthermore, if I left without you he would make sure I never saw either of you again.' Verity sniffed and dabbed at her nose with her white lacy handkerchief. 'And he meant it you know, he-'

'But surely he was just angry and when he calmed down...' Margaret trailed off as she found herself defending her father.

'No, he meant it and that actually happened to a friend of mine, Margery, from Shepherd's Bush. It was a frightful situation and because she made such a fuss her husband beat her and threw her out; she ended up with nothing as he told everyone she was an unfit mother. She never saw her children again. We, as women have no rights.'

'Yes we do.' Margaret went and stood next to the window, 'we have the vote thanks to the Suffragettes.'

Verity smiled a cold smile that didn't reach her eyes.

'A paltry number of women do. They just threw us a few crumbs to shut us up.'

'You do though. And you were thrilled at the time. I saw it in your eyes when you told me.'

'Yes. That was then. You still can't vote though, can you? You're not old enough.'

Margaret put her arm on her Mother's shoulder. 'Do you remember the day we went to that rally and heard Mrs Pankhurst speak?'

'I do. Yes, why?'

'Because it became our secret and you believed then that things could change - would change - and they have. It's an unstoppable tide. You said so yourself. Especially since the war when women had to take men's place and do their jobs.'

Verity gave a sardonic smile. 'And look how they repaid women for that. Blamed them for taking their jobs and forced them back into the home. Women who were doctors and saved men's lives working tirelessly throughout the war utterly devalued.'

'But things have to keep moving. I don't believe Emily Davison died in vain. Look at all they went through with hunger strikes and suffering to make people listen. Change did happen, and it will continue to happen. What made you stop believing Mother?'

'The realisation that it is, and always will be, a man's world.'

'I thought Father was forward thinking. He let me go to college. Why would he have done that?'

'Because I persuaded him. You were so bright as a child, constantly asking questions -working things out – that's why I took you to that rally. I saw a bit of myself in you and a bit of my mother. I wanted you to have a different life. One with choices. You aren't the same as your sisters. Take Jean, all she ever wanted to do was get married and have children and there's nothing wrong with that as she's happy. And Win, she's still young and isn't sure what she wants yet. She didn't enjoy studying as much as you. I thought you could do things differently, especially as there is a shortage of men because of the war. Not everyone will be able to get married. However, as you did, you've become your husband's property and must obey him. I can't see it ever changing.' Verity sighed.

'No! I read in the paper last week that they are considering changing the law so that all women over the age of twenty-one can vote. They need us and they are beginning to see our worth.'

'Yes dear, but men are still allowed to beat their wives with a stick, as long as it is no thicker than their thumb. They can sleep with prostitutes and give their wives terrible diseases, they can do whatever they like, they still hold all the cards. The country is run by men who all think alike and look after one another's best interests.'

Startled, they turned as the door opened and Edward walked in kissing first his wife and then Margaret.

'Hello my dear what brings you round at this time of day?' Margaret looked at her feet.

'I'm coming home Father, I can't live with Leslie anymore, I'm sorry.' She stuck her bottom lip out and stared at him waiting for his reaction.

'I see you've had a little lover's tiff, have you?' He laughed and rubbed his moustache. 'The best thing is to make up straight away isn't that right my dear?' He smiled at Verity who gave him a weak smile in return. Margaret looked to her mother for reassurance and was dismayed to receive none as she watched her leave the room complaining of a headache.

'It's not just a tiff Father. He doesn't love me and I don't love him, please can I just come home?'

'Don't be so ridiculous! What would everyone say?' Edward's face began to flush with anger, and his moustache, flecked with grey, bristled. 'It would be scandalous, of course not. I can't believe how ungrateful you are. Leslie's a real catch. There's a shortage of good men thanks to the war you know and there's a lot of women your age who would give their eye-teeth for a husband like him. No Margaret. I don't want to hear another word about it,' he held up his hands. 'Now go home, I'm going to change for dinner.' He walked out of the room without a backward glance.

THE BOLSENA RENAISSANCE
1124AD

'Creeping from her bed fully clothed, Sofia tied a scarf around her hair like a peasant. Once she had silently stuffed the feather bolster in her place she pulled the covers up to disguise her absence. Taking a candle, she stole through the shadows pausing to check her papa's snores were even and regular before scurrying along the corridor and down the grand sweeping staircase past her ancestors watching her from the walls.

The house was asleep; she could hear a low rumble from the room off the kitchen where the cook slept as he snored away. Tiptoeing into the huge kitchen she took a large key from a hook at one end and placed it in the lock of a low wooden door. It creaked as it opened and Sofia held her breath, waiting to see if anyone stirred. Satisfied, she held up her light and began to descend the narrow wooden stairs that led down into the cellar. At the bottom, she gasped as a huge olive-green toad croaked peevishly at her and hopped across her foot to escape the light. Shuddering she thought about

Marco and the last time they had met; he reminded her of a toad with his bulbous eyes and large mouth. She had only agreed to dance with him at the ball because it would have been rude not to. He mistook her assent for fervour which led to him asking her father for her hand in marriage. Sighing she remembered the aggravation it had caused when she refused. She had always hated balls, but just recently even more so as her father seemed to be trying to marry her off.

The candle flickered as the cellar opened out into the first of many rooms which ran under the length of the house. Books with broken spines and old paintings leant languorously against the clay walls. Trunks and chests were housed there full of the past; so many old things left down there to their fate as they gathered dust and mice nibbled at them to make their nests. Entering the next room Sofia felt a pang as she reached the place where her mother's things were kept. Drawn to touch the fading dresses that hung on rails forlorn and forgotten. Leather hat boxes piled up in front of them formed a barrier, so Sofia rested her candle and moved them away taking out one of the dresses. It was dusky pink, like the roses that rambled across the summer house and perfumed the air inside. Burying her face in the cool silk, she inhaled deeply, before angrily throwing it to the floor as she realised time had done its work too efficiently.

Steeling herself she walked through a further two rooms, trying to ignore the scuttling sounds and the spiders' webs that hung like dreary bunting magnified in the candle's shadows and touched her face making her shiver. Finally, she stopped as she came to the largest room, lined floor to ceiling with shelves. This was why she had come. Each shelf held rows of barrels made from dark wood. Her father's obsession was wine making, but lately he had invented a new drink, liquer al limoni, made from lemons that grew up on the hillside. He wasn't happy with the recipe yet and every week would come and taste to see if it was ready or to add more honey to it to sweeten it.

He had always been popular in the area because of this and had once been a gregarious man, the life and soul of the party, who gave the best balls. He was very happy with his family and devoted to them. Until one day, tragedy struck. His wife, Elena, died after drowning in the lake. Heartbroken he retreated into his shell. The only thing that seemed to make him happy now was his hobby of being a vintner. He was also very protective of his two beautiful daughters who looked just like their mother.

Sofia felt a twinge of guilt as she lifted the one closest to her and heaved it on to the floor, moving the two either side closer, to bridge the gap.

"What are you doing?"

Turning wide eyed she saw her younger sister, Alessia, standing in front of her.

"Nothing. Go back to bed." She glared at her.

"No. Not until you tell me what you're up to."

"It's none of your business. Go away." Sofia hissed.

"I could wake Papa up and say I can't find you..."

She smiled sweetly. Sofia wanted to hit her.

Apart from their hair, because Sofia's was covered and Alessia's was mussy, with the imprint of sleep on it, they looked identical. Both girls wore frowns and their cocoa coloured eyes flashed as they stood opposite one another, neither prepared to back down.

"Where are you going with that"' Alessia pointed at the barrel.

"If I tell you, you must promise not to tell anyone." Sofia wavered.

"I promise."

"I'm meeting Dante Sotio."

"I see. But why the barrel"'

"He's taking me to a party and-"

"Ooh can I come too?" Alessia's eyes shone in the candle flame. "Please Sofia. You know how dull it is round here." Sofia sighed.

"Well, I suppose you can help me with this."

Alessia squealed and hugged her sister.

"Thank you."

"Sh. We don't want anyone to hear."

At the end of the cellar, there was a trap door that led out into the garden. Using all their strength, and standing on a rickety old chair, the girls managed to hoist the barrel up outside and join it. Sofia had hidden a cart and some rope in the bushes nearby and they tied it securely and began making their escape.

"That was heavier than I thought. I suppose it's a good thing you're here." Sofia smiled at her sister.

The sky to the west was still holding on to its last rosy slivers of light. With the rising moon as their guide they made their way through the silvery garden past the fountains, the summer house and eventually to the enormous clipped yew hedges that circled the grounds. Slipping through the gate they began to breathe normally again as they took turns to pull.

"Where are we meeting him?"

"By the lake. The party's at Conventina Cove. We're rowing across."

"What's going on with you and Dante?"

Sofia blushed. "Nothing."

"You're lying. I've been watching you you're always sneaking off to meet him."

"We're friends that's all."

Dante was the son of their father's enemy, Count Sotio. They were enemies as a result of an old family feud, although no one could remember how it had come about. They owned juxtaposing land and ignored one another. Sofia and Dante had become friends through meeting at the lake. Sofia loved to paint and often walked down there for inspiration. Dante also enjoyed painting; his other passion was fishing and he began showing off to try to get her to notice him. They were in love and had been meeting secretly when Sofia could sneak out at night.

The party this evening was to celebrate midsummer's eve and as they neared the lake they could see him waiting on the beach next to the rowing boat. Shocked when he first saw Alessia, he was fine once Sofia explained. Helping them both into the boat he pushed off with a crunch as the bottom scraped against the shingle, before jumping in himself and gripping the oars cutting through the water with ease. The moon filled the lake with shimmering diamonds as it rose above them and the only sound was the plash of the oars as they cut through the whispering waves. Alessia sat one end with the barrel and Sofia the other trailing her hand through the cool water.

"I can see the fire", said Alessia, 'who will be there?'

"Look, I might as well tell you now. It's not just an ordinary party, we paint there and dance and tell stories. Do you know Alberto and Milo Sotio, Dante's brothers?" asked Sofia.

"Sort of."

"Well it's their family's private cove leading down from their house. They have a boat house there where we keep all our painting equipment."

"Oh, I see."

"You must keep this a secret," said Dante. "You know your sister and I are forbidden to see one another and if we get caught who knows what will happen. Especially if your papa finds out about the liquer al limoni."

"I promise." Alessia agreed, a feeling of excitement bubbling up inside her, as the boat neared the shore and the sounds of a fiddle player echoed across the ripples on the silvery lake.

"Who's that playing?"

"Adalgiso, from Civita."

Dante's younger brother, Milo, helped her from the boat. She blushed as he took her hand and lead her up towards the fire. The fine volcanic sand held onto the warmth of the day's sun as well as their secrets. Alessia stood behind her sister feeling awkward as she was welcomed by her friends. They sat around the fire as it spat and crackled burning driftwood dragged from the beach. Lemon liquer was poured into goblets and Alessia enjoyed the sweet liquid trickling down her throat. A little way off stood a young man, with long curly hair and a curly moustache, that glowed orange in the firelight. Alessia recognized him as Alberto, the older brother. Oblivious to the party, he studied his easel and daubed paint from the palette he held up flamboyantly like a waiter about to serve a plate of food. The moonlight lit the scene, making Alessia feel she had walked into a magical land. She had never experienced anything like this before. No rules or decorum. People laughing and drinking without a care for manners or stifling propriety.

As the barrel emptied wild dancing began. Figures twirling and writhing around the fire became a blur as the fiddle took control. Alessia watched the small man play with his eyes shut, inextricably bound to his instrument he allowed it to take him over, his bow flying over the strings, until suddenly he stopped exhausted letting out one last mournful note he fell to the floor exhausted, laughing. Loud clapping and cheering echoed around the silent lake and then Alessia noticed each person of the fifteen or so there became serious. Three or four took to an easel and began to paint. The rest sat under the trees and took it in turns reciting poetry to one another and telling stories. Standing back, feeling like an outsider she watched as they all fell into place as naturally as if they were acting in a play.

Silently walking to where Alberto was frowning at his picture, Alessia gasped as the moonlight washed over it. It was the most beautiful thing she had ever seen, despite it being unfinished. The crucifix as she had never seen it before. The background was a deep blue, like the Italian sky. In the centre was a golden halo which shimmered as the light caught it. It was painted with intricate blue and black patterns in the shape of a cross as delicate as embroidery. Moved to tears as she saw Jesus's face, the anguish in His enormous dark eyes made her shudder and the way His lips turned down as if He was about to cry out forced her to turn away and let her tears fall on to the gritty sand between her feet. She felt a hand on her arm.

"Why do you cry?"

"Because He looks so desperate. I've never seen Christ look like that before. He always seems so distant and strong but here you have painted Him as human and vulnerable. I can't bear the look in His eyes, it makes me feel ashamed."

"*Grazie.*" Alberto kissed her on both cheeks suddenly. "You have given me the finest compliment."

Alessia noticed his eyes were glistening.

"This is the most wonderful painting I have ever seen. What inspired you to paint something so different?"

"Bolsena is having a renaissance. We have been meeting for a while now and at first none of our creativity could be released. Until your sister started to bring the liquer and then it happened. We were inspired in a different way than ever we had been before." Alberto smiled at her.

Alessia and Alberto fell in love and he painted a wonderful picture of her, capturing her very essence through his adoration. Both couples continued to meet in secret for some time. One day their fathers met at a wedding where the liquer al limoni was flowing freely. It was as if they both had a revelation. Sofia and Alessia were dumbfounded to find them chatting like old friends with no mention of the feud.

"Life is too short." They heard their father say.

Finally, they were allowed to marry their sweethearts and did so in an extravagant double wedding, talked about for years, but they never told the secrets of the lemon tree. Alessia was the chosen one, the story keeper. She only trusted the stories to one person, her grandson, Romaine, who she instructed to keep the stories alive through the oral tradition, and to ensure he only told one trustworthy person.

"But how will I know who that is Nonna?"

"The tree will show you, just wait and be patient."

'Which is what he did. The lemon liquer recipe, perfected then, has been passed down through the generations and I believe it has special properties. Good things happen to those who drink it. For example, those in the Bolsena Renaissance circle became famous painters and that picture of the crucifix by Alberto is in Spoleto Cathedral above the altar. I have seen it.'

SUSSEX

Finally, Roberta pushed her way through to where Sarah was doing a roaring trade in front of a huge metal saucepan full of ruby red wine filling up glasses. Peering inside, Roberta saw orange cartwheels bobbing around alongside chunks of apple. Inhaling, she smelt cinnamon, cloves and other spices mingling with the scent of the Christmas tree.

'Hello.' Sarah passed her a glass. 'Careful it's hot.'

'Thanks.' Roberta sipped at it. 'It's lovely.'

Suddenly a hush fell as Giuseppe appeared in the doorway and walked over to Roberta. She blushed as the whole room seemed to stop and hold its breath for a moment before the hum of chatter resumed.

'What are you doing here?'

'I thought I'd come and walk you home, it will be dark soon.'

'Is Eva all right?'

'When I left, Papa was asleep in the rocking chair by the fire with her on his lap.'

'Ah, he's so good with her.'

Turning, Roberta noticed another of her new friends, Joan, standing beside her.

'Oh, hello Joan, this is my brother Giuseppe.'

'*Buongiornio* pleased to make your acquaintance.' Giuseppe swept off his hat and bowed at her, then took her hand and kissed it while staring deep into her eyes.

Roberta glared at him as Joan giggled girlishly.

'What?' He held his hands up in mock horror.

'It's fine, really,' said Joan still blushing.

Behind Giuseppe a queue of women stood waiting for introductions, which fortunately Joan quickly took over. Marching away Roberta bumped into Sarah.

'Where are you going?'

'I had to get away from my brother.'

'He's made a bit of a stir, hasn't he?'

'I know. He just can't help himself.'

They were interrupted by the vicar's wife announcing the raffle winners. Roberta won some lavender bath salts and Sarah, a beautiful iced Christmas cake with a snowman on top. Dusk was falling as they left and tiny snowflakes began to fall around them, decorating the hedgerows like icing sugar. Lilac clouds heavy with the promise of more to come shed a strange light across the lanes as they walked home.

'Does it snow in Italy where you come from?' Sarah stopped at the lane leading up to her farm.

'Sometimes.' Roberta nudged Giuseppe. 'Do you remember that time we went on our sledges?'

'Yes, and you fell off and cried.'

'I was only about eight! Sorry, Sarah. It does snow sometimes but not very much and it rarely lasts more than a day or two. In our country there's a saying: *Anno di neve, anno di bene*. It means A snow year, a rich year. Does it snow here a lot?'

'Yes. I think we're in for quite a storm according to my father-in-law. He's a shepherd and they're good at reading the weather. At this rate we'll all be millionaires!'
They all laughed.

'Rightio, see you on Christmas Eve for the party, 'bye.' Waving, Roberta tucked her arm into Giuseppe's as they climbed the hill to the farm.

'I hope it does settle; I love snow.'

'I hope the animals will be all right we might have to bring them in.'

'Mmm, the buffalo won't be very happy. Do you think we should go and put them in the barn?'

'Probably. They've settled in really well, but this could be a step too far, we don't want them to stop giving us milk.'

Flakes began settling on their coats and eyelashes. Enjoying the warmth of Giuseppe's arm around her as they trudged to the field, Roberta looked up at him. As they rarely got the chance to be alone she asked him something that had been bothering her.

'Do you think Corrado's all right?'

'I know he's really cut up about Giverny and feels guilty about not being able to go home.'

'It's so awful just before Christmas too and so unexpected. No one dreamed that all those headaches she was getting would lead up to this.' Roberta sighed. 'And it's so sad for the poor children losing their mother like that when they are still so young.'

'I know.'

'With Corrado, he seemed sad before all this.'

'What do you mean?'

'He just didn't seem himself. He hardly laughs anymore and always looks like he's miles away thinking of something else.'

'Maybe that's because he's in love.'

'In love. Who with?'

'She's called Margaret.'

'What's she like? Does she live in London?'

'She's lovely. I've met her and yes, she lives in London but it's complicated.'

'What do you mean?'

Giuseppe looked a bit shifty.

'She's married.'

She let go of his arm and wheeled round.

'What?'

'I told you it was complicated. She's very unhappy apparently and her husband treats her badly. But for Corrado there's not really any hope.'

'I see. What a shame, he's such a lovely man.'

'I know, but you can't help who you fall for and it seems like he's fallen hard. Don't tell him I told you, will you?'

'Of course not.'

Nothing more was said as they coaxed the buffalo into the barn and bedded them down with fresh hay. Giuseppe scratched Carlos behind the ear and talked softly to him.

'How do you like it here, eh boy?'

Carlos stretched his head asking for more.

'They've settled in well, haven't they?'

'We all have I suppose but I miss home.'

'I know. I think Papa misses it the most, don't you?'

'That's why I'm going to make it a proper family Christmas I can't wait as it's Eva's first one. And I really want to try to make Corrado feel better too.'

Giuseppe smiled at his sister before looking serious.

'I'm sure you will. I've never said face to face that I'm sorry for what I did and that it meant you had to leave, but you know I did it for you don't you? I hate what he did to you and I had to do something.'

'I know. I still find it hard to think about, because whatever he did to me I did love him and he is Eva's father. You should never have done what you did although I know you were looking out for me. I hated you at first. I was so angry and it just made everything fifty times worse, especially after what they did to Mimi.' A tear trickled down her cheek and she looked him straight in the eye. 'I've learnt to forgive you and him and his mother otherwise I couldn't bear it. Every day when I woke up I was unhappy and couldn't be the person I want to be or a proper Mama to little Eva. Now we're here, we have to make the best of it. At least we're still together and safe.'

Giuseppe hugged her to him rubbing his arms up and down her back as they both cried.

'I truly am sorry. And now I'm going to look after my family, please believe me?'

'I know. Come on let's get in the warm.'

Roberta smiled as they went inside rubbing their hands, excited to get by the fire as she saw Papa snoring in the armchair by the hearth with baby Eva asleep in his arms. As she gently picked up the baby Luigi stirred and smiled.

'Did you have a good time?'

'Yes. It was lovely. Thank you for looking after the little one. Was she good?'

'As gold, she didn't miss you at all.'

ITALY

The bar's lights spilled invitingly on to the road outside. Within, the wooden floor was dotted with square tables, each decorated with a small vase of flowers, containing sweet scented dried lavender competing with the smell of tobacco clinging to the air and hovering above the customers' heads like a blue heat haze. Down one side was a long dark wooden bar behind which Gabriella stood polishing glasses for the next day. Behind her were bottles, glasses and a menu written on the wall. The few stragglers were finishing their drinks ready to head home when three men weaved their way in laughing. Gabriella and the two old men in the corner, standing up to leave, stared as the strangers entered.

The man in front was short and sweating, wearing a pale blue shirt, whose buttons appeared to be losing the battle to keep his large stomach contained. Gabriella eyed him warily as she recognised him as one of the fascists who had been in before with one of Nicolai's brothers asking about Corrado. Behind him was a tall thin man with greasy hair and a hook nose, dressed entirely in black giving him a funereal air. The last man wearing a hat stumbled on the step and collided with the table to his left, smashing a jug, pouring water over the table and extinguishing the candle with a splutter and a puff of smoke. He held up his hands, before following his friends who were laughing as they made their way to a table at the back of the small room. Gabriella sniffed as she mopped up the table cloth and swept up the glass before slowly walking over.

'I'm about to close,' she said.

'Ah, are you here all alone? We only want one drink *bella.*' The man in black stroked his droopy black moustache and smiled at her, displaying crumbling yellow teeth.

'Your friend looks like he's had enough.' Gabriella scowled at him.

'I am so sorry please forgive me.' Slurred the culprit, sweeping his hat off in apology and narrowly missing another jug.

'Well it'll have to be quick, I need to close up in a few minutes, what would you like?'

'It's your round,' nodded the tall man across the table to his friend.

'All right, all right.' The fat man turned to Gabriella, 'three large glasses of grappa and one for yourself.' Ignoring the wink he gave her she walked back to the bar. The men watched her with approving glances. Gabriella had turned into a fine young woman with a shapely figure tapered by long slim brown legs. As she leant down to pour the drinks on the table the fat man pinched her on the bottom, making her spill the liquid on the table. Gabriella slammed down the bottle and slapped him round the face.

'Hands off!' Gabriella tossed her ringlets and stalked away leaving him spluttering and his friends laughing and slapping him on the back.

Gabriella walked behind the bar and went outside into the cold to calm down. Her hot temper often got her into trouble. Thinking of her mama as she did every day she blinked back tears. They had decided to keep the osteria open after Corrado had gone, and before Giverny had died Gabriella had been enjoying cooking in there in the evenings and using the skills Uncle Corrado had taught her. It had been a distraction from thinking about everything that was wrong. Although she wasn't looking forward to the Christmas season. She couldn't stand seeing the sadness in her papa's eyes all the time. Standing in the dark, leaning against the door she breathed deeply.

Hearing a noise behind her, she turned to see the fat man from the bar with a red mark on his face.

'What are you doing out here?' He asked with a smile.

'Nothing.'

'A pretty girl like you shouldn't be left all alone like this.' He began to stroke her arm with his fat index finger. Gabriella stiffened and moved her arm away.

He smiled at her again, like a fox surveying a rabbit. 'What's the matter? I'm not going to hurt you. I just want to ask you some questions.'

'My papa will be back soon. He's picking me up.' She tried to move past him to go back inside.

'Wait a minute. You're related to Corrado aren't you? We just want to know where he is and that friend of his.'

'I don't know.' Gabriella bit her lip. 'They moved away.'

'Bit of a coincidence don't you think? At the same time as Nicolai was murdered. You know everyone's saying it was them.'

'I don't know what you're talking about. Now let me pass.' She pushed past him to get back to the safety of the bar, but he roughly grabbed her arm.'

'Not so fast my pretty. You need to tell me what happened that night.'

Furious, she pushed him hard and tried to run inside. The scream that rose in her throat was quelled as his hand was clamped over her mouth and a hairy arm wrapped around her throat, she tried to turn around, but the arms encircling her tightened.

'Not so clever now are you?' I think you need to learn a few manners, young girl like you.' She could smell the grappa on his stale breath as he whispered in her ear. Gabriella wriggled and elbowed him in the belly feeling her arm squash into nothingness. Her dark eyes widened as a glint of metal passed before her eyes. The man held a knife to her cheek, she felt it cold and rigid against her soft skin before he pushed her down onto the hard cobbles below.

'Scream and you won't have such a pretty face much longer.'

Gabriella froze as he stared down at her and started undoing his trousers. Using all her strength she kicked out at him. He laughed as he stood over her.

Whimpering she lay there sobbing as time seemed to stand still willing her father to return or someone to come and save her.

The burning between her legs was agonizing as he roughly pulled up her skirt and plunged himself inside her, making her cry out until he quickly muffled her scream with his hand again. Tasting blood as her teeth cut into her lip, she felt as if her insides were being lacerated as he writhed inside her. His weight engulfed her trapping her face beneath his armpit where the stench of his sweat made her retch, the gravel beneath her dug into her back and broke her skin. Turning her face, she looked into his eyes and saw that they were black as inkwells and filled with hatred and desire. Rolling off her he spat in her face and walked back into the bar.

Rooted to the cold hard floor unable to think or cry listening to her heartbeat hammering and breathed she shook convulsively. Eventually she hauled herself to her feet holding onto the door frame and staggered back into the now deserted bar. Quickly locking all the doors and putting down the blinds she sat down at a table putting her head in her hands. She cried for her mother and father and for Uncle Corrado, who had to go away. She wanted him to come back, he'd always looked after her, she wanted to go back in time to when she was small, or even just to yesterday before all this. The pain inside her welled up in explosions and she ran back outside and vomited.

By the time her father came to collect her she had cleaned herself up and she quickly got in the car.

'Sorry I'm so late. I couldn't stop Andrea going on about his new cows, you know what he's like never stops talking.' Ricardo turned to his daughter.

'Are you all right? How was this evening, many in?'

'A few it was quite quiet really, I'm just really tired and need to get straight to bed.'

'Won't be long now.'

They drove home in silence and Gabriella kissed her father and went straight to bed where she lay under the quilt hugging her teddy and silently weeping as the pain inside and outside overwhelmed her in waves.

LONDON

Fury drove Margaret out of the house, it wasn't until she got into the car that she realised she was soaking wet. Putting her head in her hands she tried to devise a plan although her mind felt thick and woolly. Corrado's face swam into her thoughts and she found herself half smiling and starting the car. Stopping outside the osteria she took a deep breath as her stomach fluttered slightly at the thought of seeing him, although she didn't know what she would tell him. Gianni greeted her with a warm smile and a kiss on both cheeks.

'*Ciao*.'

'Hello Gianni, how are you?'

'I'm very well. Have you come to see Corrado?'

'Yes. Is he around?'

'He's not here, sorry, he's gone away for Christmas down to the farm, he'll be back next week.'

'Oh, I see.' She tried to smile. 'Never mind I'll come back then.' A thought crossed her mind. 'I'm going to stay at my cousins please could you write down the telephone number and give it to Corrado when he gets back?'

'Of course.' He found a piece of paper and wrote the

number on it. 'I hope you have a good Christmas.'

'Thank you, and you. Goodbye.'

Gianni waved as she got back in her car and drove slowly and aimlessly. The Christmas decorations mocked her as they lit up the windows making them look cheery and welcoming. Sighing she thought about Christmas.

What's going to happen now? I can't go home or to my parents'. Gazing out of the windscreen she marvelled at the size of the raindrops, each one landing like an explosion. She drove past a man cycling slowly, resigned to the weather. His long black coat was soaked through and he didn't seem to notice the drips cascading from his cap into his eyes and down the end of his long thin nose. Her eye was caught by a short, plump woman wearing a scarlet cape who stood out in the dreary landscape, waiting at a bus stop with a black umbrella. Mousy hair cut in a bob, a button nose, dotted with freckles above slightly buck teeth. Coming to a halt she recognised her friend, Daphne, from school. Waving at her through the passenger window Margaret motioned for her to get inside.

'Would you like a lift?' Margaret smiled at her friend who was busy shaking her umbrella before getting in.

'Yes please, it's foul out here.'

'Where are you off to?'

'Back to school. I've been to visit Mother, since Father died she gets quite lonely, so I try to go once a week, my sisters go on other days, so she has quite a lot of company.' Daphne put her umbrella in the back and took off her gloves.

'On no. I'm sorry to hear about your father. What happened?'

'The influenza.' Her lip wobbled. 'It was terrible. There was no room in the hospitals, you know so many people have it, so we had to nurse him at home. Mother got it too, but she recovered. I was in quarantine and couldn't go back to school. I've only been back a few weeks.'

'I'm so sorry. I had no idea. I feel awful for not being in touch it's just…' She tailed off.

'It's not your fault. There isn't anything you could have done.'

'No. But I've been so wrapped up in myself. I've not been a very good friend. Do you have to be back by a certain time?'

'No,' said Daphne, 'why?'

'Come for dinner, let me make it up to you. My treat?' Margaret smiled and squeezed her friend's arm.

'Oh, thank you.'

'I know, let's go to Mon Plaisir in Covent Garden, have you been there before?'

Daphne shook her head.

'It's frightfully good to see you Margaret, it's been ages.'

'I know, how's everything at school?'

'The same really, the girls all miss you.'

'Ah, I miss them too and you.'

*

Leslie sat on the side of the bed and stared at the boxes surrounding him before curling into a ball and letting the tears flow as his mother's face whirled around in his mind followed by the look of horror and disgust that Margaret had given him.

I should never have married her. I should have known this would happen. Helter skeltering his thoughts and tears came thick and fast. Staggering to the drinks cabinet and shakily taking out a bottle of whisky he put it to his lips and swigged hard. Gasping he took a breath before gulping down some more. Once the bottle was empty he slumped in the chair and fell asleep.

*

Daphne and Margaret were greeted by the French waiter and ushered to a table covered with a spotless white cloth, a candle and a coral camellia as the centre piece in a miniature glass vase. He handed them the menus with a flourish.

'Thank you', Margaret smiled and arched an eyebrow at Daphne. 'G and T's all round?'

'Yes please.' Daphne laughed, 'this was a fantastic idea, I haven't been out for ages.'

A low hum of chatter filled the room from the other diners around them, most of them couples, eating intimate dinners for two. Scents of chicken and steak cooking wafting from the steamy kitchen and made Daphne's stomach rumble as she gazed around at the walls decorated with mirrors and large pictures advertising Gauloises; a brightly coloured cockerel with tail and legs the colour of peacock feathers held a long white cigarette in his beak and his yellow body was the cigarette packet. She noticed a theme. The large wooden clock was in the shape of a chicken and on the end of the bar stood a crowing silver cockerel on a plinth. A Christmas tree filled the corner draped with silver and gold lametta strands that glistened in the candlelight. Margaret giggled when she noticed that instead of an angel or star at the top there was a cockerel.

'I'm glad I bumped into you today, Daphne, as I really need someone to talk to.'

Beginning to relax, they sipped their drinks, smoked and nattered, Margaret knew Daphne was a real friend, even though they hadn't seen each other for a while it felt like only yesterday. She really wished she's made the effort to keep in touch with her and decided to confide in her about her marriage.

Daphne's mouth became a large O. 'So, what are you going to do?' Daphne squeezed Margaret's arm.

'I don't know,' Margaret shook her head, 'what do you suggest?'

'I have no idea, but, you could come home with me tonight it'll be like old times.'

'I can't bear him, after today, when I think of him he makes my skin crawl. I used to feel sorry for him after he told me what he's been through with his mother dying, and because he's a tortured soul he has nightmares all the time about his friend dying in the war.' Margaret shivered.

'It's awfully sad that you seemed to have the most wonderful life and now this. Why don't you come back to school with me and we'll think up a plan? We'll have to keep an eye out for old Miss Mayfield, she's still as sour as a gooseberry.'

'She never liked us, did she? Always trying to get us into trouble. Do you remember that time we stayed out and she locked the doors, so we couldn't get in and caused all that fuss?'

'Exactly,' said Daphne, 'she hasn't changed.'

Slinking through the gates and into the shadows they walked on tiptoe to stop their heels clicking on the uneven cobbles in the courtyard that was surrounded by the school. A light appeared at one of the windows making them scuttle inside burying their giggles. Safely in Daphne's study, while her friend went to fetch some milk for their cocoa, Margaret looked round the small room and thought back to her own further along the corridor. The thin bed against the wall was covered with a yellow eiderdown, hers had been blue. Next to it on the bedside table was a stack of books and a half-drunk glass of water. Margaret smiled because Daphne always read several books at once where she could only read one at a time pondering on how they were both English teachers but such different people. The sulky fire smoked and sizzled brashly, but barely lit up the brass fender. Daphne's desk was heaped high with marking. Moving to the window Margaret stared out at the overcast black sky devoid of moon and stars, suffocated with dense clouds. Beneath was Daphne's bookshelf brimming with books all piled on top of one another, each fighting its neighbour for shelf space.

As Margaret felt waves of nostalgia creeping up on her, Daphne returned brandishing a bottle of gin and giggling.

'I thought this would be better than milk! Although it'll have to be neat.'

Opening a cupboard, she pulled out two bone china tea cups decorated with miniature violets and poured generous measures into each one.

'Don't think we'll bother with saucers!'

'Thanks. What beautiful cups.' said Margaret.

'They were my Grandmother's. Not sure she'd be too pleased to see us now though. Cheers!'
They both shuddered as the gin burned their throats, then Daphne hiccupped sending them into fits of giggles.

'Sh! I'll get into trouble.'

'Sorry. So how are things with you and John?'

'I broke up with him.'

'Oh, I'm sorry.'

'It's all right. It was my choice, I just got sick of sitting around waiting for him to propose. He kept making excuses about not having enough money and in the end, I decided he isn't worth it.'

'I see. Good for you, why settle for second best?'

'That's what I thought.'

'Daph, what's your favourite book?'

'That's hard. I think either *Jane Eyre* or *Wuthering Heights*.'

'I really miss our book club.'

'It's not the same without you.'

'My favourite was, or maybe still is, I don't know, *Pride and Prejudice*. At least that's what I told Corrado when he asked me.' Margaret sat up in bed her eyes shining as she talked about him. 'He's got a bet on with his friend that he can read all the Dickens books by April. I'm not sure he'll do it though.'

'You sound quite well matched if he likes reading as much as you. Why aren't you sure P&P is your favourite anymore?'

'Because I'm not sure I believe in 'Reader I married him' type endings anymore. When I first married Leslie, I was living in a fairytale world. Then I made a new friend, Caroline, she's moved away now, but she gave me some of her books and they're different – ones written during the fin-de-siècle. You know people had this feeling of hope and that change was coming at the turn of the century, particularly women and they wrote loads of short stories. There's one I love and since being married, can relate to. It's called *The Story of an Hour* by Kate Chopin.

'What's it about?'

'It starts with a woman who is told that her husband has died in an accident by one of his colleagues. He's worried about telling her because she has a weak heart. She cries immediately then goes upstairs to her room to be alone. The tone of the story changes then; as she looks out of the window at the sky she's filled with hope and begins to imagine her new life without her husband. The sky represents her liberty and she says: *"free free free"* as she smells the spring flowers and hears the birds twittering. It is as if the outside is coming in to her room to claim her. She begins to look forward to the summer and rest of the year where before she felt that it stretched endlessly and miserably ahead. In a daze she keeps whispering *"Free! Body and soul free!"* Going downstairs celebrating her new-found freedom, she reaches the hallway, suddenly the door opens, and her husband walks in. He hadn't died. It had all been a mistake. When she sees him standing in the doorway, she falls to the floor. The doctor is called but he says it is too late, she had died of heart disease - 'of the joy that kills.

'That's shocking!' said Daphne.

'I know, but now I know how she feels - trapped forever - bound to Leslie. Do you think I'll ever be free?'

As the grey light of morning began to filter through the gap at the top of the curtains, both girls were fast asleep on the bed and Margaret had a plan.

BONAVENTURA

1222AD

ITALY

'Dr Fidanza, a wealthy man was happily married to Adela, his beautiful wife. She became devoted to Francis of Assisi after he had come to Civita to preach and established a community there. For many years the couple longed for a child and were eventually rewarded. Consequently, when their son, Giovanni, was born he was cherished and adored.

One day he became gravely ill with a mysterious illness that, although he racked his brains, his father could not diagnose and was in despair as his beautiful son was close to death. Adela prayed to Francis to intercede. Prior to this, Giovanni and his best friend, Angelo, were inseparable. They loved to play together outwitting the tiny silver lizards that scuttled up the walls laughing as they caught them and their little claws tickled their hands. Finding his friend seriously ill distressed Angelo so considerably that he implored his mother to help. Swearing him to secrecy she gave him a tiny bottle of *liquer al limoni,* telling him to covertly convince

Giovanni to drink it when they were alone, which he did.

Swiftly, the boy began to recover which was accredited to the intercession of Francis. From that day forwards, Giovanni became known as Bonaventura, meaning good fortune. Angelo told Bonaventura about the power of the lemon syrup donated by his mother. Explaining that he must not reveal this to another soul, this knowledge, combined with gratefulness to his friend, formed an inextricable bond between them. They looked very similar with dark curly hair that framed their faces and were often mistaken for brothers.

Following in his mother's footsteps with his love for Francis, Adela was immensely proud when her son took the vows of the Franciscan order in his early twenties. A beautiful man with an air of serenity about him, people felt a sense of calmness overwhelm them when they were in his presence. The two friends went their separate ways when Bonaventura travelled to Paris to study at the Sorbonne and Angelo stayed at home as his was a close-knit farming family. They wrote to one another while he was away; Angelo enjoyed hearing about his friend's travels and what he was learning. While studying theology, Bonaventura met, and became firm friends with Thomas Aquinas whom he found like-minded.

In time, Bonaventura became Professor of Theology leading to him attaining the role of General Minister of the Order.

Unfortunately, the order was in dreadful moral and organisational crisis; however, Bonaventura found he had a divine given talent for negotiating and solved the order's problems with great skill. He went on to resolve a great many disputes with content on both sides, gaining him a reputation wherever he went. Called back to Rome by Pope Clement he was asked to sail to England as an envoy to arbitrate an important dispute there. Bonaventura prayed before going to bed asking God to give him the answers to resolve the disagreement. That night St Ansano appeared to him in a dream. Waking up, Bonaventura knew what he had to do and quickly returned home to Civita. After visiting his parents, he surprised Angelo, finding him ploughing a field behind a donkey. Hurrying across the furrowed field the friends embraced and Bonaventura explained why he was there.

"I have been chosen by the Pope to go to England and try to free King Henry. His country is in chaos. As a result of the Papacy expecting a huge income from England it has led to a dispute between the church leaders and the King, because he is always asking them for more money. The Earl of Leicester, a man named Simon de Montfort, rebelled against King Henry. After marrying Henry's sister, Eleanor, without permission he fled to France. Earlier this year, he returned and created an army. Marching on London he led a revolt and the King and

Queen are now trapped in the Tower of London. The Archbishop of Canterbury in England has requested that the Pope intervenes to try to restore order."

"So you are going to England?"

"Yes, and I need you to come with me. I was shown a vision in a dream. Sant Ansano told me that you and the lemons are the key. Will you come and be my right-hand man and we need to bring some of the *liquer al limoni* too, although we will be surreptitious about it. I have not forgotten the promise I made you all those years ago."

Angelo agreed and after an arduous journey where waves tossed the ship around like a toy, they arrived in a dismal foggy London. They took a boat on the Thames to the residence of Simon de Montfort. Shivering and damp they were shown into a large room. Grateful for the huge fire they warmed their hands and prayed together in low voices while waiting for their host. After some time, Simon de Montfort, a tall man, greeted them without a smile. Bonaventura introduced Angelo and said, "we have brought you a gift." He handed a flagon to Simon who took it. Removing the cork, he sniffed and stood back surprised. Pouring each of them a goblet, he invited them to sit at the table. The debate raged backwards and forwards for several hours and Bonaventura had to work harder than ever before to persuade de Montfort to agree to release King Henry and Queen Eleanor. Eventually, by the time the bottle was empty a decree had been signed and they took their leave.

"That was amazing. I haven't seen you in action before," said Angelo.

"That wasn't down to me it was the lemons. You know how powerful they are."

From that day onwards, Angelo made a vow to stay by his friend's side and travel with him, clandestinely administering the lemon liquer, when it was necessary, to aid negotiations. Many years later, the Church of Rome was being ripped apart as a result of rivalries and corruption. Again, Bonaventura was summoned to play the part of peace-maker. Unfortunately, at the same time, Angelo's father had become seriously ill, so he rushed home to his family. This had grave consequences because while Bonaventura was in Rome, alone, he was poisoned by an adversary of the Pope and died. Throughout their time together, neither of them ever told a soul and Bonaventura received all the credit. Although he knew he had to keep it a secret, this did not sit well with him as he knew in his heart that he couldn't have done it without his friend and the lemons.'

ALICE AND MARGARET

The clock chimed eleven as the red train crept into the station letting out an ear-splitting shriek. Steam shrouded the WATERLOO sign, wreathing between Margaret and the other passengers waiting on the platform clasping their cases, umbrellas and children's hands. She started as a porter wearing a peaked hat called out behind her.

'Excuse me, coming through.'

Margaret clutched at her hat, as a particularly strong gust of wind threatened to snatch it away while the porter weaved through the crowd wheeling a wooden trolley laden with precariously perched leather trunks and suitcases. A kind man wearing a navy-blue suit, removed his hat, and ushered her in front of him. Smiling gratefully, she hurried along the corridor in search of an empty carriage so she could be alone with her feelings. Finally, she was rewarded, removing her coat she laid it over the coarse material of the seat to stop it scratching her stockings and making her legs itch. Leaning her head against the window she let down her guard and opened her mind to the thoughts she had been parrying. They came with no order like a swarm of gnats - each had to be addressed -

Margaret mentally slapped them away as her anxiety heightened. First, the picture of Leslie amidst her shoes. Pushing this away it was replaced by her mother's face as she described her disappointment in her marriage, followed by her father's face.

Opening her eyes, she took some deep breaths and watched the grey, drab, enclosing walls and rooves of the London buildings give way to verdant fields of lush grass dotted with sheep and broad rivers rushing and cutting through the landscape. Her anxiousness ebbing with the clouds of steam slipping away at each station she thought back to the last time she had been to stay with her cousin Alice in Devon. It had been over a year ago, before she had even met Leslie, how things had changed in such a short time. When she had telephoned Alice, Margaret felt stronger as soon as she heard her voice.

'Margaret, so good to hear from you. How are you?'

'Well, I was wondering if I could come and stay for a while?'

'Of course. Leslie too? Come for Christmas we're having a big party, and the children will love to see you.'

'Um, no. Just me I'm afraid.'

'Oh. All right. We can have a proper catch-up when you get here.'

Picturing her cousin made her smile. Last time she'd seen her she had been standing on the steps with her husband, George, and their three children, waving their guests off after another of their famous parties. Alice looked like a Pre-Raphaelite muse - one of the girls from Margaret's favourite painting - with porcelain skin and titian hair cascading down her back. She thought back to the first time she had set eyes on the picture, in Manchester, she must have been about fifteen. They had gone to visit Aunt Elizabeth, her mother's elder sister, and Alice and her brother, Alistair for a few days. As it was Verity's home city she wanted to show Margaret around and took her to the art gallery. It was a striking building made from light coloured sandstone with thick pillars at the entrance, designed, she read, in the style of Palazzo architecture by Sir Charles Barry. Inside there was an imposing double staircase decorated with busts of Greek and Roman figures. The beauty and height of the ceiling ornamented with frescoes of angels and cherubs in bright colours had made her gasp.

This was when Margaret's interest in Victorian art and literature had been awakened. A day she would never forget after walking into the room that housed the Pre-Raphaelite collection. Initially, she was enchanted by John Everett Millais' painting of 'Ophelia' lying dead in the brook. Margaret loved

Shakespeare and had just finished studying Hamlet, so she knew the story of Ophelia, tragically drowning because she believed herself powerless through living in a society that imposed impossible expectations upon its women. Haunted with sorrow and mesmerised by the beauty of both the muse in her sumptuous gold dress, and the vibrant indigo and ruby colours of the flowers, Margaret thought she had never seen a more stunning picture, until she saw John Waterhouse's 'Hylas and the Nymphs'.

Closing her eyes, she leant back letting the motion of the train soothe her, remembering the story that she had memorised from her art book, and picturing the painting. Hylas, one of Jason's Argonauts, was sent to fetch water from an island they landed on while searching for the Golden Fleece. Finding a pool in the leafy woods, he sits on the bank amidst navy wood anemones and lowers his pitcher into the tranquil water. Before he can lift it out, he finds himself surrounded by exquisite beauty in the form of the water nymphs. With their naked, soft, alabaster skin and long chestnut tresses adorned with yellow flowers, they are mesmeric as they form the centre piece within the setting of the shadowy green water. The moss coloured lily pads crowned with creamy flowers mirror the beauty of the girls as Hylas is spellbound by their loveliness. Contrastingly, he is olive skinned, muscular and handsome wearing a rich peacock blue tunic with a scarlet sash reflecting the girls' inviting red lips. One of the nymphs, enthralled with Hylas' beauty, reaches up to kiss him; the tranquility of the scene belies what is really happening, as the others use trails of water weed as a rope and pull Hylas under the water to his doom.

Her mother had bought her the art book for her sixteenth birthday and it became her prized possession, she loved to leaf through the pages full of prints and read the history of the Pre-Raphaelite Brotherhood and its founders. This led to her discovering Christina Rossetti, sister of Dante, who she became fascinated in, devouring her poetry, and finding out as much information about her as possible. Margaret regarded Rossetti as a forerunner of the women's movement in early Victorian literature, and she was particularly interested in the fact that she had worked with fallen women at St Mary Magdalene House of Charity in Highgate, for more than ten years. She found it inspiring that she cared about the plight of women and in her own writing fought against the patriarchal, hypocritical society she lived in.

Until now, I didn't really understand why I preferred this painting with the nymphs enticing Hylas to enter the water, to Ophelia, she thought. Now I know it's because they have power. Just like Alice. She married a wonderful man in George who adores her and spends his whole life trying to please her. She gained more freedom. She's not imprisoned in the way my mother perceives women and marriage, or in the way that I am. I have no agency. I'm not in charge of my life. Trapped like a fly in a spider's web by Leslie in this marriage and my family's expectations. But not anymore; I'm breaking free. Leaving is the beginning of me taking control. I'm sure Alice will help me, she's one of those people who can always find a solution, but I'm not going back to him whatever anyone says.

There was a car to meet her when she walked out of Honiton Station. Andrew, George's very good looking, younger brother, and renowned bachelor, stood next to the large black Ford and waved before hurrying to kiss her on the cheek and take her case.

'Good journey? Alice knew I was popping into town and asked if I could pick you up.' He opened the car door and Margaret slid inside.

'Yes, thank you. I'm glad the weather's a bit better here, it was absolutely dismal in London.'

'I must say, you're looking as ravishing as ever.'

'Ha ha, you haven't changed. How's your love life? Haven't you got enough poor young women swooning over you at present?'

'Well there's a couple. Can't blame a chap for trying eh?' Laughing and chatting about family and friends they drove away from the town and out into the country. Margaret sat up as they turned up a long, curved drive in the shape of a C, flanked with rhododendrons and camellias - their pink and velvety blooms striking in contrast with the deep green waxy leaves that shone as if each one had been polished. Rounding the corner, she always loved the first sight of the house; it brought back memories of so many happy occasions of tennis and swimming parties in the summer.

'Margaret, darling.' Alice swept down the steps and crushed her cousin in a warm embrace. 'Come in. The children have been dying to see you.'
Buried under a flurry of kisses and hugs from Kitty and Lottie. Jimmy, the eldest, Margaret stood back and smiled.

'Hello. What a welcome. Gosh you've all grown so much, especially you Jim. You look so like your father, peas in a pod.'

'Everyone says that.'

'So how old is everyone now? Shall I try and guess? Jim, I think you must be ten am I right?'

'Nearly. I'm ten in May.'

'Ok you two I'm guessing at eight and seven.'

'Very good.' Said Alice. 'Now how about some tea? I'll ring the bell.'

'Tea would be lovely. Thanks. Right I've brought presents. Hold on a second and I'll get them out.'

Forgetting about Leslie, she listened to the children's chatter and drank her tea.

'Children, you need to get ready for your walk with Nanny. Come on let's give Margaret a minute to catch her breath. Be back shortly.' said Alice.

Sipping her tea and enjoying its heat on her lips Margaret sat back. She felt comfortable as she looked around the large familiar room with its striped claret and cream coloured Chesterfields and matching armchairs. The fire made the room cozy as it danced and crackled in the grate beneath a thick grey marble mantelpiece. The most striking aspect was the photographs that covered each wall. Taking pictures was George's hobby and passion. Happy children smiled down at her from the wall on her right. A proud James, stocky and broad-shouldered with blue eyes and blonde hair, wearing his whites and bowling in his first cricket match. The little girls as bridesmaids; the image of their mother, with tumbling red hair and cat green eyes. The wall opposite showed friends and family having fun at the house over the years. Margaret smiled as she saw a picture of herself and Alice taken at a summer party. The theme had been *A Midsummer Night's Dream*. They both stood at the top of the grand steps that led up to the front door, wearing cream floaty dresses and daisy chains in their hair. This party had been particularly special, as she had been seventeen and had her first taste of Champagne. It had made her all giggly at first and then she'd danced for the rest of the evening to the jazz band that played under the trees in the garden.

Startled she jumped as the door opened and Alice came and sat down beside her.

'So, do you want to talk about it?'

'I've left Leslie and I'm not going back whatever anyone says.'

'I see. What happened?'

Alice looked concerned as Margaret explained the compromising position she had found Leslie in, then her expression turned grave as she described the conversation with her parents.

'So, you see I just can't go back and I didn't know where else to go.'

'I'm glad you came here. We'll have to try to work something out. Do you mind if I tell George?'

'No course not. You two don't have any secrets do you?'

*

Sitting in bed with the covers up to her chin, Margaret began reading another of the new books that Caroline had given her. It was also written during the fin-de-siècle, by an American, and called *The Yellow Wallpaper*. She found herself getting annoyed at the way women were treated. The protagonist didn't even have a name and was utterly patronised by her husband. Flinging the book on the floor she shivered and pulled the cover up around her shoulders. The thick robin-egg blue quilt was comforting as she stared into the orange embers of the dying fire. Deciding to focus on positive things Corrado stole into her thoughts and commandeered them deliciously. She kept him in a treasure chest in her mind under lock and key. The kisses he'd given her she stored away like a squirrel with an acorn and allowed herself intermittently to recall his touch, his scent, his warmth, he was the opposite of Leslie, with his flinty eyes; Corrado's were a soft brown with black eyelashes longer and thicker than any she'd seen before.

I wonder what he's doing at the farm? Even if he had been at the osteria what could he have done? I don't really know him. I know he seems to like me but...it's impossible. Sighing she put him away and returned to her lonely room before curling up and falling into a deep sleep.

The following morning, she woke and shivered. The gap above the curtains lent an icy hue to the room. Hearing squeals from outside she got up, drew back the curtains and laughed as she saw the children playing outside in the snow that had fallen overnight. A snowman was half built and the three of them and George were packing the snow around him to make him fatter. Margaret waved and four snowy gloved hands waved back. Alice knocked on the door and came in with a silver tray bearing a green teapot, matching cup, saucer and milk jug and toast, butter and marmalade.

'How did you sleep?' she said, sitting on the side of the bed.

'Thank you for this,' said Margaret. 'It was a bit hard getting off but the bed's very comfy.'

'Did the children wake you?'

'No. They look like they're having such fun. Sometimes I wish I was a child again with no responsibilities, or decisions to make.'

'I know. I really feel for you with all this Leslie business. We all thought you were so happy.'

'The thing is,' Margaret put down her tea cup. 'It's worse than that, I think I've fallen in love with someone else.'

'Really? Who?'

'Well,' a little smile whispered across her lips. 'We became friends and I used to pop in to his osteria for coffee most days. I've been so lonely since getting married, you know Leslie made me give up my job? And now I feel worthless.'

'Why didn't you tell me what you were going through?' said Alice.

'I don't know. I was embarrassed. I felt a failure, like there must be something wrong with me, that it was my fault I couldn't make Leslie happy. I did try everything I could think of, but I now know that nothing can be done. Leslie's the one with the problem. He's got so many issues. He has nightmares all the time and shouts in his sleep about people dying around him in the war. There was one night when he seemed different, he came home early and treated me like he cared for me and then confided in me that he saw his mother die after she was pushed down the stairs by his father during a blazing row.'

'Oh!' Gasped Alice, 'that's terrible.'

'I know. So, then I felt guilty and, oh I don't know it's all such a terrific mess. It's his coldness I can't bear. Anyway, I was left alone so much and I got incredibly lonely. Corrado invited me to a party and there I met his friends, who are lovely, incidentally, and at the end of the night he walked me back to my car and he kissed me.' Margaret looked down at the quilt realising she had been twisting it between her fingers as she talked.

'I see,' said Alice. 'And then what happened?'

'It was wonderful, but I stopped him and told him I was married. I'd always worn gloves, so he hadn't seen my rings. I drove off and vowed to myself that I wouldn't see him again, but then I got home and realised I'd left my special cigarette case at the party, you know the one they gave me from work. Although I was tremendously embarrassed. I went round to fetch it and apologised. It was awful. He didn't speak to me just handed it back and I scuttled away. Then I went to a jazz club with a friend and he was there. He was so lovely, he said we could just be friends and invited me to go down to the farm in Sussex he owns with his friend, Giuseppe.'

'Did you go?'

'Yes. That evening we had a fabulous meal, he's an amazing chef, and I loved every minute. I woke up in the middle of the night feeling terribly guilty about Leslie and that it was unfair to lead Corrado on. I decided that on the way home I had to tell him we can't keep meeting. When I said it to him he told me that he's in love with me! And the thing is, I think I'm in love with him too.'

'It is all a fearful mess, isn't it?' Alice took the tray and put it on the bedside table. 'So, what are you going to do?'

'I have absolutely no idea at all. Have you got any suggestions?'

'Not right this minute. Like I said I'll speak to George if you don't mind?'

'No. That's perfectly all right.'

'Do you think you want to divorce Leslie?'

'Is that possible?'

'Well, I don't know but it does happen sometimes and as you don't have children together it may be an option. George will know.'

Shouts from outside summoned them to the window where the children proudly showed off their finished snowman sporting a carrot nose, striped blue scarf and battered fedora. They both clapped through the glass and Alice motioned that she was coming outside.

'Why don't you get dressed and come down and spend some time with the children while I speak to George, and after that we're going to have a fun day. George and the children are going to cut down the Christmas tree would you mind helping me decorate it ready for the party tomorrow?'

'No. That would be lovely and it'll take my mind off everything. Thank you.' She smiled gratefully at her cousin who gave her a hug.

'Don't worry sweetie, we'll get this sorted somehow. One

more thing, do your parents and Leslie know you're here and staying for Christmas?'

'Er, no. And I don't want to speak to them because-'

'That's fine. I'll telephone them, you don't have to.'

The call between Alice and Edward was brief, ending with him asking Alice to talk some sense into Margaret. Alice was diplomatic but made no promises. While Margaret played with the children she took her husband aside into his study.

'George, darling I need to speak with you for a moment.'

'What's up?'

'Well I need to talk to you about Margaret, but it's somewhat delicate. She's in rather a predicament.'
Once she had explained the whole story, George sat for a moment thinking.

'So, you're telling me their marriage hasn't been consummated in all this time? They got married in May didn't they?'

'Yes. Margaret categorically assured me that they haven't ever been intimate. George, she's so unhappy and now she's met someone else who says he loves her.'

'Who?'

'An Italian.'

'This Italian chap, how well does she know him?'

'She said they met last September, and he knows she's

married but has fallen for her anyway.'

'Are you sure she wants a divorce? It's all very complex with Leslie being in business with her father, what's his take on all this?'

'He thinks she's just being silly and Verity told her she'd made her bed and has to lie in it. They're refusing to listen to her, but Leslie has some deep underlying problems. It sounds like he's got a foot fetish as all he does is buy her shoes but can't make love to her. I feel so sorry for her. Edward doesn't know any of this of course, or that they don't have a sexual relationship. I'm sure he'd rather not know.'

'Oh dear. Would you mind sending Margaret in, so I can talk to her?'

Taking a deep breath as she opened the study door Margaret was relieved that George greeted her with a smile.

'It sounds like you need some help?'

'I don't know what to do, but I'm not going back to him whatever my parents say.'

'Right. I understand you've met a chap?'

'Yes, Corrado.'

'How well do you know him? What are his intentions to you?'

'He said to me he knows I'm married but he loves me and if I ever decide to leave Leslie he's willing to take it further.'

'And are you sure he is who he says he is?'

'Obviously, I haven't known him all that long, but I have met his friends. And Leonora, who's the girlfriend of Gianni who works for him, confided in me that he's never had a girlfriend since he's been in London, that he seems to be an honourable man and that he never stops talking about me and wishes he could marry me.'

'Right, I see. So, there is a possibility that you could divorce Leslie. You could go down the route of declaring that you haven't consummated your marriage.'

Margaret blushed.

'I'm sorry, Margaret, but I'll be totally frank with you. This way will also be embarrassing for Leslie and he may stand in court and try to deny it.'

'I see. Is there an alternative?'

'There might be but I will have to consider it, and ask some of my colleagues. Leave it with me. You need to think this through very seriously Margaret, because once the wheels are in motion if you believe divorce is the answer there's no going back.'

'I understand.' said Margaret.

'If you do decide that this is what you want, then I will act for you as your lawyer, although I'm under no illusions that this will cause a very large family rift which is something I don't wish to happen but may be unavoidable. You have a think and let me know your decision.'

'Thank you, George.'

'Now,' he smiled, 'there's nothing that can be done this minute, so let's get Christmas started and worry about all this in the new year.'

SUSSEX

The Italians were preparing for the evening. They celebrated on Christmas Eve and Roberta was determined to make it as like home as possible, despite the sadness that hung over them like a shroud because of Giverny's death. Luigi had spent several days carving the nativity stable and whittling the wooden figures. Decorating it with pine cones he made a star for the apex before fixing candles to the tapering sides. Baby Eva blinked at it in delight and held Mary in her little fist waving her around. Roberta was excited as she prepared the Urn of Fate. She had found just what she was looking for at a rummage sale that had been held at the village hall and pounced on it. It was a white soup tureen with a circular handle on the lid and side handles in the shape of the heads of roaring lions. It was crazed in places where slight cracks had begun to form with age and use, reminding her of the ones her mama used on special occasions, like christenings, for the dishes she loved to make. She remembered the urn her mama used with its gilt handles and how excited they used to be waiting for the moment when it was her turn to take one of the packages. Her favourite had been when she had received a tiny tea set for her dolls house; white with miniature pink roses on the teapot, cups and saucers. She couldn't wait to give baby Eva her little dolly. Humming, she began wrapping up the gifts ready to fill it for later that evening.

After Midnight Mass they trundled back to the farm along the silvery moonlit paths through the slippery snow which blanketed everything in an eerie silence. Giuseppe dragged in the *ceppo,* the yule log, from the barn, he had been saving to burn during the festive season and pushed one end into the fire. As it crackled the white walls turned rosy. Luigi lit the candles on the Nativity and dancing shadows flitted across their smiling faces. They drank a toast to friends and family, especially the bereft Hugentobler's, with wine, the colour of the blackberries that stained their fingers and mouths back home and talked about past Christmases. Corrado made his contribution known from the kitchen as his onions and garlic sizzled in a pan with the olive oil he'd brought from London. Although he'd got the best he could, it wasn't a patch on Abramo's which had an earthy smell that made him want to cook all his favourite recipes.

While preparing the mussels and removing their beards the scent of the sea took him back to cooking the lake fish with Gabriella. He remembered the last family Christmas back in

Italy; how the boys kept racing around excitedly, getting in everyone's way while Ricardo laughed and encouraged them. Giverny always loved preparing the Urn of Fate as Roberta had done for them here. And Gabby had been in the kitchen with him, helping with the cooking. What would their Christmas be like this year with a great hole left in it? He prayed for them then and sadly raised his glass in a toast, before his thoughts turned to Margaret.

I wonder what she's doing? Where is she? Will I ever see her again?

After dinner, Roberta proudly presented the urn and watched delightedly as each person took out their presents. Corrado took out a gift and finding it had Giuseppe's name on it put it back. When he found his, he opened it and was delighted to find a new wooden pestle and mortar.

'*Grazie.*' He kissed her on both cheeks

'*Prego.*' Roberta beamed.

Chuckling, Luigi found he'd been given a new tool set to help make Eva more toys and Giuseppe was happy with his new mirror.

'What are you trying to say, eh?'

They all laughed.

'So, any new year's resolutions?'

'I'm going to learn the lingo and get out and about more

next year,' said Luigi.

'You've learnt a lot already Papa. There are so many friendly people here too. It will be good for you to make friends.' said Roberta. 'Since we've been here I've been dying to go and visit London. And see the osteria.'

'I'm sure that can be arranged. 'Said Giuseppe. 'You can come and stay with me. Papa will look after Eva for one day and night and we can show you the sights.'

'Why don't you come to the New Year's Eve party at the Osteria?' asked Corrado.

Her eyes shone. 'Yes please. Would you mind Papa?'

'Of course.' Luigi chucked his sleeping granddaughter under her chin. 'We'll be absolutely fine, won't we little chicken?'

Eva opened her big eyes, yawned and snuffled before falling back to sleep.

DEVON

Margaret had spent the day in her room considering what George had told her. She felt quite sure that she wanted a divorce; but all the implications were swimming around in her mind. In the end, she gave up and went downstairs to join Alice as she watched George dragging the huge pine tree across the snow towards the house, leaving a feathery path in its wake.

'Look at James helping,' said Alice.

The little boy wore a duffle coat with matching hat, red as a robin's breast, and only visible intermittently as it bobbed up and down behind the branches. Getting closer, they saw he wore a grim look of determination as he held on to his branch trying to keep up with his father. The girls walked behind wearing navy blue coats that reached to the top of their boots and were bundled up in scarves and gloves. George leant the tree up on the wall outside and gave it a shake to remove the snow giving the children a powdery shower which made the girls giggle.

'Thank you, son,' said George. 'I don't know what I'd have done without you.'

James grinned from ear to ear.

'Now children come in and have some cocoa by the fire.' Trooping in obediently, they stood in front of the fire as Alice helped them take off their wet things, bustling around them like a mother hen. One of the chairs had been moved to make room for the tree to stand in the corner. Glass ornaments peeped invitingly from a large wooden box.

'Can we help?' Kitty pleaded.

'Well, Margaret and I are going to decorate the tree, darling. You and Lottie can arrange the nativity on the sideboard over there.'

Passing them a small wooden stable with the figures she watched as they happily began placing them inside, chattering to one another.

'What about me?' asked James.

'I still need your help. We've got to go back out and pick holly and ivy for the wreaths and the mantelpiece, come on,' said George.

As they got their coats on, Alice gave her son a hug.

'And when we're done Daddy will lift you up and you can put the star on top. Don't forget the mistletoe.'

'Some of these decorations are quite old, aren't they?'

Margaret asked as she admired a green glass bauble.

'Yes. My mother gave a box to me and one to Alistair when we got married. Some of them were her mothers and maybe Granny's too.'

'Are they spending Christmas together?'

'Yes, Ali will take his brood over for dinner.'

'Do you wish you saw them more?'

'I wish my children knew them better, but Manchester's a long way and we've got all George's family here.'

The pine aroma spiced the room as they fastened crimson bows, silver strings of beads and glistening baubles of rainbow colours to the huge tree.

'So, will I know anyone coming to the party later? I love your parties.'

'It's going to be all hands-on deck. I've invited around forty people and all George's lot are coming too. We're starting early evening, with the carol singers coming.' Glancing over at the girls who were still engrossed with the nativity, she leaned in conspiratorially to Margaret and whispered, 'Father Christmas is going to make an appearance too.'

'How lovely for them, they'll be so excited.'

'I know. Then once they're in bed the rest of the guests should start arriving and we'll serve canapes and champagne, before sitting down for dinner at 8.30. Poor Mrs. Phillips looked like she was going to have a fit when I asked her. I've got her lots of extra help though so she's calmed down a bit thank goodness.'

'It sounds like you've got it all under control, but then you are an old hand. What are you going to wear?'

'George went up to town last week and bought me a new dress as part of my Christmas present, once we've finished the tree I'll show you. What about you? Did you bring anything, or do you need to borrow something?'

'I wasn't really thinking straight when I was packing it was just after I'd found Leslie, so I threw some things in my case and left, so if you don't mind that would be lovely.'

George and James came back with a box full of glossy green holly with scarlet berries, trailing ivy.

'Well done you two, the tree looks splendid, doesn't it James?'

'Can I do the star now?'

'You certainly can.'

George passed the gold star to his son and lifted him up above his head to fasten it on while the little girls danced around his legs excitedly.

'Well children, what do you think?'

'It looks magical Mummy, and we've set up the nativity too, look.'

'Beautiful,' said Alice giving them a hug, 'go and fetch Nanny to show her.'

Once the tree had been admired by everyone, Nanny took the children off to help decorate the rest of the house with the greenery and Alice and Margaret went upstairs to look at dresses. Margaret gasped when she saw Alice's dress. It was cobalt blue silk with silver threads and beads running through it, floor length with a v neck and thin shoulder straps decorated with a floppy bow at the front fashioned from the same material.

'It's so beautiful.' Margaret rubbed the fabric between her finger and thumb. 'And so soft.'

'I know, George chose well didn't he? It's Chanel.'

'You'll look incredible in it with your hair too, are you going to put it up?'

'I don't know yet. Now let's find something for you, come on.'

Margaret followed her into a large walk-in wardrobe bursting with dresses of all different colours and fabrics. Alice riffled through them, picked three out and handed them to Margaret.

'Maybe one of these?'

The one that immediately caught Margaret's eye was a long redcurrant colour, backless with ruffles across the front.

'Can I try this on?'

Alice clapped when she re-entered the room.

'Gorgeous. And wait I've got just the thing to go with it.' She passed Margaret a white fur stole. 'Very Christmassy, perfect for the party. Excellent.'

'Would it be all right if I stay for a bit while all this business gets sorted out?'

'Of course. You can stay as long as you need.'

'Thank you. You and George are very kind.'

Outside, the gardeners were scarlet with the exertion of digging snow from the paths ready for the guests later. Delicious aromas exuded from the kitchen where the staff were cooking an enormous turkey for dinner that evening. Margaret was amazed that Alice always seemed to stay so calm, she never got flustered and took everything in her stride. The house was polished to within an inch of its life and five tables had been laid up with spotless white cloths for the fifty guests. Each table seated ten and Alice asked Margaret if she minded making the decorations for the middle. Margaret was glad to help and have something to do to stop her thinking about the mess her life was in. Putting the red candles in the tall silver candlesticks and placing pine fronds and holly and ivy around them, she wondered what Corrado was doing for Christmas. She pictured him at the farm, imagined him cooking on his Aga.

Lost in her imaginings she pricked her finger on the sharp holly and a deep red spot appeared. Tears sprang to her eyes as she wished she wasn't in Devon but in Sussex with him instead. Sucking her finger and tasting the saltiness of her blood, she gave herself a stiff talking to.

You've got to be prepared that you might never be with Corrado. In the heat of the moment he said he loves you but does he really? You don't properly know each other. Will he really want to be with me if I divorce Leslie? She began to feel giddy as her thoughts whirled around like a Catherine wheel. All I know is that whether I'm with Corrado or not, I can't be with Leslie even if that means I will be alone forever. I must be free.

Feeling shy Margaret watched the guests arrive. Half-hidden behind a door in the large hallway she watched the chandelier tremble in the breeze and the glass beads glisten and play on the walls and the dresses of the ladies as their coats were taken by the maids dressed in black with spotless white aprons. Alice looked like a goddess as she greeted everyone with a kiss. The banisters were wound round with holly and ivy, the red berries glowing in the flickering light from the candles dotted around the walls and tables. Sipping her champagne Margaret thought about Corrado for what seemed like the hundredth time that day before taking a deep breath, fixing her smile and entering the party.

The orchestra began playing *The Holly and the Ivy* which cheered her spirits. Humming away she moved closer to the grand piano and watched the man's fingers caressing the keys. She thought what a beautiful instrument it was, made from ebony and highly polished, so it looked like patent leather. The carol singers appeared at the French doors and were ushered in to stand around the roaring fire and sing. Margaret joined in when they played *In the Bleak Mid-Winter*, her favourite song, because it was by Christina Rossetti, imagining her sitting with pen and paper writing it. After they moved on, the room began to fill up with loud chatter and smoke as old friends caught up and new acquaintances were made. Feeling a hand on her arm Margaret turned to see Stephen, one of George's younger brothers smiling down at her.

'How are you, old girl?'

'Oh, hello. Very well thank you and you?'

He handed her a new glass of champagne.

'Bottoms up!'

They both laughed and as they chatted Margaret found she was enjoying herself. Stephen was very tall and handsome; with blonde floppy hair and grey green eyes like the sea on a January day. Towering over Margaret he twirled her around the floor, she noticed several girls looking on enviously at her. As they danced he confided in Margaret that he had fallen in love with a woman he had met at a party in London. The night passed by in a blur of dancing, bubbly, eating and laughing. Margaret forgot about Corrado until she went to bed. Her thoughts were addled from the Champagne; but, despite this Margaret knew with all her heart that she was going to divorce Leslie, and after that who knew what would happen.

SUSSEX

Corrado cried in bed that night. He cried for his family, for his brother, Gabriella and the twins. And he cried because he felt so lonely. Lying in bed he looked at the photograph of them all smiling. It had been taken by Abramo at the party after the lemon festival. How long ago that seemed now. At that time none of them had any idea that any of this would happen and now Giverny dead! How could she be? She was so vibrant and strong. He had never met another woman like her. Tirelessly working on the farm in her dairy, the one she was so proud of. She had loved her buffalo so much. Incredibly gentle when they were calving, easing the babies out and all the time gently murmuring soothing words to the mothers as they lowed in agony. For the first time, he really let himself go and wept inconsolably as the sense of loss drowned him. A nagging sense of guilt had been troubling him. He pushed the thoughts about the tree from his mind along with the memory of Nonna's face as she sat him on her knee and told him stories. Bubbling rage began building inside him again.

Once he could cry no more he thought of Margaret. Remembering her taste on his lips he wondered if she was sharing a bed with her husband. His fists clenched as he thought of him. He wanted to punch him hard for making her so unhappy. When they had talked about resolutions downstairs he hadn't said his. He didn't dare say it out loud. All he wanted was to hold Margaret, to show her love like a real man not like that idiot she was married to who had no idea, but it was hopeless. He couldn't see how that could ever happen. Exhausted, he sighed and lit a cigarette watching the smoke rise above his head in curls in the dying firelight.

DEVON

Alice and Margaret sipped tea and gossiped in the drawing room while the children were out for a walk. It was another crisp day although the snow had begun to melt and large drips from the icicles decorating the roof slid down the windowpanes blurring the view of the bare trees outside. Staring into the fire, Margaret was enthralled with its heat and the tiny flames flickering at a log, she remembered Corrado lighting the fire at the osteria the first time they met.

I miss him so much. I had no idea then how well we'd get to know each other. Or that Leslie would… Her thoughts tailed off as George entered the room.

'Telephone for you Margaret.'

'Oh. Who is it?' She looked worried expecting her father again.

'I think it might be your Italian chap.'

Margaret's stomach lurched as she walked into the hall and picked up the receiver.

'Hello.'

'Margarita it's Corrado. Did you have a good Christmas?'

'Yes, thank you. Did you?'

'Yes, although very sad as we found out that Giverny, my

brother's wife, has died.'

'Oh no. I'm so sorry.'

'I am telephoning to ask when you are coming back to London as Gianni is holding a party for Leonora's birthday at the osteria on New Year's Eve. She asked me to invite you.'

'Oh, thank you. I don't expect you feel like celebrating though?'

'No, not really but this was organised before, so I don't feel I can let them down.'

'Well, I would love to come. What time?'

'Eight. Oh and Margaret I forgot to say it's a masquerade party. I look forward to seeing you then.'

Replacing the receiver she shivered in anticipation at seeing him again.

Alice clapped in excitement. 'Well then you must stay at our London house and we need to go upstairs and find you something to wear.' Margaret giggled as Alice swept her upstairs and into her dressing room.

'Now, I've got just the thing' She ran her hands across the rails that held a rainbow of silk dresses. 'Wait I've got to find it.' She took down a brown leather hat box with her initials on and opened the clasps. Margaret peered inside to see an eye mask and gasped.

'It's so beautiful.'

Alice passed the mask to her; its filigree pattern was in the shape of delicate butterfly wings fashioned from silver metal and turquoise lace. Its crowning glory was a trio of long curled peacock feathers on one side. While Margaret cooed over the mask and held it up to her eyes with its long white handle, Alice took out a turquoise silk backless dress covered in glass beads and held it up.

'Try this on.'

Margaret twirled around and looked at her reflection.

'It's perfect, how can I ever thank you?'

She looked like a goddess now. Every ruche accentuated her curves. It fell just below the knee and the straps showed off her pale shoulders to perfection.

'What about shoes?'

'I've got shoes for every outfit and occasion.' Margaret grimaced.

'Are you going to go back and get some of your things then?'

'Yes. I hardly brought anything with me. I'm going to go back and ask Leslie to divorce me.'

'Really?' Alice looked worried. 'Are you sure that's a good idea?'

'Until I do, I'll be in limbo. I have to get this sorted out.'

'Well if you've made your mind up, you can stay up at the

house for as long as you need. Come and try it on then we can show them downstairs.'

'You look very nice my dear,' said George. The children came in and the girls flocked round Margaret.

'You look like a princess,' said Kitty.

'You look so pretty Auntie Margaret. Where are you going?' asked Lottie.

'Thank you. I'm going to a party in London tomorrow. Mummy's lent me her dress and mask.'

'But I thought you were staying for our party tomorrow.' Kitty looked crestfallen.

'I was, but now I have to go back to London, but I promise I'll come and visit again soon.'

Once the children were in bed, George invited Margaret in to his study.

'Are you going to speak to Leslie about the divorce?'

'Yes. I am going to ask him if he'll divorce me.'

'I hope that works, but…' he looked doubtful. 'If he does agree, getting the divorce is going to take some time you know. What are you going to do in the meantime?' He coughed and looked uncomfortable. 'I mean do you want to stay at our house in town, or come back here? And what are you going to do for money? We can help you if-'

'No. Thank you, George.' Margaret clasped his hand, 'for

everything. I know I've got myself into this dreadful mess, but I have some money saved up from when I was working and it would be wonderful if I could stay in town and try to sort it all out. It's awfully kind of you otherwise I'd have nowhere to stay.'

The following morning, New Year's Eve dawned bright and sunny melting the remaining snow while George drove them to the station. As the train chugged slowly in, Alice hugged her cousin tightly.

'Do telephone and tell me how everything's going, won't you?

'Of course. And thank you, thank you for everything you've done, both of you. I don't know how I can ever repay you.'
Alice and George waved until the last threads of steam disappeared around the bend. Alice sighed.

'I do hope we've done the right thing, George, letting her go back, and this works out for her.'

'We didn't really have a choice, my dear, she's got no one else. What do you think her parents will do when they find out?'

'I'd like to hope the they'll come round and accept her decision about the divorce, but I don't hold out much hope,' said Alice. 'A scandal like this won't be good for business or their family's social standing.'

'Yes,' George nodded. 'Margaret may find things difficult back in London. She could find she's snubbed by people she thought were her friends.'

'Maybe it will work out with the Italian chap?'

'Yes, I hope so. I just wonder about this Corrado. How is he off for money, does Margaret have any idea?' said George.

'Well, yes I did ask Margaret, although it was awkward doing so I felt like I was prying, but I wanted to make sure he could look after her properly if they end up together. She doesn't seem to really know except she said he told her he brought his inheritance money with him which is what he used to buy the farm he owns in Sussex with his friend. He seems to be doing well.'

'I suppose people will always need to eat and the same goes for the osteria too.'

'Yes, and from what Margaret tells me the Italian community seem very close-knit, they all look after one another and barter with food to sell. Let's hope everything turns out all right.'

'Indeed.'

George kissed Alice on the forehead and put a protective arm around her shoulder as they walked back to the car.

Inside the train Margaret had to share the carriage with a

studious young man with slicked back hair and glasses. He looked up from his book, smiled and nodded owlishly as she sat down and removed her hat, but fortunately for Margaret made no attempt at conversation. She wanted to be alone with her thoughts as she had before on the journey down to Devon, but this time they were so much happier. Relieved to have the carriage to herself when the man got off at Axminster she thought back to Corrado asking her to the party.

He wouldn't have done that if he didn't like me. Or love me even. Remembering back to the evening in Sussex when he had declared his love for her, she couldn't wait to see him.

Taking a cab, she tried to think calmly and asked the driver to wait. Reaching the door of the home she'd shared with Leslie she took a deep breath and opened it. Leslie loomed in the hallway looking dishevelled and wearing a scowl.

'Where the hell have you been?'

'I've come to pick up my things. I'm leaving again.'

'What do you mean you're leaving? Where are you going? You're my wife.'

'Not for much longer.'

Brushing past him she went to her room taking a case and filling it as quickly as she could.

'What do you mean by that? So this is it then? No explanation or-'

'What do you want me to say Leslie? We don't have a marriage. It's just a façade you've never loved me and if I'm honest I've never loved you. I don't know you. You've never let me close enough. We should never have got married. And I would like you to divorce me.'

'Don't be ridiculous. What will everyone say? What about your father? He won't stand for this.'

Leslie tried to stop her packing by standing in the way.

'I don't care. He's made it very clear that he no longer thinks of me as a daughter. Now excuse me.'

Margaret pushed him aside and closed the lid before dragging the case down the hall.

'Goodbye Leslie.'

Slamming the door, she hurried down the steps as the driver got out to help her with her case. Leslie appeared at the door shaking his head at her.

'I refuse to do what you're asking. Definitely not. You haven't heard the last of this you'll see.'

Sinking back in to the car, she gave the driver the address for Alice's house and didn't look back.

ITALY

1641 AD

'Father Raphael's desperation grew at the same rate as his congregation diminished. The disease was spreading like the wildfires that sometimes took over the scrubland when therehad been no rain. It always made him sad to see the golden hills blackened, ravaged and turned into something hellish. He felt like he was in hell. The whole of Civita was under attack. A swarm of mosquitoes had arrived one evening. A winged black cloud moving fast towards the village across the valley. The villagers had no time to consider what was happening until they landed on everyone and everything, biting and sucking blood, infecting anyone they touched. From old to young, they seemed to have no preference and then as suddenly as they arrived they were gone.

The first wave of sickness began swiftly, but Father Raphael's sister, Maria, and her children did not come down with it then. She went around helping those who became so weak they could not stand. They complained of blinding headaches, nausea, diarrohea and aching muscles. The itching was unbearable. The bites became infected. The Malaria was like a wild animal hunting a herd of water buffalo, the weakest were picked off first. A sickly baby died in her arms. Distraught, Maria continued tirelessly helping others, ignoring the stench and the blazing heat until she and her children finally succumbed. Father Raphael gagged as he entered the house that held so many family memories, the stench of excrement and vomit making him reel. The whole family were lying in their beds unable to move, to eat or sleep; his nephew and niece looked grey.

Constantly praying to Sant Bonaventure, Sant Hildebrand and Sant Ansano, he was in despair as his prayers seemed to go unanswered. Still families were dropping like flies and the dead were beginning to pile up. No one would come near the town as they were terrified of becoming infected. Father Raphael finally fell ill too. He felt nausea bubbling inside him as he drifted into a fitful sleep; dreaming of fires, enormous mosquitoes and bodies burning, until he was awoken by someone entering his chamber.

'Who's there?' He called out.

A man stood before him wearing a long brown habit like his own. He smiled down at him.

'Don't be afraid. I am Sant Ansano. Get up and follow me.' He led him out of the town and up the hill to the lemon tree.

'Pick these lemons. Take them back to Civita and squeeze them. Put the juice in the well and all the other water supplies that people use. Mosquitoes lay their eggs in water and soon the larvae will hatch. If that happens it will be the end for your people. Ensure you are not seen and tell no one.'

When he woke, he found himself back in bed, although he couldn't remember getting there. Rubbing his eyes he remembered the visitation during the night. Ignoring his aching muscles, he hurried to the tree with a large sack and picked as many lemons as he could fit in, fervently praying under his breath as he did so. Rushing back, relieved as no sounds came from any of the houses surrounding the square, he squeezed the lemons feverishly and sneaked to the well holding two buckets of lemon juice. Looking left then right and seeing no signs of life he swiftly tipped the contents of one into the well. The other he emptied into the fountain near the church.

Dawn began to break, the sky turned rosy and the sun peeped over the horizon. The tall cypress trees became silhouettes, like sentries looking out, their long shadows striping the tawny hills below them. Father Raphael sighed and praised God for the beautiful vista that he saw every day and as the sun rose higher and flooded the valley with light, hope grew in his heart. From that day onwards, the villagers began recovering. The lemon juice stopped the larvae hatching. It also helped the villagers recover as they drank the well water. Soon the malaria epidemic was over.'

'

ROBERTA

Excited, Roberta looked out of the window as Giuseppe drove her up to London. The snow was melting fast and everything was dripping. She sat up as the buildings became denser and the streets more crowded with buses, cars and trams and noticing that everyone seemed in a hurry as they bustled about their business, cold steam escaping from their lips like smoke.

'Almost there now.' Giuseppe smiled at his sister. 'I hope it's everything you expected. I found it quite a shock at first when we arrived, but I'm used to it now.'

'It's a lot busier than at home or Sussex, but I've always wanted to come and I can't wait to see the sights and meet all your friends tonight at the party.'
He took her to see the changing of the guard where she was enthralled by the uniforms and impassive expressions on the soldier's faces. The vastness of Buckingham Palace overwhelmed her and she could hardly take it in when Giuseppe told her it had seven hundred and seventy-five rooms.

'I've never seen anything like it. And how can one family use that much space?'

'Imagine how much it costs to run? All those servants and heating it. A lot of people feel the royal family are pointless, especially when so many poor people are struggling. We're fortunate but it's very difficult for many others, look.'
He pointed to some beggars asking passers-by for money. Most ignored them but one man in an expensive suit and top hat gave them some loose change.

Next he took her to Covent Garden to the market. Stall holders tried to drown one another out shouting about their wares. A stand selling hats with a girl of a similar age to Roberta caught her eye. She invited them over with a wave and a smile. Captivated by a white silk hat, Roberta wasted no time in trying it on. Close fitting with a low brim that covered her eyebrows it was fashioned from white silk with a large flower entirely made from purple beads on the left- hand side.

'Looks lovely with your dark hair,' said the girl.

'Thank you. It's the most beautiful hat I've ever seen.'

'I'll buy it for you. A late Christmas present.' Giuseppe ignored Roberta's protests. 'Today is your day I want to spoil you.'

'*Grazie mille.*'

Roberta put her arm through his and he led her to a stall selling cured meats and cheeses where a young Italian man spoke excitedly at break neck speed to an older Italian woman. Stopping when he saw Giuseppe he broke into a grin and embraced him.

'*Ciao.*'

'*Ciao. Come stai?*'

'Very good my friend and who is this?'

'My sister I wanted to introduce you. Roberta meet Matthias who sells our cheese and meat from the farm.'

'*Buongiornio.*' Roberta smiled at him.

'*Buongiornio.* I love your hat.' Matthias took her hand and kissed it making her blush.

'I'm just showing her around London as she hasn't been before.' said Giuseppe.

'How are you finding it?' said Matthias.

'Busy and exciting. We've just been to Buckingham Palace, I can't believe how big it is.'

They all laughed.

'Just wanted to check you're coming to the New Year's Eve party for Leonora later?'

'I certainly am. What time?'

'Eight. See you there.'

'*Ciao.* See you later.' Matthias winked at Roberta making her smile as they walked to catch a tram back to Giuseppe's flat to get changed for the party.

THE MASQUERADE PARTY

Getting ready at Alice's house, Margaret thought back to the first party she'd attended at the osteria and wondered who would be there. She had not only missed Corrado, but his friends too. The thought of seeing them all again made her feel like hugging herself with happiness. Opening a box and moving the tissue paper to one side she took out her shoes. The moment she had seen the dress Alice had picked out for her to borrow, she'd known the ones to go with it. Turquoise Mary-Jane's with a small gold buckle on the outside. Brand new and unworn, she put them on and nodded appreciatively, feeling fabulous as she headed to the party. Closing the door of the cab she stood for a moment in the street outside the osteria. Music was drifting out invitingly from inside but she couldn't see through the steamy windows. Shivering at a gust of wind she looked up at the sky noticing there were hardly any stars and the half-moon seemed a long way away. The church clock chimed ten and a pair of young lovers strolled past arm in arm through the pool of lamp light. Across the road a group of revellers were singing loudly, practising Auld Lang Syne for later. Turning a corner, their voices faded, and Margaret steeled herself, putting her mask to her eyes she pushed the door open.

One of her favourite songs was playing as she walked in. Larry Levine crooned:

"Why was I born to love you?"

Candlelight flickered across the five or six couples dancing and the buzz of laughter and chatter became a hushed silence as everyone turned to stare. Margaret stood rooted in the doorway until Leonora, dressed in a long black velvet gown with a cat mask on, disentangled herself from Gianni's arms and ran over to hug her.

'Margaret, it's so good to see you.' Kissing her on both cheeks she dragged her inside. Gianni embraced her and she was just wishing Leonora happy birthday when Corrado came from the kitchen carrying a tray of drinks. In that split second, Margaret noted how handsome he looked wearing a suit and bowtie with an eye mask with black and white squares like a chess board. Almost dropping the tray, he stopped when he saw Margaret before making his way through the pathway created by his friends, ripping off his mask and kissing her on the cheek.

Everyone wanted to talk to her and Corrado looked on proudly as she made friends with Roberta; he had always known they would get along. He nearly burnt the food he was cooking he was so enrapt. This time when he fed Margaret she kissed his fingers.

'It's nearly time.' Giuseppe opened the door and they all spilled out onto the pavement to join the crowd in the street. The bells were beginning to chime as they did the countdown

'5, 4, 3, 2, 1 HAPPY NEW YEAR!'

There was an explosion of clapping and kissing before everyone linked arms with strangers and friends alike and a loud rendition of Auld Lang Syne began. The Italians joined in enthusiastically although none of them knew the words and Corrado and Margaret kissed again and again before they went back inside and she felt enveloped by that feeling that was becoming familiar. Each time he touched her every synapse and every nerve became electrified.

'I'll be right back.' he said.

He came out of the kitchen with a huge cake and they all sang Happy Birthday to Leonora who sat there grinning throughout.

'*Grazie.*'

'Speech.' yelled Giuseppe.

'All right, all right,' she held up her hands. 'I'd like to thank you all for making this such a good party and especially to you Corrado for the cake and all the other food.' She waited for the clapping to subside before adding 'and finally I want to wish you all a *Felice Anno Nuovo,* a Happy New Year.' Loud cheering drowned out the rest of her sentence so she gave up and kissed Gianni.

'Now it's time to eat.' said Corrado.

'What are we having?' asked Margaret.

'*Cotechino,* sausage, and lentils,' said Roberta. 'We always eat them on New Year's Eve they're eaten to signify wealth to come and for good luck, that and the underwear.'

'What do you mean underwear?' Margaret looked a little shocked.

Roberta shrugged nonchalantly.

'In our country, it's traditional to wear red underwear to start the year with good luck.'

'Oh!' said Margaret. 'Even the men?'

'Of course. Everybody.'

Sat between Corrado and Giuseppe, Margaret tucked in to her food with anticipation remembering the feast he'd made her before and she wasn't disappointed. The huge sausage had been cooked for hours and was cut into coin shapes and was served on a lake of lentils that had been braised in a rich tomato sauce. Wanting to pinch herself to ensure she was actually there she listened to the chatter around her, some of it in Italian which she didn't understand and some of it which she did. Giuseppe sat back in his seat holding his stomach.

'*Sono pieno come un uovo.*'

'What does that mean?'

'It means I'm as full as an egg.' He smiled as Margaret laughed out loud.

'I've never heard that before.'

'What does Auld Lang Syne mean?'

'I don't really know, but it originally comes from a poem written in the eighteenth century by Robert Burns. Have you heard of him?'

He shook his head.

'Not many people know the words; there's something about not forgetting your old friends but I don't really know, sorry. Tell me some more Italian sayings?'

'Like the egg one?'

'Yes. And I'll tell you an English proverb.'

'*Guardati dale vipere e dale bisce e dale donne coi baffe.*'

Laughter rang around the room.

'What does that mean?' asked Margaret.

'Beware of snakes and vipers and of women with moustaches.'

Margaret giggled. 'We don't say that, we say things like a stitch in time saves nine, or a bird in the hand is worth two in the bush. Tell me another one.'

'Only if you tell me one after.'

'It's a deal!' They clinked glasses.

'This is a good one for you two lovebirds.' He nodded at Corrado. *'L'amore e come il vino nuovo se e buono invecchiando migloria ma se e gram ova in malora.* Love is like new wine if it's good it will get better as it ages if it's not it will go bad. I'm sure yours will get better. Your turn.'

'This one probably wouldn't work for Italians. We say I'm feeling under the weather when we're feeling ill because normally our weather is so rubbish. If you said it, it would have quite a different meaning, maybe that you're feeling well. Actually, it comes from when back in the olden days on sailing ships, the number of sailors who got sick was often more than the space allotted on the ship's logbook to record their names. When this happened, the extra names were usually written in the column used to write in the weather conditions. So there you are! Margaret smiled. 'Yours are much funnier, I need to learn Italian.'
Giggling she tried to repeat the words that Giuseppe taught her but gave up.

'Last one now',' he said. *'Anni, amori e biccheri di vino, nun se contano mai!* Years, lovers and glasses of wine, these things must not be counted.'

'That's my favourite one so far.' Sinking back into her chair and sipping her drink she couldn't stop grinning as she looked around at the others. Roberta and Matthias were deep in conversation making Giuseppe look on proudly as it had been his aim to play cupid.

Eventually, Corrado asked her if he could walk her back.

'Where are you staying?'

'At my cousin, Alice's, townhouse in Islington.'

He helped her into her coat and held her hand as they walked slowly through the dark streets. A chill wind gusted around them and when she shivered Corrado put his arm around her.

'So, have you decided what you are going to do about your husband?' Corrado asked.

'I don't know yet. I need some time to think.'

'Can I see you on Tuesday? I have to go back to the farm for a couple of days but I'll be free then?'

'That would be lovely. Do you want to come here and we can decide what to do?'

'I'll come at 11 o'clock.'

Lingering in the shadows they lost track of time kissing and whispering until the milk cart trundled along the road and the birds began making little trills from the trees in the square surrounded by black railings opposite the house. After a final kiss Margaret watched from the steps as he strode away, turning once to blow her one more.

*

Tuesday seemed to take forever to come as Corrado waited impatiently to execute his plan. He had decided to surprise Margaret and go to see her earlier than they had arranged and take all the ingredients for a delicious breakfast. He packed things up in the kitchen of the osteria.

'*Buongiornio.*' said Gianni. 'What are you up to?'

'I'm going to make Margaret breakfast.'

Turning the corner into her road, Corrado stopped short as if he had been shot. A man in an expensive pinstriped suit was walking out of the door. Margaret stood in the doorway in a cream silk dressing gown and he kissed her on the cheek and hugged her. They were both laughing and as he descended the steps he waved and she blew him a kiss. The door closed and Corrado stood behind a tree his heart pounding clenching his fists.

She looked at me like that when I left her here after the party. Was she just playing me? How could she? But why do that? Why would she pretend to care about me? I'm such a fool. Of course she's got other men interested in her. She's rich and beautiful and English.

Stomping back to his van he threw the bag holding the ingredients into the back, swearing as he heard the eggs crack, and got behind the wheel. The doubts he had been compressing surfaced like ripples on a lake. He hit the steering wheel with the palm of his hand.

Deep down I knew it would never work. We come from different worlds, different cultures and she's still married. That's it. I'm having nothing more to do with her or any woman. How can I have been so stupid to believe she was in love with me?

Margaret went back inside excited about seeing Corrado. It had been lovely to catch up with Stephen, George's brother, who had come up to town on business and stayed at the house. Over dinner he had asked her advice about how to propose to the girl he wanted to marry. Waiting for Corrado to come, Margaret kept reliving the party and how he had kissed her. Determination to free herself from her marriage was growing continually as she tried to devise a way. Doubts began to niggle her like an annoying itch on her back that she couldn't reach as the time for Corrado to call came and went. Maybe he's just been held up she told herself and tried to pass the time by reading her book. Swimming in front of her she couldn't take the words in. Eventually she decided to go to the osteria and try to find out what had happened. Panic set in as she sat in the back of the cab imagining Corrado had maybe had an accident or was ill or…her mind raced. Relieved to be there, she quickly paid the cab driver and opened the door to the Osteria, surprised when Gianni greeted her with a stony look.

'Hello. I'm looking for Corrado.'

'He's gone to Sussex.'

'Oh.' Margaret fiddled with her glove. 'He was supposed to be meeting me today and he didn't come.'

'I don't know anything about that. He left earlier.'

'Did he say when he would be back?'

'No. he said he could be there for a while as he needs a break.'

'I see.' Margaret's eyes turned glassy as she walked away. I don't understand. Why has he gone so suddenly and why was Gianni so beastly, he didn't smile once. What could have happened to change his mind? He told me he loved me. Was he lying when he looked at me like that? He told me he loved me and I got carried away and believed him. I thought he felt the same as me. I've been such an idiot. Her face flushed. Why would he want me and all my problems? I'm no good to him or anyone. Damn you Leslie. I hate you. Damn everything. She dissolved into tears.

ITALY

Inside they were hurting, but the family threw themselves into carrying on for one another. The twins seemed more self-sufficient as they had each other but it was Gabriella that worried Ricardo the most. Showing such resilience and strength, she reminded him of Giverny every day. Initially she was still his little girl and he felt close to her and though he couldn't put his finger on when this changed she seemed to be building barriers. Imperceptibly, like the smallest of the Russian dolls she used to love so much, she began hiding beneath layer after layer. Where once she had beautiful nails like little white almonds, now they were ragged and stumpy where she was always worrying away at them. Refusing to talk about her feelings she never smiled or laughed anymore seeming to have the weight of the world on her young shoulders. Most noticeable was the way she constantly clutched the rosary beads that had belonged to her mother and whispered prayers under her breath. He worried that she was doing too much and had suggested shutting the osteria, but she wouldn't hear of it.

'I'm determined that one day Uncle Corrado will come back and I want him to see that it's still here and we've taken over from him.'

Ricardo smiled and hugged her, but her body turned wooden, so he let her go. Keeping his doubts to himself he decided that it was probably best for her to keep busy rather than dwelling on her sadness. Cooking constantly after school and at the weekends she had come into her own. Immensely proud of her, he beamed when her dishes were met with compliments. Isabella continued to run the dairy; Ricardo didn't know how he would cope without her. At night was the only time he let his guard down. During the day, he kept up a façade of normality, but once he was alone he felt like a clown who had removed his greasepaint and sobbed soundlessly into his pillow because of the cavernous space beside him.

PART THREE

THREE MONTHS LATER
ITALY 1928

Tiny slivers of pink light burnished the sky as the birds began producing a few warbles, clearing their throats ready for their morning choir practice. Gabriella moved silently round her bedroom putting her last few belongings into the bag, leaving the letter for her father on the bed that she wished could say more. Longing to tell him about the baby she wanted to feel his strong arms around her telling her everything would be all right. Agonising for hours about what to write she was unhappy with the result as she knew it sounded so cold and matter of fact but this was the only way.

Dear Papa

Please forgive me, I am leaving to become a sister at l'Abbazia di Nostra Signora. I am sorry for not telling you, please don't try and stop me or come and see me. I have been praying constantly and believe that this is God's plan for my life and I need time alone to contemplate.
All my love

Gabriella xxx

Desperate. She hoped that he would accept it as she had been taught by the nuns at the village school and he had seen her continually clutching her beads and praying. Finally, she packed her diary and the family photograph of the five of them. Looking round the room, memories of her mother and grandmother flooded her mind, of them kissing her goodnight and tucking her in with Bobo her teddy bear. His glassy eyes glinted in the light and at the last minute she stuffed him in the top of the bag and slipped out of the door. Creeping downstairs she missed out the creaky step and tiptoed through the kitchen. Nero wagged his tail sleepily as she patted his smooth coat.

'I'm going away, you be good and look after Papa and the boys.' A sob formed in her throat as she shouldered her bag and soundlessly lifted the catch on the heavy wooden door closing it behind her before stealing swiftly down the path and up the hill behind the farm. The grass was bathed in a pink glow and the hills above were shrouded in a muffling mist as she crossed a field and a buffalo loomed in front of her. Gabriella stroked its shaggy neck as it continued grazing. Further up her pony, Belleza, whinnied as she trudged through the wet grass which polished her boots. Gabriella offered her some grass and breathed in her sweet scent. Stroking her velvety nose, she kissed her, she couldn't even say goodbye. Too many memories of glorious rides across these hills. She used to tell Belleza everything all her secrets and dreams, but not anymore. Two rabbits nibbling the dewy grass scampered away as Gabriella walked on through the field and disappeared into the haze. The birds were taking part in the dawn chorus; however, Gabriella was oblivious, blinded by her tears she prayed.

'Please God and Our Lady help me. I'm sorry for leaving but there was no other way the shame would kill Papa.'

Eventually, she arrived at the lemon tree and touched its bark, remembering what a wonderful day she'd had, lemon picking with Corrado before everything went wrong. Its leaves were ragged and crispy, she was shocked at how dead it looked. She stroked the tree and spoke to it.

'I wish I could go back. I want to be small again and still have my family. What has happened to us? You look like you're dying, just like everybody else.'

The tree sighed in the breeze as Gabriella leant her head against it before taking a deep breath and heading off to the Abbey in the distance nestling at the bottom of the hill underneath the lemon grove. She remembered from her history lessons the sisters saying it dated back to Roman times when it had been a prison. Taking a deep breath, she propelled herself forwards until she reached its circular walls and sat down outside the high wrought iron gates, trying to summon the courage to step inside. Her stomach churned, she felt as if she would vomit at any moment, gripping the round black handle, she turned it and entered a courtyard where the high stone walls were smothered in honeysuckle and jasmine.

Brushing past a large rosemary bush, she shuddered as the smell reminded her of cooking in the *osteria*. The scent followed her as she walked past beautifully manicured rose beds milk white buds and peachy blooms all bathed in the early morning sunlight. A blackbird chirruped revelling in the new day. The beauty of the hidden garden lifted Gabriella's spirits as she went up the stone steps that had been shaped and worn through the centuries. Reaching the thick oak panelled door covered in black studs she knocked. A young nun wearing a black habit with a kindly face and piercing brown eyes answered the door. Smiling at Gabriella she ushered her inside. In the dark corridor, the perfume from the flowers collided with the scent of history.

'If you could wait here, I will speak to the *Badessa*.' Gulping she nodded, blinking back tears from her big brown eyes. Tossing her head making her ringlets quiver she spoke sternly to herself.

'Pull yourself together, you have to do this.'

The walls inside were made from the same dark wood as the outer door, decorated with carvings and candle sconces. At the end stood a statue of the Virgin Mary cradling Baby Jesus. Gabriella gazed into her pale serene face imploringly and clasped her hands together.

'Please give me strength,' she whispered.

The nun returned.

'I am Sister Teresa, if you come this way I'll take you to the *Badessa*.'

The corridor opened onto a long room where at intervals square patches of light from the windows spilled on to the old wooden floor. They entered another door which led into a large study mainly furnished floor to ceiling with books. Sitting opposite a huge fireplace, behind a large desk sat the *Badessa* wearing a black habit. Her kind eyes gave Gabriella hope.

'Come in child,' she beckoned Gabriella to sit in a wooden chair as Sister Teresa quietly shut the door behind her leaving them alone. The *Badessa* wore a concerned look as she waited for her to speak. Gabriella twisted her hands together in her lap before the words tumbled out.

'I...I need your help. I'm in trouble, I'm having a baby and I don't know what to do. I have been praying and praying to God and Our Blessed Virgin and I believe that I am destined to become a nun and join your order, but I…'

The *Badessa* looked severe as Gabriella haltingly told her
the story of the night she was attacked outside the *osteria*
before reaching across the table and taking her hand gently.

'You poor child. I am so sorry for what you have suffered. I
will help you. We will pray and ask for God to grant me
wisdom and the understanding to find a way.'

'I feel so ashamed. I lost my temper it was my fault if I
hadn't slapped him then…' She dissolved into sobs and the
Badessa moved round the desk and put her arm around her.

'No. Gabriella, look at me.'
Gabriella lifted her red eyes and searched the *Badessa's* face.

'I haven't seen you lately, at church of course and I
remember your mother's funeral, a very sad day. I have heard
that you have been a great help to your father shouldering so
much responsibility for one so young. I was friends with your
Nonna too, we went to school together she was a wonderful
woman and a close friend of mine. Your family has had a
great deal of sorrow inflicted on it and I know both your
Mama and Nonna would have been very proud of you. This is
not your fault. You must believe that. Things happen in our
lives and we don't know why, we can't see God's plan for us.
We need to go to the chapel now, together and ask forgiveness
for our sins and forgive those who have hurt us as it says in

Our Lord's Prayer.'

Taking Gabriella by the hand she led her down a corridor to the chapel. As soon as they entered the cool room where the sunlight painted the stained-glass windows crimson, cobalt and gold, Gabriella felt a sense of peace wash over her. They knelt and prayed together; Gabriella asked for God's forgiveness and she let go of all the hate for her baby's father. She prayed for her father and brothers asking God to give them strength and understanding about her leaving. Opening her eyes she gazed around at the chapel. Its stone arches were decorated with icons and tombs beneath. The floor was tiled in rich warm orange, russet and sienna, flecked with white flowers and patterns. The altar they knelt at was gilded with carvings of saints and angels and candles flickered in the air mixing a waxy burning scent with the aroma of ancient wood and incense.

The *Badessa* took her to a room with a high window where Gabriella could only see out if she stood on tip toe. It was sparsely furnished with a bed, a chair and a table.

'This is where you will sleep. Everyone who lives here has duties and you will be no exception. Sister Teresa oversees the kitchen; I'm sure she will appreciate your help. Sisters Francesca and Elizabetta teach at the school as you know. Sister Benedetta does the garden; you will meet her later. We grow our own fruit and vegetables and make jams and soups to give to the poor and to eat ourselves. Now if you follow me I'll show you where to go.'

The large kitchen was full of steam as pots bubbled on the stove. While the *Badessa* took Sister Teresa aside for a moment, Gabriella peered out of the window at the garden below. A plump sister wearing round glasses was tending to a vegetable plot that looked military in its precision. Perfectly straight rows of seedlings promised cabbages, cauliflowers and broccoli. Sister Teresa made them both a drink and smiled at Gabriella.

'I hear you're a good cook?'

'I love to cook. I was taught by my Nonna and my Uncle Corrado although I'm not as good as them.' A dark shadow passed across her eyes and Sister Teresa hastily handed her an apron and a bowl before pointing to a pile of peas in pods.

'Well I'll be very glad to have help there's always so much to do. Do you mind making a start shelling them?'

In her room that night Gabriella knelt at the side of her bed and prayed for her family before climbing beneath the covers. As she thought about the future fat tears rolled down her cheeks each one representing her fading ambitions. Hoping to one day become a teacher, she had always worked hard at school. Her dream had been to travel and see the world - go to

London to visit Corrado and see all the sights he'd written to her about. He'd said he'd give her a job in his *osteria* and now this instead. A life growing inside her. She put her hands around her slightly swollen belly and sighed - partly with relief - as she no longer had to hide it. It had become almost impossible as she was getting bigger. Sickness had driven her outside. Every morning she had to sneak away from her father and brothers, although the time Alfredo had caught her she'd passed it off as a stomach bug. If Mama had still been alive she would have known for sure. Gabriella's tears flowed freely as she longed for her mother.

When Ricardo read her letter his first instinct was to go to the Abbey and fetch her. He was greeted at the door by the Badessa.

'I had a letter from my daughter saying she's come here, can I see her?'

'She is in contemplation at present and has asked to be left alone.' She smiled kindly at him.

'But she's so young. I'm not sure she knows what she's committing to. I don't mean to offend you Mother, but I really need to see her and-'

'I'm sorry but those are her wishes. Give her some time and she will find out what she really wants. She is safe here I will look after her.'

Despite repeated attempts to see his daughter, Ricardo was always turned away. The Badessa did not tell Gabriella after the first time.

DEVON

Margaret felt her old self returning. Day by day during the last few months her positive self, had indefatigably been eroded. Now she was left with the one that told her everything was bleak and she would never be happy. It had burrowed inside her like a tick, infecting her bloodstream. She remembered back in London when she had stopped going out and became a recluse. Then a murmur of a smile crossed her face as she thought about the day she had watched the ice skaters and Corrado had appeared in front of her. For a few moments she was transported back to that day in the Holly Bush Inn when she had finally confided in Corrado, about her marriage. His face entered her mind like a beacon of light but then she recalled the look on Gianni's face when she had called round to the osteria in January. 'Gone to Sussex for a break don't know when he'll be back.' She slammed the door on her memories as the tears began to well again.

Despite their best efforts, she still refused to speak to her parents, or to Leslie who had tried to telephone her there. Stuck in limbo, she couldn't move forward in her life as Leslie steadfastly refused to agree to a divorce. She didn't know what to do or where to go. Alice and George were very supportive and she put a brave face on it while the children were around but inside she felt as if she was withering like a neglected flower. At first, she had clung on to the idea that Corrado would telephone her as he had the number from when he'd invited her to the party. Each day had been full of hope fading as the time wore on and now she knew he would never call. The only thing keeping her going was her writing, she tried to sit at her desk every day and found that she could lose herself and feel free for a while.

Deciding to go for a walk in the hope that the sunshine would cheer her up, she set out. The gardens there were beautiful and immaculate due to an army of men working tirelessly to ensure no weeds reared their heads and each border was perfect. The orchard was her favourite place at this time of year. She sat amongst the golden narcissi that surrounded the fruit trees. The cherry blossom was beginning to bloom. Pink froth covered the branches clashing with the rusty lichen on the trunks. The scent of the flowers was heavenly as she sank down in the grass. Emptying her mind, she concentrated on enjoying the weak sun freckling her face from the interstices between the trees where it reached her and dappled the ground around her like an intricate piece of crochet. Closing her eyes, she drifted into sleep lulled by the distant droning of a lawnmower.

Suddenly she woke to see Alice standing over her.

'Margaret.'

Groggily she sat up and yawned.

'Sorry I must have dozed off. Is everything all right?'

'I've got something for you.'

From behind her back she brandished a letter and passed it to Margaret.

Blearily Margaret took it and looked at the front. It just said her name and bore no postmark. She didn't recognise the writing.

'Who's it from?'

'Open it and find out,' said Alice impatiently.

She ripped open the envelope, took out a sheet of white paper and began to read.

Alice watched her face as she read it in silence. Margaret turned white then blushed a rosy pink that matched the blossom.

With shaking hands Margaret passed her the letter.

Dearest Margaret,

I have missed you so much. Your cousin Alice came to visit me today and told me that you intend to obtain a divorce from your husband. Hearing this has made me the happiest man on earth. When I said to you that I would wait for you and be here if you could find a way out of your marriage, I truly meant it, Bella. I love you so much that I can't put it into words. You fill all my waking thoughts from the moment I open my eyes to last thing at night. I long to hold you, feel your soft skin and comfort and protect you. I have been such a fool, I thought you were with someone else. I came to surprise you on that day we agreed to meet, and I saw a man leaving and thought the worst. I am sorry that I doubted you, that I was so stupid. Please forgive me.

Darling Margarita, I am writing this to ask you if you will do me the honour of becoming my wife? I know there will be difficult times ahead. Alice has explained to me what is involved. However, I believe our love can weather any storm and I am prepared to do anything possible in my power to make you happy. If you agree to marrying me, come to Hampstead Heath and meet me under your favourite tree on the 12th of April at 11 o'clock. Please come, I will be waiting. I can't wait to see you again belissima.

Forever yours Corrado xxxxxxx

Alice hauled Margaret to her feet and hugged her.

'But I don't understand.' Margaret looked dazed. 'Why now? I've been here for three months. And who's the man he's talking about?'

'Well, I couldn't bear seeing you so unhappy and I wanted to find out what had happened to suddenly to change his mind back in January. I didn't want to say anything to you in case nothing came of it. You know George and I went up to town yesterday?'

Margaret nodded.

'I called in to the Osteria and started chatting to Corrado. When I mentioned you, his face lit up for a second and then he looked utterly dejected. I asked him why you were no longer friends and he told me that on that morning when he was coming to see you at our house in London, he saw a man leaving. He said he saw you blow him a kiss and put two and two together.'

Margaret looked incredulous.

'What man?'

'Well that's what I was trying to work out and then I remembered that Stephen stayed with you that night before he proposed to Audrey.'

'Of course. What you mean he was watching? Why was he there? He was supposed to be coming later.'

'He wanted to surprise you and cook you breakfast, so he came earlier.'

'And all this time he thought I was in love with someone else?'

'It seems so. Well, are you going to meet him?'

'I feel all over the place. I don't know. He's ignored me for ages. Of course it's what I've hoped for all this time but-'

'But what?'

'Now it all seems so real and fast. The 12th is the day after tomorrow and it means I have to find a way to divorce Leslie. I'm scared Alice.'

Alice took her hand. 'It's not going to be easy, but if this is what you really want then you're going to have to be strong.' Margaret stuck out her bottom lip and sighed. 'I'm going to do it and I'm going to see my parents and tell them face to face.'

THE MERLA DAYS

Spring was heralded by snowdrops blooming in drifts, and crocuses - indigo and gold – wet with morning dew, littered the lawns of the Abbey like glistening jewels. Sister Benedetta had begun to plan her new vegetable patch and badgered Gabriella to help her. At first, Gabriella had not enjoyed being outside, preferring the cool darkness of the Abbey where she felt safe and secure, but Sister Benedetta's enthusiasm was infectious and now Gabriella felt excited as she saw the first green shoots of daffodils poking through the earth and began to take pleasure in the weak rays of sun that caressed her face. Although her belly was swollen, she found she could still dig, so they worked alongside one another preparing the garden for growing potatoes. Sister Benedetta left Gabriella there while she went to school to teach and Gabriella found herself humming as she dug in the rich chocolate soil.

In front of the vegetable garden was a bird bath and her eye was caught by a female blackbird perched on the stone rim. The bird cocked its head to one side and stared at Gabriella inquisitively.

'Hello little *merla*.' said Gabriella, standing up and leaning on the fork as she rubbed her aching back. The bird gave a trill before hopping into the bath and spreading her wings wide, using them to pour the water over herself, which turned her feathers almost black, until she gave a big shake and fluffed herself up to twice the size and shook droplets like tiny shards of a broken mirror scattering the earth below. Gabriella laughed as the little bird bounced back onto the side and began preening herself, meticulously cleaning each feather one by one.

Resuming her digging she found the little bird behind her gratefully gobbling up the fat juicy pink worms left in her wake. Once the patch was dug over Gabriella drove her fork into the ground and sat on a stone bench next to the bird bath. The little bird fluttered up onto the handle and sang. Gabriella felt as if she was singing to her as she listened to the whistles and warbles.

I wish I was a bird, free, living an uncomplicated life where all you have to think about is food and having a bath and singing. She sighed and thought back to a time when she was small in the garden with her mother and another *merla*.

Gabriella could remember the day quite clearly although she was probably only about eight years old. Her mother had been weeding her flower garden; it was a spring day with the promise of real afternoon heat.

'Which flowers do you like best?' Giverny expertly pulled up a weed and smiled at her daughter who had screwed up her little nose before answering.

'Ummm, I think daffodils because they're the same colour as the sun.'

'They're a real sign of spring. I like them too.'
Above them in their old apple tree the pale pink buds of blossom were beginning to unfurl, and on a branch a bird sang sedulously. The whole garden seemed to be waking up after the winter.

'Ah, it's a *merla*, another sign of spring.' said Giverny.

'What's a *merla*?' Gabriella looked up at the bird perched on a thick branch singing its heart out.

'A blackbird.'

'But it's not black.' Gabriella looked puzzled.

'It's a female, the *merlos* are black. There's a legend that tells why she's that colour. Would you like to hear it?'
Sitting down together on the grass under the tree, the sun stippled their clothes as it peeped through the branches and Giverny put her arm round her daughter pulling her in next to her before beginning the story. Snuggled up to her, Gabriella

enjoyed their closeness and the clean citrus scent of her mother.

'Once upon a time in the olden days, it was a really cold winter. Back then, female blackbirds had the same glossy black feathers as the males, with beaks so shiny they looked as if they had been dipped in gold paint. The months were like ancient gods, they had power and form and could speak. The month of January was shorter then, lasting 28 days. January had been showing off and making his month as chilly as possible. The snow kept falling, and ice froze the ponds, streams and fountains much to the delight of the children, who wrapped up warmly and skated and sledged, laughing as they fell over and squealing with pleasure as they flew down the white hills.

People out walking couldn't feel their feet, they tried to stay indoors as much as possible. Evenings were long and dark spent by their fires telling stories and eating to take their mind off the cold. During the day, they stayed cheerful, greeting one another with the words: "it won't be long until spring is on the way." At night, they wore thick woollen socks to bed and prayed that it would soon get warmer.

The creatures were finding it hard too, especially the birds. As legend has it, there was a merla, a blackbird hen, who was desperate for some relief from the cold. She was so angry with January that she went to see him to tell him off. She visited him on the 28th, which

was the last day that the weather was under his control before he
passed the baton on to February. The merla had to fly a long way up
through the freezing air to speak to him, as January lived on a high
mountain top. When she arrived, she scolded January for making
them so cold.

"We've all had to suffer so you could have your fun watching us
shivering and going hungry, I'm glad this is your last day and now
we can look forward to February."'

Gabriella closed her eyes and remembered looking up into her
mother's face, and how her big brown eyes fringed with
smoky lashes shone with animation as she continued with the
story. And how her even white teeth were framed perfectly by
her generous mouth.

'January was furious at the bird's speech and decided to take
revenge. Before the merla flew away, he warned her that she
wouldn't have the last word. After she left, January visited February
who lived on a neighbouring mountain, and ranted and raved until
finally, February agreed to give January three more days, so his
month would last for 31 days instead of 28, and February would
have less. January decided to pay back the merla for her unkind
words and made those extra three days the frostiest it had ever been
known before in Italy. Everything was frozen solid, and everyone
was numb with cold despite their fires roaring. The blackbird wished
that she hadn't spoken out against January and was so bitterly cold

that she flew to a smoking chimney where she spent three days trying to stay warm huddled inside it. By the time February arrived, the merla's shiny black feathers had turned a grey-brown colour, even her beak had changed from gold to grey, and that is the way that she stayed.'

Giverny brushed Gabriella's hair from her eyes and kissed her daughter on the top of her head.

'So, ever since then, February has become the shortest month in the calendar, the merla is a charcoal colour, and the last three days of January are known as The Merla Days and thought of as the coldest days of the year.'

'Poor *merla*,' said Gabriella as she cuddled up to her mother, who smiled at her.

'In Pianengo, the village I come from in the north, we celebrated these days. I used to get excited when I was a little girl because weeks before, the men used to start building a big bonfire in the square. Everyone would add pieces of wood to it until it was enormous, and on the 31st, the women all dressed up in long skirts and shawls and the men would wear cloaks and light the fire. Old Eduardo played his accordion, quietly to start with as we watched the flames take hold, then louder to be heard over the crackles. We had to stand back; I remember the sparks from the fire swirling up into the dark sky like hundreds of fireflies and the scorching heat as if it was yesterday. We all held hands and our faces turned orange, you know the way we look in the sunset sometimes?' Gabriella nodded.

'We would sing songs about the *merla* and January, and celebrate the fact that spring was on the way and soon we would have more sunshine. Auntie Guilia and I got to stay up late as we visited neighbour's houses and ate traditional food. One year I was poorly and couldn't go out into the cold. After the fire lighting and singing, lots of people came to our house and mama had made a soup from cabbage and beans. The house was filled with chatter as our neighbours stood around blowing on the thick soup before taking sips between laughing and joking.'

Gabriella could almost feel her mother's arm around her, the memory was so vivid, until she opened her eyes and shivered. She felt that same sense of loss, the feeling that the world was a drearier place without her mother and nothing could ever be enjoyed in the same way she had before she'd died, like the sun being constantly behind a cloud. All that remained were memories. Gabriella looked across at the bird who sat quietly watching her and felt a wave of pain as she realised that she would never be able to tell her child stories or tuck it in to bed at night as her mother had done with her.

Wearily she picked up the fork and went inside to help Teresa make dinner.

THE SPIRITUAL LIFE

Outside, Sister Benedetta was singing 'Ave Maris Stella', the hymn they'd all sung during morning mass. Enjoying the sunshine and the feel of the warm earth in her hands, she planted some beans tending to them gently as if they were babies. Her reedy voice drifted through the open window where the smell of baking bread filled the kitchen as Gabriella and Teresa stood side by side kneading dough for the next batch they were preparing to bake. Gabriella had to stand quite far back from the counter now but she still loved manipulating the bread, pulling it towards her before pushing it away. She turned to Teresa.

'Can I ask you something?'

'Yes, of course.'

'Did you always know you would become a sister?'
Teresa shaped her bread into the tin and wiped her hands.

'No. I come from a small village where everyone knows everyone else. I had a childhood sweetheart, Enrico,' a wistful look glanced across her face for a second before she continued. 'We grew up together, my family and his family were great friends and everyone thought we'd get married.'

She began slicing mushrooms deftly each one the thickness of the last before continuing.

'I have two younger brothers and one day when I was about fifteen, I think, the middle one got the measles. He was really poorly and then he got whooping cough as well. It was intolerable listening to his little body being racked constantly as he coughed. My mama held him all the time.' She shuddered as she remembered. 'He used to lie there almost lifeless between bouts of coughing. He was ill for a few weeks, until one day he took a turn for the worse, his temperature went so high that Mama could barely bear to touch him. She kept bathing him with cool water. The look on her face was agonising when the doctor said there was nothing more he could do and that we should call for Father Benedictine to read the last rites. I felt so helpless. I didn't know what to do. Despairing, I knelt and prayed to God and Our Lady to save him and I vowed that if he lived I would spend my whole life in service. Later that day the fever broke and he slowly recovered.'

'So, you gave up Enrico and joined the order?'

'Yes. And here I am.'

'Have you ever regretted it?'

'No. I made a promise that day and now I have a wonderful life. Although it was dreadful telling Enrico. He cried and so did I. Before that I'd expected to be with him and have lots of children.'

'What about your parents?' Gabriella finished her bread off and slipped it into the oven.

'They accepted my decision although I think they were a bit sad as it meant me going away and not seeing them very often.'

'Now you feel fulfilled and happy?'

'Yes, I love teaching at the school, cooking and helping people and I feel so close to God. Before, especially when my brother was ill, I felt scared and then once I made my promise to Him, I had a vision of God as huge and all powerful. He was standing holding up his arm and I was sitting in the palm of his hand totally safe. I love to sing to Him and my prayer time is when I worship and intercede for others. I feel at one and I have never felt frightened or alone since.'

'I have asked to join the order, although I don't feel as sure as you. I'm scared.'

'Of what?'

'Having this baby, of the pain, and what I'm most worried about is that I'm beginning to love it and I can't. The *Badessa* has found a family to take it. She told me they are called the Santini's, a couple who can't have children. I don't understand, how it is that they really want a baby and can't have one and I have one that I didn't want.' Gabriella bowed her head so her long dark curls covered her face and sniffed. Teresa put her hand on her shoulder.

'Every child is a gift from heaven, even yours although it doesn't seem that way. You are giving the Santini's the thing that they have always dreamed of; this baby will enable them to become a family and they will love it and bring it up as their own. God has given you a special role to play. He loves you Gabriella, you can depend on Him always.'

Gabriella nodded and looked up at Teresa with haunted eyes.

'Will you stay with me when it's time?'

'Of course.'

LONDON

Arriving at the house Margaret was met with a stony silence broken by her father.

'So, you've come to your senses have you?'

Looking up at the painting of her grandmother she took a deep breath.

'I've come to tell you that I'm divorcing Leslie and marrying Corrado.'

Her mother gasped and her father's face turned almost purple.

'You're doing what?'

'I'm sorry, but I can't live a lie anymore. Leslie and I don't love each other. I love Corrado.'

'A bloody foreigner! Have you lost your mind?' He spluttered.

'No. On the contrary I think I've-'

'How can you do this to us? Haven't we given you everything you've ever wanted? You've had an education, I let you get a job. Paid for everything, you've never wanted for anything and you just throw it back in our faces like this.'

'Yes.' Margaret shouted. 'You gave me an education and that's when I started thinking for myself. Reading books by women trapped in this system of being beholden to men. Having to obey first their fathers then their husbands. And all the time dying inside bit by bit. I'm just a chattel to you, something you can use as a bargaining tool. You gave me to Leslie as if I was a piece of your personal property, as a bribe because you want him to take over the business.'

'Don't be so ridiculous. You wanted to marry him. No one forced you.'

'Well I made a mistake. I'm sorry, but I've made my mind up and I'm asking you to forgive me and support me because I'm your daughter and you love me.' She looked imploringly at her mother who stared at the floor.

She had never seen cold hatred in her father's eyes before as he turned and held the door open for her. He looked at her, unblinkingly, like a snake regarding its prey.

'If you do this, you will never receive another penny from me and as far as I'm concerned I only have two daughters. I never want to see you again.'

Margaret tried to hold back her furious tears.

'So your love is conditional.' She spat. 'I can only be your daughter if I toe the line and do as I'm told? How could you? If that's the case I don't want to be part of this family.'

Stalking stiffly past her father she slammed the door on her way out.

Just thinking about it made her want to cry, she shook her head and steeled herself by thinking about Corrado. Picturing his eyes at the party as he had stared at her so intensely in a way she had never been looked at before.

Margaret thought she'd never been so happy as she walked towards Hampstead Heath. Oblivious to anyone she thought again of Corrado, when they'd walked together here in the winter, as she admired swathes of daffodils, glowing and nodding in the gentle breeze. The scent of lilac clung

delicately in the air and the trees were waking up stretching

their limbs. The path was bordered with ferns; their scroll-like

leaves shyly unfurling as the sun painted them and the paths

beneath with leopard spots through the apertures in the trees.

A pair of courting yellow brimstones fluttered above her

exalting in their new-found wings. Margaret felt a jolt inside

her realising she felt more alive than she had in her whole life

as she walked towards her favourite tree trying to tame the

butterflies in her stomach. Her heart almost stopped as she

saw Corrado waiting beneath the great oak tree wearing its

pale, newborn leaves. They ran to one another and he lifted

her into the air and twirled her around until they were both

dizzy and laughing uncontrollably. Corrado took out a pen

knife and carved their initials in the tree's freckled trunk,

before turning and kissing her hard.

'Shall we go to the Holly Bush for a drink?' Corrado kissed

her again.

'Well that depends. Only if you've got a lemon in your pocket.'

'Oh no!' He frowned and patted his pockets.

'In that case, no thank you.'

'Only joking.' He pulled a huge lemon from his coat pocket and handed it to her. 'Did you really think I'd come out without one?'

Laughing they walked arm in arm to the inn.

'So today is the 12th, and Gianni's birthday is on the 16th. Who won the bet?'

'Me.'

'Really?'

'Yes. You sound surprised, but I was determined. And when I went back to the farm I couldn't bear to think about you so I read and read although I'll be very happy never to read any more Dickens ever.'

'I'm sorry you felt like that. I had no idea that you'd come early that day or anything. I just thought you'd changed your mind and I wouldn't have blamed you.'

'I'm sorry. Sorry that I didn't trust you. I should have asked you instead of jumping to conclusions. I think I was just so scared of getting hurt.'

'Have you been in love before?'

He held the door open for Margaret and they sat at the same table as before although there was no fire this time.

'No, I don't think so. There was a girl I was with, Isabella. My mama was beside herself when we got together. She kept going on about looking forward to being surrounded by babies, but it wasn't what I wanted. My papa was always telling me about the places he'd seen when I was young and it gave me the desire to see what they were like. Italy is the most beautiful place in the world, but somehow it wasn't enough for me.'

'So what happened with Isabella?'

'I had to tell her. I felt very guilty, but I knew long term it wouldn't work between us.'

'That was a brave thing to do. I should have done that with Leslie.' Margret sighed. 'I wish I had now then I wouldn't be in this fearful mess.'

'Let me get you a drink.'

'Thank you.'

Margaret smiled as he plopped a slice of lemon in her drink. 'Gin and tonic hasn't tasted the same without this.'

'I think I was scared to love because of losing all those I cared about. It felt as if everyone I loved left me and then I met you. I don't know why it was different and somehow, I couldn't stop myself. I was all over the place. I had no idea if you felt the same, but I've never felt like this before and I just knew that I had to take that chance and I'm happy I did.' said Corrado kissing her again.

'I'm so glad you did and that Alice came to see you otherwise we'd both be miserable.'

'At least one good thing came out of it. I won the bet! And on the plus side, I expanded my vocabulary. I had to keep looking up words in a dictionary.'

They both burst out laughing.

'What about *Pride and Prejudice* then? You can't have had time to read that too.'

'Ah but that's where you're wrong. I read that on New Year's Day and the day after before I came back to see you and it all went wrong.'

'And what did you think?'

'At first I wasn't sure, but in the end, I loved it.'

Margaret beamed. 'I'm so glad. It's delightful isn't it?'

'She writes wonderfully.'

'I know,' said Margaret, 'her observations are genius.'

'Mr Darcy reminds me of myself a little.'

'What do you mean?'

'In Italy everyone thought I was moody and didn't want to dance with any girls.'

'I can't imagine you being like that. You're always so friendly and lovely.'

'That's because I'm in love. I think you'll find once he found the woman of his dreams he changed too.'

'Ah, I see what you mean.'

'Now what about us. Has Leslie agreed to divorce you?'

'No.'

'Oh.' He sat back in his chair. 'But I thought Alice said it was going ahead?'

Margaret fiddled with her glove. 'He refused. Look, Corrado are you absolutely sure that this is what you want?'

'I've never been more certain in my life. I'm prepared to do whatever it takes for us to be together.'

'In that case, George telephoned me and told me he has an idea and that he thinks it is the only way Leslie will agree. He told me it could cause a scandal. But,' she gulped, 'to be with you I'm also prepared to do whatever it takes.'

It began to rain as they parted. Margaret barely noticed; she felt as if she was floating along the pavement until she suddenly saw Julia and Harriet, her friends from the knitting circle, across the road. Since Caroline left she had stopped going but was pleased to see them again so she waved and smiled, crossing the road to meet them. They looked at her then hurried away, turning their backs on her snubbing her as if she was invisible then walked on arm in arm whispering and laughing. Stung, Margaret's cheeks burnt as she pulled her hat down firmly and hurried away blinking back tears even more determined to execute her plan, now she had been made aware of the consequences.

AT THE HOTEL

The maid glanced up at the glamorous woman, her attention immediately caught by the antique brooch on her left-hand lapel. The black onyx panther on it, with its one glimmering diamond eye, stood out starkly against her camel coloured woollen coat. She stood shaking slightly, warming her hands - with their exquisitely lacquered nails - in front of the crackling open fire in the hotel lounge. The glow from the flames reflected and flickered across the onyx, setting it alight. Looking down, the maid noticed the woman's shoes, coveting them; they were exquisite, soft leather, Italian, the kind she could only dream of possessing herself. She sighed longingly. They were the height of fashion; strapped Mary-Jane's with a two-inch heel that enhanced the woman's slender, stocking-clad legs.

'I know what I have to do,' murmured the maid.

Margaret stared unseeingly at the burning coals, lost in thought, shivering, not from the cold, but from a combination of fear and exhilaration at what was about to happen. She touched her panther for reassurance, remembering her strong, calm grandmother who had given it to her. As a child, she'd always been fascinated by it. Although she'd never said anything to her grandmother about the brooch, she must have noticed because she'd left it to Margaret in her will. Margaret derived pleasure from the idea that through the brooch she might also have inherited some of her grandmother's tenacity.

Corrado strode purposefully along the London Street. Next to him a Chrysler Imperial, rain dripping off its bodywork, overtook a coal-cart sending water sheeting across the pavement. Corrado hardly noticed. All he was aware of was the clip-clop of the horse's hooves on the road as it mirrored the pounding of blood in his veins. He felt hot, dazed – he was barely aware that he was walking. All he could think about was Margaret – her glossy hair, her pinky-gold skin, the way she held her slender, energetic body, her vivacity. His mouth felt dry. He didn't see the crowds around him. Today, for the first time, he would... He would be allowed to treat her the way a husband... Pulling up the collar of his black trench coat, he swept his dark fringe from his eyes. His hands involuntarily clenched into fists, as he remembered meeting her for the first time. Back in Italy, his mother and brother had constantly been trying to marry him off. He smiled at the memory of his mother waving her arms at him in frustration, hearing her voice.

'Corrado, son, what's wrong with you? Carlotta is stunning and her mother is my friend you would have such beautiful babies...'

He had always had a thing about English girls, it's just that his arm had been twisted by that bastard. He was ecstatic to be meeting Margaret, there were still problems ahead though.

Sinking down in one of the gold brocade armchairs in the lobby, appearing to onlookers a carefree, attractive young woman. Margaret's beautiful dancing amber eyes, lit up as she smiled widely, showing her large, even white teeth, whilst remembering Corrado's comment about diving in and drowning in her. Her thoughts returned to the present and she glanced at her delicate gold watch impatiently. She found herself trawling through her mind, thinking of Leslie. The apparent perfect man - everyone thought so - especially her father. She pictured her father, serious, immovable, and aloof, imagining him giving her that piercing look over the top of his spectacles and sighing as she envisaged his disappointment in her.

'He'll never forgive me for my actions today, but I am determined to be free,' she murmured, frowning. Looking downwards her eyes rest on the engagement ring that Leslie had presented to her; an ostentatious aquamarine surrounded by diamonds that winked and glistened in the light. When he gave it to me I was the happiest girl alive, my friends were jealous I was the talk of the town. Twisting it around she hears him proposing like it was yesterday.

'Margaret will you marry me?'

'Yes, yes!' I'd replied without hesitation. Why wouldn't I? He was a catch. I felt privileged, until...'

She looked down at the slim gold band on her wedding finger that complimented the aquamarine. She regarded it as more of an iron shackle than a thing of beauty.

Taking out her notebook, the one she always carried with her full of half written poems and observations, to calm her nerves she leafed through until she found a new page. Sometimes when she wrote, the page seemed endlessly blank and wordless however hard she tried, but today was different. Margaret began to carve the poem, caressing and cajoling the words until they became a rhythm.

Suddenly she was brought back to her senses as Corrado strode towards her; she felt as if she could explode with pent-up excitement as she watched him, revelling in his handsomeness in the fact that he is Italian and dark, entirely different to Leslie, binary opposites. He took her hands in his and kissed them before pulling Margaret close and whispering in her ear.

'*Ti amo*, I've missed you so much. And,' he inhaled deeply, 'you smell *meraviglioso.*'

She sighed with relief.

'I've missed you too, it seems like an eternity I've been waiting.'

'Let's have a drink, G and T for you *Tesora*?' Nodding, she watched him summon the waiter at the bar. While he waited, with his back to Margaret, he took a large lemon from his jacket pocket and skillfully cut slices for their drinks before he carried them over and returned to the fire. Margaret sipped from the glass, enjoying the sourness of the gin as it played across her lips, feeling more determined with every resolve filled mouthful.

'Who's going to go up first?' Corrado arched his eyebrows provocatively. 'Are you absolutely sure that this is what you want?'

'Yes.' She hastily replied. 'Come to room number seventeen, up the stairs turn left and along the corridor you won't be long, will you?'

He allayed her fears by winking at her.

'I've waited such a long time for this,' he groaned. 'I've dreamed of us being alone, just you and-.'

'Stop.' She covered his mouth with her finger interrupting him and blushing slightly.

As he watched her walk out of the room, the intensity of his stare made her shudder involuntarily with anticipation. Margaret had to concentrate on walking in her shoes without stumbling. The wide stairs were covered in dense carpet, which her heels penetrated digging into the deep pile. She became aware of swirling patterns crimson, navy, indigo merging into her thoughts frowning, as she recalled her husband and his fascination with shoes. Remembering the numerous pairs he had bought for her, Margaret's thoughts swelled, overwhelming her leapfrogging one another to reach the forefront.

At first I was overjoyed, who wouldn't be? Isn't that what everyone dreams of, a considerate husband who adores you and constantly buys you gifts? He came home with a new pair of shoes almost every day, until that first day when something changed. The memory made her shudder.

'Close your eyes and hold out your hands.' Leslie's brilliant smile was intense and convincing.

'Thank you, they're gorgeous.' She'd kissed him. 'I'll put them back in the box while I finish what I'm doing.' His smile vanished; he gripped her wrist, 'try them on now I want to see if they fit.' His tone was wheedling but with an undercurrent of menace. Margaret had felt afraid. Sitting on the sofa; his weighted stare had felt stifling as she fumbled with the buckles. Once they were fastened Margaret slowly stood and looked at him. He looked excruciatingly uncomfortable.

'There, what do you think?'

Instead of replying he grimaced and quickly left the room. His behaviour had bewildered her, and from then his obsession took a more sinister turn, his attentiveness became twisted, threatening, suffocating. He made peculiar demands. Shoe related. Feet related. Margaret stared out of the elegant bay window blindly recalling how Leslie made her stand before him whilst kneeling in front of her. Gingerly clasping her slim ankle, reverently caressing it, softly, meaningfully he began to stroke her feet and shoes whilst moaning imperceptibly. He shattered her dreams as he turned into a stranger, her heart filled with uncertainty. Shivering Margaret returned to the present, back to the hotel room. Removing both her rings, she dropped them into her handbag and resolutely snapped the clasp shut.

Taking the stairs two at a time, Corrado briefly stopped to smooth his hair and catch his breath before tentatively knocking and opening the door. Halting in the doorway, he saw her beautiful silhouette gazing out at the topiary hedges clipped into dazzling designs of birds, all glossy from the rain; a glimpse of a fountain surrounded by cherubs momentarily stalled him. Margaret turned and saw him smiling; he searched her face, sensing her vulnerability calming her with a look of love, conveying his thoughts speechlessly. She flew across the room and he pulled her to his chest enveloping her, crushing her to him. As she melted into Corrado's arms intoxicated by his delicious scent, she inhaled deeply.

'Margarita, I love you.' Kneeling in front of her, he stared into her eyes with a deep yearning before rapidly removing first one and then the other of the ill-fated shoes. She held her breath as he tossed them away out of sight. Finally, she felt she could breathe freely, exhaling letting herself go, falling into him.

The maid stood at the door of number seventeen and knocked, breathing nervously, before opening the door to reveal the lovers entwined. Standing silently for a few seconds, she sensed their relief, before gently closing the door.

The couple clung to one another and their future, as the maid entered, remaining poised, poignant statues determining time, their lives, and the carefully devised plan that would enable Margaret to obtain a divorce from Leslie, through their observed adultery, and allow them to be together. Corrado loved her with his body and his tongue until she felt as if she were in a kaleidoscope of ecstasy. Finally, she was a woman after all the waiting and anticipation and she wanted to stay in this moment forever and ever. George had worked out that the only way that Leslie would agree to divorce her would be if he looked like the wronged party and he could save face. Margaret had agreed determined to be free.

The following day the maid received an unexpected gift in a box, left for her at reception. Puzzled she opened it to reveal the glamourous woman's shoes. The note read simply: Thank you.

Corrado insisted on accompanying Margaret when she went back to the house she shared with Leslie. As they had hoped, he had been at work and the maid had let them in. While Margaret collected her belongings Corrado looked at the picture of Leslie on the wall. On the sideboard stood a photo of them on their wedding day. Margaret looked radiant in her white dress and coronet of roses. He sighed. Why couldn't I have met her first, before him, and we could have had a wedding like that? He felt guilty about being with Margaret, because of his faith and wanted to marry her once she was divorced although they wouldn't be allowed to marry in a church. Despite this he believed he had to put this to one side because they were meant to be together. And in turn Margaret had rejected her family but hoped in time that her sisters would accept Corrado although she knew because of their parents it would make life difficult for them.

Margaret looked around the room one more time before calling Corrado upstairs and into the bare bedroom. Opening the cupboard door she showed him the mountain of shoes piled from floor to ceiling.

'I'm leaving all those, so we'll need to go shopping.'

'That's not a problem. I can't wait for us to be together properly. Are you absolutely sure this is what you want?'

'I've never been more convinced of anything in my life.'

'Nor have I. My family is the most important thing to me, and once we're married you will become part of my family. I hope you'll get to meet them one day.'

The platform was crowded, but Margaret and Corrado only had eyes for each other. Steaming southwards, they talked about the future. Alice welcomed them with open arms and Margaret was relieved that George seemed to like Corrado too. The children were soon won over, as Margaret found them squealing with delight as Corrado gave them horse rides on his back in the drawing room.

'We decided to give you the cottage to stay in so you can have some privacy.'

'Thank you.' Margaret smiled gratefully.

When the cousins were alone Alice hugged Margaret

'I'm so happy for you. He's very handsome, you make a lovely couple.'

Margaret glowed with pleasure.

'I still can't quite believe we're actually together. I've never been so happy in my entire life.'

'It was a very brave thing to do. What about your parents?'

'They're irrelevant now.' Margaret sighed. 'After this, we're going to Sussex to stay at the farm.'

'What will you do for money?'

'Corrado is a businessman. He has the farm and the osteria.'

'Will you go back to teaching?'

'I don't know yet. It's exciting to think that finally I'll be able to make my own choices. I know Corrado will support me whatever I decide.'

'That's wonderful. Enjoy your weekend and once you're settled in to life in Sussex we'll come and visit you. I'm dying to try his cooking you've told me so much about it.'

HEMBURY FORT

'I want to take you to one of my favourite places.' said
Margaret taking Corrado's hand.

'Where?'

'Hembury Fort. It's an ancient wood dating back to the Iron
Age. You can see where the fort used to be and this is the best
time of year to see it.'

They borrowed George's car and slowly drove through the
winding lane and up the steep hill fringed with trees - their
trunks like great statue legs - covered in velvety green moss
and orange lichen, formed a leafy awning the colour of
gooseberries caught in the light above them. Their gnarled
roots rose from the ground surrounding the car, the sentries of
the woods. Entering, Margaret felt a familiar stillness cloak
her.

'I always think about how many people have walked here
before me. Whenever I wander amongst these trees, I wonder
what they've seen. It feels as if ghosts watch you-not bad
ones- but it just holds so much history, and I suppose because
I'm a writer I like to imagine who those people were.'

'Are you going to let me read any of your writing?' Margaret turned away slightly before taking his arm.

'I don't know. I've never let anyone read it yet. Come on this way.'

They took a less trodden path, where the sun intermittently littered the leafy floor with splashes of light, laughing they dashed up and down the ramparts before pausing for breath next to trees with parasols of white fungi that Corrado said looked like pixie steps leading to the branches above. Margaret led him up a steep hill covered in tree roots and laughed as he almost slipped on the leafy mulch beneath their feet. Birds fluted in the old oaks above them, their new leaves glowing bronze where the sun smiled on them, and as they neared the top a heady intoxicating scent enticed them further.

'I'm going to cover your eyes before we get there. Keep them shut. Trust me, you're going to love what you see in a minute.'

Placing her hands over his eyes she guided him into a clearing before removing them.

'Now you can open them.'

Corrado looked around him and gasped. Before him was a dense lake of bluebells as far as the eye could see forming an indigo haze in the sunlight. Flanked by a circle of coppery oaks and tall beech trees, their new leaves lime green, and soft as the wings of the butterflies that fluttered amongst the flowers. They walked through the flowers and Corrado pulled Margaret to him kissing her passionately.

'We're free. Now we can really be together.'

Margaret smiled, then threw her head back and laughed making Corrado join in.

'Free at last, free at last.'

Echoing the words of the protagonist in the Kate Chopin story she felt a surge of relief that she had been able to stand up for herself.

Sinking into the flowers, soft as an eiderdown, she pulled Corrado down with her. As the birds trilled above them, the sun began to slide down lazily, painting the sky a fiery red which reflected in their eyes as they made love below it, totally absorbed in one another. Margaret had never experienced being wanted so passionately. She revelled in being able to stroke Corrado's chest and the tiny strip of black hair that led from his brown belly to below. They explored one another's bodies with tongues and lips and soft caresses, taking their time. As bats began to cavort above them they headed back to the car overwhelmed by the bubble of love they found themselves in.

The following morning when Corrado woke before Margaret he collected his cloudy thoughts. The past year had been extraordinary. So difficult, but now she was there with him, it was so wonderful. Turning over he smiled as he watched her sleep, her red hair fanned out on the white pillowcase like a cloud caught in the light of a particularly good sunset and captured by Monet.

In Sussex they cemented their love as they walked down by the river and sat on the bank amongst the daffodils and irises. The cerulean sky above them filled with tiny wisps of clouds like feathers escaped from a pillow. Margaret was in heaven, waking up with Corrado every day, making love, being fed breakfasts in bed and helping with the animals. It was so removed from her old life that it began to pale into insignificance. The pain when she thought of her parents was beginning to recede. Roberta and Luigi had made her feel at home immediately and she loved playing with baby Eva. She sat under the trees next to the buffalo paddock because she enjoyed hearing them lowing at one another and wrote reams of poetry.

Corrado and Margaret had taken over the old cottage where Mr and Mrs Jones had lived. They were happy to retire now that Corrado was at the farm full-time and Gianni and Leonora had taken over the osteria. Margaret had spent hours making red and white gingham curtains and sprucing it up, so that it felt like home. It was small with a thatched roof and a rickety wooden staircase that led up to the large room above. The outside was whitewashed and had the most beautiful rambling rose covering it with garnet blooms spraying out in all directions like water from a fountain. The large kitchen took up the whole of the ground floor where Corrado delighted in cooking for her. He was beginning to teach her too and she found she loved to make cakes using the golden butter they churned in the dairy and the fresh eggs from the hens. They were her favourite. Finding it therapeutic to watch them scratching around she'd taken over tending to them and delighted in the way they ran to greet her when she fed them. Collecting their eggs felt like treasure hunting as they were always trying to hide their nests. It never failed to give her pleasure when she found a little clutch of speckled brown eggs in a nest, sometimes still warm.

'Dinner's almost ready.' Corrado shouted from the door. Putting away her notebook, Margaret went into the kitchen quietly and stole up behind him hugging him as he stirred the silky tomato sauce.

'It smells divine. I'm so glad we met.' She smiled and kissed him.

'I see. Now it's all coming out. You only want me for my cooking skills!'

'Well, now you mention it.' She raised her eyebrows and pulled a face.

He wheeled around and kissed her gently on the lips.

'What about your skills? Are you going to show me any of your writing?'

'There are two poems I wrote about us, one about Hembury Fort, after we went there, I could show you them.'

Later that evening as they sat at the old, long scrubbed table with its burn marks and scratches that told stories of delicious dishes gone by, she took out her notebook and with her heart beating erratically like an out of time drum handed it to Corrado on the right page.

Pure White Basildon Bond

Her alluring scent sealed it,
'Meet me at the hotel at 4.'
Signed with an expectant M.
He became a willing conspirator
In her desire for freedom
A chivalrous cog in the
Null and void procedure
For a taste of her lips

Stained ruby red.
They teeter clinging to the

Pure White Basildon Bond

Her alluring scent sealed it,
'Meet me at the hotel at 4.'
Signed with an expectant M.
He became a willing conspirator
In her desire for freedom
A chivalrous cog in the
Null and void procedure
For a taste of her lips
Stained ruby red.
They teeter clinging to the
Precipice of respectability, before
The maid knocking sends them
Tumbling into the abyss,
Where she becomes both woman
And adulteress.

Amidst the Bluebells

We lie together in a
Sea of promise within
Undulating purple waves
Irrevocably entwined

Like the subterranean
Roots sprawling below.
You are an atlas
Taking me on a journey,

I am intoxicated from a
Fusion of your scent
And the bruised
Bluebells beneath us.

The dusky sky, no longer
Endless blue is ours.
The spring breeze drifts
Caressing brown skin and

Puckered lips
That demand to be kissed.
We become one heartbeat
Aware of every artery.

Cumulus clouds race
Across the crimson sky,
We leave our imprint, intact
As bats begin hunting and dew falls.

She couldn't look at Corrado as he read; instead she stood outside and watched the black and white house martins – the acrobats of the sky - as they soared and dived collecting food on the wing. One just missed her head as it ducked under the eaves of the house. Margaret was delighted to see a little fluffy chick peering out with open beak waiting for its mother who fed it a grub and swooped away. Turning back to the door Corrado stood with her book and a grin.

'I love them. You've captured that moment in time we spent together in the bluebells perfectly. And the other one, well, both, just paint a picture. You are talented Margarita what else don't I know about you?'
He pulled her into his arms and kissed her until she felt dizzy and led her through the kitchen towards the stairs.

'What about the washing up?'

'That can wait. I've just remembered something very important I need to do, your poem reminded me.'

Spring drifted lazily into a warm summer as they all fell into place with their jobs at the farm. Margaret had learnt to milk the buffalo, although it had been a bit hairy at the start. Soon finding she had a talent for it and where once she gingerly held Manuela's teats making her stamp and swish her tail and knock the bucket over, she became confident.

Deftly squeezed the teats and gently talked to her constantly in a low voice she leant her head against her hairy side enjoying the animal warmth emanating from her. Roberta had become a firm friend and they liked chatting together in the cool of the dairy on hot summer days as they churned the butter and made mozzarella. Margaret loved using the huge paddle to separate the curds from the watery whey. Laughing and gossiping, they formed the huge slabs of elastic curds into balls. Roberta taught Margaret to shape them by folding them in on themselves over and over again. It was so satisfying feeling the cheese coming together in her hands. Stroking and manipulating the ball until it became smooth as silk made her feel like a sculptor. Watching Corrado eat it approvingly with the tomatoes and basil they grew in the garden made her proud. Sitting together outside at the table where the scent of the roses mingled with the basil deliciously and watching the sunset was a far cry from her old life in London. Margaret felt the happiest she had ever felt, as she embraced her new life and her old one became nothing more than a distant memory.

2nd July 1928

Today I learnt that the law has changed. Hopefully as a result, the world has become a better place. A place where women can have their say in Parliament. The Equal Franchise Act has finally been passed. Yet, I feel torn between joy and sadness. The one person I would love to talk to discuss this with is Mother, but we are no longer talking. She has taken Father's and Leslie's side in all this and cut me off. I miss her. I feel tremendously sorry that I didn't get to know her better. I wish I had been aware of her hopes and dreams when she was younger. She hinted at her former dreams when I went to tell her about Leslie. I remember how excited she was when women first got the vote. It makes me so sad to think that imperceptibly, during the last ten years, she has given up hope. Now she's bitter as a consequence of Father treating her badly over the years; although, he's just doing what men do – having it all. Not anymore. Times are changing. We're moving forward, marching relentlessly to equality.

AUGUST 1928

ITALY

Gabriella woke up suddenly with a vice like pain inside. All around her was inky darkness and silence. She groaned quietly as wave after wave of pain overtook her. Holding her stomach, she gingerly sat up and got to her feet. A surge of water spilled down her legs and onto the stone floor. As she mopped it up the pain engulfed her, she felt as if her bones were grinding against one another. The pains stopped momentarily, and she sank back down on to the bed and began praying.

'It's too early. Father, help me. Our Lady give me the strength to...'

As the next wave of pain hit her she cried out.

'God why are you punishing me like this? I can't stand it I...'

Dissolving into sobs she writhed around trying to get some relief.

'Mama where are you? I need you. I'm scared all alone why did you have to die and leave me? God why do you hate me so much. Aargh.' She screamed. 'Save me, please help.'
Sister Teresa tapped on the door as the grey light of dawn crept through the small window and found Gabriella doubled up on the floor. Hurrying to her she stroked her hair back from her face which was soaked with sweat and tears.

'I'm here. Come on we need to get you on the bed and- ' Gabriella's groan interrupted her as she pulled her to her feet and placed her in a lying down position.

'It's alright, I'm going to get some towels and water I'll be really quick.'
Unaware of her surroundings the pain was overwhelming her all she could feel was white hot fire between her legs and every contraction left her writhing and crying out. She was oblivious to the *Badessa* entering the room.

'Poor child.' She took Gabriella's hand and stroked it. 'I'm going to have a look and see how close you are.'

'But it's too early. It shouldn't be here until next month.'
She dissolved into agonised sobs.
As Teresa returned the *Badessa* called out.

'It's coming. I can see the baby's head. Not long now Gabriella. You need to breathe and wait until I say to push, once the next really strong pain comes then get ready.'

Panting like a dog, she tried to obey the *Badessa.*

'Now push. Come on you can do it.'

As Gabriella rode the pain for a second, panting feverishly, she gripped Teresa's hand so tightly that her nails dug into the palm. Teresa didn't flinch, instead she stroked her shoulder.

'Come on you can do this. I'm here with you don't be afraid.'

'I can't. I'm scared. I'm going to die please help.'

Bearing down, as the pain ricocheted through Gabriella's whole body, she let out a guttural scream that echoed around the walls; a huge gush of liquid poured out followed by the baby who slithered into the *Badessa's* waiting arms. Crying as she wrapped it in a warm blanket and placed it in Gabriella's arms.

'Well done Gabriella. The Lord has given you a little girl.'

Teresa and the *Badessa* thanked God for the safe delivery and the sunlight began to filter into the little room and play on the wall. Gabriella held her tiny daughter gazing into her little screwed up face. She bent her head to the black down that crowned her head and drank in her scent before stroking her cheek gently, feeling her skin as soft as a butterfly's wing, Gabriella peeped below the blanket and counted her fingers and toes marvelling at how minute they were. The *Badessa* rested one hand on Gabriella's head and the other on the baby.

'Bless you both.'

Gabriella smiled through her tears.

'Thank you. Thank you both for helping me.'

Teresa kissed the baby and then Gabriella.

'Well done you were very brave.'

'Have you thought of a name for her?' The *Badessa* smiled down at them both.

'I'm going to call her Maria, Maria Teresa.'

Teresa beamed through her tears as she walked out of the door.

The following five days were the happiest and saddest of Gabriella's short life. As Maria suckled, she felt so proud to be keeping her baby alive, sustaining her and as she fed, Gabriella could feel her womb moving back into place. Enveloped in a haze of milk and motherhood. Maria's skin next to hers felt delicious and so right all she wanted to do was look after her forever. This was the closest she had ever felt to another human being. Gabriella sighed as she thought of her mother. She must have held me like this so close, given me life. And she thought of the Virgin Mary holding Baby Jesus just like she held Maria.

'Why do all the people I love have to leave me?'

The thought of giving her baby up was unbearable, yet she

knew there was no other way. Children were forbidden to live at the Abbey. And she couldn't bring shame on her family by returning as an unmarried mother.

The morning she was dreading arrived with a rain shower, black and grey clouds chased one another scudding across the sky. Alone in her room, Gabriella sat on the side of the bed cradling her daughter tracing the contours of her face determined to etch them into her memory for eternity. The small blue eyes that stared up at her so full of trust and love that Gabriella's eyes filled up. She stared into her daughter's eyes and whispered to her.

'I wonder what you'll grow up to be. What dreams will you have? Maybe some of them will be the same as mine, you might travel the world or be a teacher. You might have a child of your own one day to love and look after.' Gabriella stroked her little downy arm and sighed. 'I'm so sorry little one. I love you, I really do. I promise I won't ever forget you. You're going to have a better life without me. Your new Mama and Papa can't wait to meet you. They're going to love you so much and give you all the things I can't.'

There was a knock at the door and the *Badessa* entered with a grave look.

'It is time Gabriella.'

Gabriella kissed the baby, smelling her soft hair for the last time before placing her into the *Badessa's* arms along with Bobbo, her teddy bear.

'I love you.' She stifled a sob as the *Badessa* took her daughter to meet her new family.

Gabriella threw herself face down on the bed, hammering her fists into the pillow as she cried.

SUSSEX

Corrado led Margaret outside.

'I've got something I want to show you. A surprise. It's a bit of a walk.'

Following him down the lane and up a hill they entered a grassy field dotted with speedwell and buttercups; surprised russet coloured cows showed off their long lashes as they blinked at them indolently before returning to their cud. Eventually, Corrado pointed to a field in the distance.

'I'm intrigued. I've never been up here before. It's very out of the way.'

'I know. There's a reason for that, which you'll see in a minute.'

As they entered the field, Corrado ushered her into the middle to a large, long, stone hay barn with a wooden door. Suddenly, Corrado took her hand and squeezed it. Margaret noticed that he was shaking. Behind the barn a large glass house had been attached to the back and a small sapling was growing inside. Corrado's eyes were shining as he turned to her and his words tumbled out.

'You know all the stories I've told you about the lemon

tree? Well for the last year I've been growing this tree from the seeds of the lemons I got from back home. I had no idea whether it would take or not as I know the climate isn't the same here, that's why it's under cover. But as you can see it seems to be working. And look.' He pointed to the bottom of the tree where a tiny lemon hung on a branch. 'I know I can't go back to Italy. My place is here with you, so I may never see the lemon tree back at home again, so I'm so excited that I can grow lemons here. As you know from the stories I've told you the lemon tree is special, so I felt it was my responsibility to try to continue the line. There's something I want to ask you too.'

Margaret looked up in surprise at the seriousness in his voice.

'Do you miss London? Would you like to go back to being a teacher like you were before?'

'I haven't really thought about it. Alice was asking me if I would consider going back to teaching and part of me would like to because I felt like I had some worth then, but I'm so happy here with you now.'

'I know that you were unhappy when you were with Leslie, as you missed your job, and you just said it gave you a feeling of self-worth.'

'I did, but now being with you I don't feel like I need anything else. I'm so contented.'

He smiled at her and kissed her gently.

'What about your writing? You once told me that was your dream. I see how happy you are when you write. You become totally absorbed, feverish almost and I love that about you. I really believe you are an amazing writer and I've got an idea if you'll agree.' He took Margaret's hands in his and stared into her eyes. 'I want you to write our story. Not just our story, but all the lemon tree stories as well. Now I've gone from Italy, they could be lost. I don't know why, but those stories were entrusted to me. Ricardo wasn't so interested, but they have always fascinated me and made me feel as if I am part of something much bigger than just the here and now. When Nonna told them to me she made me promise that I would pass them on, so they are never forgotten. They have become like legends and always been told in the oral tradition but now I have met a writer! Please will you write them and make them into a book Margaret?'

'If that's what you really want. I had no idea! I suppose our love story is quite unusual too. I would like my future relatives to know that I stood up for what I believed in despite losing my family and social standing. When I used to read about all the women emotionally enslaved by men and the Suffragettes doing something tangible to change things, I wanted to be like them and do something too. I haven't done anything to change the world, but I have stood up for women in my own small way.'

'So you agree?' he kissed her. 'I'm so proud of what you've done. It took integrity and enormous courage to follow your heart and not settle as so many other women would. Thank you. Once the stories are written down they will be kept forever. I always thought that my niece, Gabriella, would become the next keeper of the stories, so if you write it, I will send it to her. I believe the lemon tree has brought us together. And now these new trees are planted here, its lineage will live on and new chapters in the story will begin.'

'So apart from ours, have you told me all of them now?'

'There is one more I'd forgotten about. It's not a secret one in the way the others are. Back home, or rather I should say in Italy as this is my home now, we have a festa. In the church there is a statue of Our Lady and we have a procession and then a big lemon festival afterwards to celebrate the fact that our relatives suffered a huge fire…'

Sitting together in the field amongst the flowers Corrado told Margaret the final story.

ITALY

Gabriella refused to leave her room. Every night she dreamt of her baby. The dream was heavenly. In it, she could feel Maria suckling, hear her little snuffling noises and smell her sweet head until she woke and realised she was alone, feeling the agony of loss as fiercely as the day Maria had been taken away, penetrating her heart. The *Badessa* visited her and prayed for her healing. After a week had passed Teresa came to Gabriella and held her hand.

'I can't imagine what you are going through, I hate seeing you like this but staying in here is just going to make you feel worse. Get dressed and come for a walk with me.' Ignoring her protests, she passed over Gabriella's clothes. 'I'm going to stay here until you're ready there's no point arguing.' The young sister had a determined look in her eye as she crossed her arms and stood up.

Dazed, Gabriella dragged on her clothes. Her eyes were red and puffy and face was chalky white. Following Teresa outside she blinked in the sunlight which filtered through the trees across the garden. Sister Benedetta was digging in the distance, Teresa picked up a large wicker basket and they left the grounds and began walking up the hill.

'We're going lemon picking.' Teresa hooked her arm through her friends and pulled her upwards. Walking in silence, they listened to the sounds of the birds and the low hum of insect life.

'When the birds sing like that I always think they're praising God,' said Teresa.
Gabriella smiled a half smile and sighed.

'I don't think I'll ever be able to praise God again after this.'

'You need to be healed, we are all praying for you, I know God won't leave you feeling like this forever, and of course you're sad you have every right to be, but the God that I love is full of compassion and love for you Gabriella, you have to let Him in.'
They walked past a huge sage bush in full bloom its aromatic aroma following them up the hill. In the distance there was the sound of a woodpecker drilling a tree, and a startled herd of goats scattered erratically their bleats echoing around the hillside.

'I used to come up here with my Uncle Corrado,' said Gabriella, 'he was always telling me stories and making me laugh with his jokes, he said he can remember helping his

Papa to plant some of the trees. When we came here all those years ago we could hear singing coming from the Abbey, it sounded so beautiful. I had no idea then that I'd end up living there.'

'No, I suppose none of us know where life will take us, but when you first came you said you wanted to devote your life to prayer, and now you can. Giving your life to God is not easy, we have to suffer as He did for us and like Mary who had to watch as her poor son was crucified. God has given you a great role to play and an opportunity to come to understand Him more by entering into the world of suffering. I believe that you will come through all this closer to Him and with true devotion knowing that this all happened for a reason and that He is standing with you, not letting you fall.'

'I think you are right.' Gabriella turned to her friend. 'But this pain inside me is strangling my love for God I feel as if I'm losing my faith, I'm losing everything.' She buried her head in her hands and sobbed.

Teresa held her and rubbed her back praying soothingly as Gabriella cried out all her fear and pain. Once she had settled down Teresa passed her a handkerchief and continued to stroke her until she was quiet and peaceful.

Reaching the tree where Gabriella had sat with Corrado they stopped.

'Oh no.' Teresa touched the brown leaves. 'It's suffering, look. There aren't any lemons.'

'What's happened? I remember Corrado telling me it's more than a thousand years old.'

'The other trees are all right. I don't understand it.'

'Maybe it's the end of that tree's life. There's nothing we can do. Now, we need to do some picking. I love the smell of lemon trees there's nothing else quite like it, it makes me want to make so many lemony things when we get back.' Gabriella laughed.

'You sound like my uncle. What are you planning to make?'

'Did you know that for hundreds of years, lemons have been used as a type of medicine? They have great healing properties for all sorts of things.'

'What sort of things?'

'Skin complaints, headaches, some people claim lemons can help just about anything. You could try putting drops of lemon on your hanky and breathing it in, when I feel sad I do that and it always makes me feel better. My Nonna used to put it on our cut knees and make us drink it every day. I can hear her now: "cleanse yourselves from the inside out." It could just be an old wives' tale, but I still do it every day.'

'I might try that,' said Gabriella as she put the last lemons she could reach into the basket. Carrying it down the hill together, Gabriella enjoyed the feel of the sun on her back and breathed in the scent of the flowers and the lemons as they walked through the grass. Suddenly Teresa stopped, put her fingers to her lips and pointed. There below them stood a stag. Majestic. Crowned with huge antlers; haunches, taut and rippling, it sniffed the air before turning away from them. Both young women were silent, in awe of the magnificent creature as they watched it. Once it had disappeared they walked on.

'He was so beautiful,' said Gabriella. 'I'm so glad you dragged me out today, I feel a lot better. Thank you.' She squeezed Teresa's arm.

*

Frowning, Ricardo looked in the mirror at his suit; he barely recognized himself as it hung off him. I can't go. I look like a clown, he thought. And I can't talk to anyone. I hate the way everyone gives me sympathetic looks I know it's because they care but - he sighed I'm lost without them. Why didn't I just say no? I've turned down all the other invites since they've gone.

Looking at the photograph of his laughing wife and daughter he thought back to the day it was taken. They had gone on a picnic up to the lemon grove. The boys had been off trying to catch butterflies and Giverny and Gabriella had been lying together in the sunshine while he was saying silly things to make them laugh so he could get a good picture. And it had worked. Pushing down the pain inside that threatened to engulf him he loosened his tie and took a glass from the cupboard and a bottle from the larder. Her writing loopy - and confident - just like her, covered the label. Pouring himself a glass he knocked it back. The sweet lemon liqueur slipped down his throat and warmed him all over. He refilled his glass three times. His doubts about going to the wedding became fuzzier. Returning to the mirror he smoothed his hair down, fixed his tie, picked up some flagons of liquer al limoni and walked down the track towards Civita.

Walking past the buffalo as they lazily swished their tails he thought of Giverny again and how proud she was of the dairy and their herd. Now it was Isabella who kept it all going. He didn't know how he'd cope without her. She was a true friend and would be there today. The only one he could talk to. As Giverny's best friend she felt the loss almost as deeply as the rest of them.

Awash with anticipation the town square bustled. Boys dressed in their best played football near the church steps, and girls sat in little groups playing pat-a-cake. The twins, playing with the three angels, waved at Ricardo and he waved back. Walking up the cobbled path, his heart sank as he passed the sad peeling osteria sign. Deep longing engulfed him. The desire to go back in time before it was boarded up to the days when he and his brother sat outside drinking coffee without a care in the world. Back to when his boys had their mother, when his little girl still laughed, when they were a family. He desperately wanted to feel her little warm hand in his again. His thoughts began to strangle him. He turned around and walked fast back down the hill, until he heard footsteps running behind him.

'Ricardo, wait.'

He turned as Isabella, caught his arm.

'Where are you going?' She panted trying to catch her breath.

'I'm sorry.' Ricardo looked at his feet. 'I can't face everyone. I thought I could but-'

'But everyone's so looking forward to seeing you. Right wait here.' She pushed him into the alleyway that led behind the square and made him sit on a step. 'Don't move.' Dashing off, she returned a couple of minutes later with two glasses.

'Let's have a drink.'

Ricardo sighed as he poured them both a glass of the liquer

that glowed in the sunshine.

'I just want to feel normal again and seeing the osteria like that brought back so many memories and seeing everyone happy it's hard. I don't think I'll ever be happy again.' Isabella sat next to him and took his hand. 'I can't possibly imagine what you're feeling after everything that's happened, but I do feel something as Giverny was my friend and I loved her too and miss her every day. What I do know is that she would want you to try to be happy and to continue to be part of this community, if not just for the boys' sake. We all love you and want to help. You know what it's like here we all look out for each other, let us in. Stop pushing everyone away. Sergio is one of your oldest friends and he was so glad when I said you were coming. Apart from the fact that we're all very excited about drinking this.' She put her glass to her lips and sipped the drink shivering at its coldness savouring the sweet and citrus combination as it slipped smoothly down her throat. 'If I promise to stay by your side for the whole day will you stay?'

Looking into her hazel eyes intense with hope, he relented before following her up the hill.

In the square old friends surrounded them hugging him and the two wizened sisters kissed him on both cheeks. The bells began to ring out and all attention was turned to the bride arriving in a cart adorned with creamy roses the colour of mozzarella, pulled by a pretty white pony who trotted proudly into the square. Her bridle was decorated with ivy and sprays of baby's breath. Dressed in a white suit, the driver clicked his tongue and pulled the reins stopping in front of the church steps. The congregation filed into the church and saw Sergio, sweating and looking like he was going to lose his breakfast. The bells rang out again as they had for hundreds of years at every wedding, christening and funeral giving Ricardo a feeling of hope. He smiled at Sergio and mouthed 'good luck.'

A vision in white, Estella entered the church on her proud father's arm walking up the same aisle where he and her mother had married. Sergio's nerves left him as he gasped and thought himself the luckiest men alive. His wife-to-be looked more beautiful than he'd ever seen her in a silk gown, her long her in elaborate plaits pinned up and fastened with cream rose buds that glowed against her caramel skin. They didn't stop smiling all the way through the ceremony. Looking around the church Ricardo couldn't help laughing at all the women holding handkerchiefs to their eyes. Nothing changes here. He remembered his own wedding and the wonderful life he and Giverny had known. Next to him, Isabella caught his eye and smiled, he smiled back.

Liquer al limoni was the choice for the toasts and got the party going. Ricardo found he was actually enjoying himself as he sat down between Isabella and Santo at a long trestle table in the square in the sunshine. The twins were seated opposite him eating heartily and chatting to one another. Above them the balconies dripped with greenery and flowers. Honeysuckle wafted on the wind and mingled with the smell of the spit-roasted lamb stuffed with mint and rosemary. It melted in his mouth, washed down with good red wine made from Mario's vineyard.

He helped to clear the tables as the band tuned up. The bride and groom took centre stage, whispering to one another, before everyone else joined in. Isabella politely refused to dance with Santo saying she was tired as she determined to keep her promise and not leave Ricardo alone. Seated in front of him on the step he found himself gazing at her bare shoulders glowing in the sunset. The fiery sky seemed to be showing off, trying to outdo the bride's beauty at the same time enhancing Isabella's. Ricardo felt as if he was looking at her for the first time. She was wearing a pale pink dress, the colour of his mama's favourite rose bush in a Grecian style that fell loosely across her curves. Those shoulders kept drawing him back. Examining her closely he noticed the smattering of freckles that covered her back matched the ones that sprinkled her nose and the way long tendrils of her hair fell in little curly wisps around her ears reminding him of his mama's, her curls were always escaping. How she would have loved today.

Surrounded by his friends again gave Ricardo an intense feeling of belonging. It was, he realised, as satisfying as taking a swim in the cool lake after a long hard day's work in the fields under the searing sun as he and his father used to. Overwhelmed suddenly with the love he had received in his life from his family and his friends he knew his boys gave him the reason to live. When his papa died he felt that he couldn't go on, but with his family and friends' support he had survived and he knew at that moment that he would also survive this and live again and hopefully in time, be happy.

Rounding up the sleepy boys Ricardo and Isabella wended their way home as the crescent moon rose high in the sky, the twins went straight to bed where Ricardo tenderly tucked them in kissing them goodnight. Going back downstairs he realised how little affection he had shown them since all this had happened and resolved not only to hug them more but to give them his time. Every day had been so laced with grief he had lost sight of the fact that they needed him and he needed them too.

Collecting another flagon of liquer from the cool larder he found Isabella in the garden. Handing her a glass they sat side by side on the stone bench next to the roses, inhaling the sweet smell of the countless blooms that had grown back after being so cruelly cut the year before.

'So much has happened in the past year, I can hardly believe it.' said Ricardo.

'I know. In one way, it seems to be such a short time but in another a lifetime.'

'Thank you, Isabella, for today. If you hadn't called me back I would have come home and been miserable on my own. Instead I had a wonderful evening with friends.' He lit a cigarette and moved to lie in the cool grass gazing up at the sky. 'I've been too busy looking down at the ground I haven't noticed so many things, like these stars, there are thousands of them.'

Isabella lay down in the grass too.

'When I was little I used to try and count them, but tonight that would be impossible.'

A tiny sliver of fire on the horizon was all that was left of the sun as it finally said farewell to the day.

'It's strange that we know barely anything about what's above us, like those stars so faint that you can only see them as you look away from the corner of your eye as if they're teasing you.'

The chirruping crickets filled the air, still warm without a whisper of wind.

Suddenly Ricardo sat up and leaned on one elbow.

'Have you ever been in love?'

'When I was with Corrado I thought I loved him, but I think deep down I always knew he was holding back although I didn't know why.'

'I know. You seemed to be the perfect match. Mama was so happy when you got together, but in a way Corrado was brave to break it off with you as everyone started talking about marriage and babies. He knew he wanted to travel and couldn't settle for that life, so I don't think it was about you. It was about him.'

'When it happened, I felt totally rejected but as time went on I began to understand. And it's true that time is a good healer.'

'I know. I felt my world ended and nothing would ever be the same when Papa died, but life goes on. Today at the party I felt more like my old self for the first time.' He looked up at the sky. 'Giverny used to say that when people die they become stars and look down on us so they never really leave us. I know it's not true, but it's a comforting thought.'

'Well I know for a fact that if it was, Giverny would have been proud of you today and so would your parents.'

'Today I realised that I will love again.' He took Isabella's hand. 'And I believe that you will too in time.'
The mutual silence spoke volumes as they clasped hands and looked to the future aware that they would spend it together.

Gabriella visited the lemon grove daily after going with Teresa, loving being there and having time to reminisce and just breathe in the citrus aroma. Although the dying tree made her sad. She had taken Teresa's advice and begun drinking lemon juice in the mornings as soon as she got up before she said her prayers. She felt herself growing closer to God and Our Lady and as if her healing had begun as she prayed.

'I was so unsure that this was the path for my life, and I hated you for letting this happen to me but now I am beginning to see that you did have a plan for my life after all and to serve you is what you want. I want to do your will and with Our Lady's help I can be a better person, I'm so sorry for doubting you and thank you for not giving up on me.' Gabriella fingered her rosary beads. 'Mary, holy mother of God please look after my baby, make her happy wherever she is now.' Fat tears rolled down her face and landed on the beads she clasped in her hands. Wiping them away she grew contemplative and closed her eyes praying silently until she was disturbed by a twig snapping. Opening them she saw her father standing in front of her with a huge smile. Leaping into his strong arms she felt safe for the first time in months. Ricardo buried his face in his daughter's tangle of curls and let his tears fall as he smelt her scent.

'I've missed you Gabby.' Ricardo held her away from him and gazed into her face, thinking how much she looked like her mother, before hugging her again. 'How are you?'

'I am happy Papa.' Gabriella made up her mind not to tell him about the baby, she knew it would kill him. 'I'm sorry I left like that without telling you.' She hugged him tighter and buried her face into his chest feeling like a little girl again.

'I'm so proud of you, *Cara*, you always had such an independent streak. Even when you were tiny, you used to boss me around all the time, and your poor brothers, well…' He laughed.

'Are they all right? How's the farm?'

'They're fine and the farm is going well, you should come and visit us sometime, they'd love to see you and-'
Stormily she shook her head.

'I've made my promise to God and the only time I leave the Abbey is to come here and pray. I'm sorry.'
Ricardo and Gabriella sat under the tree and hugged one another in companiable silence, punctuated by the trilling of a

merla in the lemon tree above them which made Gabriella smile. As they hugged to part, Gabriella looked up and saw to her delight a brand new green leaf growing on the tree above her. Walking home the bird followed her from tree to tree and Gabriella felt loved, loved by her father, loved by the angels, loved by Our Lady, loved by God and through the *merla* loved by her mother. Her spirits soared as the sun warmed her face and the burnished grass around her seemed to glow.

EPILOGUE

TWO YEARS LATER

ITALY

Gabriella was making marmalade. She had collected the lemons the day before on her visit to the tree. It had finally fully recovered and grew lemons bigger than ever before. She was breathing in their aroma as the sunlight flickered across the wall next to her. Looking out into the garden she smiled at her little *merla* friend splashing about in the bird bath with her offspring. She brought them there every morning having nested in the plum tree. Gabriella had delighted in watching her teaching her babies to fly and found she could think about her own baby now without welling up and having truly dedicated her life and taken her vows she felt at peace. Suddenly Teresa burst through the door breathlessly handing her a package wrapped in brown paper.

'You've got a parcel from England.'

Heavy in her hands, they shook as she fumbled with the coarse string that tied it. Teresa handed her a knife. Ripping off the paper revealed a large book with a painting of a lemon grove on the cover. There was a letter on top addressed to her. Instantly recognising Corrado's handwriting she tore it open.

Sussex, England.

Dear Gabriella

I am sorry I have not been in touch. I want you to know that I still think about you all the time. I hear from your papa that you have become a sister. He is very proud of your dedication. So am I and I know that your mama and Nonna would be too. I have enclosed something very special for you. When I was a boy, Nonna told me the secret stories of our history with the lemon tree. I gave my word that I would keep them safe and do my absolute upmost to pass them on to someone I trust when the time came. I always believed you were the next keeper of the stories and now is the time for me to fulfill my promise.

When I was in London, I met a wonderful woman called Margaret and we are now together living on a farm and very happy. She is a writer and because of this, I have relayed the stories to her so that for the first time they can be written down instead of being told in the oral tradition. As well as our family ancestry, you will find our story in there, the struggle that Margaret and I have been through in order that we can be together.

I hope you enjoy reading it and please promise to keep it safe as I am now handing the baton on to you. You are the new keeper of the stories and when the time comes you will know who to pass them onto. The lemon tree will choose that person and present someone to you. You don't need to worry about it as it is not in your hands. Trust the tree.

I know that you and your papa often meet in the lemon grove and I enjoy picturing you both there. I miss you all so much and I miss the tree, but something amazing has happened. Here in England, despite the rain and cold, I have grown a lemon tree under glass from the seeds of the lemons sent over after I moved away. Now its legacy is twofold. You have its history back in Italy and I have replanted the tree so it can continue to tell its stories.

I hope that one day we will meet again, but in the meantime God bless you.
Sending lots of love Corrado xx

Printed in Great Britain
by Amazon